Case of the Wayward Son

Tales from the P.I.T. Crew

J.M. Tilbury

ISBN: 978-1-960534-30-9 (Paperback)
ISBN: B0F7L66NF3 (Ebook)

Written by J.M. Tilbury
Edited by Kasey Kubica
Cover art by Susan Russell

Published by Grendel Press LLC
www.grendelpress.com

To Ashton: With hard work, you can be whatever you wish.

Chapter 1

H ITTING A NUMBER ON my smartphone, I put it to my ear.

The other end picked up. *"Da?"*

"Just checking in, Stravinsky."

"You have found ghoul?"

"Yeah, I have it in an abandoned warehouse out in Weed. I'll check in once I'm done."

"Very good, Doctor." The call terminated.

Rain pelted the run-down warehouse in the distance. Lightning flashed and thunder sounded overhead. I parked across the street and cut the engine. The fresh smell of petrichor and pine hung in the air as I braced myself against the October downpour. I quickly closed the door of my metallic silver Porsche 718 Boxster Spyder to keep water off the black all-leather interior. The lights flashed and the alarm chirped as I locked it and slid the keys into a pocket.

Small strands of pine and other conifers intermixed with the dark buildings that stood along the lonely road. Loose gravel crunched softly under my feet as I made my way across. Sparse streetlamps created ominous shadows as rain scattered the light back onto itself, making ghostly halos that did little more than ruin one's night vision.

I had followed a taxidiótís ghoul, or taxi ghoul as I called them, from a nearby graveyard before losing sight of it in the storm. The cemetery created a steady, if not suboptimal, food source, like having a fast-food joint close to home: It may suck, but at least it provided sustenance. Combined with the obscurity of the place, it made perfect sense as to why the thing had preferred this spot to roost.

My agency had been intercepting reports from the local police blotter of grave robberies and a few missing persons. Mainly the type of people easily overlooked or dismissed, homeless and vagrants and such. With a small amount of research, I had easily put together the taxi ghoul theory and nailed down its hunting territory. Then it became a waiting game until the thing showed its melty face.

I made my way across the street and slunk up to the chain-link fence, complete with padlock and a "No Trespassing" sign hanging loosely from the front gate. Picking the lock and pushing it open, I winced at the squeak it made. Ghouls had excellent hearing, but maybe the storm had provided me some cover. I crept to the rusty, metal warehouse door and gave the knob a tentative wiggle. Shit, locked as well. How the hell was it getting in and out?

I couldn't see much of anything through the rain and darkness—no obvious open or broken windows, nor did there seem to be any other way in besides the front door. Trying to be as quiet as possible, I opened the lock with a loud clunk that made me wince again. Drawing my silver Desert Eagle steadily from its shoulder holster, I pushed my way in, the door creaking in protest. I made a mental note to add a spray bottle of olive oil to my field kit for future rusty hinges.

This building should have been demolished a long time ago. A ton of dusty wooden pallets were stacked to one side in a haphazard fashion and a rusty flatbed truck sat to the other with a single open doorway looming in front of me leading to a loading area. The air smelled stale and mildewy as rainwater collected into puddles on the floor, the drips echoing through the darkness. Cobwebs, rust, and grime decorated the aluminum siding that made up the ceilings and walls. It felt drafty, damp, and dark, just the kind of dump you'd expect to find a ghoul in.

As I moved farther in, the sickly stench of death assaulted my nose. In the distance, I could hear slurping, crunching, then a burp. I peeked around the corner and into the loading area. A raised platform with more planks littering it, and some large, steel double doors on the far side with a big chain and padlock made the room. The ceiling had several missing aluminum panels, and rain poured in through the resulting hole. Among the clutter, I saw what looked like a homeless man hunched over a dead person, gorging itself on the remains. I almost threw up. No wonder it hadn't noticed me.

Ducking back around the corner to wait until it became full and slow, I thought myself in a good position when something stupid happened.

A rusty screech announced two blues pushing into the warehouse. One called into the distance, voice echoing. "Hello?"

I must have tripped a silent alarm, son of a bitch.

The ghoul's munching stopped. I hid behind some pallets, hoping the officers would go away, but no such luck.

Two lights cut through the murk swiveling back and forth. "We know you're in here. We have backup on the way, so best to come out now."

Why the hell would a dump like this have a silent alarm? Why the hell would they want backup on a routine trespassing alarm? Must be rookies. Of all the stupid, dumbass luck. A scurrying sound that could have been mistaken for rats came from the dock area. Nevertheless, it drew their attention.

"Hello?"

Their flashlights finally caught sight of the half-eaten corpse. "Holy shit, John. We got ourselves a dead body!"

The swish of metal against leather echoed through the darkness, both men on high alert. "Alright! Whoever's here, come out with your hands up."

I didn't have time to take another breath. The ghoul came out of the shadows like a professional stalker.

"John? Holy shit, John!" There came a ripping sound and blood splattered the ground.

"Stop right there, motherfucker!" Gunfire, another hair-raising scream, more blood.

I had to act.

Coming from behind the pallets with my weapon leveled, I saw one officer on the ground bleeding out, his heart ripped from his chest. The other tangoed with Señor Nasty, the thing ripping his throat out with its fangs. I squeezed off a round, blowing a good-sized hole in its shoulder. Black ichor oozed from the wound.

It turned and took a supernatural leap backward, hissing and shying away from the silver weapon.

Another voice joined the party. "Freeze!"

The situation suddenly became way more of a mess than I had bargained for.

The newcomer's flashlight illuminated the ghoul for half a moment, enough to get a glimpse of what looked like a homeless guy covered in blood with his face melting off. "What the fuck?"

The creature hissed again and leaped straight up through the hole in the roof.

I looked up, rain pelting my face. "Well, I'll be damned. That's how he's getting in and out."

The officer drew his weapon on me. "Drop it and get down on the ground, now!"

"I'm an agent."

His eyes darted around the building as if expecting something else to jump out of the shadows at any second, and his voice quaked. "Fuck that. Get down on the ground, now!"

I carefully placed my gun on the ground without another word, keeping my hands up and open. No sense in getting shot over something like this.

RED AND BLUE LIGHTS flashed as the county sheriff, an ambulance, a medical examiner, and a few other officers swarmed the warehouse. My arresting officer searched me and removed my weapon, phone, badge, extendable baton, portable apothecary, and my hat to hold it all in. Then the officer none too gently shoved me in the back of a cruiser, setting my belongings on the front seat next to him.

We took a short ride to a modest precinct where the officer parked and frog-marched me through a set of glass doors. Concrete walls glistened with an ugly high-gloss yellowish paint bathed in fluorescent lighting. Dark brown rubber molding created a border between the walls and the floor. Two holding cells and a huge metal desk with a brutish looking sergeant glaring at me completed the whole *Shawshank Redemption* motif.

My escort dumped everything but my badge on the desk. "Log this stuff in for me, will ya, Collins? Then bring me a cuppa joe. I have a feeling it's gonna be a long morning."

The place smelled of floor wax and strong coffee. My shoes clicked against the scuffed but freshly buffed dark brown tile floors. He pushed me down the hallway past an old rickety vending machine and a corkboard full of missing person posters and other pinups, shunting me in front of a camera. The marks on the wall behind me told him I stood at 5'11".

His face remained granite. "Remove your hair tie, please."

Taking the tie from my long, dirty-blond ponytail, I shook my mane out and scowled at the camera intensely until it flashed so bright I could feel the light singe my five o'clock shadow. Sure to be a keeper, I'd have to ask for a copy before I left.

He led me to a lone desk with nothing but a phone on it. "Make it quick."

I picked up the receiver and dialed a number I used in emergencies like this.

An electronically garbled voice answered, "Yes?"

"I'm looking for a good neighbor."

The garbled voice confirmed. "Weed, California police precinct? We'll be there as soon as possible." *Click.*

The officer chuckled. "You waste your one call on State Farm there, buddy? Seems like Jake didn't wanna talk to you."

I hung up the receiver and gave a long sigh.

He laughed as he led me farther back and dumped me into a white brick interrogation room, complete with a rickety metal table, two uncomfortable looking chairs, no windows, and no two-way mirror.

Two silver bars glinting on each lapel and the gray in his hair marked him as a captain. A round-faced, clean-shaven guy, he had a slight pudge from sitting behind a desk most of the day, but his pristine uniform echoed a meticulous attention to detail. From his shiny leather shoes to his heavily starched and creased shirt and trousers, this guy seemed all business.

Rolling my eyes toward the ceiling, I muttered, "Perfect."

His face scrunched up. "Excuse me?"

I remained silent as he shut the door and plopped himself down opposite me. He set a digital recorder on the table and pressed the record button.

As he bit at the inside of his cheek, he continued to glare at me. "This is Captain Stanley Monroe for the Weed County Sheriff's Department, taking a verbal statement from one detained suspect. Please state your full name and date of birth for the record."

I leaned into the recorder. "For the record, I don't remember offering to give a verbal statement."

He shrugged. "Are you asking for a lawyer? 'Cause if you wanna sit in a holding cell till the arraignment happens in three days, fine by me."

I sighed. "My name is Dr. Darrell Diamondback. My birthday is eight, six, seventy-seven."

His eyes didn't leave me. "May I ask your profession, Mr. Diamondback?"

I craned my neck and scrunched up my left cheek, eyebrows folding in on themselves. "Doctor, if you please. I didn't spend six years studying at UC Berkeley to be called mister, did I? Now, you say this statement is 'for the record'?"

"I'll ask the questions, Dr. Diamondback."

I smiled like the Cheshire cat. "Well, if it's 'for the record' then I'm afraid the answer to that question is above your pay grade."

He leaned forward. "I see. Does this mean you consider yourself above the law, Dr. Diamondback?"

I shook my head slowly. "Not at all, but I'm not sure you have the proper security clearances to discuss what it is I do. If you'd kindly provide me with a complete personal profile that includes all federal security clearances you might have before we proceed, it would be appreciated."

He folded his arms. "So you're saying you work for the feds?"

I kept my silence.

He started to rise out of his seat. "A tough guy, huh? So maybe I put you in a cell, tough guy, and you can spend the night thinking about answering my questions."

I snorted and looked away. "I wouldn't if you value your job."

He paused and squinted at me again. "Are you threatening me, Mr. Diamondback?"

"It's doctor, and no, just stating fact. 'For the record,' all your questions will be answered when my lawyer gets here."

"As this is currently just a simple trespassing charge, Dr. Diamondback, I was hoping to avoid a nasty trial, but if you wanna wait for State Farm to save you… I didn't know they dealt in law." He chuckled at his running joke.

Leaning forward, I laced my fingers together in front of me and rested my hands on the table. "I suppose that depends on what you'd like to know, Captain."

The seasoned officer didn't blink. "What were you doing in that warehouse?"

"Like I told you before in the police cruiser, I was conducting my own investigation."

"Because you're a detective."

"Yes."

"Who has a PhD?"

"Yes."

"Who doesn't have any legitimate credentials?"

"Just because you've never seen a badge for my agency doesn't make it false, Captain."

He smiled as he glanced at the table and chuckled, then looked me in the eye. "You're honestly gonna sit there and expect me to believe that this Department of Paranormal Investigation and Education is legit?"

"As real as I'm sitting here."

He took my badge and ID out of his uniform pocket, considered them for a moment, then tossed them on the table. "These could easily be a forgery. It looks like you found 'em in a Cracker Jack box. What, did you get a decoder ring too?"

I looked him in the eye as I nodded. "And that proves what I do is completely above your pay grade."

He came out of his seat, his face red, the corner of his left eye twitching slightly as he pointed a finger in my face. "I'm a captain, and there's nothing above my pay grade here!"

I gestured for him to sit back down. "Very well. You win. Have a seat."

He settled back in his chair. "That's more like it."

I gave a pause for effect while shifting around in my seat, trying to make myself comfortable. "At this point, Captain, it's imperative that I ask you a question."

He blew out a long breath. "Okay, I'll humor you. Shoot."

Shifting my eyes back and forth, I brought the back of my hand horizontally to my mouth and asked him in a quiet voice, "Do you believe in ghosts?"

He snorted. "You've gotta be shittin' me."

"I'm dead serious, Captain."

"So what? You want me to believe that you're some sorta federal spook hunter or somethin'?"

"It sounds derogatory when you say it like that. I prefer federal agent with a PhD in forensic psychology and a self-studied paranormal psychologist."

His face screwed up. "You're a fuckin' what now?"

I looked down, shaking my head. "The key words there are 'federal agent,' Captain. Though the question remains: Do you believe in the supernatural?"

He slammed his fist on the table as his eyes bore into me. "Look, wiseass. I just had two officers torn limb from limb by something I can't describe. It looked to me like a maniacal, homicidal maniac on crack and PCP. You were there, unlawfully I might add, and witnessed the whole damn thing. Now I want answers or so help me I'm gonna lose my fucking shit real fast."

I hung my head. "I truly am sorry about your officers, Captain. But they had no idea what they were dealing with."

He strained his bottom lip against his teeth and rubbed his chin. "And I suppose you do?"

"Yes."

"Care to enlighten me?"

I shook my head. "You're still evading my question, so I have no confidence that your attitude toward the situation will change."

He leaned back in his chair and folded his arms. "Yet you're still talkin'. Maybe you try me and let me be the judge'a that."

"It was a taxidiótís ghoul."

"A taxi-Dorito what?"

I enunciated every syllable like speaking to a child. "A tax-i-di-ó-tís ghoul, Captain."

"I see."

I cocked my head and scrunched my face in annoyance. "No, I don't think you understand the gravity of the situation at all. The taxidiótís ghoul, also known as traveling ghouls or taxi ghouls as I call them, are beings that can teleport between dimensions. They have sadistic, scavenger/predator-type personalities and are extremely ruthless when feeding. As far as we know, they are not, nor have ever been human. They seek to study, harass, scare, and hurt humans, as they find fear and pain to be equally humorous. They tend to hang out in seedy parts of town, like the abandoned building we were just in. You can also find them in drug houses, homeless encampments, hospitals, anywhere there are sick or dying people, and of course they feed off us, or our dead, at any rate."

The captain's mouth hung agape as he let it all sink in. "So let me get this straight. There's some sort of… monster out there, dressin' up like a bum?"

I nodded.

He began speaking with his hands. "And uh… it's… it's torturing people, to… to get its jollies?"

I kept nodding.

He leaned in. "Then it kills 'em… and eats 'em?"

I looked him in the eye. "That, or he digs up a dead body in your graveyard to eat. Why do you think you've had all the missing persons and grave robberies lately?"

He nodded slowly. "And you… you were just tryin' to stop it."

"Now you're getting it, Captain."

He let out a barking laugh as he pointed at me. "Oh, man! Do you fucking hear yourself right now?"

I sighed. "This is exactly why you have two dead officers. It's not like we're talking about your run-of-the-mill zombie, for fuck's sake."

He went rigid. "Are you fucking for real right now?"

"You caught a highly intelligent, multidimensional being in its lair while feeding. What did you expect it to do, invite you to pull up a chair?"

His face went red like a thermometer as a vein throbbed at his left temple. "We got a routine trespassing call. We found… someone eating a corpse that turns out had been dug up from the local cemetery. My men had every right to be there!"

"This isn't about right or wrong, Captain. It's more about home invasion really, and the natural reaction of any sentient being when feeling trapped or threatened in their home."

He gave a nervous laugh. "Why do you speak like that? Speak English."

My brow knitted. "Because I'm a doctor, you twit. Please, do try and keep up with the conversation."

He put his finger in my face again. "You know, I have half a mind to throw your wise ass in a cell and let the judge sort you out."

Rolling my eyes, I drummed my fingers on the table. "Bluff all you like, Captain. You're not fooling anyone."

His eyes popped. "You think I'm bluffing?"

"Absolutely. That's the third time you've made the threat to put me in a holding cell. I'm surprised actual criminals take you seriously."

He stood, reaching for me. "Whatever, buster. Come on. Get up. I'm done with you."

"Besides, I saved your life."

His fingertips found the table between us as he leaned in. "You did what now? Look, buddy. The only thing I saw was you obstructing me from taking down a perp that killed two of my officers. That's what I saw!"

My voice dripped with venom. "You also saw what that thing did to your officers, Captain. What chance did you honestly have against it? You would have wound up dead next to them if I hadn't stopped it. Do you still honestly believe that what you saw tonight was, in fact, a homeless man?"

For the second time, his voice quaked with fear. "I don't know what the hell I saw."

"That's right. You don't know what the hell you saw! So, the best thing you can do is let me go, make something up, go home, have a bourbon, and forget this whole damn night ever happened."

"Are you out of your fucking mind? Let you go? Those were good men! They deserve better than the bullshit you're peddling."

I tried stern empathy. "They deserve justice and peace, which they will get if you let me go. The longer I sit here, the farther away it gets and the greater chance of it killing someone else."

"The crazy thing is, I honestly think you believe what you're saying."

I slammed my fist on the table. "It's probably hopped dimensions by now! You and your men cost me weeks' worth of research."

There were mushroom clouds in his eyes. "I cost you?"

The door opened and a smooth Russian accent interrupted. "*Pozhaluysta*, do not say another word, Dr. Diamondback."

The captain spun around. "What? Who the fuck are you and who the hell let you in here? I'll have their goddamn badge!"

I held my cuffs out to the captain, rattling them.

He pointed at Stravinsky, then at me. "You, get the fuck out of my interrogation room. And you, stay where you're at. I'm not done with you yet."

My handler clasped his hands behind his back. "*Nyet*, Captain. I do believe that you are done with the good doctor."

The captain growled like a rabid dog. "Look, buddy. I don't know who the fuck you think you are, but... Mayor?"

A balding, older gentleman dressed in a tailored suit and a tan trench coat stepped through the door. He appeared shaken and groggy from having been woken up in the wee hours of the morning. He gestured to the captain's chair. "How's it going, Stan? Have a seat."

My handler cocked an eyebrow at the newcomer. "I trust all is in order, Mayor Thomas?"

"Of course, Agent Stravinsky, of course. Stan, uncuff the good doctor, now."

I rattled my bracelets at him again as he sputtered at the mayor, but finally moved to remove them.

Stravinsky picked up the tape recorder and turned it off. "I will be taking this and the recording from the bug planted under the table, if you please."

"Hey, wait!"

The mayor waved his hand. "Very good. You and Dr. Diamondback are free to go, and the city apologizes for any inconvenience we may have caused you and your department. Please, in the future, if you're ever working in Weed again? Give us a goddamn heads-up, will ya?"

I stood, rubbing my wrists, then took my badge off the table. I put it back in my pocket and adjusted my black Italian silk suit, straightened my magenta silk tie, and smoothed my leather overcoat. I flashed my perfect teeth in a smile. "*Au revoir*, Captain. I do hope your morning gets better, and again, I *am* sorry about this mess."

The indignation in the captain's voice rang clear as a bell. "Mayor, please. You can't be serious about this."

The mayor gestured to the chair again as Stravinsky and I turned to go. "Sit down, Stan. We need to talk."

Chapter 2

Weed City Precinct Parking Lot, Weed, CA—0334 hours

AFTER PICKING UP THE rest of my belongings from the disgruntled desk sergeant and returning them to their proper places, I donned my wide-brim leather fedora. The sergeant informed me they hadn't towed my car yet, and after thanking him for a pleasant stay, I headed toward the exit. Relieved I wouldn't need to wait for the impound lot to open, I gave a silent huzzah for American laziness. Stravinsky followed me out in his gray silk suit, red silk power tie, and dark gray tweed overcoat. His slick, wavy black hair and Vandyke beard appeared neatly trimmed as always.

His thick Russian accent riled with disapproval. "This is third time this week I am saving your *zadnitsa*, Doctor."

"Hey, taxidiótís ghouls are tricky, Stravinsky, even for the best of us. I can't help it if the cops screwed things up."

Stravinsky's face held no sympathy. "Our mutual friends? They are not so convinced. They want you to take on team."

It had quit raining and my highly shined Oxford wingtips clicked against the wet pavement as we walked from the precinct out into the parking lot. "I told you, and them, no. I work better alone."

Stravinsky scratched his bearded chin. "Perhaps if you spent little less on wardrobe, there would be *dengi* in budget to hire team."

I gave him a hurt look. "What's wrong with the way I dress? I'll have you know I have sensitive skin, which appreciates the touch of real Italian silk."

"Some might say you are *izbalovannyy*."

I cocked an eyebrow at the staunch Russian lawyer. "Spoiled? Come on Stravinsky, you don't want me to break out in hives, do you? Besides, have you seen that dump of a hotel you put me in? I'm surprised Norman Bates hasn't paid me a visit."

Stravinsky sighed. "Here are files of potential candidates."

I scowled like a liberal at an antifur rally. "Why the hell didn't you email them to me? Come on, Stravinsky, save a damn tree."

"I did email them. Last week."

"Then you can trust I looked them over and decided against it."

He eyeballed me. "This is not up for debate, Doctor. Please do as asked this time."

Staring across the street, I made to pull out my phone for an Uber. "I'll get right on that. Now if you'll excuse me, I need to get back to my car."

He grinned. "I will be giving you ride, *da*? You can look at profiles whilst I drive."

I gave him a sour expression as I climbed into the passenger seat of his black Range Rover, mocking his Russian accent. "I thought this taxidiótís ghoul was 'top pree-or-i-tee.'"

"That was before trail went cold, *moy drug*, and things change. Do try and, how you say, 'keep up.'" Stravinsky chuckled as if he had made a good joke.

"Har-dee-har-har. You know, Stravinsky, you and I have been friends for a while now, and I must say, sometimes it's extremely difficult being the smartest guy in the room."

"I am sure it is, Doctor. Now, to business. First person you will need is computer specialist by name of Charles Mopps."

I kept my voice ambiguous as my eyes scanned over the file. "I take it his parents are Irish? What's so special about him?"

"Top grad at MIT. Works as security specialist. Also moonlights as small-time hacker. Goes by handle 'Spook.'

Has never done anything big or FBI noteworthy, but we feel there is much potential."

Stravinsky wasn't really selling me on this guy. "If he's never been in trouble with the feds, how good can he be?"

"Do good hackers get caught? Besides, you had never been picked up by feds, yet we hired you. Now, you are arrested constantly. Give him time."

I flipped to the next file. "Inconsequential, and you're still not funny. What about this… Jaiden Fox? Really, Stravinsky? A reporter? I thought we wanted to keep the snoops away from this."

He gave me a quick sideways glance. "Or you hire one to put out story you want and is better for business. Also, with press badge and connections, reporter should be able to get into some places that you wouldn't be able to otherwise. We are willing to bet she will be large asset to operations. Graduated from Northwestern University, you know."

"You couldn't have picked a bigger skeptic."

"Sometimes skepticism is healthy. She also has taste for unexplainable occurrences, so should take to this line of work very easy."

I riffled through to the last profile. "Yeah, right. What's with Mountain Man Mike? Looks like he went off the grid a couple of decades ago."

Stravinsky nodded. "Ah, Staff Sergeant Edward Anderson. Weapons specialist in Marine Military Police. Awarded Golden Lifesaving Medal and Medal of Honor in Afghanistan for saving comrades life and for 'valor above and beyond call of duty.' All-American hero and a very worthwhile person to have in back pocket. You can see from file why he is perfect fit."

I looked at him dubiously. "He fought a djinn and lived, huh? And you're serious about all this?"

Stravinsky shrugged again. "Mutual friends at agency think this is good move. Will make you more productive."

I pointed. "Ha! So, you admit I'm productive all by myself."

He tapped the steering wheel with an index finger as his eyebrows caved in on themselves. "You still need team. Like was said, this is to make you more productive. Mutual friends are indeed about results."

"They can take their results and shove them where the sun doesn't shine."

My handler's face became stern as he pulled up next to my Spyder. "If you do not reach out to team as instructed, my help may not be so, eh… forthcoming, next time you need friend, *ponimat*?"

Scowl lines massaged the foremost parts of my skull. "Yeah, I hear you."

He looked around at the neighborhood, still gray in the pink of the early dawn. The dark and rain had indeed hidden several broken windows high in the warehouse walls. Layers of faded spray-painted sigils jostled on most of the buildings, looking like the bastard children of van Gogh and Pollock, making any original meaning impossible to discern. Discarded syringes, broken bottles, and bits of latex littered the concrete slabs holding up the buildings, mixing with the gravel or peeking from beneath the mud wash nibbling at the edges of the foundations.

Stravinsky spat out his window into the road. "Now, *moy drug*. I believe this is where I leave you. *Spasibo a do skorava*, Doctor. Until we meet again."

"Later, Stravinsky. Thanks for the ride."

A sigh escaped me as I got out, shut the door, and watched him drive away. I spoke to the chill morning air. "Friends. Who needs 'em?"

As I opened my own car door, a greasy voice sounded from the lingering shadows. "I knew casin' this car would pan out."

I glanced over my shoulder at a welcome distraction. Two degenerates appeared out of a narrow alley between two buildings. "You ladies out for an early morning stroll?"

The first one, tall and lanky with ripped jeans, a T-shirt, and a light jacket, looked hungrily at me. A switchblade appeared in his hand. "Look here, Billy. We got us a pretty boy comedian. How's about I cut them fancy digs from yer dead body, pretty boy? Then I'll take yer car out fer a little joyride."

His friend, shorter, heavier, all flannel and blue jeans, smiled a methamphetamine-ridden grin while slipping on some brass knuckles.

I shut my car door and slid the keys into my pocket as I turned to face them. "Honestly? I don't think you could handle her."

My extendable baton easily slid from my wrist sheathe and into my hand. With a flick of the wrist, it extended to full length. I pulled down my hat tightly to right above my steely gaze as I eased into a fighting stance. "Normally I wouldn't give you girls the time of day, but since I got stood up last night, I'm in the mood to dance."

They circled, trying to flank me, but I had training and experience fighting more than one person at a time, and I wouldn't exactly call these guys professionals.

Lashing out with all the frustration the last few hours had mustered, I easily relieved the taller douchebag of his weapon with a rap on the hand. I stepped into him, hooking his extended arm, and preceded to hip-toss him to the ground.

The second douchebag, who took a clumsy swipe at me, received a counterstrike across his face, my baton knocking a couple teeth that had managed to stand up to his drug habit into the street. My assailant lay on the ground, bleeding from his mouth, as I used the tip of my baton to squash his fat nose. "I'm sure you have medical insurance with your line of work?"

He wisely decided not to press the issue. Grabbing his winded buddy, they took off back down the gravel road. Ah, meth heads. Even so, that hadn't really been much of a workout. I would have to hit the gym later.

A streetwalker with a suspiciously deep voice eyed me curiously from around a corner as I returned my baton to its sheathe. "Thanks, sugar daddy. Those two were bad for business. You wouldn't be lookin' for love, would ya?"

I scowled at her. "Beat it, Lola, before I get the blues."

"Your loss." She turned her nose up in the air and sauntered away in search of an unsuspecting john.

I climbed into my Spyder as the morning sun began to peek from behind the mountains. Time to head for home base and regroup.

The Good Night Inn, Weed, CA—0459 hours

ONE THING ABOUT PODUNK towns is they only have podunk hotels. Let's just say I wouldn't have been surprised to see two old men in rocking chairs, chewing tobacco, and playing "Dueling Banjos." The dilapidated shack functioning as my current home away from home reeked of mildew, stale cigarettes, and bad taste as I rattled open the bright orange door. Stained brown carpeting worn black in high traffic areas, wood-paneled walls, and brown plastic molding provided cover for at least seven generations of roaches. The seventies wanted this place back sooner rather than later.

I couldn't wait to check out. I missed my high-rise apartment in the middle of San Jose's Santana Row. Sighing, I set my keys on the small, round table by a window with ugly cotton curtains adorned with teal and olive baubles and hung my jacket on one of the old wooden chairs with orange vinyl seat cushions.

If Stravinsky had the right of it, the taxi ghoul had gone underground, and the Department of Paranormal Investigation and Education, or PIE, wasn't bluffing about me taking on some deadweight. Since they paid the bills, I had to put up with their bullshit.

You would think that I'd be more bummed about the news, but in truth, partners never lasted with me. Not many people had the stomach or the head for this line of work because 99.9 percent of the time people weren't taking it seriously. Oh, sure, at first their excitement knew no bounds. Wannabe ghostbusters, ghost hunters, and nerds, oh my! I even had one dildo show up with a fake proton accelerator on his back. Every single one of them a fresh-faced rookie who had never left the sanctity of their parents' basement and wanted to get paid for playing pretend, but then found out this shit could actually kill you.

I wish I had a nickel for every person who thought this to be a skate job, a dream job, just to wind up getting their head ripped off by a téras—a monster ghoul. Even something as simple as getting possessed by a poltergeist for the first time, they'd flip the fuck out. Then I'd have a heap of messy separation paperwork to do after checking them into a morgue or worse, a mental hospital. Still, occasionally PIE got a wild hair up its ass and tried to push them off on me. Ah, the stupidity of bureaucracy.

I blamed the name of the organization. PIE. Who the fuck thinks this shit up?

Their suggestion of a full team this time intrigued me, though. Truth be told, I wouldn't mind a little competent backup. Maybe they could have stalled the cops back at the warehouse and kept them alive.

I pulled my suitcase from a closet whose door clung to its hinges for dear life and began packing. No sense in hanging around this dump. I wouldn't be able to sleep a wink for fear that the Roach King would carry me off in my sleep.

I stopped by the front office, handed my key to the blurry-eyed-with-moonshine clerk, threw my suitcase in the back of my car, and sped off into the rising sun.

As it turned out, this Charlie Mopps guy was my neighbor. Ha! Charlie Mopps. I shook my head. Who the hell would be mean enough to name their kid after a character from Irish drinking lore?

Charlie's Apartment, Santana Row, San Jose, CA—1200 hours

A CHIME SOUNDED AND I exited the elevator on the first floor of my apartment building, entering a hallway with textured cream-colored walls, dark stained wood trim, and blue industrial carpeting. Ambient lighting set into a dark brown ceiling illuminated the row of stark white doors with black numbers mounted on them. Stopping at number six, I collected myself, rapped with a knuckle on the door, then clasped my hands behind my back and waited. After a moment or two, it opened.

"Who the fuck are you?" I liked him immediately.

I stood nose to nose with a young man in his early twenties wearing a solid black T-shirt, baggy jeans, and a dark green beanie with a mop of straw-colored hair hanging out around the edges. A set of black headphones complete with mic were parked on top as he stared at me with sleepy hazel eyes and a stoned grimace. He reminded me of me in my twenties during my college years. "Undead" by Hollywood Undead blasted in the background, making it hard to hear.

"Do you mind turning down the music?"

"What?"

"Can you turn down the music, please?"

"What?"

"I asked if you could turn down the music!"

He shook his head. "Hold on, I can't hear you over the music! Alexa, music off!"

The music abruptly stopped.

I stuck a finger in my ear and wiggled it. "Much better."

"Not really."

I jerked my thumb upward. "I live four floors above you."

"So, what, is the music too loud? What the fuck do you want, Grindelwald? I thought you were the pizza guy."

My arms folded as I gave him a smirk. "I can tell from the reek of pot smoke you were hoping I was the pizza guy, but alas, no."

He snapped his fingers and then shook one at me. "Then you *are* the stupid motherfucker who keeps complaining about my music being too loud."

"Again, no. I actually enjoy Hollywood Undead."

He continued to stare blankly at me. "Then my question still stands. What the fuck do you want?"

"May I come in, Mr. Mopps?"

"Why?"

"*Sakes begorra*, Charlie. Ta' have a cuppa tea, ta' be sure."

He scowled. "Now you're just being a douche. I hate that fucking shit."

I gave him my best smile. "In all seriousness, Mr. Mopps, I have something to discuss with you, and I'd rather discuss it indoors."

He remained stubbornly skeptical. "I just have one more question."

"Shoot."

"How the fuck do you know my name?"

"It probably wouldn't help if I said I work for the government, would it?"

He instantly went rigid. "Whoa, man. You ain't got shit on me."

"No, no, nothing like that."

"I work for a legit business, dude."

"Mr. Mopps…"

"Pro Tech, Inc. Look 'em up. Besides, I never signed anything that says I wouldn't take clients on the side."

"Charlie!"

"What?"

I nonchalantly studied my well-manicured nails. "I don't give a fuck that you go by the handle Spook or that you can crack a bank security system in nothing flat, and thus far…"

"Dude, they were paying me cash to crash test their shit. It's not illegal if they know about it."

"…*thus far*, have flown under the FBI's and CIA's radars. Those are some of the reasons why my agency is interested in you. Now, may I please come in to discuss things further, or are you not interested in the opportunity of a lifetime?"

Staring at me like a teenager in trouble, he opened the door a little wider. His apartment boasted hardwood floors and beige stucco walls with wooden trim. A glass-top coffee table with an old bohemian rug under it sat in front of a black leather couch. A cherrywood entertainment center complete with wall-mounted flatscreen TV and video game console dominated the center of the front room. Several variously sized pieces of equipment with blinking lights and a rat's nest of cables occupied a solid oak computer desk in the corner which also held a double-wide flatscreen monitor, a mouse, and a keyboard. A glass ashtray that had a few roaches in it and a half-full glass of Hawaiian Punch littered the rest of the desktop. An empty pizza box stuffed with garbage and a laptop sat on the coffee table and unfolded laundry littered the couch.

My eyes darted to the kitchen full of dirty dishes. "Now that I have your attention, can I trouble you for a glass of water? I find myself to be a bit parched."

He gestured. "I might have a clean glass on the counter somewhere."

I wrinkled my nose. "Never mind the water. Down to business."

"Suit yourself."

Looking around, I added, "Maybe you have a place to sit?"

He gestured again. "There might be a clean spot over there somewhere."

I clasped my hands behind my back for fear of touching anything. "Standing, then."

He sat down in a high-backed black leather chair by the desk and crossed his arms.

I inhaled. "Basically, you'd be working for me."

He continued to study me as if I had six heads. "That's not much of a hook. If you haven't noticed, you're kind of an old *Castlevania* reject."

I winced at the age crack. "I figured I'd lead with the good news. The bad news is…"

"I'd have to dress like that?"

I winced again. "No, but I'm certainly reconsidering my offer."

"Whoa! Hold up, boss. I'm sorry. I just get a bit salty when my blood sugar's low. So, what's this job?"

I gazed appraisingly at him. "Yeah, on second thought, I'm not sure you have what it takes to do this."

He folded his arms and scowled. "Hey, man. I was top at MIT."

My shoulders gravitated toward my ears. "So what?"

"I'm one of the best in my field."

"Any monkey can run a bit of code."

His scowl transformed into a smirk. "If any monkey could, you wouldn't be here."

"Touché. Alright, so you're good at the keyboard. What about your stomach?"

He patted his modest belly. "Hang around and you can watch me eat a whole fucking pizza. At least, I think I ordered one."

The room seemed to darken as I kept my voice even and ice cold. "That's not what I mean. I'm talking about when you're out in the field, Mr. Mopps. What happens when you're out in the field and the shit goes down and there's fucking gore and guts everywhere and you can't fucking see because you have your partner's blood in your eyes because his fucking head was just ripped off? What do you do then, Charlie?"

He leaned away from me in his chair. "You sure you're not fucking with me?"

"Actually, Mr. Mopps, I'm dead serious."

"Dude."

I let out a laugh. "No, of course I'm just fucking with you. It won't be like that at all. Just some light freelance computer work when I need it. You'll be on call. After each job completion you'll get a check in the mail, and no questions asked. Think you can handle it?"

"I have a question."

"See? I knew you couldn't handle it."

He squinted. "How much are we talking?"

"Depends on what I need, but you'll be amply compensated for your time."

He shook his head. "Nah, I still have questions."

"You're a tough one. Here I'm trying to be as vague as possible."

"And it's fuckin' annoying."

I tugged at my collar. "It helps keep the whole cloak-and-dagger facade."

He bit his lower lip. "You mean the whole spy-versus-spy bullshit? Yeah, that shit is stupid. What agency did you say you were from?"

I raised an eyebrow. "Did I?"

"You still haven't told me your name either."

I sighed. "Also true. So do you want the job or not?"

"Am I just supposed to call you Grindelwald then?"

My eyes popped as my jaw fell. "What?"

"Since I'm taking the job I gotta call you something."

"Wait, you are?"

He snapped his fingers in excitement and pointed at me. "Hey, I know. Bosley. You're from that era, right?"

I snorted. "You're no Angel."

He rolled his eyes. "Whatever, Van Helsing. Remember, I better get paid, or you may find your weird-ass freaky business all over TikTok and YouTube. And I'm not exclusive. I'm not dropping any of my existing clients and I reserve the right to pick up new ones as I see fit. Do we understand each other?"

He might be able to give PIE a run for its money if the information in his file held any truth. I shook my head and gave a mirthful chuckle. "You have no idea, and call me Dr. Diamondback."

"Get the fuck out, you're a doctor?"

"Yes."

He folded his arms. "A doctor of what?"

I opened the front door to leave. "You're still asking questions."

"You didn't give me a business card or anything."

"Correct, Mr. Mopps. Don't call me, I'll call you." I closed the door behind me.

If this guy was worth his salt, he'd find the number I had planted online for just such an occasion. Before I could reach the elevator, my phone rang. My eyebrows lifted in surprise as I picked up and listened. That had been rather expedient.

Charlie sounded irritated. "What? Is this like some sort of stupid fucking test?"

I continued walking down the hallway. "If it had been a test, would you be passing, Mr. Mopps? You can't even seem to follow simple directions."

"Are you sure you even exist? I can't find shit on you."

"Still with the questions, but bravo for finding my number so quickly. We'll be in touch." I killed the call.

My phone rang again. I spoke first this time. "You can't take a hint, can you? No wonder you're single despite that baby face of yours."

Charlie's voice came back at me as he whistled. "Okay, I admit your schooling's impressive. A Berkeley graduate with a bachelor's in forensic science, double master's in criminal justice and toxicology, and for the cherry on top, a PhD in forensic psychology. With all that, shouldn't you be working for the FBI as a criminal profiler or some shit?"

I paused by the elevator. "The department I work for also deals in parapsychology, which is more of an interest to me."

"Parapsychology?"

"Paranormal psychology. The study of paranormal entities and their activity."

He thought for a second. "So you went from being a CSI golden boy to a dead-end job psychoanalyzing Casper the Friendly Ghost and his three uncles?"

"In lamest terms, I suppose."

He chuckled. "Sucker."

"Though you're not far off from the 'dead end' part."

"Hey, as long as you're getting paid, right?"

"Money isn't everything, Mr. Mopps."

His keyboard clicked furiously in the background. "Yeah, well it's everything to me and I still can't find anything on where you work or who you work for. I wanna makes sure my checks clear."

I hit the call button to go up. "Trust me, you won't, but you'll learn soon enough."

"One last question before I go."

I stepped into the elevator as the doors opened. "What, Mr. Mopps?"

"Can ghosts use computers?"

I hung up and mumbled as I pressed the button for my floor. "Fucking kids."

Affidavit from Charlie Mopps: Evidence ID#: SJ-0003 Charlie's Apartment, Five Seconds After the Doctor Left

CHARLIE MOPPS HAD ALWAYS been secure in the realm of what he considered sane. He believed in ghosts and the supernatural, hence his handle Spook. It was funny on a few different levels. The truth? He had seen ghosts every day of his twenty-three years on this earth and had long ago accepted that he saw the world differently than most people—a secret he guarded very closely. He couldn't talk to them, couldn't interact with them, but he could see them and could normally tell the difference between the living and the dead. It was in the way they moved.

The ghost that had come in with the doctor had unhinged him. A little girl, no more than seven, in a pink jacket, light blue shirt, blue jeans, and light-up *Care Bear* LA Gear's, which hadn't been seen since the early nineties. It had taken Charlie a minute to even identify her as a ghost. He had secretly been hoping for Girl Scout cookies when they first showed up, but no such luck. He found it rather ironic that the doctor had no idea he had a ghost attached to him considering what he did for a living.

She hadn't done anything, just stood next to the doctor, staring up at him with an expression of admiration on her face. With her blonde hair and blue eyes, she looked like a real guardian angel.

When the doctor left, though, she did something Charlie hadn't expected. She walked— floated? He wasn't sure—toward his computer. She stuck her hand through it, and when she pulled it out, there on the screen plain as day was a single word following the command prompt: "Help."

Then she waved at Charlie and disappeared.

That, for sure, remained a first.

Who the fuck was this guy?

Chapter 3

A MURDER OF CROWS isn't an odd thing to see at a park in California, especially in October. I remember the cawing and cackling in any season. Milling around on the ground or nestled in tree branches they perched, preening, watching, waiting.

Like something out of a Hitchcock movie.

As a teenager, I had been blissfully ignorant, but now I understand the significance of their congregation.

They gather to bear witness.

Growing up, I lived in an upper-class neighborhood where nothing ever happened. We had a two-story house, a pool in the backyard with a waterfall, and Dad often took us on his business trips to LA so we could spend the weekend at Disneyland, or there was the one time we went to Hawaii for two weeks. Things came so good, so easy, I had no fundamental idea of the darker, harsher realities of the world. Sheltered living had made me arrogant. Why would I think anything bad would happen to me or those around me?

One day, with Mom cooking dinner and Dad still at work, I had taken my younger sister to the park for some fresh air and exercise. As the older brother, our parents had always trusted me, even expected me to be responsible with her. She loved the playground. Surrounded by tall pines and other trees, it had swings, slides, and even one of those old steel merry-go-rounds that some older kid would spin so fast that all the other kids would tumble from it like water drops from an aspergillum, a few throwing up in the tanbark from dizziness. I could see the baseball diamond where I played little league at the other end of the park from the bench where I sat. My nose intently glued to my new handheld video game console while my sister hung upside down from the monkey bars by her legs, singing the *Gummy Bears* theme song at the top of her lungs with her face turning red as she swung back and forth.

Only seven years old, Daisy had golden hair and sky-blue eyes set off by her pink jacket and blue jeans with a rainbow on the back pocket. She positively glowed because Mom had bought her the light-up *Care Bear* LA Gears she wanted.

The sun raced toward the western city skyline as it started to grow colder. Children whining to stay had been grabbed up by mothers and fathers or else jumped on their bikes to race home before sundown to avoid a scolding. The rustling of feathers from the crows joined the rustling of trees in the wind as the streetlights flickered on.

I called out, "Time to head home, Day! It's almost dinner!"

"Hold on, Dare! I'll be there in a minute." She pulled herself up, grabbed the bar, and went into a backward flip for a dismount.

"Show off!"

She stuck her tongue out and ran around to ride her favorite slide one more time before we left. I turned my attention back to the game console in my hands. The wind, the crows, and light traffic off Quimby Road meshed with the noise from my game as it grew darker. The streetlamps flickered on and off as the console screen went fuzzy. I whacked the side of it to get it to work again. "Come on, damn it, not now. Stupid batteries."

It came back into focus.

I had died because of the power failure. "Aww, son of a bitch."

The crows squabbled and postured as the lights flickered continuously and my game died completely, forcing me to look around. Finally, the last ray of sunlight disappeared as the wind whipped up strong and frigid.

"Day?"

Nothing but the cawing of crows and the howl of the wind. I jumped as a fat, black rat skittered across the tanbark.

I stood. The empty swings squeaked back and forth in the breeze with "ghost kids," as my sister and I called them. "Daisy? Come on now, Mom's gonna kick my butt if we don't get home and then Dad will kick what's left of it."

I made my way toward her favorite slide. She wasn't there. Just a rat standing on its hind legs, twitching its whiskers at me. "Daisy Marie Diamondback, this isn't funny!"

The crows went berserk.

I shielded myself with my arms from a cloud of black feathers that exploded in front of me. As they cleared, I squinted in the low light, finally catching sight of the blinking lights on her shoes in the distance.

"Day, what the heck…" Once my eyes came into focus, I saw her caught in the middle of every kid's nightmare. She had been slung over the shoulder of some creep silhouetted by shadows, trying to make off with her.

Dropping my game to the ground, I sprinted to the rescue. There had been no scream, no call for help, which meant this guy had to have taken her by surprise. He had probably done this thousands of times, but with seven years of wrestling and martial arts under my belt, I felt confidence swell in my chest.

He stopped as he heard me coming, glancing over his shoulder, still cloaked in shadow.

I flew at him like the Man of Steel. "Hey, dickweed! Let go of my sister."

I noticed Daisy had been rendered unconscious as I tried to punch and kick every inch of him. I might as well have been trying to move the boulder of Prometheus. My fisticuffs bounced off the hulking mass in front of me, landing me on my ass more than once as he stood there.

Still, I kept popping up to press the attack when his backhand hit me like a planetesimal. On the ground once more, I felt my eye and lip swelling and tasted the blood in my mouth. I didn't care as I reached deep down inside myself and channeled the inner willpower to stand back up.

This was my hero moment.

From the flickering streetlamp, I could tell I faced no ordinary child molester, but a monster that urban legends were spun from. Over eight feet tall with massive bedrock limbs, he looked like Andre the Giant in a Halloween costume. The hood of his unzipped jacket fell away to reveal a mop of dirty black hair that hung loose over his face like greasy jungle vines. His skin looked pale and lumpy like milk left out on the counter during a hot summer day. Dingy yellow nails and teeth to match looked jagged and crooked as he glared at me. Grubby dungaree overalls covered in dirt and shit, a filthy white collared shirt, and soiled work boots that smelled like a used port-a-potty mixed with a smell I would come to recognize much later in life, the stench of death. But it was his eyes that I remember the most. Twin burning-red orbs of pure, unadulterated hate.

He sniffed at me with a fat, crooked nose. His voice sounded like stone grinding on stone. "You? You're too old for Daddy to play with."

I set myself in a side stance and pointed a finger as blood trickled down my chin from a busted lip. "I'm not playing. I'll… I'll fuckin' kill you, motherfucker. Stay away from my sister!"

He smiled a crooked-toothed grin that made my blood go cold and dropped Daisy to the ground with a thud. "Oh well, Daddy will have fun breaking… breaking your neck on the Darkside. Your sister isn't going anywhere."

Grinning, he beckoned me with both hands upturned in a sloppy square stance. I gave a primordial war cry as I charged. He should have been easy to overcome with no technique, but again, his sheer mass sent me back to the ground.

Adrenaline remained my best friend as I rolled out of the way of his boot speeding toward my face. My toes dug into the grass as I scrambled toward my sister. I had to get her to safety.

My outstretched finger brushed her jacket before his boot came out of nowhere again and caught me in the ribs. For such a big guy, he moved with the speed and agility of a UFC champion. A sickening crunch sounded in my ears. He picked me up off the ground by the neck and put his face into mine as I wheezed for air.

Drool ran from his cracked smile as breath like a men's restroom hit me harder than the boot. His laugh sounded deep, gravely, and hoarse. "Stupid boy, you can't! You can't hurt Daddy. You're weak, weak, weak! You're nothing without the Darkside, nothing! You're a pathetic excuse for a human being."

I fixed him with my good eye and spat blood in his face. A bloated, purple tongue licked it off his cheek without breaking his maniacal grin. "Is that the best… the best you got? Some big brother you are."

He didn't see the lock-blade knife I had drawn from my pocket. I plunged all three and a half inches right into his eye. Thank my lucky stars for being a Scout: Always be prepared.

He dropped me to the ground and grabbed at his eye. I smiled a bloody smile, quite proud of myself, until I figured out his screams of pain were really fits of laughter. The chortling stopped and the hand came away from his face. My knife protruded from his eye as he looked straight at me. No blood seeped from the wound. He reached up, ripped it out, and tossed it away without a care. "That's right, boy. Nothing can hurt Daddy!"

In that moment, the stark reality of my situation came into sharp focus. I knew exactly what I faced. The very thing that parents have warned their children about since the invention of language. It would come in the night to kidnap little children and drag them away, never to be seen again. It would torment those who didn't eat their vegetables or pulled their little sister's hair because she messed up their science project. It lurked under beds and behind closet doors, grinning with malice, waiting for darkness to thin the veil between reality and the nightmare where it dwelled so it could slither out, approaching its young, fear-stricken victims with a predatory inexorability. It collected children who had been painted red and placed on street corners, though now I realize that the paint was their own blood that it lusted for. It embodied stranger danger and the ever-present threat of evil in this world, used to discourage the petty evil acts of childhood while attempting to teach caution and vigilance. Now it wanted Daisy and me. Like all children, I knew its name.

As death came for me, a hiss caught my ear. Then another harmonized with it. Turning my throbbing head, my blurred vision made out four alley cats, backs arched. Spitting, hissing, and growling they moved in front of me, as if forming a wall. The creature shied away at first, then took an angry step forward. "You won't stop Daddy, stupid cats! Stupid, stupid cats!"

I tried to move toward my sister, despair forcing me to feel every wound and ache, making me slow.

He reached out to stop me, but one of the animals raked his hand with its claws.

He snatched it back, howling. Black ectoplasm ran down the wound as his eyes flared.

The cats began to stalk toward him like they would a rodent, tails bristled as I collapsed to the ground unable to move any further.

He picked up my sister with his uninjured hand and slung her over his shoulder once more, backing away from the cats. "Maybe they can save you, but they can't save you both from the Darkside, Big Brother."

He laughed, and then Daisy's voice came from his mouth. "Goodbye, Dare. Goodbye forever!"

The last thing I saw before giving into unconsciousness felt like something out of *Tales from the Crypt*. His maniacal laughter mixed with the frantic cawing of the crows, and the gleeful squeaking of rats rang in my ears, as pain, grief, and failure overwhelmed me, forcing my body to shut down.

I AWOKE SWEATING DESPITE the frigid air and tried to sit up. A hand gently pressed on my shoulder to keep me from rising as a voice I didn't know spoke. "We need to restrain him so he can't move. If he thrashes around anymore, he's liable to injure himself further."

I tensed and tried to defend myself but found I couldn't move my arms. I wanted to turn my head, but something prevented me from doing so. My bedroom looked like a hospital. People I didn't know hovered over me dressed like medical staff or police officers. There was a steady beep of a heart monitor and the mixture of murmuring voices as a blood pressure cuff buzzed to life and tightened around my left arm.

"He's awake!" My mother's voice rose above the others, but then I drifted out again.

The next time I came around I knew I wasn't dreaming. I still wore the whiplash collar and the blood pressure cuff. A fentanyl drip had been hooked up to my right arm. My hands and feet had been strapped down so I couldn't thrash about. The pain in my ribs throbbed in time with my heartbeat and my face felt as numb as my wits. I scanned the room and saw Mom asleep in a chair nearby. I gave a dusty croak. "D–Daisy?"

Mom stirred and looked up. "Darrell? Darrell! Honey?"

"M–mom?"

"Oh my God. He's awake!"

Tears streamed out of my eyes as my parents stared down at me with tears streaming out of theirs. My father's voice sounded choked and forced. "Easy, son."

I struggled. "Dad, he's got her!"

"Darrell, stay down."

"No! He's got her."

My dad put a hand on my shoulder to try and calm me. Their tears fell rapidly as my mom spoke. "Do you know who has Daisy, Darrell? What happened?"

"We have to find her!"

My dad grimaced. "Calm down. The police are looking for her right now. Just tell us what happened."

I continued to try and push myself back up, but I didn't have the strength. "No, you don't understand. He... he has her."

"Who, son? You know who has Daisy?"

"The bogeyman." I passed out again.

My Apartment, Santana Row, San Jose, CA—0815 hours (To Date)

I AWOKE IN MY leather recliner, listening to rain pelting the window mingled with the sounds of morning traffic on Stevens Creek Boulevard. The venetian blinds to the balcony hung open, and I blinked against the overcast morning light streaming in. Staring for a moment at the smoky blue colored walls with white wooden trim and a textured white ceiling, I stretched my arms and groaned.

I hated that memory.

When I had finally been able to tell the full story, things didn't go over so well. Miraculously, no one had witnessed my epic fight except for the crows and alley cats, and evidently, they weren't talking. Hell, I almost didn't believe me. Thank goodness my parents never put me in a mental institution. Sure, I saw a psychiatrist for a while. She told me my mind had been so stressed out over the events that I couldn't remember things clearly, but that tripe was total crap and I knew it. She even wanted to put me on medication for a while, though I refused to take it.

I wasn't crazy.

After a few weeks, the cops quit searching for her. After a few months, my mother quit speaking to me and dove into a bottle as my father buried himself in his work. He wouldn't even look at me anymore, and I had been his golden boy, his legacy. Kids at school thought me weird or a liar, so they avoided me. Even the goths and emos kept their distance. It was the worst of times as my nightmares grew more intense, but at least I had Gizmo, our cat. He slept with me every night until I moved out on my own. Even now I liked to have a cat around the house because they kept rats away. *Rats are* his *pets.* I started hanging out in libraries, especially the ones at universities, looking up everything I could on stress and trauma and their effects on memory. Nothing could explain away my truth, what I knew I saw, what I knew I had been through. Since nobody cared enough to watch me, I kept going back to the park and looking for clues. Those fucking cops might have quit but I never would. I still go by the park from time to time to trace over my steps.

I looked over at my bookshelf that held glossy new volumes of titles like *How to Analyze People* by David T. Abbots or *Coping with Trauma* by Kleber, Brom, and Defares, intermixed with several dusty old tomes Stravinsky had given me while I worked as a crime scene investigator for a missing persons unit. We met when he came as a guest speaker during my five months at the police academy. I had a lot of questions about some of the more unorthodox investigative techniques he had described in his address such as the use of salt, silver, and the usefulness of UV rays when attempting to detect and trace paranormal entities. The other attending officers mocked him until I made them all look like fools, leaving him and me alone in the room to continue our discussion. The day of my graduation from the academy, he had taken me to lunch and gave me a trunk full of ancient, brittle volumes relating to a field he referred to as "paranormal psychology" as a graduation present. Some of them had been obvious handmade copies of other works yet were so old I had to use cotton gloves and tweezers to turn the pages lest they fell apart. Many of the original works read like stereo instructions or the mad rantings of an ancient conspiracy theorist. I devoured every page, committing them to memory.

My stint with San Jose Missing Persons lasted thirteen months, during which I prevented a zombie apocalypse; but that's another story. Stravinsky and I kept in steady correspondence the entire time, the bulk consisting of me begging him to bring me on to work for an organization that I knew only one thing about: They went looking for the paranormal and found them.

I took out the picture of Daisy from my breast pocket where I kept it, alongside a gold heart locket she used to wear. Her face carried a prize fighter's victory smile as she proudly showed off the big-girl gaps where her top incisors had come out just before the picture had been taken. Twin braids rested on her shoulders looking like the golden rope from Rumpelstiltskin's loom. It happened to be the same photo that had been scanned into her cold-case file that sat in a manila folder on my desk at the bottom of a pile of my more recent work. The only difference being the photo in my pocket had a white crease cutting across the top left corner. Several years ago, I had been wrestling with someone possessed by a poltergeist, leaving me with a scar on my back from a kitchen knife and a creased picture of my sister. I put it away not wanting to drudge up that memory.

The morning grew long, and I had an interview to conduct before my superiors pitched a fit about me not trying to build this team they seemed to think I needed. My Bombay cat, Nicodemus, slept in my lap and I shifted to give him a hint. He stretched, arched his back, and began kneading my leg with his claws. Big yellow eyes bored into mine as if to say, "Don't you dare."

His short, solid black fur felt like satin beneath my palm as I ran my hand down his back. "Okay, you win."

I sat there for a while, scratching him between the ears as he purred like an industrial generator. I had found him as a kitten entangled in a basket of yarn while raiding the home of a sea hag. After causing his owner's demise, I ran a few tests to make sure he wasn't some demon from hell. Afterward, I felt compelled to take him home and raise him as my own. Sometimes I wasn't sure I had performed those tests correctly, but he was mine now.

I sighed looking at my iWatch. It was noon and I had things to do. I whispered an apology to Nicodemus and set him on the carpet. He gave me a sage look and an indignant meow, then slunk off in search of another warm place to curl up.

I took a shower, changed, put food and fresh water out for the cat, then left. Time to meet the second person on Stravinsky's list.

XYZ News Building, San Francisco, CA—1334 hours

T HE NEWS BUILDING BUZZED like a hive of angry wasps. Everything harmonized in the chaotic symphony of a high-pressure work environment. As I stepped off the elevator, I discovered a completely untapped source of psychological research. A balding guy in bifocals wearing tan slacks, a checkered sweater vest, and a green brimmed visor ran some paper through a paper shredder while muttering to himself about the genius of his prose and how sorry they would all be when he left. A lady in a pink blouse and gray skirt didn't try to hide the fact she wasn't paying attention as she stared at her smartphone, letting endless copies spill onto the floor. A guy in a blue collared shirt with his sleeves rolled up rested an elbow on his desk, forehead in hand, begging someone at the other end of a cell phone not to leave him. Littered with cubicles, offices, corridors, and ugly green paisley industrial carpeting, ink coupled with strong coffee and burnt popcorn hung in the air as I made my way to an office nestled in the corner of it all.

I knocked on the faux wooden door adorned with a name placard. "Ms. Jaiden Fox?"

Storm-gray eyes in a sea of flawlessly made-up olive skin glanced through the open door from behind a pair of pink-marble Marbella Vogue eyeglasses. She looked far younger than the thirty-something accusation in her file. An untamable lock of raven-black hair kept falling over her right eye and she continuously pushed it aside while typing with all the speed of a stenographer. The back wall displayed an array of journalistic awards, personal pictures of her and her boyfriend, and her college diploma from Northwestern University. She wore a black Ralph Lauren tuxedo jumpsuit, a pearl necklace, and a matching bracelet on her right wrist. As I stepped into her office, her Chanel No. 5 limited edition lingered in the air.

She scrunched her nose without taking her eyes off the screen. "I'm sorry, you are?"

I realized I had been staring. I shook it off and cleared my throat. "I understand you're very busy, Ms. Fox…"

She cut me off. "If that were true, you wouldn't be distracting me, Mister…"

I handed her a card. "Doctor, actually. Dr. Darrell Diamondback."

Her eyes hardly brushed the card as she set it aside and continued typing. "What exactly is it you think I can do for you, Doctor?"

"I'm wondering if there's a more private place we might, um, talk?"

She barked out a mocking laugh and pushed the lock of hair back from her face again, then returned to typing. "I'm sorry, Doctor, but I'm taken."

I clasped my hands behind my back. "Oh, nothing like that. I know you're dating that Bigfoot hunter reality star. Oh, what's his name… Jakob Barr? Star? Something like that. He seems alright, if you like that sort of thing."

The typing abruptly stopped as she glared at me. "That's Marr, and if you came here to discuss my love life, I'm sure security can help you find your way out."

"No, Ms. Fox, it's your skill sets not your love life that interests me. I came here to offer you a job."

"I have one of those too."

I shrugged. "And I'll bet you're about as happy with it as the others are, judging from the numerous failed relationships around here. Did you hear the guy on the phone three cubicles down? He's practically on the ledge. Some personal days would probably help him out."

Fury flashed in her eyes like lightning. "You've got to be kidding me."

"I assure you I am not kidding. That's why I'd like to get away from this office. This place could suck your soul out through your nose it's so depressing."

Her lips went thin as she reached for the receiver on her desk. "Okay, jackass. You've wasted enough of my time. I'm calling security."

I held up my hands. "No, wait, please. I'm sorry about the soul sucking thing, but I am serious about offering you a job."

Her hand hovered over the phone as she frowned at me. Finally, she snatched up my card, scrutinizing it. "It just has a name and a phone number."

I blinked. "Naturally, that's how you contact me once you accept the job."

"But there's no other information on who you are or who you work for."

"That's true. I can see why my agency is interested in you."

She gave a snort of a laugh as she shook her head.

I produced a lopsided grin. "Though I wouldn't mind going over some of the finer details, say, over coffee? My treat?"

She sighed, smiled wryly, and toasted me with a mug bearing the XYZ logo, then went back to typing, the lock of hair falling in her face again. "As you can see, Doctor, I have coffee, a man, and a job that I'm quite happy with. Now, if you'd kindly quit wasting my time, I have a deadline to meet."

My face fell. "You haven't even listened to my offer."

"Nor do I plan to."

I scrunched my nose and shrugged. "Keep the card, just in case you change your mind."

She picked it up off her desk and threw it into the garbage can without missing a keystroke. "Yeah, I'll do that."

I scowled. "The thing is, Ms. Fox, it would be imperative for you to keep your job at XYZ if you were to accept my offer. We're looking to recruit a person with your skills and resources. I assure you there would be no conflict of interest between the two, so I do hope you'll reconsider. Sorry for the interruption to your dead… line. Have a pleasant day."

As I spun on my heel to leave, I could feel her eyes on me, the rapping of her keyboard stopping a second time.

The Sewers near Douglass Playground Picnic Area, San Francisco, CA—1810 hours

RATTLING FROM THE TRAFFIC above, a maze of pipes that lined the concrete ceiling dripped into a trench full of murky water. Two burning red eyes sat in the darkness surrounded by rats scurrying to and fro on the slimy concrete floors. Scrambling over grimy work boots, sitting on his deformed head, clinging onto his hooded jacket for dear life then falling back onto the pavement, their squealing and shrieking echoing throughout the gloomy tunnels.

He lifted one on a huge finger to eye level. "Daddy... Daddy is hungry. You will show Daddy when the sun has set on the Darkside so he can hunt. Go, go now!"

The rat scurried off.

His head twitched as if he had water in his ear. "The rage, it... it hurts." He clenched a fist as his eyes flared. "Daddy needs to hunt. Daddy needs to feed... feed on the innocent. He needs to taste their fear... fear! He needs, needs, needs their anguish, their bloody blood for the Darkside."

A big fat rat from the masses raised up on its hind legs to consider him, whiskers twitching.

Turning his attention on it, he bellowed. "Do you know what the mean old bastard did to the poor little guy? Do you? No, no, no! Of course you don't. You weren't there, were you? On the Darkside? How could you possibly know? How could a stupid rat know... know anything about the Darkside?"

The rat sniffed at the air.

A dirty, pale hand pushed the oily locks out of his face as he glared at the tiny creature. "Fine! Fine, fine, fine. Do you really want to know? Do you? What happened on the Darkside? Then Daddy… Daddy will tell you about the Darkside. The… the mean old bastard used to get drunk and beat the poor little guy, kick the poor little guy, crush cigarettes on the poor little guy's arms, burning him. One time… one time, the mean old bastard slammed the poor little guy against the walls of his room, then threw the poor little guy on the bed and whipped the poor little guy! Whipped him on the Darkside! Whipped him across the back with a belt until the poor little guy bled, all because the poor little guy woke the mean old bastard up. Anything, anything the poor little guy did wasn't good enough. Anything the poor little guy said was wrong! Wrong, wrong, wrong! Anything the poor little guy ever… ever tried to accomplish was met with ridicule and scorn. The mean old bastard never wanted a son, only a punching bag, that mean old bastard. And the selfish bitch? The selfish bitch. She let the mean old bastard do it! Just stood there and watched, like the selfish bitch enjoyed it on the Darkside. Until the selfish bitch got a taste of the mean old bastard's medicine. Didn't she? Then? Then the selfish bitch cared. Can you believe it?"

The rat waved its front paws and chittered.

"Daddy knows, Daddy knows everything! And then… and then other people were no better. Laughing at the poor little guy, taunting the poor little guy, hurting the poor little guy's feelings, hurting the poor little guy on the Darkside." His head jerked again. "We don't know why the poor little guy was different, he just… was, and… and they hurt him for it."

The rat hunched over and sniffed at one of its own.

He pointed a sallow finger and roared as his eyes flared like a bonfire beneath his hood. "Don't ignore Daddy when Daddy's talking to you, or Daddy will knock you into next week! Do you understand Daddy?"

The rat snapped back to attention.

"That's more like it. You show Daddy proper respect. Always show Daddy proper respect on the Darkside."

He blinked, then smiled as he rubbed his hands together. "Daddy can see it's almost sunset. Daddy hates the sun, hates it… hate on the Darkside. It stings the poor little guy and burns his skin and that makes Daddy mad, mad, mad. Daddy hates this world. It's evil, and mean, and stupid, and uncaring on the Darkside!"

He slammed a fist on the floor making the rats around him run for cover while others that had been too slow went flying. "Well if they don't care about Daddy, then Daddy doesn't care about them! They'll all pay for the hurt that poor little guy felt, they'll pay in rivers of blood, bloody blood… blood on the Darkside."

His stomach growled. "So hungry, but we need to watch for the cats who hunt the poor little guy, the crows that tattle on the poor little guy, and the dogs that can see and smell the poor little guy. And the people… people on the Darkside! The people that might get in Daddy's way when Daddy finds new meat to tenderize and stew in anguish… sweet, sweet anguish"

His hand shot out grabbing the rat he had been talking to and shoved it in his mouth. The shrieks and crunching of bones stopped after a few moments of chewing, then he swallowed and burped. "It's… it's not enough. Not enough! Daddy needs the pleading cries for mercy, the torment and fear, the marring of an innocent soul until it breaks just like that poor little guy did when Daddy was born on the Darkside. That's what Daddy craves, and that's what Daddy will have… soon."

Finally, the last rays of the sun disappeared as his laugh echoed loudest of all through the sewer. "It's time, it's time! Hurry, hurry to the surface. Now it's time to choose a new playmate."

He disappeared into the darkness as the rats all split in different directions, leaving only the echo of dripping water behind.

I AWOKE WITH A start to find Nicodemus curled up at my feet in a dark room. The softness of a warm mattress under me proved an eerie contrast to the cold wet concrete of the sewer. My silk sheets clung to my drenched body as I lay there panting and sweating. I flung them to the side and sat up, drawing a haughty look of derision and an irritated yowl from Nicodemus as he hopped off the bed. I clutched my head and stood. That had been so lifelike, it felt as if I had been there, watching him. I could almost smell the sewer gas still assaulting my nose. Dreams like that occurred for me often enough, but this had been so vivid I couldn't help but feel jumpy. I marched to the bathroom and threw on the light. I looked in the mirror as I pulled at the bags under my eyes with a finger and stuck my tongue out at my reflection. Not noticing anything immediately wrong, I clicked the light off.

I was having difficulty pushing this one away. On my way back to bed, I glanced at my refrigerator through the open bedroom door and chuckled. As I crawled underneath the covers, I figured it must have been a mild psychosis induced by a late-night snack of pepperoni pizza mixed with past trauma, nothing more. I settled back down to try and pick up a little more sleep.

Chapter 4

J AIDEN APPEARED ON THE screen with a playground behind her, the unruly lock of hair streaming along the right side of her head in the blustery oceanic wind. "Good morning, San Francisco. This is Jaiden Fox for XYZ, the last word in news. Our story this morning comes to you live from Douglass Park, where another tragedy has struck our fair city. Yet another child has gone missing yesterday evening, making it the fourth one in four months. This time it's five-year-old Maddison Bell, and like the other three children, circumstances are rather bizarre."

The news feed cut to a bust shot of a soccer mom with styled bleach-blonde hair, Chanel sunglasses, and lips that had been engorged from collagen with a boob job to match. "Keren Dolittle: eyewitness," popped up below her image. "Well obviously we're all just so devastated around here. *I* was in the parking lot at the time it happened, so I heard the whole thing. But Betty-Jo, who knows Peggy, who knows Janice, said she's just devastated. One moment her and little Maddison were walking to their car, she unlocked and opened the door, and then, *bam*! Supposedly little Maddison just disappeared like magic, without a trace."

Footage cut to an overweight individual with greasy brown hair, droopy eyes, and a day or two of growth on his face. He blinked into the camera, shaking like a blender set to frappé. Sporting an olive-green groundskeeper uniform, "John Diggle: eyewitness" appeared below.

He looked past the camera. "Now? You… you want me to talk now?"

One could hear Jaiden hissing in the background. "Yes, *now!*"

He bobbed his head as he centered his gaze, wringing his ball cap in his hands. "Oh, okay. So, uh, yeah… so I was takin' out the trash by the parking lot last evenin' and… and my momma said, she always told me, 'Johhny, Johnny don't you ever lie,' so that's how you know I ain't lyin'. But I was takin' out the trash, and… and I-I saw that little girl disappear right from behind her momma. *Whisk!* Just like that! Scariest <*beep!*> thing I'd ever seen in my life."

The image switched to Jaiden in front of the park again. "The disappearance happened at six thirty yesterday evening according to Maddison's mother, Janice Bell, just after sundown right here in Diamond Heights at Douglass Playground. An amber alert has already been issued for Maddison who was last seen wearing purple pants, a black shirt, a pink hoodie, and white sandals."

A shot of a middle-aged woman in a white blouse and red jacket with blonde hair, blue eyes swimming in tears, and a red nose from blowing it, sniffled into the camera. "Janice Bell: victim's mother" appeared at the bottom of the screen. "Please, please who ever took my baby, please just bring her back. Please? I'll… I'll give you anything, anything! Just… please bring her back to me… please?"

The poor woman broke down crying as the footage cut to a shot of four different pictures of children with their names and ages stenciled underneath. Jaiden's voice continued in the background. "The family has provided us with a recent picture of Maddison that we're showing now. She's the latest in a string of disappearances, and we're putting all their pictures up on screen, including young Ian Johnson, age five, abducted from George Christopher Playground back in July; Kayla Sanchez, age seven, abducted from the parking lot of Whole Foods Market in August; six-year-old Montel Evens, abducted from Diamond Heights Shopping Center in September;

and now, Maddison Bell, taken less than twenty-four hours ago at Twenty-Seventh and Douglass."

The footage cut back to Jaiden still standing in front of the park. "Police have not commented on this ongoing investigation, but one might conclude that we have a serial kidnapper on our hands, and a crafty one at that. There's no word on whether the FBI will be involved, but the police are advising people to keep two eyes on their young ones and to be inside by sundown with windows and doors locked, though they are not enforcing a mandatory curfew at this time. Police Chief McNair stated that extra patrols are being issued for Diamond Heights and all surrounding areas."

A hotline number appeared at the bottom of the screen as the video focused back on Jaiden once more. "If anyone has seen anything or has any information on the whereabouts of any of these children, they are encouraged to come forward. You can even call in anonymously to the hotline number at the bottom of the screen. We here at XYZ News would like to send our thoughts and prayers to all the families affected by these travesties, and we will keep you, the viewers, updated on this story as more unfolds. This is Jaiden Fox for XYZ, the last word in news, saying: Stay safe, San Francisco. Now, back to you, Anna."

The video feed stopped.

Starbucks on Santana Row, San Jose, CA—0927 hours

I HAD JUST TREATED myself to a venti white mocha with a double shot of espresso from Starbucks when my phone began to play "The Imperial March" by John Williams. I picked it up. "Happy's House of Hamburgers, what's your beef?"

A garbled voice came from the other end. "Very funny, Doctor. We have a problem in San Francisco. We need you and your new team on it."

"Yeah, umm, about that…"

"You did reach out to your team, correct?"

"Charlie Mopps is a tentative maybe."

"What about Jaiden Fox?"

"Working on her."

My director didn't seem amused. "Work harder. She's on this story. Use that as your angle. What of Mr. Anderson?"

"Hey, I can only do so much in a day."

"Remember, I want results this time, Doctor. I'm sending some files to Mr. Mopps. You'll understand your assignment after reading them."

"Yeah, sure." I hung up.

It seemed I would have to have round two with Ms. Fox after all. First things first: Best to give Charlie a heads-up that he would be receiving some important files.

After a few rings, he picked up, his voice groggy. "H–hello?"

Pushing my way out of Starbucks, I headed toward the carport. I chirped into the phone, "Rise and shine, cupcake. The early bird gets the worm, you know."

"Fuckin' Doc? What the fuck? Didn't I tell you not to bother me until noon?"

I took a noisy sip of my coffee. "No."

"Oh, well I meant to."

"Just giving you a heads-up. You have some important files coming your way."

He yawned. "What kind of files?"

"Frankly, I have no idea. Check for me, would you?"

He moved around, then there was the clicking sound of keystrokes. "Yeah, yeah, keep your pants on. Looks like some video footage and four dossiers. Let's see…" *Click, click, click.* "Ian Johnson? This guy's just a kid, Doc. This one too: Kayla Sanchez? Why do these names sound so familiar?"

I remembered the news reports. It seemed like PIE knew something the SFPD didn't. "Do you watch the news?"

Charlie sounded less than engaged. "Sometimes, I try to stay away from politics, to tell you the truth. I figure the asshole is always gonna win."

"The news isn't all politics and gloom. Sometimes there's actual worthwhile information, but let me guess: the last two files are those of Montel Evens and Maddison Bell?"

After a short pause, Charlie's voice came back. "I guess that's why they pay you the big bucks, huh? So what the hell am I supposed to do with all this?"

"How do you feel about solving a multiple kidnapping?"

"Why not leave it to the police and let me go back to sleep?"

"Obviously my agency feels there's something that they won't be able to handle and there's no rest for the wicked. You mentioned there's video feed, Mr. Mopps?"

"Yeah, of a Whole Foods parking lot... Very boring."

"Just keep watching."

"Whoa! The little girl just disappeared. Like, one minute she's standing behind her mother, then the next she's gone."

"Did you see anyone or anything approach?"

"No, she's just there one minute, and then she's not."

Finally reaching my car, I opened the door. Getting in, I set my drink in a cup holder and closed the door behind me. "Here's your new mission, Mr. Mopps. Tweak that video and see if you can get a clear picture of what we're dealing with."

"What the fuck do you think I'm gonna find that the police didn't?"

I put my key in the ignition and started the engine. "I don't know. Look for something that isn't there. This is where you earn your bread and butter with me, Mr. Mopps. Give me a miracle and come up with something I can use."

"You're insane."

I chuckled. "Welcome to my world. What's the address to the first victim? Ian Johnson."

"His mother still lives in an apartment building in Diamond Heights. I'll text you the address."

"Thank you, Mr. Mopps. You've been extremely helpful."

"Like I said, Dracula. I better get paid for all this." He killed the call.

I shook my head as I backed out of my space and set a course for San Francisco.

XYZ News Building, San Francisco, CA—1106 hours

"**H**ow would you like to crack this story wide open?"

Jaiden jumped in surprise. She had been intently reading a piece of paper in her hand. Sliding her glasses down the bridge of her nose, she gave me an appraising look. "Mr. Diamondback, wasn't it?"

"Doctor, actually."

"Well, Doctor, you're going to have to be more specific."

I ticked names off on my fingers. "Ian Johnson, Kayla Sanchez, Montel Evens, and Maddison Bell."

She pushed her glasses back up and blew the lock of hair out of her eye. "What do you know about four missing children, Dr. Diamondback?"

My lopsided smile came out. "Nothing yet. That's where I hope you'll be able to help me."

She studied me intently. "You don't look like police."

"True."

"You don't look like FBI either."

A look of genuine horror landed on my face. "I should hope not."

"I've never seen you in a press pit."

"There's a reason for that."

"Do tell."

I shrugged. "I'm not a reporter."

She continued to look down on me from her seated position. "That begs the question, Doctor: What are you, exactly?"

I flipped out my shield. "Besides extremely good looking? Special federal task force."

Her eyes went wide as she studied my badge. "You've got to be joking. What's PIE? Like a special victim's unit?"

I nodded as I tucked it back in my pocket. "You could say that, and no this is not a joke. I know you're on this story too, Ms. Fox, and my agency feels it a good idea to work with the press for some reason."

Her face set as if had been chiseled from marble. "To try and control the story?"

I clutched my hands to my chest as if wounded. "Not at all. More to make sure the right story gets out to the public. That's why I wanted to hire you in the first place."

She gave a dismissive snort. "Still not interested."

"Aww, come on, give it a chance. If you don't like the way I operate, you're always free to walk away."

She put down the report she had been reading and folded her arms. "Okay, I'll play along for now, but I don't work for you."

I brightened. "Excellent! My agency will be excited to know you're willing to work for free."

Her glare could have melted the sun. "Very funny. Alright then, Doctor, where do we start?"

Standing up straight, I adjusted my attire. "A wise man once said, 'Start at the beginning, and when you get to the end, stop.' Grab your purse, please, Ms. Fox. We're going to the beginning."

She wrinkled her nose and called after me, "Wait a second, it was the Mad Hatter who said that."

The Johnson's Apartment Building, Diamond Heights, San Francisco, CA—1235 hours

WE PULLED UP TO a gated apartment complex. The outside had been painted cream with dark brown trim, and a set of double glass doors led inside. A Hispanic gentleman pushed a lawn mower, throwing the aroma of fresh cut grass into the air and making my hay fever twinge.

Jaiden glowered at me, a tinge of exasperation in her voice. "This is not the beginning. It started at George Christopher Playground."

"If the crime scene weren't four months cold or we had footage from a camera, I would agree, Ms. Fox. As the crime scene *is* four months cold and we don't have any camera footage, the best we have is the word of the parents, or in this case, parent. The only witness left to the abduction: Ian's mom."

As I got out of my car, she followed suit. "Don't you already have the statement she gave the police? The poor woman has probably recounted it enough already."

My voice became airy as I entered the building. "Imagine the press concerned over someone's feelings about being bothered. I'm sure you didn't have that attitude when you sought her exclusive."

She gave me an offended glare. "Hey, I'm extremely sensitive to all my story subjects."

We walked a short distance down a corridor with ugly orange walls, tan rubber molding, and dark brown industrial carpet.

I filed into an elevator and pressed the button for the third floor. "The fact you call them subjects…"

She crossed her arms. "Now look here, you judgmental prick. I have an impeccable approach when it comes to being sensitive."

A bell went off, and the elevator doors opened into a hallway. "It shows."

"I don't have to take this shit." She hit the elevator button to ride it back down.

My palm came up. "*Shh!* Do you feel that?"

She stuck her arm out to keep the doors from closing and stepped out. "What are you going on about?"

"The temperature. Don't you feel it getting colder?"

Jaiden put her hand out toward a nearby air vent. "The AC is probably broken. So what? Happens all the time."

Starting down the hall, I glanced over my shoulder. "It makes sense to you that it's significantly colder inside the third story hallway than the lobby or elevator? If the AC were running, this whole place would be a winter wonderland."

She still had a scowl on her face, but followed. "Okay, so what do you think it is?"

"*Shh!*"

"If you shush me one more fucking time, I'm going to snatch you bald!"

"No, seriously! Listen."

As we approached the apartment, there was soft weeping coming from behind the door. A rime of frost made the carpet crunch beneath our feet. I looked at my iWatch: thirty-two degrees Fahrenheit and dropping. Taking a quick glance behind me, Jaiden's breath wafted into the air and a rose color appeared in her cheeks.

I crept forward and knocked at the door. "Ms. Johnson?"

Only the crying answered.

Trying the handle, I found it locked. I called a little louder, "Ms. Johnson?"

The lock clicked, the handle turned, and it swung open of its own accord.

The carpet crunched behind me as Jaiden took a step back. "Doctor…?"

I raised my hand again for her to hold her silence.

The modest apartment with tan walls, off-white carpet, and stained wooden molding sat unnaturally dark. All the windows had been closed, curtains drawn, and a thick, inky-black cloud of negative energy hung in the air like a dense fog. The water of a fifty-five-gallon fish tank along the far wall had expanded upon becoming ice, littering the carpet around the wooden cabinet holding it up with broken glass.

The crying intensified. It came from one of the bedrooms down the hall.

I made my way farther in and peeked into a doorway to my left. There on the floor sat the bluish outline of a lachrymose woman, looking like one of the holograms in a *Star Wars* movie. Clutching a child's blanket to her chest, she wept uncontrollably. She had become an emoji ghost.

"Oh, Ms. Johnson, no."

Jaiden's voice came out hoarse and shivery. "A-am I seeing w-what I think I'm seeing?"

I kept my eyes on the haunt. "That depends on what it is you think you see, Ms. Fox. Emoji ghosts, or haunts as they're more classically known, are ghosts that focus on a single moment in time and a single associated emotion: fear, anger, sadness, et cetera. They intensify and personify it. Usually, they're the product of some horrific event, like a suicide or murder, and they're generally harmless unless provoked. Unfortunately, attempting to get rid of them normally provokes them. The trick? Find what's anchoring the thing and destroy it. This is sometimes easier said than done, of course."

"H-how are you doing this? How did you s-set all of this up?"

I glanced back at her. "You think I had something to do with this?"

"If not you then who?"

Suddenly, the apparition gave a long, loud wail, and looked in our direction. "Why?" Her ghostly voice sent chills down my spine and rooted Jaiden to the spot. A riptide of crippling misery threatened to drag me into its depths.

I put my hands up passively as I shook my head to clear it, trying to rebuke its empathic barrage. "Easy, Ms. Johnson. We just want to talk to you."

The haunt whispered, though her voice reverberated as if inside an echo chamber, "Such a good boy. He didn't deserve to die."

"How do you know he's dead, Ms. Johnson?" I kept my voice low as my eyes darted around the room looking for the anchor. The room must have been Ian's, unless Ms. Johnson had a thing for race car beds and clowns. A wooden toy chest sat at the foot of the bed and a bookshelf with titles like *Nobody Likes a Goblin* by Ben Hatke or *The ABCs of D&D* by Ivan Van Norman and Caleb Cleveland was pushed up against the far wall. A full laundry basket lay next to a wooden dresser, ready to be put away, and the sliding closet stood open, revealing a baseball, glove, and an aluminum bat leaning against the wall with shirts, jackets and hoodies hanging on the crossbar. A small wooden desk sat in front of the window so one could gaze out into the city while sitting at it.

The spirit sobbed. "A mother knows!"

Another wave of overwhelming grief radiated from her. I glanced back when I heard Ms. Fox gasp for breath and hit a knee, tears streaming down her face. "Wh-what's g-going on with m-me?"

My own knees buckled as a tear ran down my cheek despite my training at keeping my emotions in check. "This is why I call them emojis. They radiate their personified emotion like a white hole."

Then I noticed over in the corner next to the nightstand, partially obscured by the bed, lay the body of a woman, the inky, unnatural darkness filling the air emanating from her. The poor woman had opened her wrists and pools of frozen blood stained the floor. A light-blue blanket with a teddy bear embroidered on it remained grasped in the corpse's hand.

"There you are."

The emoji followed my gaze. "No!"

An icy wind whipped up from nowhere, buffeting Jaiden and me without stirring the cloud of negative energy. The effect made me feel disorientated.

Holding on to my hat, I tried to move toward the body. "Ms. Johnson, please."

"No!" The wind grew stronger as the toy chest and dresser drawers popped open. Objects began flying at me. Toys, clothes, books—I ducked a metal Tonka dump truck that crashed into the wall behind me. Luckily no furniture yet, but I had been through worse before and knew it remained a matter of time.

Then I heard Jaiden call above the howling wind. "Ms. Johnson, do you remember me?"

The squall immediately stopped and the haunt considered her. "You're that nice reporter who said you would help find him. You seemed different from the others, that's why I talked to you. You seemed to care more about finding Ian than the story."

A look of relief washed over Jaiden. "That's right."

The haunt's face distorted with rage. "You never found him. You lied!"

I put my arms up to protect my head and face. "Shit, here comes the furniture."

The wind whipped back into a frenzy, smashing a child-size chair into the wall near Jaiden. Ms. Johnson focused on her now. The reporter covered her face with both arms and screamed as LEGOs, blocks, and crayons pelted her. I fought toward the blanket as the ghost continued to fling objects around in her fury.

Yelling over the howl of Ms. Johnson, Jaiden tried to keep the emoji engaged. "I know, but we're trying, Ms. Johnson. We're trying to find out what happened to Ian."

Ms. Johnson calmed at the sound of his name. "I–Ian?"

The wind subsided to a chill zephyr as I stumbled forward and twisted my ankle due to a lack of resistance, but quickly caught myself. Keeping an eye on the emoji, I continued to inch my way toward the corpse at the far end of the room so as not to attract attention. The last few feet seemed like miles.

Jaiden peered out from between her arms, keeping her voice calm and soothing even though she shook more than a vibrating bed at a cheap motel. "That's right. Ian. We're trying to make sure what happened to him doesn't happen to any other children. Please, Ms. Johnson. Please help us."

I had to hand it to her, she had guts.

The haunt's ire roiled. "How do I know you're not lying to me again?"

Jaiden screamed as a lamp smashed into the wall next to her. "Ms. Johnson, I swear to you we'll find the truth, please!"

Taking it slow and easy paid off. I yanked the blanket out of the corpse's hand.

An invisible force shoved me against the wall, dazing me for a moment, and held me there. The spirit wailed again. "No! I want Ian! Ian!"

I croaked at Jaiden. "The blanket! It needs to be destroyed."

Ms. Johnson went berserk as a cyclone formed in the center of the room. It ripped drawers from the dresser and bashed them around, their corners knocking chunks of gypsum from the walls. Jaiden dropped to the ground, narrowly dodging the race car bed. The desk flipped up on its end and slammed into me, squashing me harder against the wall.

"No! Give me Ian! Give me my son!"

A barrage of stuffed animals pelted me in the head as I struggled against the desk. The Class 5 room-tornado had taken my hat as well. I watched it swirl around the room as my brain quickly calculated the lazy arc of its path. I followed it for two more passes to make sure I had it right, then looked at Jaiden. Down on the floor, hands laced over the back of her head, she kept stealing glances at me then covered back up and screamed whenever something crashed around her.

"Jaiden! Catch!" Hoping that the wind wouldn't steal my words like it had my hat, as she peeked out from under her arms again, I released the blanket into the spinning vortex of junk. It whipped around the air column like a bullet. I wouldn't even have time to blink before she missed it.

With reflexes worthy of a ninja, her hand shot out and snatched it from the air. As it snapped in the raging wind like a victory flag, I grunted again as the desk threatened to push me through the wall.

"You have to destroy it!"

Jaiden struggled to her hands and knees, keeping a death grip on the blanket. She yelled over the whistling wind, "How?"

"Rip it, burn it, I don't care. Destroy it, now!"

A dresser drawer narrowly missed her head. It smashed into the wall behind her, causing her to scream and shield her face as an invisible force seized the blanket, attempting to yank it from her hands.

Ms. Johnson continued to wail. "Give me Ian! Give him back!"

Grabbing the blanket with both hands, Jaiden yanked and pulled. The screaming from the emoji drowned out the sound of her voice, but I could read lips and saw hers form the unmistakable word "Fuck!"

The haunt's power stretched thin, the pressure from the desk lessened and I slid out from behind it, letting it slam against the wall, but a jack-in-the-box rang my bell and caused a nasty gash over my right eye.

Noticing my break for freedom, the knife on the floor next to Ms. Johnson's body came alive and shot straight at me like an arrow. "Die!"

I caught the blade between the flat of my palms, the hilt catching on my pinkies to prevent it from going any farther as I struggled with it. "Hurry!"

Ms. Johnson's psychic grip on the blanket went slack as the force from Jaiden's final tug tumbled her back into the hall.

The haunt opened her mouth to a gaping black hole, like that painting *The Scream* from Edvard Munch. *"Iiiiiiiaaaaaaannnn!"*

The knife began slipping through my grasp, millimeters from my sternum. Having sliced into one of my palms, it wiggled back and forth as blood ran between my fingers, the wind splattering it all over my jacket and suit.

"Nooooooo!" The pressure from the knife subsided as Ms. Johnson spontaneously combusted. Her scream continued to gain in pitch and became so loud I thought it might burst my eardrums. Finally, she exploded into a shower of sparkly blue particles that drifted away like dandelion fluff on a gentle breeze.

Then all was quiet. The wind had died. The knife went limp between my sweaty, bloody palms and the inky darkness lifted. I dropped the knife to the floor as the room began to lose its chill. Releasing a sigh of relief and retrieving my hat, I made my way out of the bedroom.

I found Jaiden in the kitchen standing in front of a gas stove, burner still lit, the blanket aflame in the sink. Glasses slightly askew, her hair stuck out like a harpy's nest, yet the stubborn lock still hung in her face.

Nodding, I took a clean dish towel and wrapped my bloody hand. "Nice work, Ms. Fox."

She gave me a look that defined incredulity. "What the fuck did you say you were a doctor of again?"

Chapter 5

Ms. Johnson's Apartment Building, Fremont Street, San Francisco, CA—1401 hours

WE SAT AT THE rear of an ambulance in silence, police swarming the scene. My hand and forehead had been freshly bandaged, my bruised ribs had been taped up for support, and my twisted ankle from stumbling had been wrapped in an ACE bandage. Used to stuff like this, I winced as I turned my head to look at Jaiden.

She sat with a blanket wrapped around her, staring at the ground. Shock had set in and her teeth chattered, as if trying to fight off the cold from the apartment. Her hair still looked like an '80s do gone wrong, her skin was sallow, and her eyes were glassy. She needed to lay back and elevate her feet to keep from passing out, but I decided not to press the issue unless her breathing became quick and labored.

Oddly, the police had believed my story for once. I didn't even have to show my badge. Having been alerted to the scene by neighbors, I hadn't needed to call them. We told them Ms. Fox and I, a private investigator hired by XYZ, had come calling to ask a few follow-up questions of Ms. Johnson, which wasn't entirely a lie. That's when we found her dead and the apartment trashed, most likely from a rage-fueled fit, which wasn't entirely a lie either. The coroner correctly named it suicide, but incorrectly called her time of death at a week ago. She had no way of knowing about the supernatural freezing conditions that had preserved the body for a week or more. It had all come together quite nicely, except Jaiden's broken psyche.

I finally broke the silence between us as I drew some Godiva dark chocolate from my pocket and offered her a piece. "Are you okay?"

Her head rotated up and her glassy eyes stared through me like a zombie when attempting to process sensory information. Frozen in that position for quite a long time, the edge of panic rose in me. Was I going to have to check this one into a mental hospital already? Then her eyes flicked briefly to the chocolate.

I gave an inward sigh of relief. "Come now, Ms. Fox. Take it. It'll help."

Jaiden didn't move, eyes still on me.

I opened it, broke off a piece, and popped it into my mouth, then held it back out to her. "It's always difficult your first time, but it gets easier."

Jaiden finally reached up and took the chocolate. She looked at the ground again. "I'm sitting here questioning my sanity, and you tell me it gets easier? How do I know this shit isn't laced with the hallucinogens you've been taking?"

I swung my legs back and forth over the bumper of the ambulance. "Are you saying you were tripping too?"

"Maybe you slipped me something."

I shook my head. "Welcome to a larger world, Ms. Fox. Believe it or not, you're doing better than most others have in your shoes."

She looked at me sideways. "Others?"

"You're not the first teammate I've had."

She cast her eyes back toward the ground. After a pause, she asked, "What happened to them?"

This time, I looked down at the street as well. "A few quit. A few had to be committed. A few... weren't so lucky."

She scoffed. "Committed? And here I thought you worked alone because you're pigheaded and hard to deal with, I didn't know you drive people to the point of mental breakdowns. And you want to talk about my work being high stress?"

I laughed. "You got me there, but there does tend to be a reason for everything I do."

She watched the bustle of the first responders for a while before finally giving in and taking a healthy bite of the chocolate. Her face visibly brightened as she took another bite. Chewing thoughtfully, she spoke around it. "I'm beginning to see that."

"Thanks."

After a few moments of silence, a tear ran down her cheek. "That poor woman. She was still alive a month ago. Sure, her husband had left her over it all, but it really seemed like she would pull through."

I bulged my eyes out and exhaled through pursed lips. "Hell hath no fury like a mother's sorrow."

She gave me a perplexed look as she flipped her hair out of her face. "I thought it was 'a woman scorned.'"

"That too."

We sat watching the cops hustling in and out of the apartment complex with evidence bags and going door-to-door to question neighbors who didn't have a clue. At last, she spoke. "I want in."

This time, I looked at her sideways. "Even after all that?"

She locked eyes with me. "People deserve the truth."

"You'd give up your career for a tinfoil hat and a blog?"

Squinting, her lips thinned. "You said you needed me to keep my job at XYZ, right? Besides, I think I can juggle both."

Laughing, I shook my head. "I can read the headline now: XYZ News Golden Girl Goes Mental."

"Are you trying to piss me off?"

I continued to laugh as I held up my hands defensively. "No, Ms. Fox, the job still stands. I suppose this means I'll need to take you and Charlie in for fingerprints, background checks, and IDs at some point."

"Charlie?"

I nodded. "A newcomer to the group like yourself. Mr. Mopps will be handling all our technical needs."

Her face scrunched up as she snorted. "Charlie Mopps, huh? Your IT guy is a drunk? You're in worse shape than I thought."

I scratched the stubble on my chin. "Actually, he seems to be more of an herbalist."

"That's not reassuring."

"Comin' in Hot" by Hollywood Undead interrupted our conversation. I took out my phone and looked at the screen. "Speak of the devil and he shall appear."

Jaiden brushed the lock of hair out of her face as I hit the answer button. "I take it that's him now?"

"Mr. Mopps, we were just talking about you."

Charlie sounded confused. "We? You have more than one personality now or some shit?"

"No, Mr. Mopps. I happen to be speaking with our team's newest recruit, Ms. Jaiden Fox."

"You mean that hot-ass reporter from XYZ News San Francisco?"

"The very one."

"Dude, why the fuck are you on the phone with me?"

"I was hoping you found something I can use."

His voice dripped with disappointment. "I knew you had no game."

"The video footage, Mr. Mopps."

He sounded excited, yet hesitant. "Yeah. So, I took your advice, and I think I found something."

"Do tell."

"I ran the footage through a video spectral comparator for shits and giggles, and you were right, there is something that grabs the kid."

"Did you get a clear image?"

"Not really, but maybe you should come see for yourself."

Finally, a breakthrough. "Excellent. We'll be there in a few."

A note of panic broke into Charlie's voice. "What do you mean 'we'?"

"Ms. Fox and I, of course."

"You're bringing a hot chick with you?"

"Yes."

His voice squeaked. "Here?"

"Yes."

"Awww, shit."

I laughed out loud. "What's wrong?"

"I gotta go, Doc. I gotta clean this fucking shithole." The line went dead.

I continued to chuckle as I put my phone back in my pocket.

Jaiden looked at me perplexed, the lock of hair hanging over her eye again. "What was all that about?"

I couldn't shake my smile. "Oh, he just needs to prepare for guests is all. Shall we?"

Charlie's Apartment, Santana Row, San Jose, CA—1532 hours

AFTER FIXING OURSELVES UP the best we could, we took my car back to San Jose as hers was still in the XYZ parking structure. Arriving at Charlie's, I almost didn't recognize the place when the door opened. Evidently, Charlie *did* own cleaning supplies, for his apartment now smelled strongly of Pine-Sol and nag champa. The only clutter remaining was the network of equipment by the desk, and even that had been dusted and straightened up. Leaning suavely against the doorjamb, he greeted us at the entrance wearing a magenta silk smoking jacket with gold trim and matching pajama bottoms with black slippers, trying to put some bass in his voice. "Welcome to Casa de Charlie."

One of my eyebrows elevated slowly. "Mr. Mopps?"

His mop of straw-colored hair had been combed and parted down the middle and he carried a full martini glass nestled in his left hand. He ushered us inside. "Doc. Charmed, I'm sure."

"What are you…"

He hardly gave me a second glance as he turned his full attention to Jaiden, extending a hand. "Ah! The illustrious Ms. Jaiden Fox. Charlie, Charlie Mopps, at your complete and utter service."

Her eyes widened until her forehead crinkled and the left side of her upper lip curled. Then a laugh escaped her as she fixed him with a quizzical eye. "Really, I'm very flattered, but… um, how old are you?"

His baby face cracked into a demure smile. "Old enough to know my own mind."

Trying not to laugh myself, I stepped in. "I hate to interrupt your embarrassing display of toxic masculinity, but I'd love to see that video footage, if you please."

He waved me off, his eyes never leaving Jaiden. "Yeah, sure, Doc, in a second. Can I offer you a drink, Ms. Fox? Or may I call you Jaiden?"

She put her hands up. "Ahh, no thanks, on both accounts."

He wiggled his eyebrows. "A dirty martini, perhaps?"

Jaiden shot me a look of desperation. "Does he have an off button?"

I held up my index finger at her, then whispered in his ear, "You know she has a boyfriend, right?"

For the first time, he turned his full attention to me. "Really?" He looked back at Jaiden who nodded vigorously. "Well… shit." He set the martini glass on his computer desk and plopped himself down in the chair, muttering, "Man, some guys have all the luck."

Jaiden rolled her eyes and blew at her strand of hair.

Charlie glanced over his shoulder as he unlocked his computer with his fingerprint scanner. "So, what the fuck happened to you?"

"Occupational hazard. Please stay focused."

Charlie brought up the video of the Whole Foods parking lot on his computer. "Whatever. Okay, so check this out."

He ran the normal video. I watched as the little girl disappeared from behind her mother who stood just inches away while putting groceries into the back of a dark green minivan.

"I'm still waiting for the good stuff."

"Never show the money shot up front, Doc. Now watch it when I slow it down and run it through a video spectral comparator app."

He brought up the video again, but this time I was viewing it in the infrared spectrum. The heat signature of Ms. Sanchez and poor little Kayla, and there—a hulking dark spot on the video. It enveloped the girl as her heat signature disappeared off camera.

Jaiden spoke up. "What the fuck was that?"

I rubbed my chin. "I have no idea, Ms. Fox, but it's our job to find out."

Biting his lower lip, Charlie continued to moon at Jaiden. "So what now? I'm not feeling the same excitement off a cold front that you are, Doc."

"Now, Mr. Mopps, you go put on some appropriate attire and we go to the scene of the crime."

He swiveled around in his chair. "You mean you want me to go out there with you?"

I nodded.

"In the field?"

I nodded again.

He thought for a moment. "Is she going?"

I shrugged. "I don't see how that makes any difference, but we came together so I would assume so."

He sprang to his feet and ran to his room. "Be right out."

I gave Jaiden a look of amusement as she returned one of open-mouth shock. "I think he likes you."

Whole Foods Parking Lot, Diamond Heights, San Francisco, CA—2045 hours

"**H**OW THE FUCKING FUCK did I fuckin' let you fuckin' talk me into this fucking bullshit, Doc? I could be at fuckin' home all cozy on my fuckin' computer, playin' fuckin' video games, but nooooo! I'm fuckin' out here in the middle of a goddamn fuckin' parking lot, it's fuckin' cold, and for fuckin' what? Fuck this fuckin' shit is fuckin' fucked!"

The wind whipped around the deserted Whole Foods parking lot, blowing leaves and other debris around in a swirl. A few cars still sat idle as the few remaining staff closed the store. The lights from the sign and the parking lamps helped illuminate the immediate area against the dark clouds overhead that blotted out the moon and threatened rain.

Charlie pouted in his dark green beanie, ratty high-top Converse, and baggy jeans with holes in the knees. The edges of a black-and-white checkered flannel hung out from beneath his black bomber jacket as he shook his head and wrapped his arms around himself to keep warm. "I better get fuckin' travel expenses for this bullshit."

We had taken his van as my car wouldn't fit three people. I wasn't used to having other people drive, but I found it gave me time to think about things. Maybe I should ask Stravinsky for a chauffeur.

We parked in the exact spot where Ms. Sanchez had parked the day of Kayla's abduction. "There's one thing I want to check, Mr. Mopps. Then we'll be on our way to warmer places."

Jaiden cast her eyes around the empty parking lot, the light from the lampposts reflecting off her glasses. "What exactly are you looking for, Doctor?"

I took out a UV flashlight and switched it on, shining it around on the ground. "I'm looking for a residual trail."

The reporter watched me with a puzzled expression. "Do ghosts leave trails?"

"Everything leaves a trail if you know how to look for it, Ms. Fox. UV light can expose ectoplasm much like it can blood or semen, though it can't be seen with the naked eye and is commonly mistaken for one of the latter at crime scenes. The decomposition rate for ectoplasm, luckily for us, is months… Ah, here we are."

Charlie stared at the faint, ghostly image that reflected off the pavement. "It looks like a footprint."

I rubbed the stubble on my chin. "Something the size and intensity of what we saw in the video, it's no wonder the trail is still here. Whatever we're dealing with, it's powerful."

Charlie's jaw dropped. "That's gotta be a size seventeen work boot at least. Are there more?"

"A very good question, Mr. Mopps." I shined my light across the parking lot. Sure enough, a faint trail led away from the spot where we stood.

Jaiden pointed. "It looks like it goes back toward the loading docks."

The hairs on the back of my neck suddenly stood on end. "Maybe you two should wait here."

Charlie looked longingly at his van. "I'm for that."

Jaiden fixed me with a haughty stare. "Absolutely not. I can handle myself."

"Well, shit. If she's going, I'm not ready to turn in my man card yet."

Sighing, I drew my Desert Eagle. "Stick close then and stay behind me."

Charlie's eyes widened. "Badass! When do I get one'a those?"

"Put in some more fieldwork and we'll talk. Now, *shh!*"

Jaiden folded her arms, raising her eyebrows. "My question is, why do you think you'll need it?"

I gave her and Charlie both a handheld UV flashlight and a spray canister from one of my jacket pockets. "You never know what you're going to encounter in the dark, Ms. Fox. Best to be prepared."

Charlie looked at the flashlight and bottle like someone had just handed him a pair of skid-marked undies. "You get a silver cannon and I get a dumbass squirt bottle? What the fuck, man?"

"It's full of silver water. Just point and spray, you'll be fine. Now, *shh!*"

His face crinkled. "Whatever."

Jaiden followed my lead. She pointed her UV light and brought her spray canister level with it.

As we rounded the corner of the building, the parking lights dimmed and flickered. A growl sounded from the empty loading docks, joined by another, then another. I moved my team in a wide circle to approach the docks from the side, where the elevated position blocked our view of what lay beyond.

The wind hit full gale as the lights continued to flicker like mad until their bulbs popped, making Charlie and Jaiden jump. Only our UV lights illuminated the area. I caught a brief glimpse of what looked like a dog leaving smoke trails behind it, darting in and out of the shadows, trying to stay out of the light. It had dark purple fur and burning-red eyes. My grip tightened on my weapon. "I should have known. Shadow hounds."

Jaiden's voice shook more than an imbalanced spin cycle. "W-what is a sh-shadow hound?"

"Scavengers of the paranormal akin to coyotes, they feed off anything dead and rotting along with minor paranormal entities. Most likely they were following the same trail we are, looking for food. They can be quite lethal and have been known to kill when threatened or cornered, much like we have them now."

Jaiden blinked. "Well… shit."

"The UV lights will slow them down and keep them from phasing in and out of shadows. The silver water and my weapon will hurt them, so at least we can protect ourselves."

Charlie groaned. "That's comforting… Not."

"Stay facing them, don't make any sudden movements, and back away slowly. One should never run from the immortal. We'll be fine just as long as—"

"Aaaaaawwwwooooooo!" An earsplitting howl cut the night.

"—that doesn't happen."

The shadow hounds charged.

My Desert Eagle flashed as it discharged a round, hitting the alpha in the shoulder. It stumbled face-first into the concrete as black ectoplasm gushed from the wound.

The second went for Jaiden, snapping and growling. Showing off her amazing reflexes for the second time today, she sidestepped its jaws and sprayed it full in the face with the silver water. Red blisters sprang up around its muzzle and eyes as it yelped in agony and tried to back away from her light, unable to phase.

Charlie howled in pain as I spun to see one of the creatures had slipped past his light and clamped its powerful jaws on his leg. As I attempted to line up my shot, it cringed and darted away from my UV beam, dropping him. Before I could take a shot that didn't risk hitting Charlie, it darted away into the darkness.

While the alpha struggled to rise on its bad leg, Jaiden hit the blinded hound again with a sustained blast. Its face became one big pustule and exploded, showering her with black ectoplasm. She let out a screech of disgust.

As Charlie rolled on the ground holding his leg and wincing in pain, the uninjured shadow hound leapt at me. I aimed and fired, hitting it square in the chest. It burst into a mess of black ectoplasm as well.

The alpha, now on its feet, loped toward Jaiden snarling, strings of poisonous neon-green drool dangling from its jowls. Jaiden leveled her canister and sprayed. It dodged and sprang at her with an eerie wail that made my blood run cold.

In my peripheral vision, I saw her close her eyes and turn away from the jaws of death flying toward her. I took aim at its head and fired. I didn't lead it enough and my shot missed, puncturing into its rib cage instead, delivering a perfect kill shot to its black heart. It exploded into a mess of ectoplasm all over Jaiden as she screeched again.

The wind died down, but the chill still hung in the night air.

Holstering my gun, I toggled my flashlight from UV to normal and knelt by Charlie to assess his leg. The wound bubbled with green ichor that mixed with his blood near the surface of the wound.

I scowled in concern. "Shit, it's setting."

Charlie rocked back and forth gritting his teeth. "It burns like a motherfucker, Doc."

"The bite of a shadow hound can cause necrosis unless treated right away."

I pulled a small leather case full of vials that held various liquids from my inside jacket pocket. Ticking through them, I came across one full of an opaque yellowish concoction. I uncorked it and dumped the whole thing on his leg. "This is useful for most wounds inflicted by the paranormal. It should clear this up quite nicely if I'm in time."

Charlie winced and let out a yell as the wound smoked. "What the fuck is that stuff, more silver water? It smells like some sort of shit you'd find at Bath and Body Works."

I kept my attention on his wound. "The stuff they sell there is too synthetic. This, you might find at an herbalist shop or a high-end day spa. It's a tincture that has tea tree, lavender, and germanium infused into it."

"You dumped a bottle of cheap perfume on me? You're no doctor, you're a fucking quack!"

At last, the poison began to drain from the wound, and his leg took on a healthier color. I cocked an eyebrow at him. "Am I? Essential oils and alcohol have been around as healing entities since the dawn of time for a reason, Mr. Mopps."

He grimaced. "Well I'll be fucked. I think it's working."

As I waited for the full effects of the tincture to kick in, I looked over at Jaiden. She stood unmoving with her arms held out away from her sides. Black goo dripped onto the pavement from her clothing, pearls, hair, glasses, and just about every other place on her person. She looked like the photograph negative of a bukkake session gone wrong.

"Jaiden, I didn't see you get bit. You alright?"

Her jaw trembled as her voice came out in a sob. "I'm currently questioning every single one of my life choices up unto this point, Doctor."

"You poor dear. Here, let me help." I got up and walked over to her, producing a handkerchief from my pocket. Her eyes scrutinized my every movement as I removed her glasses and tried to wipe most of the goop off. Smears of ectoplasm remained as I placed them back on her face. "There, is that better?"

Jaiden exploded to life, pounding her fists on my chest and getting ectoplasm all over me as well. "Better? *Better?* No, it's not better, you fucking asshole! It's as far from better as you could possibly get! This is ten times worse than the emoji ghost! My Ralph Lauren is ruined!"

Retreating, I shielded myself with my arms. "Hey, this isn't my fault!"

"Of course it's your fault, you son of a bitch! You never told me it would be like this."

"What did you think it was going to be, EMF meters, noise recorders, and cameras?"

"That's just it, I don't know what the hell I was thinking when I joined up with you!"

"I can pay for your dry cleaning."

"That's not the goddamn point and you know it! *Ooo!*" She quit hitting me and turned away crossing her arms.

My eyebrows folded. "Are you mad at me?"

Charlie scowled, looking between us. "Uh, hey guys, over here. The guy with the fucking dog bite is bleeding to death."

I gave Jaiden one last look before kneeling to attend to Charlie's leg further. "Sorry, I had to wait for the poison to drain."

The right side of his face scrunched. "Yeah, sure you did."

His leg had finally lost the gray tinge, so I slathered some Neosporin on the bite and bandaged it with gauze and medical tape. "There, it should heal just fine now."

Jaiden's despondent attitude didn't help brighten our surroundings. "So, what now, Doctor?"

I sighed as I gingerly helped Charlie to his feet. "Well, with the presence of shadow hounds, that means this lead has gone cold as well."

Charlie whined. "You mean I got bit for nothing?"

"I wouldn't say for nothing, Mr. Mopps…"

A voice cut my thought short. "What in the hell is going on here?"

I could feel the officer's gun trained on me. I put my hands in the air slowly, trying not to make any sudden moves. "I'm an agent."

"Oh yeah? Let's see a badge."

Turning around slowly to face him, I eased into my jacket pocket with two fingers and pulled out the leather wallet that contained my badge and ID, tossing it toward his feet. "Here you go, Officer."

He bent down just enough to grab them, his weapon still trained on me. "I got a call from the store manager that there were gunshots coming from back here."

"There's a logical explanation for that."

The cop opened my credentials, giving them a long, hard look. "Oh yeah?"

I moved sideways, letting him have a better view of Charlie. "My friend got bit by a dog, see?"

"What the fuck is PIE? Is this a joke?"

I sighed. "The Department of Paranormal Investigation and Education. It says so right there."

Disbelief and dismay filled Charlie's voice behind me. "Wait, you work for a federal agency named PIE? Oh shit, we're fucked."

"Mr. Mopps, please, not right now."

The cop raised an eyebrow at me. "You say you were shooting at a dog?"

"Only to scare it away from my associate here."

His eyes went wide at my shoulder holster. "With a cannon like that?"

I shrugged.

The frown on his face became more pronounced. "Must've been one helluva dog."

I shook my head with my hands still in the air, eyes on him and not the weapon he had pointed at me. "You have no idea."

"What happened to your hand?"

"Cooking accident from lunch. And they say you fine gentlemen don't care about the public you serve. Gold star for you, buddy."

He scowled then looked at Jaiden, still drenched in ectoplasm. He lifted his chin. "What happened to her?"

Charlie piped up before I had a chance to speak. "She got fuckin' slimed."

I spoke out of the side of my mouth. "Still not helping, Mr. Mopps."

"Slimed?"

"Unfortunately, the poor dear accidentally slipped in some garbage. We were about to bring her home so she can clean up."

He squinted, trying to find something out of place in the dark. "What about the lights? What happened to them?"

I looked around in the still darkness. "The wind blew them out. It *is* a bit blustery tonight."

The cop looked at me in disbelief. "Is that a fact?"

I gave him a dazzling smile and shrugged again. "Strange weather we're having?"

A few minutes after calling in my information and getting very little back from dispatch, he seemed to come to a decision. "At least your concealed permit checks out, and these do look rather authentic."

"Does this mean we're free to go?"

I could see his wheels spinning because he couldn't find anything illegal with the scene. He finally holstered his weapon and tossed my credentials back to me. He took out his flashlight and ran it over the place to be sure. "Tell you what. I'm gonna go this way…" He pointed in one direction, then he pointed in the opposite direction. "And all of you are gonna go that way. And when I get back…" He pointed his light at us. "None of you are gonna be here. Do I make myself clear?"

Letting out a sigh of relief, I dropped my hands. "Crystal clear, Officer." As he walked away, I turned to see my companions staring at me. "Shall we?"

Shuffling toward his van, Charlie looked over his shoulder at Jaiden. "You best not get that shit all over my van either."

Jaiden glared. "Come here, you little fucker. How about I get this shit all over you?"

He smirked. "Actually, it's kinda hot when you say it like that."

She lunged. "Oh, it's hot, is it? I'll show you fucking hot!"

He attempted to quicken his pace despite his limp. "Hey, what the fuck are you doing? I got fuckin' bit, that's not cool. Where's your sense of decency?"

I stepped between them. "Charlie, that's enough! Jaiden, ignore him. Let's get you home so you can get cleaned up. Doesn't that sound good? Mr. Mopps, your keys if you please. I'll drive so you can rest that leg."

Charlie pitched his keys to me as he made his way to the passenger side. "And grab that old blanket in the back for her, would ya, Doc?"

Jaiden opened the side door, jumped in, and began wiggling all over the bench seat. "Fuck your upholstery, motherfucker. Fuck your fuckin' upholstery."

Charlie stood observing her with his mouth hanging open. He finally closed it, shook his head, and climbed in. "You're fuckin' lucky you're hot, lady, 'cause you got a dark side off camera."

I sighed as I started the van and took off toward Jaiden's apartment.

Chapter 6

CONSIDERING HER PARKING PASS, Jaiden wasn't worried about leaving her vehicle at work overnight as she had done so many times before. We dropped her off at her apartment to clean up, decompress, and maybe get a good night's sleep if she could. Not many people had two paranormal experiences in less than twenty-four hours unless they found themselves in the line of work, like me.

Still in the driver's seat, I bobbed along with "This Love, This Hate" by Hollywood Undead on the radio. In the passenger seat, Charlie stared out the window with a perplexed look on his face.

Finally, he ruptured the silence between us. "PIE? Are you fucking for real?"

"Don't look at me. I didn't think that shit up."

He snorted. "It could have been something cool like Mystery Inc., or Ghostbusters, or Myth Inc., some shit like that."

I shrugged. "I believe all of those names have trademarks to them."

His face scrunched up. "Since when does the federal government give a shit about trademarks?"

I laughed. "Since they don't like getting sued. Besides, most federal agencies are three letter acronyms."

"Still, someone should fix that shit."

Frowning, I glanced down. "How's the leg?"

He winced. "Hurts like hell, but I'm sure I'll be okay."

I nodded. "Good, let me know if it begins to burn or becomes further inflamed, please. If you begin to feel feverish or lightheaded, those are bad signs as well."

He looked back out the window. "Back in my apartment, you weren't fucking with me, were you?"

"No, no I wasn't. You had me rather worried, Mr. Mopps, but you dealt with everything rather stoically. May I say, almost like you've seen paranormal activity before."

For the first time since I knew him, Charlie went silent. After a moment, he looked down. "How'd you know?"

I kept my eyes on the road. "Well, the first thing that tipped me off was your handle, Spook. Also, you didn't run away screaming or wet yourself at the sight of the shadow hounds. As a matter of fact, the only reason you got bit is because you were looking at something else."

He gave me a meek look that seemed a bit unnatural on his face. "Was it that obvious?"

My eyebrows folded. "I don't mean Ms. Fox's rear end!"

He smiled with a dreamy look. "She *does* have a great tuchus."

I glanced over. "Mr. Mopps, not only have I studied forms of verbal and nonverbal communication, but I've also studied basic psychology, abnormal psychology, child psychology, paranormal psychology—"

"Is paranormal psychology even a thing?"

"Mr. Mopps!"

"What?"

An exasperated breath escaped me. "What were you looking at?"

His face turned sour. "You're not gonna let this go, are you?"

I shook my head. "As your team leader, I have to know your head is in this."

"More than you realize."

Slapping my hand on the wheel, I made him jump. "Charlie!"

He folded his arms and glared at the dashboard. "Fine! I can see ghosts, okay? Go ahead and tell me I'm crazy."

Maybe he wasn't as seasoned as I had thought. "I was recently reading an article from Clarkson University: 'Why Do We See Ghosts?'"

Charlie's glum expression didn't change. "Yeah?"

"It mentioned that sometimes the death of a loved one or kids who get bullied often or are exposed to dangerous situations when they're young can cause a sort of sight. They conveniently leave out that having a paranormal experience can also trigger it, but the whole paper is rather biased."

"You left out the latter part where they mention that if you do see ghosts, you're a fucking whack-a-doo and should be medicated. I read the same fucking article."

Finding myself in troubled waters, I had to tread lightly. "I did, because that's what pharmaceutical companies tell us to believe so they can push drugs on people, but we both know that's bullshit, don't we, Charlie? There's a much bigger world out there than most people are willing to let themselves believe."

He gave a snort of derision. "I know that a fucking hell hound took a hunk out of my leg tonight."

I shook my head. "Hell hounds are different, more fire and brimstone, but that's a start. If it makes you feel any better, I see them too. So does Ms. Fox. Now Ms. Fox had her first experience earlier today, but she seems to be processing okay... I think."

Charlie shook his head. "You guys don't see them like I do."

My eyebrow went up. "Whatever do you mean by that?"

He finally looked at me. "There are some paranormal phenomena that can be seen by the naked eye as long as you're paying attention."

I nodded. "Specters and some spirits that are anchored here by a tether."

He looked back at the dashboard as if he wanted to kick it. "Right. Well, I can see spirits too, the ones we can't see on a normal basis."

"You mean you can see into the prime material plane?"

"The prime material what?"

"That's a rare gift, Mr. Mopps, you've been holding out on me. There is something interesting about you."

"You're a dick."

"How long?"

He refused to look at me. "How long what? How long have you been a dick? Oh, I don't know, probably your whole life."

"No, how long have you been able to see into the prime material plane?"

"What's that?"

"It's the realm ghosts and spirits really exist on. You might find it referred to as 'Purgatory' in religious texts. When we can see them here in the physical world, it's normally because they have an anchor or are so strong that they can draw on enough spiritual power to manifest themselves in this plane of existence. The specter or spirit drawing power is what causes lights to flicker, temperatures to drop, wind or even gales, and of course the telltale black ink cloud of negative spiritual energy."

He finally turned his scowl on me. "So you're telling me if I read the *Dungeon Master's Guide* for Dungeons & Dragons, I'll get what the hell you just said?"

I scowled back. "No, but… maybe."

Charlie slouched even more in his seat. He looked down with a glum expression. "Ever since I can remember. One of my earliest memories is me standing in my crib watching the spirit of a little boy playing with a ball on my bedroom floor. As I grew, we became friends of sorts. My parents freaked the first time I tried to tell them about my imaginary friend. I called him Tommy. They were gonna have me committed until I finally convinced them I'd been joking. Guys in white coats were about to drag me away and chuck me in a padded room to start electroshock therapy when my mom took pity on me and put a stop to the whole mess. I was five. Scariest fuckin' time in my life."

I tapped the steering wheel with my finger. "Very interesting."

"What? That my parents were gonna have me committed and tortured?"

"No, the fact you can see on that plane of existence. That's amazing."

"Yeah, amazingly awkward."

I thought for a moment. "What did you see? Back there on the loading docks."

Charlie winced. "I'd still rather not say."

I squinted and my left cheek scrunched. "Why?"

"I'm just not used to talking about it, okay? You're, like, the first person I've ever talked to about this who didn't think I was nuts. And while that should make me feel better, it doesn't."

I needed to lighten the mood. I gave him my best Cheshire cat impression. "You may have noticed that I'm not all there… myself."

This time he laughed. "Alright, that was pretty good."

"Thanks."

Pausing for a moment longer while biting his lower lip, he finally looked at me. "Fine, but you may not like this."

"What do you mean, I 'may not like this?'"

"Well, I'm pretty sure it has to do with you."

"What are you talking about?"

"She's only around when you are."

A chill ran up and down my spine. "She?"

Charlie nodded, bringing the palm of his hand to his chin. "Yeah, a little girl. Now that I think about it, she tried pointing to something back on the loading docks.

I didn't get a good look, and she disappeared when the dogs attacked."

"Is she here now?"

He looked around nonchalantly. "Nope, but then again, she's not always around when you are. She flits in and out, if that makes sense."

My mouth went dry. "What… what does she look like?"

"Blonde hair, blue eyes, pink jacket, white shirt, blue jeans with a rainbow on the back pocket, and light-up *Care Bear* shoes. LA Gears, like total old school."

Charlie screamed as the van veered right toward the shoulder, but I quickly regained my composure and corrected it.

"Whoa! What the fuck, man? I take it you know her?"

My heart dropped into my stomach at the thought of her as I clung to my composure for dear life. "My… my sister."

He gave me a sheepish look. "What happened?"

I studied the road intently. "She… she was murdered, a long time ago."

"The cops never found out who did it?"

My mouth moved even though my brain screamed for it to shut up. "I know who did it. No one believed me."

"Hey, if you're fucking with me, it's not funny."

"It was the bogeyman."

Charlie sat up straight in his seat. "Holy shit, you're fucking serious. You mean to tell me the fuckin' bogeyman is fucking for real?"

Wincing at the memory, I gripped the steering wheel. "It's why I work for the department I do. He gave me three broken ribs, a concussion, and kidnapped my sister. I owe him."

He put a hand up at me and laughed. "Whoa, whoa, whoa, hold the fuck up: You went toe to toe with the fuckin' bogeyman?"

"I was only fourteen at the time."

"And you're not fucking with me?"

"Ask my sister the next time you see her."

He sat back in his seat and stared out at the highway. "Now I don't feel so bad about making my parents check my closet and under the bed all those times, and it doesn't work like that. I can see them. I can't hear or speak to them. Except…"

"Except what?"

"Well, one time, your sister left me a message on my computer."

A memory came back to me—and here I thought he had been mocking me. "'Can ghosts…'"

"'…use computers?'" He finished for me, nodding. "You remember."

I could hear the anxiety in my own voice. "What did she say?"

He fidgeted with his fingers in his lap while staring at them. "'Help.'"

My throat tightened up to the point I couldn't speak anymore, so we drove in silence for the rest of the way. I parked the van in the garage beneath our building and helped him to the elevator.

As we stepped inside, Charlie finally broke the silence. "What was her name?"

I had to swallow a lump in my throat. Saying her name remained difficult, even after all these years. "Daisy."

In no time, his floor came up. "This is me."

I gave him a curt nod. "Have a good evening, Charlie."

As he limped off the elevator, he looked back. "Hey, Doc?"

"Yeah?"

He jerked his chin. "Just so you know? She never stopped believing in you. See you in the morning."

As the doors closed, I couldn't stop the tears from flowing.

Bank of America off Diamond Heights Boulevard, Diamond Heights, San Francisco, CA—0128 hours

T HE POURING RAIN SLOWED to a drizzle and traffic had become nonexistent on Diamond Heights Boulevard. Streetlamps offered scant lighting as they flickered, attempting to fend off the darkness best they could. An icy chill hung in the air as the bay wind whipped up, blowing leaves and litter around in a swirling gust. A hulking shadow turned by the bank to go down a side alley. The bogeyman swung a deceased cat around by the tail in one hand as he clutched a bottle of Jack Daniel's in the other. "Daddy caught this one by surprise… surprised on the Darkside! Heh, did the poor little guy see the stupid look on its face when Daddy broke its neck? Mmm, Daddy loves that sound. The sound of the Darkside."

His head ticked as a rat on his shoulder sniffed at his ear. "But, the poor little kitty."

Red eyes flared as he smacked the cat against a wall, throwing the rat from his shoulder and onto the ground. It scurried off as he continued to rant. "Have you forgotten? Did you forget? They're the enemy. They're all Daddy's enemies on the Darkside!"

"What about our friend, down in the cage? Can we go play with it yet?"

He took a pull from the bottle in his grimy hand. "No! It sleeps… sleeping, sleep on the Darkside. Daddy needs it to be awake so we can play more. Now Daddy walks. Daddy drinks. Daddy waits… on the Darkside."

"Do we have to hurt this one? The screaming and the crying make me sad."

He smacked the cat carcass against the wall again. "Yes! Yes, yes, yes, Daddy must hurt them all, you know that. Daddy is so hungry for the Darkside and… and for what they did to the poor little guy, they'll pay. No matter the skin, no matter the blood bloody-blood, no matter the breed, they… will… pay!"

A few rats scurried around his feet. He lashed out, grasping one by the tail, and shoved it squealing into his mouth. He chewed and swallowed. "Daddy craves fresh, tender, tender meat."

"Do… do you think this one will get away, like that other one? That one time?"

He roared, still flinging the corpse around. "No, it will never get free of the Darkside! Never, never, never! Daddy will see to that. Yes, Daddy likes the fear they spread, like a sickness. There… there are stories. Stories of the Darkside, stories of Daddy, whispers of the Darkside that herald Daddy's coming from the ones who get away. But if it gets away, then Daddy must find another playmate. And that takes time. And Daddy is *so* hungry."

"Do… do you remember the story of how the poor little guy died?"

He took a long pull from his bottle and wiped his mouth on a grimy sleeve. "Daddy remembers, Daddy remembers everything."

"Can… can Daddy tell us the story?"

The bogeyman dangled the dead cat in front of his face. "Do you remember how the poor little guy died on the Darkside? Do you? No, you're already on the Darkside! You can't even think, stupid cat!"

He began swinging it in an elliptical pattern and took another pull from his bottle. "I'll tell you how the poor little guy died. That mean old bastard choked him out, that's how! Wrapped his hands around his neck and squeezed until the poor little guy couldn't breathe, couldn't think… thinking, the thinks you can think on the Darkside. Then *snap*! Broke the poor little guy's neck in two. That's how the poor little guy died. Poor little guy."

"Then, the Darkside came."

"Yes, Daddy knows the Darkside. That's where Daddy found the poor little guy. Suffering, alone, scared. Daddy promised to protect the poor little guy, always, always, always. To make sure the poor little guy never gets bullied, or picked on, or hurt, ever, ever again."

"Do… do you remember the poor little guy's parents?"

"Bah! That mean old bastard and the selfish bitch? They had it coming. They had it coming on the Darkside. That's why Daddy hurt them, brought them to the Darkside. They killed the poor little guy!"

"Do… do you remember… the poor little guy's name?"

"What does it matter? Daddy is the only one that matters, Daddy and the Darkside! And Daddy will drench this world in blood bloody-blood and bones for the pain that the poor little guy felt."

He brought the bottle of booze to his cracked lips for another drink and found it empty. "Shit!"

The evil specter threw the bottle against a fence opposite the bank. As his temper flared, two security cameras blew their fuses in unison. A voice sounded from beneath a pile of cardboard. "What the hell are you doin'?"

The bogeyman paused as the streetlamps continued to flicker.

A homeless man crawled out from where he had been sleeping. "Motherfucker! Watch where you throwin'… Aww shit."

Eyes burned red in the darkness of his hood as he considered the newcomer. The squealing of rats echoed through the alley. He let go of the dead cat's tail, sending it spinning away.

The man began to back away. "Hey, I don't want no trouble."

The bogeyman cocked his head and mimicked his voice. "Hey, I don't want no trouble."

"W-what the fuck?"

He stuck his face in the old man's, clenching his fists as his eyes flared, his own deep voice rumbling. "Maybe you don't want no trouble, but you've found Daddy and the Darkside."

With the speed of a professional boxer and the glee of a child with a newly obtained toy, the bogeyman threw a right cross, connecting with the man's face. Blood squirted from his nose and dribbled from his mouth as he landed on the wet pavement. "Aww, fuck."

A huge work boot came down and connected with the man's genitals. Groaning, he tried to curl up in a ball. Giggling, the bogeyman picked him up and flung him into a wall. The crack of bones breaking reverberated through the alleyway as his blood sprayed everywhere. His voice came in a wheezing, raspy whisper. "P-please."

The bogeyman laughed as he kicked the guy again in the side. "No!"

He grunted. "S-spare… m-me."

The evil specter stooped over and yelled in his face, "No! There's no mercy from Daddy! Mercy is stupid! Mercy is weak! Put… put up your dukes, dukey-dukes! Is that the best you got? Is it? Freak! Weakling! You'll never amount to anything! Now defend yourself!"

"S-someone… a-anyone, h-help."

He kicked him in the face, smearing blood on his filth-covered work boot. "Daddy doesn't even know why Daddy lets you live on the Darkside! You're nothing but a burden to Daddy, nothing but a useless, worthless parasite! We hate you!"

The homeless man had a few more teeth missing, still bleeding from his nose and mouth as he lay crumpled on the ground, curled up in the fetal position, shivering. The flash of red and blue lights lit up the walls of the bank.

"Who dares to disturb Daddy's fun on the Darkside?"

"The… the police. They… they could hurt the poor little guy."

"Daddy will make sure they don't." He melted into the shadows.

Two flashlights cut through the darkness like beacons of shining hope as a voice called out, "Hello?"

The homeless man groaned.

A rat scurried across a light beam as it came to rest on the bloody old man lying broken in a heap of trash. One of the officers called to the other, "Batista, over here!"

Officer Batista ran over, waved a rat away, and knelt to check his pulse. "What the hell? Sir, how did this happen to you? Can you speak?"

He groaned, trying to motion with a compound fracture in his arm.

Both flashlights flickered.

Officer Batista looked up. "Clemens, radio for an ambulance! This guy is banged up bad. Hold on, sir. We're gonna get you an ambulance."

Officer Clemens clicked the talk button on her walkie-talkie. "Unit ten to dispatch, we have a 10-49 on Diamond Heights Boulevard behind the bank…"

A huge hand with gnarled, yellow fingernails and sallow skin covered her mouth and pulled her into the shadows, her scream muffled.

The homeless man's eyes bulged and rolled. "Uuuuuuuuuhhhhhhhh…"

Officer Batista shined her flashlight where she thought her partner to be. "Clemens?"

Two rats quarreling over a bit of trash drew the beam of her flashlight to the other side of the alley, making her jump. "What in the hell is with all the rats?"

The light flickered again before it fizzled out. Officer Batista smacked at it with an open palm. "Goddammit. Clemens? Didn't we just change the batteries in these things?" The beam came back as she called into the night again, flashlight searching wildly. "Clemens? Come on, where'd you go? This guy's bleeding out and I think I put bad batteries in my flashlight. Clemens?"

A scream.

A sickening, wet, ripping sound.

Then the crack of bone breaking came from deep within the gloom of the alley.

She whirled around, finding a pool of blood but nothing else. "Oh my God, Clemens!"

Nothing but the sounds of heavy breathing in the darkness and the steady drizzle of the rain.

Batista drew her weapon. "Clemens? Clemens!"

Another rat scurried across her foot as she pointed her gun at it, quaking.

Out of the blackness, a deep, echoing voice came from the shadows behind her. "It can't hear you because Daddy is done playing with it. It's on the Darkside!"

Officer Clemens got dumped to the pavement in front of her partner. Her neck had been broken so that it lolled limply to the side like a rag doll as blood seeped from around the flashlight that had been shoved through her uniform and up her rectum.

Officer Batista screamed as years of training took over. She fired her weapon center mass at the hulking brute that now stood towering over her.

After the third round, the bogeyman swatted the pistol from her hand. He grinned crookedly as he drooled, his red eyes flaring under his hood. "You think you can hurt Daddy? You can't hurt Daddy! Nobody can hurt Daddy on the Darkside."

Fear snapped Officer Batista like a brittle branch. Tears streaming down her face, she looked up. "W-what are you?"

He grabbed her by her shirt and drew her close as her eyes bulged and her breath came in quick, shallow gasps, his crooked, bulbous nose just inches from hers. "I'm… the bogeyman!"

She screamed as he plunged a hand deep into her chest and ripped out her still-beating heart. With a malicious grin, he showed it to her as her eyes rolled up and she collapsed on top of her partner.

He threw the bloody organ among the other refuse on the street as he went over to the old man. He stomped a foot and shouted after nudging him with a boot. "Why? Why do they always go to the Darkside when Daddy still wants to play? Why, why, why?"

Officer Clemens's radio drew his attention. "Unit ten, dispatch… Come in, please."

Sneering, he stomped on it, silencing the garbled voice with a crunch.

His head ticked. "Maybe… maybe our friend will be awake and now we can play?"

Red eyes flared as he rubbed his hands together greedily. "Good! Good, goody-good idea. Then Daddy can play some more before he eats."

Up along the tops of the building, crows had gathered to witness the spectacle like they always did, cawing and cackling, just out of reach. He stomped his foot on the dead man's head, squishing it while sneering up at the birds in defiance. Gray matter splattered the wall and his boot. "Stupid birds! See that? See? See what Daddy did? Daddy doesn't care. Go! Go tattle. Go tattle on Daddy. Daddy is going home to the Darkside for more fun where you can't see him, and no one can save it."

His echoing laugh sent the crows scattering as he melted into the darkness.

I AWOKE DRENCHED IN sweat. Once, I felt a fluke, but twice? I glanced around my room, but everything from the closed window to the bedroom door being ajar seemed to be in order. Nicodemus lay on my feet as usual. He opened his eyes lazily and blinked to decipher if my problem seemed worth his time. His snaggletooth smile and motorboat purring made me instantly feel better. I put my head back on the pillow, but "The Imperial March" began playing on my phone, causing me to jump.

I fumbled for it on top of the nightstand, disturbing my cat as he bolted from the bed. Hitting the 'Answer' button, I spoke irritably into the receiver, "Do you ever sleep?"

The distorted voice of my mysterious director garbled in my ear. "Ahh, Doctor. You're awake."

I sighed as I sank back down into my pillow. "It's five in the morning, but if I wasn't before, I am now. What do you want?"

"We have an incident that needs your attention in San Francisco. I need you up there as soon as possible."

I yawned loudly. "Yeah, sure. Let me get right on that."

"You need to respond to the Bank of America in Diamond Heights off Diamond Heights Boulevard."

"Sure, sure. Bank… Diamond Heights… Diamond Heights Boulevard… Got it. Now if you'll excuse me…"

"Three victims have been accounted for, but there's a fourth one I think you'll find most interesting still among the refuse, behind the building in the alleyway."

The asshole knew how to pull on my heartstrings. I started to get up. "Alright, alright. I'm movin', I'm movin'."

"Very good, Doctor." The line went dead.

Chapter 7

JAIDEN STOOD IN FRONT of the bank. "Good morning, San Francisco. This is Jaiden Fox live with XYZ's breaking morning news. I must warn you, what you are about to see may contain information or images that may be shocking or disturbing to some people or age groups. Viewer discretion is advised."

The camera panned off Jaiden and around to some light traffic on the boulevard. A few police officers had cordoned off the alleyway behind the bank with police tape and some looky-loos milled around on the sidewalk craning their necks to see or recorded the scene with their camera phones. An ambulance driver closed their rear doors and took off down the street. Police cars lined up with their cherries going and orange traffic cones were set out to block off part of the road.

"It's a somber mood here in Diamond Heights near the bank off Diamond Heights Boulevard at the scene of an incident that police are saying happened earlier this morning. A triple homicide was committed in a back alley, with two of the victims from among San Francisco's finest: Police Officers Jill Clemens and Candice Batista."

The footage showed a picture of the two young women dressed in their blues with their names written below.

Jaiden continued. "The third person, I'm told, police are attempting to find more information about and is believed to be a homeless man. Unfortunately, due to the severity of his injuries, he has not yet been identified. Police Chief McNair had this to say."

The shot of an older, very stern-looking gentleman in a police uniform stood in front of a podium with a microphone attached. Cameras flashed as he cleared his throat, a tear running down his cheek. Even though his hands trembled, he kept his composure the best he could. "First, I'd like to take the time to send my condolences to the families and friends of these two fine officers. They will be deeply missed. To the public, I say this is an ongoing investigation, so I cannot disclose too much information at this time, but what I can say is: Worry not, as the San Francisco Police Department will not rest until the person or persons that committed these heinous acts are brought to justice. To the person or persons that enacted these atrocities, I say, we are coming for you, it's only a matter of time. To the press, I'm not taking any questions or making any other comments at this time. Thank you."

Jaiden stood in front of the bank again, a slight breeze ruffling her hair. "I'm told that there are no witnesses or suspects at this time. What's even odder, there appears to be no footage from bank cameras that mysteriously shorted out at the same time the incident occurred. People are being encouraged to come forward if they have any knowledge about this horrifying turn of events and to please call the hotline at the bottom of the screen with any pertinent information. This is Jaiden Fox for XYZ, the last word in news. Now, back to you, Anna."

The video feed stopped.

Bank of America off Diamond Heights Boulevard, Diamond Heights District, San Francisco, CA—0715 hours

THE CAMERAMAN GAVE JAIDEN a thumbs-up. "And... cut! Beautiful as always, Ms. Fox."

Jaiden handed over her microphone. "Thanks, Matt."

She finally noticed me watching her from over by the police tape. I raised my coffee cup and smiled, calling out as she approached, "You're up early, Ms. Fox."

Folding her arms, she raised an eyebrow that made the lock of hair in front of it rise as well. "That's my job, Dr. Diamondback, but one has to wonder why you're here."

I took a sip of my drink. "It just so happens I have an interest in one of the victims from last night."

Her eyes widened behind her glasses, then narrowed. "You think this is connected to the kidnapping case? That's kind of a long stretch even for you, Doctor. This was a triple homicide, not a kidnapping."

"True enough, but I intend to prove it was the same person, or at least the same thing."

"If you're interested in the victims then why are you here? The victims have all been moved to the morgue."

Ducking under the police tape, I made my way toward the alley. "Not all of them, Ms. Fox."

Jaiden hissed as she ducked under after me. "What the hell are you doing? Are you trying to get yourself arrested?"

Looking over my shoulder, my brow furrowed. "I have a badge."

She looked around nervously. "Yeah, because it worked so well the last time."

"Oh, come now. We didn't get arrested, did we? Where's your faith?"

As luck would have it, no one paid us much attention. The crime scene had died down as we slipped around the building, where a hazmat crew already worked at cleaning up the biohazardous material. I flashed my badge and began to survey the area, muttering to myself, "Where are you?" My eye caught something in a corner by some boxes, completely untouched and forgotten. "There you are."

Jaiden's voice oozed disbelief as she peered over my shoulder. "A cat? Really?"

"Yes, Ms. Fox, a cat. Every living being deserves respect and notoriety, especially when it dies as violently as this poor fellow did."

She smirked. "I've heard of being an animal lover, but this is ridiculous. Just what do you think a dead cat is gonna tell you?"

A male voice rang out behind Jaiden. "Yeah, just what do you think a dead cat is gonna tell ya?"

Jaiden's eyes closed as she sighed. "Just great."

A man wearing a button-down shirt with a red and gray striped tie and a tweed jacket with elbow patches strolled toward us. His belly hung over his jeans making push-ups improbable, and his balding head glinted in the morning light. His piggy eyes fixed on Jaiden and me. Following close behind came a lady with a no-nonsense look about her in a black pencil skirt, a crisp white button-down blouse, and a black blazer. Her hairdo made her look like Aunt Vivian from *The Fresh Prince of Bel-Air*, and judging from her swagger, she held the confidence of a professional who had fought her way up the ladder of success.

I gave them my full attention. "Ahh, you must be the resident detectives."

The lady detective gave me all the consideration one would give an annoying fly. "We know who we are. Who the hell are you?"

Jaiden extended a hand. "Jaiden Fox, XYZ News."

Both detectives ignored her hand, but the male shook his head, disappointment thick as sausage gravy in his voice. "We know who you are. And may I add, as a reporter, you should know better than to be here, Ms. Fox."

"I…"

He began sizing me up and down. "Now, with you. I'm not sure whether I should arrest you for tampering with an active crime scene or for being weird and unusual in public."

Flipping out my credentials, I scowled. "Dr. Darrell Diamondback, special federal task force."

The lady detective stepped in front of her partner. "We haven't heard about any special task forces working in the area."

"I'm not surprised. Being a federal agent, I like keeping a low profile."

Her voice carried all the snootiness of a rich bitch at a cabana club as she folded her arms. "That's out of protocol, you know. You could have at least given us a heads-up."

I frowned. "I do apologize for my informalities, but I'm quite sure both of you fine officers are too busy to be bothered with the likes of me. It's evident from the fact you haven't introduced yourselves or shown me some form of identification. Seeing as how I'm on a time-sensitive case, I thought it best not to bother your office."

The other detective sounded perplexed as he attempted to process. "What in the hell is PIE? Is this a joke?"

Jaiden brought her fingers to the bridge of her nose and sighed.

I turned my grimace on her. "The Department of Paranormal Investigation and Education."

Aunt Viv put her hands on her hips as she snorted in disbelief. "Paranormal? You mean to tell me you're a federal ghost hunter?" She and her partner looked at each other and laughed.

The gloves came off. "I'm still capable of giving both of you an all-expenses paid vacation to Lompoc Federal if you'd rather."

They both stopped laughing as their mirth turned to scowls. Then the female detective brought her finger up. "Now look here, wiseass…"

Fixing her and her partner with a glare, I pointed to the cat. "No, you look here, Detective. The victim you've blatantly overlooked is extremely telling in the mindset and demeanor of the perpetrator we're looking for."

She made a sputtering noise of derision with her lips. "A dead cat? Get the fuck out of here, Sherlock. There must be one of those down every alley in the city."

I took out my silver writing pen and pointed at the cat's neck, my voice full of venom. "Oh ho, look who knows so much. First off, as its still fresh, the time of death had to be around the same time as the other three victims. Now, notice the broken neck. This is what killed the poor little guy. Notice also that this animal had his vertebrae from C1 to T1 crushed, rather than snapped. Just let me know if I'm going too fast or using too large of words for either of you."

Jaiden's jaw rose and fell as she blanched.

I continued to point. "Next, notice the petechial hemorrhaging, pointing to the fact he was abused further after he died, probably swung by his tail and used to hit things. Now add the state of the cat with the broken Jack Daniel's bottle over there and the ghastly contents of the crime, and you have evidence of a self-medicating level four antisocial personality disorder, with possible bipolar and schizotypal disorders, emotional lability, and negative impulse control. A very large and strong one to boot."

The male detective folded his arms, a hint of mirth in his voice. "A what now?"

I put my arm around his shoulder as if we were drinking buddies. "As you might call it, my fat friend: a psychopath. My furry victim here was killed by someone with a bully mentality and a flagrant lack of empathy. The fact that this person can prey upon those they consider weaker with no sense of remorse, like the homeless man and the cat, while taking out authority figures like the two police officers, proves this was intentional and not just some fit of rage. These killings may have been opportunistic or some part of a larger plan, but this was not the result of some trigger or provocation. That's how you know they're not a sociopath—this was fun for them."

The detective pushed me off, continuing to glare. "Didn't know there was a difference."

Turning to Jaiden, I tucked my pen back in my pocket. "This is why I believe it to be the same person who has been kidnapping children in this very area. Only a monster could prey on children, cats, and homeless people with no sense of remorse."

All three of them stared at me as the lady detective spoke up, her anger on edge. "The feds didn't think we'd come to these conclusions by ourselves?"

"I'm sure you and Sergeant Taggart over there would have arrived here sooner or later, but what's really going to leave you baffled is the fact that one of the officers, Batista I would imagine as she was murdered second, fired off three rounds at point-blank range into the subject since whatever it was tore her apart before she could finish emptying the clip, and hit nothing but that brick wall over there."

"So what does any of that have to do with ghosts?"

"So your trained officer has all the accuracy of an Imperial storm trooper unless there's a better explanation for how this happened where she didn't miss. To make matters more interesting, there's no blood but that of the four victims, Officer Batista's heart was ripped right out of her rib cage, and Officer Clemens's neck was crushed in a very similar manner to this cat's neck, establishing something of a modus operandi. Also, Clemens had her flashlight shoved right through her uniform and… well, we all know what happened to her flashlight. Now, what type of human would have the strength or size to perform so many inhuman feats, hmm?"

She matched my gaze. "Your wise ass seems to know an awful lot about this case, mister."

I tugged at the lapels of my overcoat. "Doctor, and as I told you before, it's nothing you and J. L. McCabe couldn't have deduced if you had sharper eyes."

"That's it, buster. You're coming with us." She reached out and grabbed my shoulder to spin me around and cuff me.

A new voice sounded from behind us. "Hold that thought, Detective."

Both detectives looked around, dumbfounded. "Chief?"

An older officer in an impeccable uniform came strolling up with a man I knew very well in tow. I looked at Jaiden's confused expression and smiled while brushing off my shoulder.

The male detective began to protest, "But Chief…"

He nodded in the direction of Jaiden and me. "Save it, Roberts. I have it on strict orders to leave these two alone."

The lady detective let go of my shoulder. "But Chief…"

His stern look made it clear he wasn't budging. "No, Washington! No 'But, Chief' on this one. You are to forget that Dr. Diamondback and Ms. Fox were ever here. Have I made myself clear?"

Washington and Roberts grumbled in unison, "Yes, Chief."

He gazed sternly at both detectives for a moment, then rested his stony old face on me. "In the future, Doctor, it would be nice if you gave my department a heads-up when you're in the area, so we don't… almost make the same mistake twice. Yes?"

I nodded. "My apologies, Chief, but time is of the essence on this one. Children are at risk."

He nodded back. Then turned to Stravinsky. "Well, Mr. Stravinsky, I believe that is all?"

Stravinsky gave me an inquisitive look. "Doctor, you are finished here?"

Taking in the alley once more, I nodded. "Yes, though I'll probably be back later tonight after the hazmat team has cleared out and the lighting is better."

He turned to Jaiden. "Ms. Fox?"

She looked around helplessly and shrugged. "I didn't want to be here in the first place."

The police chief frowned. "Then if there's nothing else, please kindly remove yourselves from my crime scene."

Stravinsky gave a curt nod and raised a well-manicured eyebrow at us. "As you wish, Chief McNair. I do hope you and detectives have pleasant day. Doctor? Ms. Fox? Shall we?"

Chief McNair turned on his heel and began to make his way back to his patrol car.

The two detectives shot daggers at me as they trailed behind their captain. I gave them a grin and a small wave goodbye. I scooped my victim into a shoebox I had brought with me so I could bury him properly, then set out after Stravinsky.

"It is no wonder you are making *druzhina* wherever you go, Doctor."

"Stravinsky, it's good to see you too."

His voice carried a sardonic tone. "Doctor, as always."

I looked at my iWatch. "You're a bit early, though. Normally you're my one phone call."

He turned to Jaiden and brightened. "Well, we couldn't have newest team member getting booked into jail, could we?"

My nose scrunched. "I thought you said getting booked into county was a rite of passage with this job."

Jaiden gave Stravinsky a long, wide-eyed blink. "Who... who are you?"

He straightened himself. With a small bow, he handed her a card as we passed back underneath the police tape. "Ah! Please allow me to introduce myself. Vladimir Stravinsky, at your service."

Jaiden reached out to shake his hand with enthusiasm. "Well, Mr. Stravinsky, thank you so much for helping back there. I've found that *some* people have no knack for diplomacy."

Stravinsky shook his head, still smiling. "*Ne dumay ob etom, devushka.* Think nothing of it. Is all part of job. Besides, what do people, especially authorities, think when one identifies themselves as hunter of paranormal?"

She looked dumbfounded, jerking a thumb at me. "So, part of your job is to get him out of trouble?"

Stravinsky shrugged. "More or less, am handler for PIE."

She chortled as she shook her head. "You're a saint."

His eyes went wide as he let out a full belly laugh and pointed at me. "Oh? Ha-ha-ha! See? She already knows you. Eh, Doctor?"

My expression turned sour. "Very funny."

Stravinsky wiped a tear from his eye. "So, Doctor, what is next move?"

Sighing, I lifted an eyebrow at my long-time friend. "Well, my dear Stravinsky, the threat level has clearly elevated. If the subject is willing to take big risks like this, who knows what's next? Things generally don't improve without some form of indulgence at the peak of the manic cycle, which means the subject will become more and more violent as time progresses. In that light, I would say it's high time we bring in the final member of our team."

Stravinsky nodded. "Very good to hear you say. I will inform mutual friend of this."

Jaiden looked confused. "Final member? Mutual friend?"

I raised an eyebrow. "Exactly. Say, do you mind driving this time?"

Somewhere in the Hoover Wilderness between CA and NV—1838 hours

I FOLLOWED JAIDEN TO her apartment so she could change and then had her follow me back to San Jose so I could grab some gear for our upcoming wilderness romp. I changed into some black Levis, a black polo, and black hiking boots, though I still wore my overcoat and fedora. Leaving my car behind, we took her red hybrid Lexus SUV out to the middle of nowhere. It had been a while since I had been in the rough. Breathing in the fresh, piney air, I could hear the trees rustling in the breeze. A Steller's jay screamed at us as various other wildlife rustled throughout the thick brush. I could really see the attraction of just leaving civilization behind and moving out to a place like this.

Maybe when I retired.

We had to abandon Jaiden's Lexus a way back and hike in on foot to the coordinates I had from the dossier. It had been since my years as a Scout that I had to do any real land navigation, but it came back to me easily enough. I soon regretted not asking Stravinsky for a chopper. It would have been much easier on my feet, and possibly my ears, if I had just flown in.

"If I get towed, I'm going to tie your ears in a knot, and then I'm going to take the towing and impound fees out of your ass."

I wasn't sure how many times I would have to listen to her threaten me about that. Dressed in blue jeans, a white blouse, and some dark brown hiking boots with red trim, Jaiden snorted like an angry minotaur as we trudged along.

I sighed as I pushed a branch out of our way, being cautious not to let it whip back into her face. "It will be fine, Ms. Fox. Nothing is going to happen, and even if it does, Stravinsky will handle it."

"Just what in the hell do you hope to find out here in the middle of all this… nowhere, Dr. Diamondback?"

"Not what, whom."

She paused for a moment. "You mean someone lives all the way out here?"

"Yup."

"On purpose?"

"Evidently."

"Have you considered that perhaps they don't want to be bothered?"

"The thought had crossed my mind, but seeing as how I was told he's the best man for the job, here we are."

Jaiden gave a dismissive huff. "Do you believe everything everyone tells you?"

"Not at all, which is why we're out here. I want to see for myself if he's the best man for the job."

The sun had begun to disappear in the tree line behind us as we stumbled into a clearing. A small cabin sat at the center, chimney smoking. A freshly cut woodpile sat near the front door and the porch had an old rickety rocking chair sitting on it. Bushes dotted the area and an old blue, gray, and silver Chevy Silverado sat parked nearby.

I brought my voice to a whisper. "Make sure to keep an eye out for booby traps."

"Booby traps?"

"Get down."

Jaiden glowered at me from behind her glasses. "What in the ever-loving hell are you talking about?"

Blam!

A rifle echoed through the forest as birds erupted from the canopy, filling the sky, then quickly dispersing.

Jaiden squealed and dropped like a pair of panties at a gentleman's club. "What in the actual fuck?"

Another shot rang out. "Well, it seems I was correct."

Jaiden's eyes bugged out of her skull. "Correct? Correct about what? That whoever this is has lost their goddamn mind?"

I rubbed my chin, peeking from around the tree I sat behind. "He won't shoot a female if he can help it."

"Wait, what? How the hell do you know that?"

"He missed you. From what I hear, he never misses. Now, *shh!*"

"I swear, if we get out of this alive…"

I took a pair of binoculars out of my pack and scrutinized the surrounding area, muttering, "Where are you?"

A thick southern drawl cut through the clearing. "Attention, trespassers! Y'all got 'xactly five seconds ta' turn yer carcasses 'round'n go back the other way!"

The echo made him impossible to pinpoint, so I cupped my hand to my mouth and called out, "Mr. Edward Anderson?"

"Four… three…"

"Mr. Anderson, if I could just have a moment of your time."

"I don't give a rat's ass 'bout ma' extended car warranty!"

"Mr. Anderson, I've been sent by the government…"

Blam!

This time, I felt the wind and heard the whistle of the bullet as it lodged itself into the tree, spraying my face with small pieces of bark.

"Y'all ain't helpin' yer chances none, hoss!" I heard the click from the bolt of his rifle chambering another bullet.

All at once, Jaiden did something I didn't think either of us expected. She stood, hands raised, eyes shut tight. Her face winced as if she expected to be shot at any second. "We need your help, Mr. Anderson!"

There came a long pause. "Maybe I don't wanna help!"

Jaiden opened a wary eye. "There are children involved, Mr. Anderson. Please, just give us a moment."

"What makes y'all think I care 'bout a bunch'a soft, snot-nosed brats?"

I yelled back, "Because a man who risks his life and military career for a couple of Afghani kids might do the same for American ones!"

A few moments passed before he responded. "How the hell'd y'all git inta' ma' service record? It's supposed ta' be sealed."

I slowly stood with my hands raised like Jaiden. "Perhaps, if we could find a better place to conversate?"

Forty feet to my left, a bush stood as well, the muzzle of a Remington .300 rifle trained on me. "Quit yer fool yellin'. I can hear ya just fine. An' don't git no ideas 'bout pullin' that side cannon'a yours. Read me, hoss?"

I nodded. "Wouldn't dream of it."

He motioned toward the cabin with his rifle. "A'ight then, let's have us a lil chitchat as ta' why Uncle Sam is dumb enough ta' come'a courtin'."

Chapter 8

Ed Anderson's Cabin, Somewhere in the Hoover Wilderness between CA and NV—1919 hours

E D SAT ON AN old wooden barstool across from Jaiden and me at his own personal bar, looking between us. His rifle rested within easy reach against the gleaming wood counter, and I would bet dollars to doughnuts that he had a loaded shotgun behind there as well. Jaiden and I sat at a small kitchen table, facing him.

The spit-shined cabin looked like something out of an animal activist's worst nightmare. Hunting trophies and pictures of Ed catching wild game hung on almost every wall, intermixed with a few religious items. A crucifix hung over the bedroom door and a sign hanging in the kitchen area read, "Everyone blesses this home, some by staying, others by leaving." The Marine Corps flag had been draped over the wall behind his bar directly above his framed service medals prominently displayed on a shelf. Pictures from his time served and awards of meritorious mass had been framed and posted up beneath the shelf. Rustic rugs adorned the hardwood floor and a fireplace at the far side of the cabin gave it a cozy feeling. A lime-green couch and an old tan La-Z-Boy near the fireplace acted as the centerpieces to the living room. I saw no TV, but a radio sat on the bar warbling out the country song "(You Let the Blues Move In) Now I'm Moving Out" by The Rouse Brothers. Beneath the music, there was the hum of a generator outside.

Ed was about my height, five ten or so. Without the ghillie suit, he looked to be about my age as well, early to mid-forties. A ball cap with the Bass Pro Shop logo on the front hid most of his neatly trimmed brown hair. A red-checkered flannel shirt with a white undershirt poking out around the neckline, camouflage cargo pants, black jungle boots, and a camouflage hunting vest, this guy screamed conservative values. His mustache had been trimmed with a slide ruler to Marine Corps regulation, pencil thin and off the lip. He studied us with ice-blue eyes as cold as the expression on his face. Opening a mini fridge next to him, he removed a beer, cracked it open, and continued to stare at us, twitching his mustache before he took a drink. His directions were as simple as he was. "Go."

I figured I had till the end of his beer before he decided what to do with us. "Um, Ed... May I call you Ed?"

His voice remained flat. "No."

"Well then, Mr. Anderson…"

He squinted. "Yer a Democrat."

My face mashed up in confusion. "I hardly see how my political affiliation makes any difference to the situation."

"'Cause ya sound like a damn Democrat ta' me."

"Actually, I'm Independent."

His rifle seemed to teleport into his shoulder as he pointed it at me. "Yer a damn Communist?"

I rolled my eyes and threw up my hands.

Leaning forward, Jaiden interjected, "Mr. Anderson, perhaps it's best if you just talk to me."

He lowered his rifle, sizing her up. "Say, don't I know y'all?"

Jaiden brightened with hope. "Do you watch… er, listen to… XYZ News?"

Ed took a sip of his beer and shook his head. "Nope. That crap's fake news."

Like that, it disappeared. "Well, regardless, Mr. Anderson…"

"Call me Ed."

"I thought you told Dr. Diamondback not to call you by your first name."

Ed took another sip of his beer as he nodded to each of us in kind. "He can't call me Ed, but y'all can."

Jaiden cleared her throat nervously. "Well, Ed, the doctor here and I are looking for some missing children."

He shook his head, chuckling. "Y'all'r tellin' me he's a doctor? Well, don't that beat all. I thought doctors normally wore white coats, not all black like some namby-pamby goth kid."

My brow wrinkled. "That's a rather trope statement, Mr. Anderson."

He ignored me, squinting at Jaiden. "Y'all ain't implyin' they're here, are ya, missy? 'Cause if that's what y'all'r thinkin', y'all can just turn yerselves right around."

Jaiden backpedaled, shaking her head and upturning her palms. "No, nothing like that. We could use your help in finding them is all."

"Why me?"

Jaiden's face screwed up in confusion as she looked at me. "Actually, that's a wonderful question. Why him?"

It seemed I would get a chance to speak after all. "Because the nature of this case matches perfectly with your military background." Ed continued to stare at me in silence. I sighed. "Because there are things you experienced in the military that qualify you for this job, Mr. Anderson."

He sipped at his beer, never taking his eyes off me. "I understood what'cha said, yah condescendin' jackass, but jus' 'cause y'all got some file on me, y'all think ya know me, hoss?"

I matched his gaze pound for pound. "I would never pretend such a thing, Mr. Anderson. What I do know is that you saved a group of children in Afghanistan from a djinn against orders. That not only gives you the heart but experience in combating paranormal entities, which is exactly what I need. Now you can sit here posturing and being difficult all you like, but I have some children to find. So, are you in or not?"

"Hold the phone here. Y'all'r tryin' ta' recruit me fer somethin' relatin' ta' spooks?"

Nodding, I tapped my finger on the table impatiently. "I showed you my badge, Mr. Anderson. What did you think the word paranormal meant?"

Rubbing his chin, he glanced to the side. "Welp, I suppose it makes sense as the federal gov'ment keeps tabs on alien activity'n such."

"Indubitably."

He dropped his head, looking at the bar. "Truth is, I don't rightly know what the heck I saw that night. All I 'member is the fire."

Jaiden leaned against the table. "Look, Ed…"

He brought his glare up. "Now y'all'r askin' me ta' git wrapped up in somethin' I been tryin' ta' ferget 'bout all these years? Why should I? The military done kicked me out 'cause I seen what I seen. Said I was plumb loco'n that I needed ta' be put out ta' pasture in that flab-nabbin' report'a theirs."

I tried to reach him with empathy. "I understand it's a lot to process."

He took a sip of his beer, staring hard as if he could look through me and see into my soul. "Do ya? Do ya really?"

Steepling my hands, I never broke his gaze. "I've done my fair share of time in the trenches, Mr. Anderson."

Jaiden leaned toward him, arm resting on the table. "Ed, in the last twenty-four hours, I've experienced things that still have me questioning my sanity. Assuming they're real, and I've got to at this point, that leaves me with no alternative but to get involved. I wouldn't be able to look myself in the mirror if I walked away and left the victims to fend for themselves."

"Welp, that's you, ain't it?" Her eyebrows folded as her lips formed an indignant O. He considered both of us for a long time before he spoke again. "A'ight, let's say fer a second that I believe what y'all'r sayin' is true. What's that Taliban demon from hell gotta do with y'all's case'n what makes y'all think I wanna leave God's green earth fer hell's kitchen?"

A smile crept across my face. "As for your second question, because the call of duty and the chance to serve your country again on the front line are too much for a man like you to ignore. As for your first, I think you already know the answer to that question, we went over it earlier."

He dropped his head and shook it. "Still don't like it. That stupid thing nearly burned us all alive when it done found out it couldn't control me. Still don't understand how I survived."

I shrugged. "Sometimes faith in something is all we need, Mr. Anderson. It couldn't possess someone strong or steadfast in their beliefs."

Ed squinted and his shoulders hunched. "Horsepucky."

Jaiden spoke up. "Think of the children."

He slammed a palm on the bar top. "Damn them kids! They ain't ma' responsibility."

Jaiden's scowl put his to shame. "They're just kids, Ed, and if you can help us find them, then it's your duty to do so as… as a patriot and an American citizen."

He sniffed, dropping his voice to a civil level. "'Sides, it was carin' 'bout them darn kids in Afghanistan what got me discharged from the military in the first place."

I tried to reel him in. "You did the right thing, though, Ed. When it came down to it, you did the right thing no matter what it cost you."

His voice came out choked. "It done cost me everythin'."

"Just like you'll do the right thing now, because you understand the words: honor, courage, and commitment."

He dropped his gaze to the bar again, the empty can of Busch Light in his hand clunking as he set it on a wooden coaster. "I gotta sleep on this. Y'all can see yerselves out."

Jaiden looked out the window. "It's dark."

"Ain't ma' fault y'all decided ta' call so late. Bridgeport's near here. Go'n check in at the inn there. I'll have an answer fer ya in the mornin'."

I nodded. "Thank you for your time, Mr. Anderson."

It seemed the best I could hope for at this point, but as I left, I happened to glance back at a man at odds with himself. I wasn't so sure I'd be able to count on his help after all.

Report From Ed Anderson's Military File: Evidence ID#: SJ–0006 Zargari, Afghanistan—1836 hours (Ten Years Ago)

THE SUN APPEARED AS a molten semicircle setting behind the rocky hillocks that made up the barren Afghan terrain, layering the sky with brilliant yellows, oranges, and reds, making it look like a tequila sunset. A US supply truck and two Humvees silhouetted against the sun kicked up dust signatures on the long dirt road into the village of Zargari. One Humvee had an M2 .50 caliber machine gun mounted on top, the other a Mark-19 rapid-fire grenade launcher. The Marines had been out on a circuit trying to satisfy some basic needs of the people: food, blankets, medicine. Needing relief because of oppressive Taliban forces, the innocent would starve to death without aid and no way would the Marine Corps, America's finest fighting force, allow that to happen.

As they pulled into their last stop for the evening, chickens scattered, children scrambled, and goats bleated as the vehicles killed their engines in the middle of the dusty streets. A rush of people came out of their mud-brick shacks to greet the soldiers, crowding the supply truck that they had come to depend on. Staff Sergeant Edward Anderson helped in passing out supplies to the thousand or so people all begging for help.

The supply officer with him, a second lieutenant by the name of Miller, was about as useless as tits on a boar. He spent his time sitting and complaining about the heat, drinking most of the water, and never lifting a finger to help anyone, let alone do his job. He had the makings of what most Marines would call "a shit bird."

At least Anderson had the operation down pat, so no need for an officer gumming up the works anyway. Newly appointed to staff sergeant, Ed took his rank, his job, and his Marines seriously. His dedication and attention to detail helped everything run smoothly. Around the time they made ready to leave, a lance corporal by the name of Riggs got his attention. "Hey, Top."

Ed nodded. "What'cha need, Riggs?"

Riggs got a little closer. "Do you hear something… weird going on?"

Ed checked his watch. "Ain't it time fer *Isha*?"

Riggs shook his head. "Naw, this is different. I've heard that stuff a thousand times already, hell, I could probably recite it myself. I don't know why, but this don't sound right, Top. The cadence is all… wrong."

Ed looked around. "Welp, where's it comin' from?"

Riggs pointed. "I think old man Gul's house."

A soft glow emanated from the dwellings window, but they could see no one inside. Ed cupped a hand to his ear and could faintly hear a steady chanting, but not like the three-to-five-minute prayer from the Quran. This sounded different, deep, repetitive, spooky.

Riggs eyes went wide. "Do you think it could be an enemy code, Top?"

Chills ran up and down Ed's spine as he climbed out of his Humvee. "Good ears, Marine. Grab Corporal Dukes'n let's go check it out."

A voice sounded behind Ed. "Go check what out?"

Ed's facade turned to stone before he did an about-face, coming nose to nose with Lieutenant Miller. He gave a salute that the second lieutenant mirrored back, then cut, "Evenin', sir. Nice night."

Miller's voice made it clear he wasn't in the mood for small talk. "You didn't answer my question, Staff Sergeant. Go and check what out?"

Ed bit his tongue before he answered, "Well, sir, Riggs here heard somethin' out'a the ordinary. I was 'bout ta'… request permission ta' take one more Marine'n check it out."

Miller shook his head. "It's probably just their evening prayer. We're due back at the TCP. Let's roll out."

Ed's eyebrows sharpened. "With all due respect, sir. What if it's an enemy code? Riggs is right, this ain't like the *Isha*."

The lieutenant looked confused. "Like what?"

"The *Isha* is their evening prayer, sir."

The officer indulged his staff sergeant for half a second, putting a hand to his ear, then brought it away shaking his head. "I don't hear anything."

This time, Riggs spoke up. "Sir, how could you not hear that? It's getting louder."

"Stay out'a this, Lance Corporal! So, yer denyin' ma' request ta' bring two Marines with me to check on a possible hostile situation, sir?"

Miller glared at Ed, crossing his arms. "I'm denying you permission to go investigate at all."

Ed stepped away, grabbing his M27 rifle. "Sorry, sir. Didn't hear ya."

Miller made to grab Ed's shoulder. "Staff Sergeant…"

He never saw Ed's right cross coming. Scowling down at the unconscious officer sprawled in the dirt, Ed grumbled, "Don't ever touch me, yah fuckin' boot." He spun on his heel in the direction of the noise. Footsteps fell in behind him. "Y'all lookin' fer a court-martial too, Riggs?"

"I ain't lettin' you face this alone, Top."

Corporal Dukes sounded off as well. "I ain't either, Top. We got your back."

Ed grinned and shook his head. "You too, eh, Dukesy? Welp, then we'll all face a court-martial together."

They continued toward the two-room mud-brick hovel. Ed gave Dukes and Riggs silent hand signals to flank the open doorway and both Marines scrambled to his direction, keeping low and silent. Ed posted himself by the door, Riggs at his back, stealing a quick glance into the open doorway.

What he saw made his blood run cold.

Candles softly illuminated both quarters, reinforced from a fireplace crackling in the front room. A simple, dilapidated table and chair sat in front of the fireplace and an old straw mattress lay in the far corner. Old man Gul stood in the far room with his back to them. He chanted something in Arabic, his arms spread out wide in front of him. A pentagram inside a circle had been neatly drawn in powdered chalk on the dirt floor. In the center lay a small, unconscious boy dressed in rags. Two other children, similarly dressed, cowered in the corner of the room, staring at the old man with expressions of dread.

As Gul's chanting intensified, fire leaped from the candles and began to encircle the old man. Ed blinked a few times to try and clear the impossible from his vision. It didn't work. Steeling himself, he breached the doorway and leveled his weapon. "What kinda devil worshippin' shit's goin' on in here, Gul?"

The old man turned toward him, revealing a visage so ghastly, it rooted Staff Sergeant Anderson to the spot. Fire flickered from Gul's eye sockets and flared from his mouth as he chanted. It even danced in and out of his long beard as it continued to spin in a hypnotic elliptical pattern around him.

The two children cowering in the corner looked to their would-be savior and began shouting a word of warning, fear in their voices. "Djinn! Djinn!"

The djinn looked at them and roared, scaring them back into silence.

Riggs and Dukes appeared beside Ed. "What the fuck?"

"Light 'em up boys!"

Riggs happened to be the first to react, firing a burst from his rifle at the flaming old man. The bullets exploded into showers of molten steel and brass. The djinn bellowed and shot a burst of flame back at Riggs, setting him ablaze on the spot. The Lance Corporal screamed and dropped to the ground.

"Oh my God, Riggs!" Dukes opened fire without thinking and the monster shot another jet of flames at him. It hit his rifle, melting it around his hands. Dukes' screams replaced those of Riggs, now just a charred husk on the floor.

The djinn considered Ed for a moment. A ghostly voice rang in his mind as it began to advance on him. *You would do nicely as a vessel. Relax… relax.*

Even with the fire burning around him, Ed felt drowsy. Rather than deadly, the warmth was so inviting. Maybe he should relax and sleep as the old man suggested. His rifle went slack in his hand.

His rifle…

In a flash, Ed's mind snapped back into focus as he began to mumble, "This is my rifle."

The djinn stopped advancing, an odd look on his face.

Ed's words gained momentum. "There are many like it, but this one is mine."

The djinn's surprise turned to fury at Ed's words as it spoke aloud. "What are you doing? I said, sleep!"

Ed's voice gained volume. "My rifle is my best friend, it is my life!"

The djinn roared, "Enough!"

He began screaming at the old man. "I must master it as I must master my life. My rifle, without me, is useless. Without my rifle, I am useless!"

The old man howled and shot a stream of flame at Ed, but he dodged the blast. As he jumped out of the way, his rifle clattered away from him.

Ed continued yelling despite the smoke and flame that threatened to choke him. "I must fire my rifle true. I must shoot straighter than my enemy who is trying to kill me. I must shoot him before he shoots me. I will!"

Another jet of flame shot toward Ed, who again leapt to the side. He fell behind the small table and chair near the fireplace, which took the brunt of the blast and caught fire, adding to the flames already running rampant throughout the dwelling.

The creed he had spoken so many times continued to flow from him. "My rifle and myself know that what counts in this war is not the rounds we fire, the noise of our burst, nor the smoke we make!"

Old man Gul burst fully into flames in his rage. "If I can't have you, then I'll destroy you, mortal!"

Ed's hand found something on the floor—an iron poker. "We know it is the hits that count!"

He came up to a knee as the djinn raised its hands to shoot another burst of flames and threw the poker like a javelin. The iron poker didn't melt like the bullets and struck true. "We will hit!"

The djinn screamed in agony as its fire began to die out, smoke and blood pouring from the wound in its chest.

Ed scrambled over to retrieve his rifle and began slowly advancing on the wounded creature. "My rifle is human, even as I, because it is my life. Thus, I will learn it as a brother. I will learn its weaknesses, its strengths, its parts, its accessories, its sights, and its barrel!"

"How… how do you resist me?"

He stood over the specter with the rifle muzzle pointed at its head. "I will forever guard it against the ravages of weather and damage, as I will ever guard my legs, my arms, my eyes, and my heart against damage!"

Once more, Gul looked like a harmless old man, blood trailing from his mouth. "P-please…"

Ed didn't listen as he continued to yell at the top of his lungs. "I will keep my rifle clean and ready. We will become part of each other. We will!"

A shot rang out and blood painted the wall of the hovel.

Ed's voice dropped to a normal pitch. "Before God, I swear this creed. My rifle and myself are the defenders of my country. We are the masters of our enemy. We are the saviors of my life."

He swooned a bit as the two children from the corner screamed and ran from the burning home. "So be it, until victory is America's and there is no enemy…" Ed fell to the ground. "…but peace."

The burning face of the djinn filled his vision right before his world went black.

Chapter 9

Affidavit from Ed Anderson: Evidence ID#: SJ-0007 Ed's Cabin, Somewhere in the Hoover Wilderness between CA and NV—0001 hours

ED JERKED AWAKE. A KA-BAR he had forged out of pure iron appeared in his hand from a sheathe on his belt. He looked around the cabin.

Nothing.

He and Corporal Dukes had been pulled from the fire by their fellow Marines, along with the unconscious child. In the end, it had been Corporal Dukes's testimony at his court-martial hearing that had saved him from time in the brig and had gotten him discharged with full honors.

He took satisfaction in knowing that the colonel who oversaw the hearing had decided that Lieutenant Miller hadn't acted accordingly in a dangerous situation and ended his military career as well. Dukes had a full medical separation because of the damage done to his hands.

Ed had always felt responsible for that.

Then the government swept it under the rug as they always did. Now these two yahoos invade his home out of nowhere, wanting to suck him right back into stuff that made no sense to him. He had hardly escaped that night with his life. What in the ever-lovin' hell did he know about spooks, other than out here in the wilderness they didn't seem to bother him? Maybe they couldn't find him? He didn't care which, he just wanted it to stay that way.

His white-knuckled grip on the iron knife loosened as he slid it back into its sheathe. Damn fools! He didn't owe them or anyone anything. On the other hand, if that were true, then why did he have this nagging guilt at the back of his mind?

Ed heard the words again: Honor, courage, commitment. "Damn that Democrat fer gittin' in ma' head."

He got up, grabbed his keys from the key box by the door, closed and locked it behind him, then headed out to his truck, resetting a few trip wires as he went.

Jaiden's Car, Somewhere in the Hoover
Wilderness between CA and NV—0002 hours

AFTER A LONG HIKE by flashlight back through dense trees and thick foliage, of which I got turned around a time or two, we finally got back to her SUV.

"See? Nothing happened to it."

She shot me a look that would have curdled milk. "Yeah, but something could have."

My eyes rolled. "Because there are so many people out here to report it."

She clicked her key fob alarm button and threw open the door. "I lose a day at work to drive up to the middle of nowhere, hike through the woods from hell, just to get shot at by some crazy-ass redneck…"

"If you would just…"

She got in and slammed the door. "All to be thrown back out, having to hike back to my car in the middle of the goddamn night…"

Scowling, I shut the door behind me and buckled my seat belt. "You're acting like that was my fault."

She started the engine and put it in reverse while looking over her shoulder to back up. "You, sir, are lucky you're not walking your happy ass to Bridgeport!"

I tried not to laugh. "You know, most women would kill for a moonlit walk through the forest."

"*Ooooooo!*" She whacked me in the shoulder with the back of her hand as I shied away and chuckled. We drove the rest of the way to Bridgeport listening to The Beatles in silence.

A neon sign claiming vacancy greeted us as we pulled into a rustic-looking motel. The main office had been made to look like a log cabin and the rooms had been sectioned off to the right. It boasted a single glass front door with light streaming from it. A few old, chipped garden gnomes, mismatched pairs of rubber galoshes, some old deck chairs, a faded welcome mat, and a beat-up welcome sign adorned the porch. The attached restaurant on the left sat dark. Jaiden parked the car and we went inside, a bell chiming upon our entrance.

The inside looked much like the outside. Rustic furniture littered a cozy common room. A chandelier of deer antlers hung from the ceiling, accented by other lamps placed haphazardly around the office. Flat, worn-down rugs lay on the hardwood floor, and a moth-eaten bearskin sat in front of a flickering fireplace. Paintings and sepia photographs decorated the walls, desperately trying to give it a vintage feel. Not the worst place I had ever been in, but it reminded me very much of a failing antique shop.

A lady in her fifties with curly blonde hair, cat eyeglasses, and too much makeup stood behind the counter. She worked her way through a crossword puzzle in a magazine as she listened to "Toes" by Zac Brown Band playing from a radio on the counter. As we approached, she still hadn't looked up from her crossword. "Can I help you?"

Jaiden leaned against the counter. "We need two rooms for the night, please."

"Just so ya know, honey, we only got one room left."

Jaiden shot me a glacier of a look as if it were my fault they didn't have accommodations to her satisfaction. "I don't suppose it has two beds?"

The clerk finally looked up from her magazine and immediately began sizing me up. "Aww, come on, honey. He couldn't'a messed up that bad."

"Excuse me?"

She gave Jaiden a wink. "Besides, he's kinda cute."

Jaiden turned redder than a box of tagalongs Girl Scout cookies. "I... uh... no, it's... nothing like that."

I stepped in. "We just need a room for the night. Any room will do."

Straightening up, the woman smiled. "That'll be a hundred and twenty-four dollars for the night, please."

Jaiden stiffened. "A hundred and twenty-four dollars? For this place? It looks like my grandmother's house threw up in here."

The clerk's face fell.

I quickly pulled out my company credit card and gave it to her with a grin. "Don't worry. It's on me."

She gave me a coy smile and batted her eyes as she took the card and ran it. "Well, if she doesn't want you, handsome, you know where I'm at."

I continued to grin. "Thank you, but I'm rather unavailable at the moment."

She handed me my credit card with some keycards and a sigh. "Suit yourself, if that's what'cha like. Outside, down the main walkway. It'll be on your left, number one oh eight."

Jaiden's fists clenched at her sides, and I was sure steam would begin whistling out of her ears at any moment. "What?"

I nodded. "Thank you very much."

She gestured toward a sign in front of a dark dining room. "Restaurant opens at seven in the morning, just so you know."

"Again, thank you."

She went back to her crossword puzzle, a smirk sliding onto her face. "You folks have a nice night now, and uh… try not to make too much noise."

Jaiden brought a finger up. "Now look here, bitch…"

The clerk's head came up as her eyes slotted.

I put a hand on Jaiden's shoulder and steered her outside. "Come, come, dear. You're making too much noise."

"That lady had some nerve!"

"I don't know, I thought she was kinda nice."

She snorted and pushed my hand away. "You would."

We walked the rest of the way to our room in silence. As we stepped inside, it held no surprise that the room, much like the office, had been decorated with antiques. Wooden floors with worn rugs, a rickety wooden table with two chairs sporting flat, tatty cushions, and a moth-eaten easy chair stood opposite a queen size bed. A small UHF TV with rabbit ears sat on a small stand near a closet door. A door opposite led to a small bathroom.

Jaiden turned to me. "So, how does this work?"

I plopped myself down in the easy chair. "Well, you've seen the movies. Go ahead and take the bed. I'll be fine."

"Thank you." Kicking off her boots and flopping herself down, she rolled to her side and soon afterward, was lightly snoring.

I made myself as comfortable as possible in my chair and tried to get a bit of shut-eye as well.

SOMEONE SCREAMING WOKE ME up.

My eyes flew open as I searched the room. Jaiden wasn't on the bed or in the bathroom.

Over the wind howling outside, I heard another scream.

I jumped out of the chair and flew out the door, taking in my surroundings.

The parking lot was full of cars and wind. I didn't recall the weather forecast calling for a gale-force storm today as I strained against the icy bombardment, searching for my teammate. Then I heard another scream to my left, away from the office and toward the dumpster near the back of the restaurant. I fought against the windstorm as I sprinted toward the screams. Rounding the corner, I stopped dead in my tracks and looked up.

A ten-foot trash golem loomed over Jaiden who was trying to push herself up from the pavement near the rear of the building.

I shook my head. "What the hell? There's no such thing as a trash golem."

The vortex had drawn up the restaurant's dumpster, using a bunch of the garbage from it to create a vaguely humanoid form held together by a network of miniature tornados. It continued to gain mass as it vacuumed up more trash, dirt, leaves, and other debris from the surrounding area. Dark-purple orbs of energy hovered like eyes, considering Jaiden as a twisted, crumpled stretch of newspaper beneath them bent into what looked like a wicked smile.

I racked my brain for ideas about what the hell it could be and how to bring it down. It certainly wasn't an air elemental. Elementals didn't look or act like this.

It roared, and from its garbage-crafted fist, a bolt of dark-purple energy struck Jaiden. She collapsed to the ground face down, her body twitching.

"No!" I drew my gun and fired at the trash bags the thing used as a head.

The garbage flew apart, but some invisible force brought it back together like a magnet. It laughed and swiped at me with a trash-bag fist. I ducked as it whooshed over my head. The monster was necessarily slow, but I still had to find its weak point.

I chanced a glance at Jaiden. She still laid on the ground, body convulsing infrequently. My mind briefly toyed with how to fix her, but it didn't matter—I needed to focus.

The trash monster roared again, this time spraying a bunch of cans that knocked the weapon from my hand.

I fell back, taking a defensive stance. "What did you do to her, trash heap?"

It laughed again and shot a beam of sizzling, dark-purple energy at me.

I threw myself to the side as it missed me by inches. As I did, I noticed my Desert Eagle laying a few feet away. The creature must have noticed my gun, too, because it began trying to suck it up into its mass. The firearm scooted away.

"No, no, no." I chased it, trying to keep from losing my only defense against this monster. Long before I reached it, a blast of trash knocked me off my feet. I landed with a thud on my ass, covered in refuse. It must have knocked some sense into me because I came up with a revelation: I had been looking at this all wrong. It wasn't a monster. It happened to be a specter. The wind and the temperature change, both telltale signs. The only thing missing seemed to be the cloud of negative energy.

I slapped myself in the forehead.

As a matter of fact, it had to be a skoupída specter, also known as a junk specter. Very rare, these invisible forces wandered the land unnoticed and docile until they decided to feed. That was when a skoupída specter became dangerous and could often be mistaken for a small tornado. The spook would pull anything to it like a magnet, to build a large, intimidating body. It fed off fear and pain, which is what this one happened to be doing to Jaiden, locking her inside her mind in a nightmarish state with that negative energy blast. It concentrated and utilized negative energy in a particular fashion for feeding and defense. A skoupída happened to be one of those exceptions to the rules, as even though they are classified as a specter, they had an anchor.

Cursing myself for being stupid, I pulled myself off the ground. Its attention on Jaiden, it began to drain her life force by shooting her up with negative energy. I could only hope that she wasn't a vegetable yet.

She screamed again.

I needed to find that anchor, fast.

Behind me, I heard the screeching of brakes and lights lit up the area like the Vegas strip. The junk specter howled against the halogen lights, halting it from feeding. I made a mental note of the light sensitivity.

Then the sound of semiautomatic rifle fire split the dawn, piercing the dumpster in a tight group. "I give y'all a simple task'n this is what'cha came up with?"

I yelled over the wind, "Keep it busy, Ed!"

Another three-round burst sounded from his rifle. "What'n the hell ya think I'm doin'? An' don't call me Ed, yah damn Democrat!"

I charged it.

Ed continued to pump lead into the thing. "Git some, hoss!"

For a moment, the specter seemed to be split on which one of us was more dangerous. With a roar, it chucked a huge branch at me. I easily ducked beneath it.

Seeing I hadn't stopped, it sprayed another stream of trash. I leapt to my left, barely avoiding it. It took Ed's bullets, ignoring him completely. A negative energy bolt emanated from the trash-bag hand. I dodged again, leaping at the last second and grabbing onto the dumpster, hoisting myself inside.

Ed quit laying down cover fire. "What'n tarnation'r y'all doin'?"

The trash monster roared again. The wind around it intensified, trying to blow me out of its makeshift body. Trash hands grasped at me as I searched for its anchor, but they were too large and unwieldly to fit.

Inside the dumpster, the wind felt substantially diminished, but used paper napkins, wrappers, and other trash still skittered around. It smelled unbearable, like sweaty yeti armpits mixed with ass, though if that was because of the skoupída specter or something it had attracted, I couldn't say. As my eyes scanned the immediate surroundings, I heard a strange thumping, like a steady rhythm contrasting with the sound of the trash beating against the outside of the dumpster. There, among the filth, lay a bag of dirty diapers beating like a heart, surrounded by the ghost's negative purple energy.

I tried to grab the bag o' nasty, but got shocked. "Shit!"

"Might wanna hurry up in there, hoss!"

I poked my head out of the sliding door of the dumpster and called over the howling wind, "Do you have anything explosive?"

"Is a frog's ass watertight?" Digging into a big silver toolbox in the back of his truck, he came up with a homemade pipe bomb.

I jumped out of the thing, rolling toward Jaiden, trying to shield her with my body. "Into the dumpster! Throw it into the dumpster!"

He lit the fuse with a Zippo lighter from his pocket and threw it. As the monster lifted its huge hand to crush Jaiden and me, a muffled explosion sounded from inside the bin. The thing stopped, smoke pouring from its body. The wind died down and the unnatural chill lifted. It wailed as the purple orbs went dark and the dumpster fell five feet to the ground with a loud crash, cracking the cement as garbage rained down around us. Using my overcoat as a shield, I tried to protect us the best I could.

Once things settled, I shook the garbage off me and turned my attention to Jaiden, checking her vital signs. Unconscious, she had a heartbeat, but her breathing came rapid and shallow. Her body continued to spasm as her eyelids fluttered and her eyes rolled, showing the whites. If she started foaming at the mouth, I was fucked.

I called hoarsely to Ed, "Orange juice! I need orange juice!"

Ed jumped down from his truck slinging his rifle over his shoulder. "What'r y'all on 'bout, hoss?"

"Please, orange juice! Her life is in jeopardy!" He blinked a few times, but as it was just after seven, he ran inside the restaurant. Jaiden's head lolled in my lap. "Hold on, Jaiden. Just a bit longer."

Ed finally came back with a to-go cup filled with orange juice and handed it to me. "Y'all owe me three fifty."

I ignored him as I took the cup and put it to Jaiden's lips. "Come on, drink."

The liquid dribbled down her chin, but I hoped enough had slid down the back of her tongue to make it into her stomach.

She lay motionless as Ed and I stared at her. "Come on, come on..."

Suddenly, her eyes popped open and she looked around wildly. Her shivering hands involuntarily grabbed onto me. "W-what... what happened?"

I let out a small sigh of relief, but I knew we weren't out of the woods yet. "What's your name?"

"J-Jaiden Fox."

"How many fingers am I holding up?"

"T-three?"

"What city are you in?"

"Bum-fuck Egypt?"

I shone my flashlight in each of her eyes, checking the dilation of her pupils. "I'll accept that answer. And my name is?"

She crinkled her nose. "Asshole, I'm still mad at you."

Ed nodded. "Yup, seems okay ta' me."

I scowled at him.

Jaiden shook her head gently, trying to clear the cobwebs. "Wh-what happened? I-I remember coming out for a walk, and there was this big trash can. Then nothing but pain, and Jakob, he... he..."

I shoved the cup of orange juice into her hands. "You had a nasty, and I emphasize *nasty*, run-in with a trash specter. Here, sip this please."

Ed squinted at me. "Yer one'a them fellers who thinks he's funny, ain't'cha?"

Jaiden clutched the cup as she frowned. "You're trying to tell me there are trash monsters? Really?"

"Its scientific name is a skoupída specter, a dirty piece of business and nothing to take lightly. So, what happened?"

The paper cup trembled along with the rest of her. "I-I couldn't sleep. I just c-came outside for a walk to… to clear m-my head."

"Drink. Trust me, you'll feel better."

She finally took a sip and began to cough.

I turned my attention to Ed, extending my muck-covered hand. "Thank you, Mr. Anderson. If it wasn't for you, I'd hate to think what would have happened to us."

He shook his head wearing a sour expression as he backed away. "Don't touch me."

Jaiden swallowed hard from another sip. "Ed? When did you get here?"

He sniffed as he looked down. "Somewhere between y'all goin' down'n Dr. Venkman here gettin' buried in a heap'a garbage. Ya feelin' any better there, missy?"

She nodded as she continued to sip. "Why is this helping?"

"The vitamin C and the sugar help to counteract what it drained from you."

Ed folded his arms. "All I jus' heard was a bunch'a mumbo-jumbo hippie crap."

The back door to the restaurant opened and an older man poked his head out, surveying the area. "What the hell is goin' on out here, World War III? My dumpster! What the hell happened to my dumpster?"

If it wasn't one damn thing, it was another. I sighed inwardly. "You didn't hear the wind? Those crazy California gales, I tell ya."

His eyes popped out, smoke still rising from the burning husk that had been his trash bin. "The wind didn't blow the fuck out of my dumpster!"

Ed yelled back, pointing a finger, "Hey! Don't cuss in front'a the lady."

The old man noticed the semiautomatic rifle slung over Ed's shoulder. He crouched, covering his head with his hands as if the action would protect him. "Don't shoot me!"

The corner of Ed's mouth twitched. "If I was gonna shoot ya, y'all'd already be shot, yah kooky ol' geezer. Don't tell me y'all ain't used ta' people openly carryin', what with all the hunters y'all see?"

I leaned in close to Ed and spoke out of the side of my mouth. "Just so you know, open carry is generally illegal in California."

His face contorted in disbelief. "No foolin'?"

The restaurant owner stood hesitantly. "I'm… I'm gonna call the police!"

My badge came out. "No need, sir. I already have this situation under control."

"Then what the fu—" He stopped himself, looking at Ed's rifle again. "—heck happened to my dumpster?"

Giving him the best friendly voice I could, "Well, sir, that's classified."

One could see bewilderment on his face. "Classified?"

Ed spat on the ground and looked the man dead in the eye. "Yup. I could tell ya, but then I'd have ta' kill ya."

We began laughing as if sharing a joke, and the man joined in.

Abruptly, he stopped. "No, seriously. I think I'm going to call the cops."

Jaiden spoke up. "Please, sir, no need for the police. I was attacked, and these two men saved my life."

He looked down at her. "What happened to my dumpster?"

Ed replied, "Same dirtbag who done attacked this here lady threw an M80 in it, tryin' ta' cover 'is 'scape."

The wheels began spinning in the old man's head. "Well… the city should replace it then." Ed nodded. "And… and I can have Elmer pick up the trash." I nodded. He looked at Jaiden. "You sure you don't want the cops called?"

"No, thank you." I helped her to her feet

He considered us for a minute. "You folks are a mess. Are you patrons of the hotel?"

I nodded. "Room number one oh eight."

"You're stopping in for breakfast, then, I hope?" Fixing us with a stern squint, his voice hinted that it might help him forget about the situation if we did.

Looking between my company, I shrugged. "After we get cleaned up and check out, I could use a cup of coffee."

My partners nodded as well.

The owner gave us a warm smile. "Well, then we'll see you folks shortly."

I looked around for my gun and found it amid the refuse. I mumbled to myself as I cleaned it off the best I could, then stuck it back in its side holster. "Don't want to forget this."

Ed's eyebrows went up. "Sure is a purty lil piece ya got there."

I nodded at him. "Thanks. Come on everybody, let's go get cleaned up."

Chapter 10

Helm Camera Footage from Sewer Technician
Manny Delgado: Evidence ID#: SJ-0010 San
Francisco Sewer System, Diamond Heights,
San Francisco, CA—0715 hours

A HELM CAMERA SWITCHED on showed me the steering wheel and dashboard of a work van, then swiveled to an empty fast-food bag in the passenger seat and a travel coffee thermos in the cup holder. He grabbed the thermos, took a drink, then put it back.

"Aww man, I love this song." He started singing along with "Nuthin' but a 'G' Thang" by Dr. Dre and Snoop Dogg on the radio as the engine continued to run. Finally, he turned off the van, halting the music, stuck the keys in a pocket, and opened the door. Jumping out into the street, he closed it behind him and went around to the back.

The click of a button and the squelch of a mic could be heard. His voice spoke out while throwing open the back doors. "George, this is Manny, over."

George's voice crackled back. "Go ahead, Manny."

He retrieved an empty garbage sack, a stick with a nail on the end of it, a net, and a couple of orange traffic cones, then closed the door. The tennis courts and pine trees in the background belonged to Douglass Park. "You know, I've been working this job for a year now, and it's still as shitty as the day I started."

"Very funny, Mr. Comedian. And stop cussin' over the radio. How about you do my poor soul a favor and quit?"

Manny shook his head as he headed toward the manhole in the middle of the street. "Why would I do that? City jobs are cushy in all the right places, like a good woman. Good pay, full benefits, 401(k), and the union gives total job security. Besides, now I'm a big playa in San Francisco's underground life."

"You're killin' me here, seriously. You should consider yourself lucky your uncle practically handed you this job."

Manny laughed as he set the orange cones around the manhole. "Never hurts to have family, man."

"Yeah, yeah. Just get those water-intake grates cleaned or we're gonna have problems. Read me?"

He removed the manhole cover with a crowbar and the helmet light clicked on. "Gettin' on down now."

The supervisor's voice came back laced with skepticism. "You're already on the second one?"

Manny scoffed. "Man, the first one hardly had anything in it. You guys are seriously misusing my talents."

George sounded as if he had been born devoid a sense of humor. "I'll be checking your work, you know."

"Check all you like, boss. All you're gonna find 'round these here parts is perfection."

The voice on the other end crackled. "I have you descending at oh seven twenty, over… and they better be clean, Delgado."

"Yeah, yeah. Manny out."

Manny reached the bottom of the ladder, the camera panning his surroundings. Water dripped from the pipes running along the ceiling as rats and cockroaches scurried away from his light. The traffic rumbled up above and the tunnel shook as a semi passed over head. He picked his way along the thin concrete walkway drenched in sludge. A lone rat got brave, standing its ground on its hind legs in the light, whiskers twitching. He kicked at it and sent it scampering away. "Get outta here, ya nasty-ass critter."

His helm camera looked down, showing stagnant sewer water overflowing onto the walkway, getting on his work boots. He shook a leg. "Ugh, disgusting. Alright, let's see why you're not with the flow."

The trench led to a small opening with a set of bars at a dead end. A bunch of rubbish floated in the water, clogging the intake grate. A cluster of rats squirmed and squealed over each other in the corner, but as his light fell on them, they disbursed further into the shadows. "Best stay away you black-plague-ridden bitches."

He took out a large sack and a long stick with a spike on the end and began stabbing at the garbage that clogged the intake and put it into the trash sack. "Cardboard box, baby wipes, tin can, human bone… What the hell?"

A long but relatively small bone floated to the surface. It had been tangled up in a tarp he fished out of the water. As he pulled it up onto the walkway, a small skull fell out as well, rolling around and landing so it faced him. "Oh fuck!"

Manny hit the button on his radio and yelled, "George! George! I fuckin' found something!"

George sounded sarcastic. "It wouldn't be work ethic, would it? And I thought I told you to quit cussin' over the radio or I'm gonna write you up."

A voice echoed from the darkness. "Daddy doesn't like visitors. You? You're not welcome… welcomed on the Darkside."

The camera shook as it swiveled back and forth, his light showing nothing but pipes and slime-covered walls. His voice shook. "Who… who the fuck said that?"

George's voice crackled from the radio. "Manny, you still there?"

George's voice parroted from the murky depths. "Manny, you still there?"

Manny screamed as his light fell on something blurry that knocked his helmet to the ground. It rolled until it showed him floating in midair, suspended by an invisible force, his eyes popping out like a deep-sea fish brought too quickly to the surface. Suddenly, there came a great popping crack. Blood trickled from his mouth and his head flopped to one side. The blotch considered the body for a moment before George's voice echoed again from it. "Manny, you still there?"

I watched as the body was flung against the wall as a laugh joined the squeal of the rats.

George's voice kept calling out from the radio attached to Manny's shoulder. "Manny? Manny, this isn't funny. Is everything okay? Manny? Come in, Manny."

A crunching sound echoed in the darkness as something stomped on the helm camera and the video feed went to snow.

Cozy Bridgeport Inn Restaurant, Bridgeport, CA—0841 hours

W E HAD CLEANED UP the best we could and went to check out at the front office. After handing the room key to the clerk, Jaiden turned to leave in a huff. The lady behind the desk slid me her phone number with a wink, brought her hand to her ear, and mouthed, "Call me."

I smiled, dropped my head, and shook it.

The restaurant portion of the place appeared just as rustic and cluttered as the rest of the hotel. A sea of freshly mopped hardwood floors ran beneath our feet. Fishing rods, a stuffed moose head, and a set of rowboat oars hung on the wooden walls, none of it saying much about the theme of the place. Booths near the windows and faded but well-kept brown vinyl covered chairs sat around a stretch of wooden tables that created a path back toward the kitchen, where the old man poked his head through the swinging door of and waved at us vigorously.

A young girl greeted us by rolling her eyes. Sighing, she set down her smartphone on the hostess podium and showed us to a booth. Her voice was monotone and rehearsed. "Welcome to Dick's Diner. Can I start you folks off with something to drink?"

Jaiden spoke up first, turning over the coffee mug in front of her. "Coffee for me, please, and a glass of orange juice."

I spoke up next. "Coffee, please."

Ed turned over his mug too. "Uh, coffee'n a water, please."

"Three coffees, a water, and an orange juice." She rolled her eyes again as she turned away to get our beverages.

We all sat in silence listening to Alan Jackson's "Don't Rock the Jukebox." The hostess brought the orange juice and the water first, then stomped back to get the coffeepot. After pouring three cups, she glared at us. "Is there anything else I can get you?"

Shaking my head, I looked at the other two. "Uh, no. No thank you."

"Your server will be with you in a second." She returned the coffeepot to the hot plate then stomped back over behind the podium, picked up her phone, and resumed texting.

Jaiden stared at the table as she broke the silence. "Does this sort of thing happen to you every day, Dr. Diamondback?"

Ed looked between us as he jerked a thumb at me. "Y'all was serious? He's a doctor?"

I nodded. "Of forensic psychology."

"Is that even a thing?"

I sputtered my lips, rolled my eyes, and became extremely interested in my coffee.

A pretty, voluptuous, blonde-haired waitress with blue eyes and a bright smile flounced up. She wore a tight black polo, black stretch pants, a pair of black Skechers, and held a notepad and pen in hand. "Hi! My name is Marni and I'll be your server today. What can I get for you folks?"

Jaiden handed her menu to the girl without looking at it. "Just the coffee and orange juice for me, thank you."

I shook my head. "Actually, you should eat something."

She gave an exaggerated sigh, making the lock of hair over her eye flutter. "Fine then. Um, how about a side of mixed fruit and cottage cheese, please."

The waitress turned to me and batted her eyes. "For you?"

I handed my menu right back as well. "A short stack with a side of sausage, please."

She turned to Ed. "And for you, sir?"

Ed studied the menu intently. "I'll take the breakfast special. Eggs, scrambled with 'Merican cheese. A side'a bacon, hash browns extra crispy, 'n sourdough toast, thank ya kindly."

After taking our order, every part of Marni bounced away to give it to the kitchen.

Jaiden addressed me again. "You never answered my question, Doctor. Does this sort of thing happen to you every day?" I opened my mouth to speak, but she cut me off. "Because things like this never happened to me before I met you. This is the second set of clothing I've had ruined since I started working with you. I've never seen a ghost before in my life. Now, suddenly, I've seen them thrice in forty-eight hours."

Ed scrunched up his face and mouthed the word, "Thrice?"

I scowled, clutching my coffee a little tighter. "You still think I had something to do with this? Come on, Jaiden. I was asleep in the room for goodness' sake."

"I've had more showers in the last two days then in a week of going to the gym."

Ed's eyebrows raised toward the brim of his cap as he reared his head back.

"Hey, I was covered in garbage too you know. Did I plan that?"

"Maybe, most of your plans are stupid! All I know is I had maggots in my hair, Doctor. Maggots, do you understand me?"

Ed looked between us both. "Now hold yer horses there, missy."

Jaiden's gaze snapped up, her lips as thin as dental floss.

Ed stirred cream and sugar into his coffee with a spoon. "Believe it 'r not, I just seen a man risk 'is life ta' save yers. Now I don't know much, but I know 'e didn't have nothin' ta' do with that there da'gone thing. He took a big risk tryin' ta' put it down."

Jaiden slouched in her seat, staring at her coffee. "I'm not crazy."

He sipped at his own. "No one said ya were. Y'all think I'm crazy 'cause I seen what I seen?"

I reassured him, "Not at all. There are plenty of other reasons, but not because you had it out with a djinn."

Ed turned his scowl on me.

Sighing, I studied the frazzled bundle of nerves before me. "As I've said before, Jaiden, welcome to a larger world. Once your eyes are open to it, it's almost impossible to close them again. Like when you buy a Jaguar and suddenly you notice every other Jaguar on the road."

Jaiden muttered, "I've never even owned a damn Jaguar."

"Perhaps not, but you can grasp the analogy, I'm sure. They're easier to notice now that you've been exposed."

Ed brought his eyes heavenward. "Amen ta' that."

I turned my attention back to the southern gent across from me. "You decided to join us after all, Mr. Anderson?"

Ed shook his head. "Not at first."

My brow wrinkled. "Then what prompted you to leave, 'God's green earth fer hell's kitchen?'"

He gave me half a smile. "I done saw what a cotton-pickin' mess ya was makin'a things."

Sighing and dropping my eyes toward my coffee, I silently wondered if he might be right.

We sat in silence until our food came. As Ed took the pepper and salt shakers for his food without tasting it, he finally asked, "So who ya workin' fer, hoss? The Agency? The Bureau? Homeland Security?"

I stared at my breakfast. "Nope."

He considered me for a second. "Y'all sure ain't military."

I pushed my sausage around on the plate with the fork, my appetite suddenly eluding me. "I'm federal: the Department of Paranormal Investigation and Education."

Ed mulled it over. "Sounds Deep South ta' me. Wait, so them Cracker-Jack credentials y'all showed me was real? Y'all really work fer an agency called PIE?"

I slathered my pancakes with butter and syrup, hoping it would spark my appetite. "Don't look at me, I didn't name it."

He dumped ketchup on his hash browns and smiled while shaking his head. "I seen better acronyms on a bathroom stall. Who'n the heck thinks up this crap anyways?"

I chuckled along with him. "It gets me into more trouble than it gets me out of, to be honest."

He swallowed a mouthful of eggs with cheese. "So what would y'all call it then?"

No one had ever asked me that question. I cocked my head to the side and scrunched my brow. "Well, I suppose if I had the liberty…" My phone began to play "The

Imperial March" from inside my pocket. "One moment." I excused myself and went outside where there were fewer ears. I pressed the answer button. "Go ahead caller, you're on the air."

The mysterious, garbled voice of my director sounded on the other end. "What are you doing in Bridgeport?"

I leaned against a support beam. "Hello to you too, sunshine. I'm in Bridgeport because I'm trying to put together this team you seem to think I need. What do you want?"

"We have a lead for you."

"I don't want them."

"What are you going on about, Doctor?"

"You heard me, I don't want them. They're too much of a liability and they'll only wind up getting in the way."

The voice remained silent for a moment. "What happened?"

"A skoupída specter. It almost killed Jaiden."

"Obviously it didn't, so why are you whining at me?"

"That's not the point!"

"That's exactly the point, Doctor. Even though Mr. Mopps got bit by a shadow hound, he's still alive and a useful asset due to your quick thinking. Ms. Fox is still alive and mentally sound from the looks of it, even after tangling with a skoupída specter, again thanks to your quick action. It also appears you have Mr. Anderson playing along as I instructed. I don't see the problem."

I began to scrutinize the surrounding area. "What? You got eyes on me?"

"To be precise."

I wanted to reach through the phone and throttle the guy. "Look here, you heartless fuck. Their names are Charlie, Jaiden, and Ed. They're not just numbers, they're real people with real feelings and real lives that had nothing to do with this shit until you forced me to drag them into it. My job is tough enough without more baggage to worry about. Besides, I'm the one who's gotta watch them die if they screw up, or on the off chance that I do, or check them into a clinic when a spook drives them mad or attend a funeral when the inevitable happens. Not you, me. So, tell me I'm whining again, you arrogant son of a bitch, and I'll find your ass and cram this phone down your throat."

"You can turn in your resignation anytime you like, Doctor." I glowered at the parking lot. "Good, I'm glad you've decided to accept responsibility for them after all. Whether you want to admit it or not, your success rate has gone up since you've had these people in your corner, and that's saying something. I expect great things from you and your team."

"I'm glad someone does."

"As I was saying before being rudely interrupted with emotional fiddle-faddle: I have a lead for you and your team. I believe that whatever is kidnapping the children is hiding in the San Francisco sewer system."

I took out my leather-bound notebook and pen. "What makes you say that?"

"Another dead body and the remains of a child. Check the San Francisco Medical Examiner's office as soon as you're able. You're looking for a Manny Delgado, a sewage plant technician. The child is a John Doe."

Scribbling down the information, I sighed. "Got it. Anything else?"

The line went dead.

"Guess not, fucker." I put away my pen, notebook, and phone.

Turning to go back inside, I found Ed staring at me, a toothpick hanging out of his mouth.

I glared at him. "It's not polite to eavesdrop you know."

"Ya care."

I gave him the evil eye. "So?"

His face wore a frown, but he nodded. "So that's ninety-nine percent'a what makes a leader."

Snorting, I shook my head. "I'm no leader."

Ed squinted. "Oh really? Keep thinkin' that way'n we all gonna die, hoss. Think on it."

"Yeah, sure."

He flicked the toothpick into the street and turned on his heel, going back inside the restaurant.

I gave a deep, soul-cleansing sigh and followed him back inside to finish my breakfast.

After paying the check, Jaiden took off for her place so she could finish cleaning herself up and change. I told her to meet Ed and me at the San Francisco Medical Examiner's office as soon as she was able. Ed gave me a lift home to San Jose, then we bounced back to San Francisco before the office closed. We barely made it.

I looked over my shoulder while exiting the vehicle. "Coming, Mr. Anderson?"

He fished a *Guns & Ammo* magazine out of his glove box and began to thumb through it. "Nope. A morgue's fer dead people. I'll wait here fer Jaiden ta' show, thank yah very much."

I shrugged. "Suit yourself."

I double-timed it through the glass doors and into a long hallway. It had a cold, solemn feel. Gray walls with shiny white-tile floors and scant abstract art prints hung from the walls to try and make the place less sterile. Ahead, a police officer sat at a small greeting desk with "San Francisco Medical Examiner's Office" stenciled above it in gold leaf. She had a fit figure, tan skin, and curly, mousy-brown hair. Her big brown eyes lifted from her smartphone and slitted at my approach. "We're closing in five minutes."

I flashed my badge. "I won't be long."

She rolled her eyes and huffed. "That's what they all say. What do you want?"

"To speak to the doctor on staff, if possible."

The officer shook her head. "Come back tomorrow. They've all left for the day."

I gave her my best pouting face, which normally worked with women. "Isn't there anyone here who can see me? This is important."

She dug her heels in. "So important you couldn't have shown up a half hour ago? No, I'm sorry, but…"

A feminine voice sounded behind me. "I might be able to help you."

The officer straightened up. "Oh, hey, Dr. McCormick. I didn't know you were still here."

I turned around and came face-to-face with one of the most beautiful women I had ever had the pleasure of laying eyes on. Her curly, fire-red hair was up in a bun with a pencil holding it in place. Emerald-green eyes with long, luscious eyelashes blinked at me behind black bedazzled Gucci frames and together with her pale skin, suggested an Irish background.

Slender fingers with long, red nails extended themselves in greeting. "Dr. Emily McCormick, and you are?"

I floundered for my badge. "Umm, yes, I'm… I'm Dr. Special Federal Task Force."

She laughed.

My mouth suddenly felt dry, and I blinked at her, smiling weakly. "I mean, I'm Dr. Darrell Diamondback, special federal task force."

She gave me a slow smile. "So what can my office help you with, Dr. Diamondback?"

Me throwing her over the guard desk and having my way with her flashed in my mind. I forced my brain to snap back to business. "As it happens, you just might be in possession of one Mr. Manny Delgado and the remains of a young John Doe whom I have an interest in. They would have come in this morning."

She slid her glasses to the bridge of her nose, eyes sparkling. Her glossy lips parted as she considered me. "Oh, do you now? So, tell me again why I shouldn't make you come back tomorrow like my officer suggests?"

The officer sat up a little straighter in her chair, beaming at the doctor.

I turned my pouting face on her, but my best efforts felt awkward rather than endearing. "Please, Doctor, my case is time sensitive. If you could do me this small favor, I'd be forever in your debt."

Her laugh sounded like wedding bells. "I like the sound of that. Follow me then, Dr. Diamondback."

The officer eyeballed me suspiciously. "You want me to stay, Dr. McCormick?"

She scrunched up her dainty nose. "No need to, Shelly. Just make sure to lock the door on your way out."

The officer's disappointment showed clear on her face as she pulled a lunch pail out of her desk and stood. "You got it, Dr. McCormick. Have a good night and see you tomorrow."

She hurried down the corridor to the double glass doors, the click echoing through the hallway as she locked them on her way out.

Dr. McCormick turned down a hallway leading deeper into the building. "Follow me, please."

I inhaled her perfume deeply, like a rose garden in spring with a hint of jasmine as I gave her a dreamy look. "To the ends of the earth."

"What was that?"

I shook my head. "Oh, uh, nothing. Lead on, please."

She led me through another set of double glass doors and down another long hallway, this time, office doors were staggered on either side of us. As we walked, she asked, "If I may be curious, what are you a doctor of?"

I continued to fight the urge to wrap my arms around her waist and nuzzle her elegant neck. "Forensic psychology, but I have a background in criminal justice, toxicology, forensic science, and parapsychology: the study of paranormal entities."

The hallway opened and we passed by a bunch of cubicles en route to an elevator. She pressed the call button. "Impressive. Which school did you study at?"

The thought of us slow dancing cheek to cheek filled my mind as my body yearned to feel her pressed up against me. My lips trembled, craving to feel those luscious lips of hers. "UC Berkeley.

"What agency did you say you worked for?"

She turned toward me and my eyes frolicked over her erect shoulders and full, perky, voluptuous breasts that begged me to plant my face in them. "The Department of Paranormal Investigation and Education. They call themselves PIE, but I hate the name."

The elevator doors slid open and we stepped in. As she turned to do so, my brain melted, and I gave an auditable gasp having been presented my kryptonite. A small waistline and a firm, thick, heart-shaped derrière that the lab coat just couldn't hide. My face became hot as I quickly folded my hands in front of me, shifting from foot to foot as I settled in next to her.

She giggled as she pressed the button for the basement. "I see. Well, I think we have what you want here in examination room two."

We road in silence as I tried to regain focus on the job rather than the fantasy experience of her. When the doors opened, we stepped out into a well-lit hall and made our way down to a drab metal door. Before we entered the examination room, I absentmindedly reached into my pocket and took out some Vicks VapoRub. I unscrewed the lid and dabbed some under my nose, a trick used to block out the smell of cadavers, then offered her some. She accepted, dabbing it under her nose as well.

An examination room comprised of white tile that covered the floor, walls, and ceiling had two big stainless-steel tables, one holding a cadaver with a sheet over it, the other empty. Two big lamps hung overhead to provide better lighting for observational purposes and a stainless-steel tray sat nearby full of cold metal instruments. The far wall held a bunch of stainless-steel drawers for other cadavers.

Handing me a clipboard that had been hanging on the wall near the door, Dr. McCormick beamed at me with her big green eyes. "First, if you could sign here? Protocol, you know."

I smiled, scribbling my name down on the sheet. "Of course."

She led me over to the cadaver table and pulled back the sheet revealing a young Hispanic male in his early twenties. His head lolled to one side like a rag doll and his eyes were missing, making him look even more grotesque. His mouth remained stretched in a silent scream.

Dr. McCormick shook her head sadly as she looked at the body, putting on some latex gloves. "Someone or something used this poor guy as a squeeze toy."

I donned some gloves myself. I noted the top vertebrae of his neck had been crushed, not simply snapped.

I brought an eyebrow up to full mast. "Something?"

She shrugged. "I don't even know if a bodybuilder has enough strength to pull off what we're looking at, Dr. Diamondback. In my opinion, this had to be accomplished by a machine or some kind of heavy object like a tree or a boulder. The police said they found him near a clogged sewer drain but didn't mention anything heavy found on his neck."

I nodded. "It is strange. As I understand it, the body was found on a walkway with the safety helmet crushed to fragments nearby. For a person to accomplish that, they would have to have above average height and strength."

The medical examiner used a pen to point at the neck. "You can see a partial handprint here, but anyone with hands that big would have to be a giant, seven feet tall at least."

"When was time of death called?"

She adjusted her glasses. "His boss said last time he had spoken to him was seven thirty-five in the morning. Considering the core body temperature when he was found, I'd say he died soon after."

I nodded.

"Other than that, I'm not sure this one has much more to offer us."

After examining the body a little further, it became clear he had told me all he was willing to tell. "How about the UID child?"

Dr. McCormick's face scrunched up. "I hope you haven't had dinner yet, Doctor."

I clasped my hands behind my back. "I'm sure my stomach can handle it. Thank you for your concern though, Dr. McCormick."

Carefully opening one of the stainless-steel drawers, she unzipped a child size body bag. It contained the skeletal remains of a child reconstructed as best as possible. I hung my head for a moment in silent lament.

She traced the pelvic bone with her pen. "We know it's a male because of the hip structure. It's smaller than a female, even at this age, and judging from the more rectangular eye sockets, wide nasal aperture, flat nasal bridge, and the fact the jaw protrudes from..."

I finished for her. "The maxillary prognathism. This is a young African American male. Judging from the overall size of the skeleton, the lack of permanent teeth, and the fact that the cranial plates haven't fused yet..."

Dr. McCormick smiled and nodded at me. "He's no more than five to six years old at most. You know your forensics, Dr. Diamondback."

I continued to look over the remains and noticed something missing. "These were the only bones found for the top of the spine?"

She nodded, pointing to the femur. "What's even more interesting is that you can see teeth marks."

I shrugged. "Not uncommon, all sorts of animals roam the sewers."

She shook her head. "Look again, Doctor. These look like human bite marks."

Sure enough, the grooves were inconsistent with those made by any animal that could have come across the bones: rats, dogs, cats. They went deeper, wider, and covered almost the whole span of the bone, like someone had been gnawing on a drumstick long after the meat was gone.

I examined the occipital bone at the base of the skull, as it had been damaged. "He still hasn't been identified?"

The doctor grimaced. "No, not yet. We sent a sample of the bone tissue to see if we can get a DNA match from SFPD, but we may be waiting awhile for results. Some parents don't register their children at all, so we may be looking at getting an inconclusive back."

I finally nodded. "Thank you very much for your time, Dr. McCormick. I think I have what I need."

She zipped the body bag full of bones closed and pushed the drawer shut. "I'll escort you out."

We exited the exam room and made our way back to the elevator, riding up in silence, though her eyes shifted on to me once or twice. Thankfully, I had better control over my impulses. Dr. McCormick was insanely attractive and just my type, but I remained baffled as to why she had brought out the animal in me earlier. The door opened, and she led me through the office space we had come through previously and into the main hallway.

She looked up and smiled as she unlocked the front door for me with a key from her pocket. "It was a pleasure, Dr. Diamondback. I daresay we should do this again sometime."

I handed her my business card. "Then I don't suppose you would mind giving me a call when those test results come in?"

She looked at it then slipped it into her pocket. "It would be my pleasure."

Tipping my hat, I smiled. "Thank you for everything, Dr. McCormick. I hope you have a lovely evening."

She gave me a small wave. "You as well, Doctor."

I heard the door close and could feel her eyes on me as I made my way out into the parking lot.

Chapter 11

San Francisco Medical Examiner's Office Parking Lot, San Francisco, California—1700 hours

THE EVER-PRESENT SOUND OF traffic could be heard in the Bay Area evening. Overhead, a collection of dark clouds drifted lazily by in the October sky. The parking lot stood empty except for a Barbie-pink Corvette and Jaiden standing next to Ed, leaning against his truck.

I looked around. "Where's your SUV?"

Jaiden stood up straight, arms folded. "Getting detailed. I took an Uber here from the dealership, that's why I was running late. So, what did you find out?"

I stared at the ground, lost between thought and answering. "I think I know where our killer is hiding. I also believe I have discovered the fate of poor young Mr. Montel Evens, Ian Johnson, and Kayla Sanchez."

"Do tell."

"I'm not so sure you want to know."

She tapped her foot. "Of course I want to know, I'm a reporter."

I blinked a few times, something nagging cryptically at my mind. If Montel had been eaten, that meant Ian and Kayla had probably shared the same horrific end. Yet I had seen at least a couple of things as bad or worse during my years with PIE—a sea hag eating babies being one of them. Horror couldn't explain the damn mosquito buzzing around the wrong side of my ear.

Jaiden's hands slowly gravitated to her hips. "Look, whatever it is, I can handle it."

I sighed. "It seems that our kidnapper... ate Mr. Evens, and the others as well."

Ed's face became as serious as woman's suffrage. "Le' me git this straight. Y'all mean ta' tell me there's somethin' runnin' 'round the sewer system... eatin' kids?"

I finally looked up and nodded. "That's about the size of it, Mr. Anderson."

He looked between Jaiden and me for a moment to make sure I wasn't pulling his leg, then brought his hand to his forehead in disbelief. "Well, paint me green'n call me Gumby. It's crap like this why I live in the da'gone country."

"Funny enough, Mr. Anderson, most cannibalistic serial killers such as Albert Fish and Jeffery Dahmer preferred urban settings because it was closer to their food source, so you may be on to something."

"The fact ya know somethin' like that's disturbin'."

After a moment, Jaiden shook her head, her nose scrunched up. "It all sounds like something out of the bogeyman myth."

My eyes came up. "Say that again."

She scowled. "What? It does. The urban legend of how he would kidnap…"

"And eat little kids. Jaiden, you're brilliant!"

Her eyebrows formed a straight line as her jaw dropped. "You mean you're taking me seriously on this? 'The bogeyman got them,' that's your working theory? God, when I say it out loud…"

My heart raced as fast as my mind. I spoke silently to myself, "That fits everything, even Delgado and the police. How did I not see it before? I even know where he is."

Ed held his hands up. "Hold up there a second, hoss. Y'all'r tryin' ta' tell me we're huntin' the bogeyman?"

Sighing, I leaned against his truck and folded my arms. "That seems to be the long and the short of it."

He laughed. When neither Jaiden nor I joined in, he stopped abruptly. "Y'all'r serious?"

My stomach ached and clenched like it had just been punched hard. I closed my eyes against the acute vertigo. "This can't be happening."

Jaiden gave me a curious look. "What?"

I swallowed back tears and vomit. "It's already been four days since Maddison Bell's abduction. If our kidnapper really is the bogeyman, and at this point I believe that to be the best working theory, he's been active with off-type killings recently. Meaning his last five victims were fun, not food."

Ed folded his arms. "Which means what?"

"I believe this is ritualistic, something he does before a feeding to psych himself up, or it could be him expending energy, something he would do… after a feeding."

Ed squinted at me. "Yer sayin' there's a dead kid at the end'a all this?"

Jaiden's voice held a note of panic. "Or maybe if we hurry, there might finally be a live one. Where do you think she is, Doctor?"

"Somewhere in the San Francisco sewer system."

Ed removed his ball cap and ran his fingers through his hair, then replaced it on his head. "Ain't no way we gonna cover ground like that in time, hoss. We need ta' narrow it down."

Jaiden looked down at the street, creasing her brow, holding her chin between her thumb and index finger. "The main office to the sewer treatment facility is closed by now."

I raked my hands down my face. "I could have asked Mr. Delgado about his route. Unfortunately, the dead don't speak. Manny Delgado's route…"

Both looked at me waiting for me to finish my thought. "What?"

"…has to be in a computer." I whipped out my phone and hit speed dial.

After a few moments, Charlie answered. Rifle fire and explosions sounded in the background. "Doc! I was beginning to think you had forgotten about me."

"Sorry, Charlie. How's the leg?"

"Never better. Thanks for carin'."

"Come on, cut me a break. I've been busy. Besides, I knew you'd be fine. I do need something, though."

"There it is."

"Charlie, I don't have time for this."

"Sheesh! Fine, so… What's up, Doc?" Maniacal laughter followed.

"Charlie."

"Man, I always wanted to say that."

I exploded. "Will you quit fucking around, Charlie! I'm trying to prevent more dead kids. I need you to find the work schedule for a San Francisco sewer technician, one Manny Delgado."

The noise from *Call of Duty: Black Ops* ceased. "Who's he?"

Pinching the bridge of my nose, I responded, "Most recent victim, though not consistent with the general MO. The killer seems to be decompensating."

The sound of rapid-fire keystrokes ensued. "This job has me decompensating. Okay, San Francisco city workers. I've never needed any information from them before, so this is gonna take a few minutes. You got a social security number, employee ID number? Anything like that I can use to track this fool?"

"Not exactly. Can't you just… find him?"

"Come on, Doc, this ain't the fucking movies. Give me an address, a phone number, a birthday, *something*. Throw me a fucking bone here, man. Do you know how many Delgados there are in San Fransisco? One hundred and fucking thirty-seven. Now, ninety-two of those for sure don't work for the damn city, but if I gotta dig through the other forty-five of 'em, it's, what… after six right now? I'll see you in two fucking days tops and you'll owe me a zip and a case of Monster on top of my normal rate."

"Hold on, I'll call you back."

After contacting Stravinsky and having him send everything we could get on Delgado, I heard the unbroken rhythm of keystrokes when I called Charlie back. "Did you get it?"

"Yeah. I gotta say you're connected, Doc, I'll give you that. Okay, password security standards haven't changed in seventy fucking years and still nobody follows 'em, especially bosses. There, got his work schedule, route, and all the video from his helmet cam. Their IT guy is good: He streams all the employee feeds right to a Hitachi Storage Area Network…"

"Charlie, let's focus on the children for a moment."

"Yeah, yeah. Everyone says they give a shit about the children until they fucking don't. Now what?"

I felt giddy at my turn of luck. "Now, Mr. Mopps, we go hunting. Please print up a map of the surrounding sewer system for that area, including Delgado's work route, and meet us at Douglass Park in San Francisco as soon as you can."

"On it, Doc." He killed the call.

The Intersection of Douglass and Clipper, San Francisco, CA—2100 hours

STANDING AT THE SIDE of the road, I felt lucky there was minimal traffic at this time of night in the intersection. Near the tennis courts in Douglass Park, the fresh smell of conifer trees nearby hung in the air. Streetlamps illuminated the area as we prepared to embark upon the biggest case of my life. I spread the map Charlie had brought over the hood of Ed's truck. When

Charlie heard what we were up to, he pumped the brakes. "The bogeyman? In the sewer? Eating kids? Why the fuck do I have to be here again? I'm the computer guy, the eye in the sky. I should be at home, or at least back in the van."

Ed eyed Charlie with mild interest. "Who's the whiny meathead?"

Charlie crossed his arms and scowled back. "Look here, Brawny Man…"

I cut Charlie off before he could make things worse. "Gentlemen, please! Ed Anderson, Charlie Mopps, intelligence specialist."

Ed folded his arms, the faintest hint of a smile at the corners of his mouth. "What? Like the guy who done invented beer?"

I gritted my teeth. "Charlie Mopps, Ed Anderson, military and tactical specialist."

Charlie sneered. "You mean like the old guy from *Beavis and Butt-Head*?"

"Whats'a matter, there, meathead? Did yer maw'n paw not pay 'nough attention ta' ya when y'all was younger?"

Charlie gave an astonishingly accurate imitation of the cartoon character's throaty twang. "Large fries, pie, large coffee, pronto. Ya got me, good buddy? Y'all got that in there?"

Jaiden stamped her foot. "Stop it, both of you! You guys are giving me a headache already and this is not the week to be fucking with me."

I looked between them both. "To make matters worse, we're about to go hunting an urban legend. So, please, let's try to work together so no one gets killed, hmm?"

Charlie and Ed continued to glare at one another but fell silent.

Jaiden's glasses slid down her nose. "Are you sure you have the right place, Doctor? He could have been anywhere along his route. How do you know this is the place to start looking?"

I tugged at the lapels of my leather overcoat. "Elementary, my dear Jaiden."

Charlie nodded and chuckled. "I see what you did there."

I tapped the map Charlie had marked Manny's route on. "Time of death puts him here. Also, according to the managers' report, this was the last place he checked in at. This is the park where Maddison Bell went missing. Here are the sites of the other kidnappings. The center of the circle is right here in this little maintenance cutout, which, according to Charlie's research, hasn't been in use since city workers went digital. It just makes sense."

"That's a fine bit of detective work." Sergeant Roberts and Sergeant Washington stepped out of the shadows of the park.

"Oh goody, more complications." I glowered at them.

Ed raised an eyebrow. "Friends'a yers?"

Leaning into Ed, I whispered out of the side of my mouth, "Not exactly."

Washington put a hand on her hip and gyrated her head in a circular manner. "What was that, agent?"

I forced a smile. "Detectives! How are you this evening?"

Sergeant Washington gave me her own mock smile. "Well, if it isn't San Francisco's resident ghostbuster."

Stepping toward her, we came nose to nose. I lost my smile. "I live in San Jose, actually, but the federal government has a long reach."

She sneered and looked away.

Sergeant Roberts gave a nervous chuckle. "Whoa, whoa, whoa, Doctor. This doesn't need to turn into a pissing match, does it?"

Charlie's voice sounded off behind me. "I'm sure Medusa would win."

The hefty detective snapped a glare in Charlie's direction. "Aren't you out past curfew?"

Charlie shrugged. "Your mom is like 7-Eleven: open all night."

Roberts turned red. "Look here, you slimy little twerp…"

"I needed a slurpee, if you know what I mean."

"Why, I'll…"

Washington called over her shoulder. "Roberts! Don't forget yourself."

The red-faced sergeant glowered at Charlie, still muttering and flexing his fingers.

She turned her attention back to me. "Look, we should all be on the same side, right?"

I gave her a dubious look. "You mean 'the enemy of my enemy is my friend' and all that?"

She smiled like a shark. "That's it. We all want the same thing, don't we? We want to catch this guy as much as you do."

Looking down at my nails, I nonchalantly rubbed them on my jacket. "Unfortunately, I feel you may interfere with my investigation, and I don't want to be held liable for your safety."

The detective brought herself even closer so I could smell the oil and red vinegar dressing she had on her salad that evening. "Like it or not, bucko, this is my jurisdiction. I can follow you if I want, and if you step a toe out of line, I'll be there to bust your sorry ass."

Rolling my eyes, I sighed. "Are those your schoolyard rules, Washington? Very mature."

She ticked off on her fingers. "You won't work with us, you treat us like we're stupid, and I don't like the fact that there's something going down in my yard that I don't know about."

Taking a breath, I counted to five. "Look, Washington, I don't think you're stupid. I just feel that your mockery of my work and your level of skepticism about what I do will interfere with my investigation and put you and your partner at unnecessary risk. Now if you want to tag along, fine, I can't stop you, but don't say I didn't warn you."

Ed's mustache twitched. "Ya sure this is wise, hoss?"

"No, but I really don't see any other option."

Washington looked me up and down like she had won the argument. "Now that we're on the same page, what's this all about?"

I looked between the two officers, stepping back and toward my team. "Well, at least you're here for the briefing."

The detective stepped back toward her partner, folding her arms. "Briefing?"

Roberts brought his hands up in a mock-spooky manner, wiggling his pudgy fingers and sniggering. "So, uh, who are we after? The bogeyman?"

I looked him dead in the eye. "As a matter of fact, yes."

Both detectives gaped at me wide-eyed. Washington's hands found her hips. "You've gotta be shittin' me."

Roberts covered his mouth with a fist as he sputtered, "Do... do you have a description?"

My team stared them down like WWE superstars getting ready to rumble.

I held a hand up to keep them from charging. "He's eight to nine feet tall, over three hundred pounds, black hair, white skin…"

The detectives began laughing raucously and Roberts gasped. "Stop it, just stop! I can't!"

I continued to try to ignore them. "Not much is known about the bogeyman's weaknesses, if there are any…"

Washington started slapping her knee. "I'm dying!"

I looked around as casually as I could to everyone who was paying attention. "So keep on your toes. Is everyone armed?"

This time, Charlie spoke up. "Do I have to hold up the Super Soaker of silver water with these two hyenas hangin' around?"

"Bwahahahahaaaa!" Roberts and Washington were now both staring at each other in disbelief, doubled over with uncontrollable laughter.

I doggedly plowed on. "Everyone has their UV flashlights?"

Three nods, everyone too on edge to speak.

"It's the closest thing we have to sunlight, which we know he hates, so it could be useful for defense."

Washington giggled. "What, no proton packs?"

I gave her a droll look. "Those are so nineteen eighties."

"Don't pay 'em no never mind, hoss. Stay focused."

I looked at him. "Mr. Anderson, you have the iron-tipped bolts for your crossbow?"

He patted the quiver at his hip as he turned his head and spat. "Call me Ed."

Charlie glared at the crossbow in Ed's hands. "Why the fuck don't I get a crossbow?"

"Learn how to shoot one, then we'll talk."

Roberts, hyperventilating, held his sides. "D-do w-we have a h-holy hand grenade?"

Jaiden held up a water balloon full of silver water. "Might save your life. Want one?"

Washington sputtered her lips and they both fell into fits of laughter again.

I passed around my Vicks VapoRub. "Dab some under your nose, it will help with the smell down there."

Ed nodded at me as he accepted the jar. "Now that's an idea."

I let out a breath and rubbed my hands together in anticipation. "Remember, if it starts going south, run and don't look back."

"We ain't leavin' our own behind, hoss."

"Yeah, what he said," Jaiden confirmed.

Charlie pumped his Super Soaker. "Fuck runnin'."

I sighed as I looked gravely at the two laughing detectives. "Alright, folks. Let's do this."

X

The Lair of the Bogeyman, The Sewer System,
San Francisco, CA—2130 hours

"DADDY IS fiNALLY READY to eat."

Jagged concrete created the maintenance alcove among the water and pathways that crisscrossed each other through the disgusting labyrinth of rusty pipes, dripping water, and scuttling cockroaches. The steady sound of trickling water from a larger pipe in the wall dribbled into a trench below. A bottle of whiskey and a flickering lamp sat on a small end table next to a grimy, decrepit armchair. A broken TV sat dark on a stool with the rabbit ears bent out of shape, the plug dangling in the murky water behind it. An old '70s wooden stereo cabinet sat along the far wall with a framed news clipping hanging over it. In the far back corner, two animal cages, one holding a small whimpering girl, sat dirty and forgotten in the shadows. He took a record from the cabinet and placed it on the old vintage player. Turning it on and placing the arm on the record, music began to echo through the chambers, making the rats around him stir and squeal.

The specter picked up his bottle of booze from next to the lamp and took a pull. "This is Daddy's favorite song from the Darkside. Music from the Darkside.

Daddy always plays it before Daddy eats to honor… the Darkside."

"Why… why do we drink?"

"Because that's what Daddy does! Don't question Daddy or Daddy will make you sorry. Do you understand?"

His head jerked as if listening for a noise. He put down the bottle and began twiddling his fingers nervously. His eyes shifted to the cages. "Now all our friend does is cry. It's boring."

His eyes blazed underneath his hood as he clenched a fist and roared at the girl, "Shut up, you're giving Daddy a headache!"

That only made the crying intensify.

A noise drew his attention.

He put an ear up. "What's that Daddy hears?"

"We don't know. It's… it's hard to hear over our friend crying."

"Of course you don't know! But Daddy can hear everything: whispers and footsteps echo… echoing in the hallways of the Darkside."

"Should… should we look?"

He kicked the cage that held the sobbing little girl. "If you don't shut up, Daddy will kill you!"

The sobbing turned to sniveling.

He put his ear to the air again. "Sounds… sounds like… more friends are coming."

"More friends? No! No, no, no! Daddy doesn't like guests. Daddy doesn't like guests on the Darkside. Daddy will make them go away!"

"But… but maybe they would be fun to play with. Ooo, a dinner party! Doesn't that sound like fun?"

"A dinner… party? Party… dinner party? Maybe, Daddy has never had a party. Daddy might like a party for dinner on the Darkside. Come, let Daddy prepare for Daddy's new friends." Red eyes gleamed with excitement as the bogeyman phased into the shadows.

Douglass and Clipper, San Francisco, CA—2130 hours

"DOCTOR?" JAIDEN'S VOICE CAME as a harsh whisper in my ear, her perpetually stray lock of hair tickling my neck.

I shook my head to clear it. We had stacked at the same manhole Manny Delgado had entered the sewer on his final job. Charlie and I stood on opposite sides, shining our UV flashlights into the dark as Ed descended the ladder.

I felt her hand on my shoulder. "Are you okay?"

Ed, already partway down into the manhole, looked up at me. "Y'all ain't narcoleptic, are ya?"

I shook my head again and pumped my fist twice in the air for him to continue. Technically, every member of the team came combat tested, and we had come well prepared, but I still had a nagging feeling inside as if something were wrong. He gave the "all clear" and the rest of us descended into the disgusting depths of The City's underbelly.

Murky water flowed down the center of two thin walkways, threatening to spill over. The water pipes ran overhead, dripping into the nastiness below. Cockroaches and rats scurried from the six beams of light searching in the dark. The noxious smell of sewer gas still overpowered the Vicks. Not exactly a place where one wanted to wear their Sunday best. I shined my UV light on the walkway before us and it lit up with a trail of ectoplasmic residue. Ed looked back and gave a curt nod, then shined his light on the trail and began to follow it.

The disgust dripped in Jaiden's voice like the grimy water from the pipes above. "*Ugh!* Why did we come down here willingly again?"

"Hey, baby, if you want to go back up to Charlie's van of love, we can do that."

"On second thought, I'd rather have a summer home down here."

Washington's voice echoed. "God, it smells. What a waste of time. Really, what the hell do you think is down here besides a bad case of dysentery?"

Roberts answered, "Hey, hey, Washington, I bet the smell is Charlie's mom."

"Hey, on the real? Fuck you, Muffin Man! Your mom's so fat she throws her back out every time she wipes her ass."

"Why I ought'a…"

"*Shh!*" I shushed them.

He could be anywhere down here.

Only Ed and I had any tactical experience. Since he moved silent as a panther, I gave him point. I followed, my Desert Eagle at the ready. Next came Jaiden and Charlie; Statler and Waldorf brought up the rear. Through a maze of twists and turns, we picked our way along the cement path. The walkways were slick, and we had to watch our step so we didn't fall in the nasty, foul-smelling water in the trench beside us.

Ed put his fist in the air, and I echoed this movement making sure those who cared had seen it. It didn't work and a pileup ensued.

Jaiden hissed, "Get off of me, Charlie."

Charlie whispered harshly over his shoulder. "Watch where the fuck you're going, Uncle Grandpa."

Roberts raised his voice. "Shut your fucking trap, yah loud-mouthed little punk."

Washington chortled loudly. "Look at 'em! Pppffftthhhhh… usin' hand signals. What the hell do you guys really think is down here, huh?"

Ed never looked back, but I could hear the scowl on his face over the bunch of undisciplined turds behind him.

The trail of ectoplasm began to get brighter. I whispered back to the other four, "We must be getting close. Ed and I are going to scout ahead. Stay quiet unless something happens, then scream like hell."

Jaiden looked about nervously. "I don't think…"

I looked at Jaiden and Charlie imploringly. "Please, it will be fine. Just stay here, and for Pete's sake, be quiet."

A soft light flickered in and out up ahead, like a lone candle dying against the darkness. We both killed our lights. Whatever element of surprise we had left, we wanted to take full advantage. Music warbled eerily through the tunnels with the quality of an old record player: "Folsom Prison Blues" by Johnny Cash.

We came upon the small maintenance alcove that had been turned into a makeshift room. An old, moldy armchair sat at the center with an ugly bit of puke-green shag carpeting sitting in front of it like a mat. An end table had been placed next to the chair and had a half-empty bottle of Jack sitting on it. An old, busted TV sitting on a stool with bent up rabbit ears, plug dangling in the water, had been placed strategically in front of the chair. The record player sat along the far wall with a picture frame containing a news clipping hanging over it, and a little way back, some dirty animal cages were in the farthest corner. The rat population boomed here and they didn't appear to fear us. Scurrying and squealing across our path, we had to be careful not to trip over them. Ed nodded toward the cages. Over the squealing rats, I heard a soft sobbing coming from them. The hairs on the back of my neck stood.

This all seemed too easy.

I heard Roberts's voice in the distance behind us. "Hey, Washington, do you hear music?"

I heard a woman reply, *"Mmmph!"*

Chapter 12

ROBERTS HAD A PATRONIZING inflection to his voice. "Okay, Washington. Ha ha, very funny, you can come out now. Washington?"

Quick footsteps came up behind me. Jaiden's face appeared illuminated by her UV flashlight, giving it a ghostly look as she kept her voice at a low hiss. "We're not staying back there with those two idiots."

Charlie looked at me, eyes wide and gnawing on his bottom lip. "Yeah, fuck those guys, Doc."

"Douse your lights, we don't want to tip him off."

Both turned off their UVs.

Roberts's normal flashlight swept back and forth in the darkness down the corridor. "Hey! Where'd everybody go?"

Whether this had been a trap from the beginning, or our position had been compromised from too much noise, I felt sure the bogeyman had turned the tables and hunted us from the shadows.

"Fuck." I ushered everyone into the main area. Better to get some walls at our backs as opposed to being in a corridor and easy pickings.

Roberts finally came into the area with his pistol drawn. His arms flailed around wildly after he walked through some cobwebs. "*Ugh!* Washington, you over here?"

Ed whispered in my ear, "We need ta' git 'im under control, hoss. An' is that what I think it is in them cages o'er yonder?"

I nodded. "I'm open to ideas, and yes, I believe that sobbing to be our victim, which means she's still alive."

Roberts shook his head in my peripheral vision. He looked around nonchalantly. "What a fuckin' shithole."

Jaiden looked between Ed and me. "Why won't he listen and… is that crying I hear?"

Charlie shrugged. "How about we use a rag full of chloroform on the douche?"

Roberts shook his head. "This is just great. Hey, Washington, do you think they're gonna make us start sweeping down here for homeless encampments? They don't pay us enough for this shit."

I continued to keep my voice as low as possible as I studied the cages. "Ed, can you pick a lock?"

Ed shook his head, still scanning the shadows with his crossbow.

Jaiden raised her hand timidly, then slowly pulled a bobby pin from her hair when I glanced at her.

I nodded, then pointed at the cage. Her eyes went wide then closed briefly. She scurried over, dropped to a knee while setting her water balloon beside her, and began trying to pick the lock with the bobby pin while softly shushing the whimpering child inside.

Roberts squinted, lowering his weapon. "What is *with* you guys? Did any of you see Washington come this way?"

I made a slashing motion across my throat, but he ignored me.

"Holy shit, where the hell did all these rats come from? Aren't any of you worried about rabies?"

I put my finger to my lips. *"Shh!"*

"So, we found a homeless guy camping out down here. So what? He just better not have hurt Washington, or I'll have his ass."

I hissed, "Roberts..."

He kicked the TV, knocking it over with an echoing smash. "Stupid homeless, always causing more work for us."

Charlie had his Super Soaker at the ready, standing back-to-back with Ed while covering Jaiden. He didn't try to keep his voice low. "Hey, dumbass. Take a hint. Doc is politely trying to tell you to shut the fuck up."

Roberts finally turned, noticing the captive child and Jaiden concentrating on the lock. "What the fuck?"

A growl came from the shadows near the tunnel we had just come through. "Daddy's TV!"

A feminine scream and a sickening, wet ripping noise followed by a crack echoed through the sewers.

Roberts spun around on his heel, shaking and pointing his gun into the darkness. The beam from his flashlight trembled and his voice quaked as he spoke meekly into the void, "N-nothing's g-gonna happen, right? Washington?"

His back exploded in blood and gore as a huge, sallow fist emerged from the depths, grabbed him by the spine, and pulled him screaming into the dark.

Aiming my gun, I lit up the area with my UV light. "Holy shit, Roberts!"

The UV light flickered as the temperature around us fell to below freezing. Then, a putrid breeze stirred up and whipped through the tunnels.

Jaiden screamed and dropped her bobby pin.

Charlie dropped his Super Soaker to the ground and threw up.

Ed continued casing the room with his crossbow, breathing hard through his nostrils.

Roberts's body flopped out of the shadows in a bloody heap five feet from where he had been grabbed. His lungs, heart, and kidneys hung out of the jagged hole in his back, and his lower spine had been crushed. Washington came after, followed by her dismembered arms. She twitched and groaned like she might be alive, but nothing would prevent her from bleeding out in the next few seconds.

A voice I remembered from my nightmares reverberated from the shadows as my light died. "It's not polite to come calling without being invited to the Darkside." Then it seemed to come from somewhere else entirely. "It's not nice to break other people's things. It's not, it's not, it's not!"

I swiveled, pointing my weapon in that direction.

An evil chuckle echoed throughout the chamber so I couldn't get a beat on him. "Naughty, naughty. Daddy's gonna teach you all a lesson you'll never forget on the Darkside."

I called back, "Since when do you care about manners, someone who kills with impunity like you do?"

I heard a shifting in the dark. "One! One has the courage to speak to Daddy?"

"I'm here to end you, bogeyman."

Heavy breathing sounded from everywhere. "Fool! Foolish fool, don't you know the Darkside when you see it?"

"Show yourself, coward! I'm not scared of you."

A deep inhalation sounded in the darkness, then he laughed. "Liar! Daddy can smell your fear, smell it! Like a stink! And… and something else."

My mind flashed to Boggini Park thirty years ago.

He sniffed the air again. "A-a smell that Daddy hasn't smelled since… Big Brother?" I lay on the ground, broken and bloody, the crows squawking. The elation in his voice made my hair stand on end. "Have you really been hunting Daddy all this time on the Darkside? Like hide-and-seek? Daddy didn't know we were still playing." The bogeyman had my sister slung over his shoulder, his laughter echoing in my head. "What fun."

I lay in a hospital bed with three broken ribs and a concussion, the sound of my heart monitor beeping in my ears.

Daisy's voice addressed me. "It's been a long time, Dare."

I fired a few shots randomly into the darkness. "Don't you use her voice, you bastard!"

His laughter intensified. "Foolish, foolish boy. You still haven't learned, have you? You can't hurt Daddy! Daddy is eternal! Daddy is the Darkside!"

Ed held steady. "Don't let 'im rent space in yer head, hoss."

Charlie stared at something hanging on the wall, trying to recover from heaving his guts out.

Jaiden had retrieved her bobby pin and continued to work at the lock of the cage as she brushed the hair from her face, hands shaking. "I-I can hardly… see."

The bogeyman charged out of the darkness. "You shouldn't touch another person's food. Now? Now you and your friends are gonna get it, Big Brother! You're gonna get it from Daddy!"

I froze.

Ed fired, hitting the bogeyman's shoulder.

He roared and smacked the weapon from my hand, burning his own. His other hand came around and hit me full in the face.

I fell to the grubby floor, my bell rung. It felt as if I had been hit with a two-by-four strapped to a backhoe. I tasted blood in my mouth, and it dripped from my nose. He held his hand, but he concentrated on the smoking bolt sticking from his arm. His red eyes shifted to me and flared as our gazes locked, staring hate at one another for what transcended into eternity, though in truth, only lasted a heartbeat. Then I noticed, seeping from the smoking wound, the same black ectoplasm I had seen when the cat scratched him all those years ago. He screamed as another crossbow bolt lodged itself right beneath his clavicle.

The bogeyman trained his flaming-red orbs on Ed, his face contorted in vexation as he ripped the crossbow bolts from his body, black ichor seeping from the wounds. "You… you hurt the poor little guy?"

Ed made to load his crossbow again.

The monster threw the bolts to the ground, and with supernatural speed, crossed the floor and swatted Ed's weapon from his hands. Grabbing him by the throat, the specter bellowed in his face, "Daddy's gonna send you to the Darkside first!"

The specter shoved him back into Jaiden, knocking her into the cages and halting her progress on the lock yet again. Maddison screamed.

"Leave my friends alone, ya freaky-ass fucker!" Charlie came up behind the bogeyman and smashed Jaiden's water balloon on his back. Smoke poured off him like a doused campfire as he howled in pain, the silver water working its magic.

He spun around and backhanded Charlie, knocking him into the wall. "All of you are going to the Darkside! All of you!"

Ed came up with Charlie's Super Soaker in his hands and sprayed the bogeyman full in the face. "Eat hot death, yah sumbitch!"

The bogeyman emitted an earthshaking bellow of pain, hands covering his smoking face.

Finally, the room quit spinning. I started trying to haul myself up. There, to my left next to Washington's armless body, lay my gun.

If I could just get to it.

The demented specter roared as he blindly kicked out at Ed. Getting lucky, he knocked him back into the wall. Ed grunted as he dropped the Super Soaker and held his ribs.

The monster grabbed the cage with Maddison in it as easily as a child would lift a block, screaming in defiance, "It's Daddy's!"

I dove for my weapon. "Not again!"

I spun onto my back and aimed.

Our eyes locked.

I whispered as I cocked the hammer, "Never again."

I fired, hitting his shoulder just before he disappeared with Maddison in a cloud of inky-black smoke.

He breathed hard in the darkness, just out of reach, taunting me with Daisy's voice, "You… you failed again, Big Brother. You failed again. Ha ha ha ha!"

I let loose a primordial scream as I rolled up to my knees and slammed a fist against the concrete. Jaiden wept uncontrollably behind me.

I couldn't move. I couldn't breathe. My chest tightened as if it would burst. I remember someone helping me up, but I couldn't tell who. Everything was in a haze and moving in slow motion. All I could think of was Maddison Bell and how I had just lost her, just like I had lost Daisy.

Ed's voice sounded in my ear, "We gotta git out'a here, hoss."

Charlie strained, trying to help Jaiden up. "Come on, Jaiden. Use your damn legs."

Ed finally slapped me. "Hoss!"

I snapped back into reality. "Ed?"

"I done said, we need ta' git the hell out'a Dodge!"

Looking around, I felt completely lost. Tears welled up in my eyes. "Right… out."

Charlie groaned as he helped support Jaiden's weight. "Come on, Doc. Snap out of it."

Ed finally pushed me in the direction I needed to go. I stumbled along blindly as my face throbbed, Ed following close behind with his flashlight out.

"Ed… Ed, I failed."

"Pull it together, yah damn Democrat!"

We floundered along until I got to the ladder. I stopped again. "The detectives…"

"Ain't nothin ya can do fer 'em now."

I tried pushing past him. "No, I've gotta go back. I can still save her. I can't just leave them."

He stopped me, grabbing on to my jacket to shake me, blood running from his nose and lip. "She's gone, 'n' so'r them damn detectives! Now git it t'gether 'fore that damn thing comes back'n finishes us all off, hear?"

Charlie grunted as Jaiden continued to sob on his shoulder. "For once, I agree with Ed."

I looked at Charlie's black eye and bloody lip, wincing. "This was all my fault."

"It's gonna be yer damn fault when I put ma' foot in yer ass, now move it!"

Climbing the ladder, I broke into the world above. Jaiden followed next, falling to the ground in a heap as soon as she cleared the surface, then Charlie, and finally Ed came crawling out.

I pulled my phone out, scrolled to a number, and pressed it. "I-I need to call… headquarters."

A garbled voice sounded over the phone. "Yes?"

My throat grew tighter as I tried to speak. "I…"

The voice sounded confused. "Doctor? Is everything alright?"

The floodgates opened as I forgot all protocol. "No! Everything is not alright."

"Doctor…"

Tears streamed down my face. "I have two dead detectives, the bogeyman got Maddison Bell, and now they're in the wind!"

"Calm down, Doctor."

I gave a maniacal chuckle. "Calm down? I just blew this whole fucking operation, and you're telling me to calm the fuck down?"

"We're sending reinforcements. Sit tight." The call cut out.

I spiked my phone on the ground. "Fuck!"

The other three sat there, staring at me. I sat and covered my face with my hands.

"Hey, Doc?"

"Hush, son. Leave 'im be fer a moment."

I don't remember how long I stayed like that before four black SUVs pulled up and cut off the surrounding area. Agents in black polyester suits jumped out and began setting up a tactical control point. No one had weapons showing, but the bulges under their jackets said they were armed and all had their shields exposed. A crew in hazmat suits went down the manhole. I almost cared enough to stop them. I think Charlie tried.

Everything felt miles away. Agents approached my team to lead them away for debriefing. I remember them trying to stay with me. I think Jaiden might have been trying to comfort me at one point, crying on my shoulder. I remember Ed trying to remain with me but became surrounded by service agents who finally dragged him away kicking and screaming.

I wasn't sure why any of them wanted anything to do with me after such a colossal failure. They deserved better than I could give.

A voice I knew all too well sounded from behind me, snapping me out of my fog. "Doctor?"

I didn't look up. "Did you know?"

Stravinsky sounded confused. "Did I know what?"

Standing and still not facing him, my voice came out in a horse rasp. "Did you know what we were dealing with?"

His jacket rustled. "Even if we did, what exactly would you have done with information? Especially considering past."

My teeth and fist clenched. "I could have been better prepared."

"*Khernya!* How you say, bullshit! You think one can be prepared for what you and team just went through, Doctor? *Nyet!* You would have taken information and let it cloud judgment, as you just did. Besides, as you say, time was of essence."

I spun around, about to explode, when an agent approached us. "I'm sorry, sir. They found Maddison Bell's remains."

Stravinsky nodded and waved the agent away.

Tears streamed down my cheeks. "That's too many lives lost, Stravinsky."

"*Moy drug…*"

I looked at my shoes. "Don't 'friend' me. I–I can't handle this anymore, I can't."

Folding his arms, he looked at me like a father would a stubborn child. "*Chert voz' mi*, Doctor, snap out of it! You are best man for job. Hell, you are only man for job. You think anyone can step in and do what you do?"

I shook my head. "This is shit, Stravinsky. You and the goon squad you work for seem to think there are acceptable losses on this, and there's no such thing."

He pointed a finger. "That is unreal expectation of situation, Doctor, considering what we are dealing with. Were mistakes made? *Da*, of course, but did you learn from them? I should hope so, or you are not as smart as you think you are."

"I don't care anymore."

"*Da!* Yes, you do! What would *sestra* think if you quit now, eh?"

My fist cocked back. "Don't you dare talk about Daisy!"

Stravinsky didn't flinch. "You are mad? Is *khorosho*. Now use anger to make right decision."

Dropping my fist, I slumped my shoulders. "Maybe I just need time to process. I'm… I'm sorry, Stravinsky."

He nodded. "This is best idea, Doctor. Go home, get rest."

"Yeah. I–I think I just need some time off is all."

He led me to one of the SUVs. "Agent will take you home, and *moy drug*, do not do anything rash." He patted me on the back as I climbed into the seat. "We will be in touch soon, Doctor."

The door closed to the SUV and it whisked me away into the night.

Somewhere in the San Francisco Sewer
System—2300 hours

H IS SCREAM OF RAGE shook the pipes.
      "We're... we're scared."

"Don't be scared, poor little guy. Daddy will protect you. Daddy will protect you from the Darkside."

"But Big Brother and his friends... hurt Daddy. They... they hurt him. I saw."

The bogeyman grabbed a rat and threw it against the wall as hard as he could, black ectoplasm still dribbling from a wound in his shoulder. "No! No, no, no! They never hurt Daddy, they only hurt the poor little guy. How? How did they hurt the poor little guy on the Darkside? How?"

"They... they didn't play fair."

He slammed a fist on the cracked pavement. "No one can hurt Daddy!"

A rat dislodged the bronze bullet, letting it fall to the ground as the wound began to close.

"And our playmate..."

"Daddy didn't get to finish eating because of them and now it's on the Darkside!" He snatched up the rat doctor and shoved it into his waiting maw of crooked yellow teeth, swallowing it whole.

"The crows, and the cats, and the dogs are bad enough, now we need to worry about Big Brother and his mean friends?"

The bogeyman bellowed in frustration again, grabbing the rat he had sent to make sure Big Brother wasn't pursuing him, and squashed it in his ire. He rocked back and forth in the dark, wrapping his arms around himself. "No, Daddy doesn't need to fear Big Brother and his horrible friends, they need to fear Daddy because Daddy is going to show them the Darkside! Daddy will hunt them down. Daddy will make them pay. The Darkside is coming for them. The Darkside is coming."

I SHOOK MY HEAD, the sound of the agent's voice startling me awake. I looked around blearily.

I had fallen asleep on the way home.

The agent looked at me in his rearview mirror. "I said we're here, sir. Do you need help to your apartment?"

I shook my head and rubbed my temples. "No, no thanks. I-I'll be fine."

I got out of the car and stumbled toward the double glass doors of my building and my fortress of solitude.

Footage from PIE Surveillance Cameras,
Evidence ID#: SJ-0015 Somewhere in San
Francisco, CA—2342 hours

CHARLIE LOOKED AROUND THE empty room. A table and chair sat at the center of it and an observation camera attached to the ceiling in the corner recorded his every move. A huge orange metal door, locked no doubt, provided the only way in or out. The walls were stark and unadorned concrete, like a government interrogation room from the movies. A huge white screen along one wall with a silhouette behind it considered him in silence.

Charlie slouched in his chair and drummed his fingers on the table as he scowled at the silhouette. "Look, asshole. I told you for the hundredth time: Doc is the only reason any of us are alive right now, and considering I just had a sack thrown over my head, was dumped in an interrogation room at an undisclosed location, especially after what I just went through? You want any other information? You can go ahead and go fuck yourself."

The video cut to Jaiden sitting in a room like Charlie's. Her head lay on the table as she bawled. "I-I couldn't pick the l-lock. I-I just couldn't. I-I tried to save her!"

The video cut again to Ed putting up more of a fight. His distorted face loomed in the camera while he stood on a chair, shaking his fist. "I know my constitutional rights!

I want a lawyer! I'm a 'Merican! Y'all can't hold me here against ma' will! I know what this is. This here's a black site y'all got us at, yah damn Democrats! Jus' y'all wait till I write ma' congressman 'bout this!"

The video cut to a fourth room with red carpet where two men stood observing all three people from a laptop on a desk. An older man in a purple corduroy suit, a crisp white button-down collared shirt, and a thin gold tie stood next to Stravinsky. The man had thick, wavy, white hair and a long, full beard to match. His stern dark-brown eyes squinted as he swished the ice cubes in a cocktail he held in his right hand. "A very interesting team you've put together, Stravinsky."

Stravinsky nodded. "They are best people for job. They have proven this tonight, I think."

He knitted his bushy eyebrows at the Russian lawyer. "You still feel the doctor will come around?"

Stravinsky nodded again. "There is no question, Director."

The man in the corduroy suit turned his attention back to the video feeds on the computer and swirled the ice cubes around in his cocktail again. "The good doctor has already proven he doesn't have to do anything he doesn't want to. You know I don't like unpredictable, Stravinsky."

The handler considered the screens in front of him. "I have faith. Team will help."

"You'd best be right. We've invested a lot of time and money in this project. Waste is the only thing I hate more than unpredictability."

"We already have results. Give more *vremya*."

The wizened man sighed. "We may be running out of time my friend, but very well, let them go."

Ed's voice came piercing through, his face still in the camera. "I'll sue!"

The video feed ended.

Chapter 13

Santana Row, San Jose, CA—0910 hours (Two Weeks Later)

I HAD JUST POURED myself a cup of black coffee and put a shot of Jameson Irish Whiskey into it when my phone began to play "Mi Mi Mi" by Bemax. I smiled at the screen: Dr. Emily McCormick. One of the few people I would answer the phone for these days. I picked it up. "Hey there, good lookin'."

Her sultry voice tickled my earlobe and sent shivers down my back. "Hey, Tiger. What'cha up to today?"

I took a sip of my Irish coffee. "As little as possible."

Her voice became pouty. "Aww, I hate that you sound so sad. How about I drop by and try to cheer you up tonight?"

"I'd like that. What do you feel like for dinner?"

"Umm, anything but pizza. We had that last night."

"How's Mexican grab you?"

"Ooh, that sounds good. You know what I like."

Grinning, I couldn't remember the last time my mind was on something other than work. "One chicken taco plate, comin' up."

"Oh, and please don't forget to put Nicodemus out. You know I'm allergic."

"You got it."

"See you tonight then, Tiger."

"Later, sexy."

She hung up.

I sighed, love on my mind. It seemed to be the only thing on my mind as of late. When Emily had called me back to confirm my fears that the victim John Doe had indeed been the young Montel Evens, we had gotten to talking. I asked her out, she said yes, and the rest was history. She could speak to me on an intellectual level that I rarely found in people. She had wit, charm, grace, and the sex drive of a female bonobo. So far, things were fantastic.

I hadn't talked to the agency since speaking to Stravinsky after the sewer fiasco. I hadn't even spoken to the team. They all kept calling, mostly Charlie, but I couldn't bring myself to answer. You would think living in the same building, it would be difficult to avoid each other, but I hadn't seen him at all.

I just wasn't ready to face them yet. It still hurt.

I don't think I had been out of my apartment in the past two weeks either. This was probably the most time I had spent here since… ever. I never took failure well, even as a kid, and I was failing too often at this job as of late. I wasn't ready to fail at it again.

Then came a knock at the door. Looking through the peephole, I saw Charlie's distorted head looking back.

He knocked again. "I know you're in there, Doc. I seen your car."

I kept quiet.

He knocked again. "You're gonna have to come out sooner or later."

Obviously, he had no idea how stubborn I could be.

He rapped on the door, harder this time. "Quit being a vagina and open up."

I threw open the door, glaring at him. "What, Mr. Mopps?"

Charlie pushed his way in. "Dude, there you are. Nice place you got here."

I shut the door and folded my arms. "Again, what can I do for you, Mr. Mopps?"

He looked back at me and blinked as Nicodemus sniffed him and swiped his leg in greeting. "Oh, we're back to, 'Mr. Mopps' now, are we? You're fuckin' joking, right?"

I stood, rooted. "No, I'm on leave right now."

Charlie faced me and folded his arms as well. "Is that right?"

Nodding, I looked away. "So I apologize, but whatever you want will have to wait."

"Nah, it ain't about what I want anymore, Doc. It's about doing the right fucking thing." I opened my mouth to reply as he put a hand up. "Nah, shut the fuck up and listen for a second. You got us all into this shit, and now you're pussin' out?"

"I'm not 'pussing out,' and I'm not a vagina either."

His pointer finger poked me in the chest. "Get over feeling sorry for yourself already. Fuck, man, we were all down there, and you were the only one to throw in the towel. Even Jaiden wasn't this bad, and she was *bad*."

I hung my head. "How is she?"

Charlie gave me a dirty look. "What the fuck do you care? You're on fucking leave. You talked to me about having the stomach for this shit. Well, what the fuck happened to you? You think any of us feel good about losing Maddison? Even Tweedledum and Tweedledumber? It sucks they died, but like you told me at the start of all this, that's part of the job, right?"

I stuck my finger in his face. "It was my fault, Charlie! It wasn't your fault, it wasn't Jaiden's fault, it wasn't Ed's fault, it was mine. I'm the one who's responsible for all of you, even Roberts and Washington. So don't come in here and lecture me about shit. I've been doing this crap longer than any of you."

"And?"

I dropped my hand and lowered my voice, looking out the window. "And maybe I don't want to do it anymore."

Charlie blew out an exasperated sigh. "Maybe, but I know we wouldn't have hurt him if it wasn't for your knowledge. I also know we wouldn't have made it out of there alive without you, and I know we can't bring him down without you."

"Bring him down?"

Charlie scoffed. "Duh, he's still out there."

"Well, yeah, but…"

"Yeah, but nothing. You're honestly gonna sit there and tell me you don't want to bring this guy down?"

I couldn't think. "Of course I do, but I don't know if I can just yet. I need more time."

He looked at me in disgust. "Yeah, well, when you find your balls and want to figure shit out, we're up at Ed's cabin."

I turned away, clutching my drink.

He moved to leave. "Oh, and Doc? Just remember, you give up now, you let Daisy down too. Think about it."

I winced again as he slammed the door shut, leaving me alone with my drink and my broken pride.

L ATER THAT NIGHT, A super burrito with carne asada from the local taqueria, cuddling on the couch with Emily, and a Netflix movie took the edge off so I could stew objectively about my encounter with Charlie. Emily nuzzled up to me as the credits rolled. "What'cha thinking about, Tiger?"

Charlie's words came back to me for the umpteenth time. *You give up now, you let Daisy down too.*

I blinked. "Actually, I was thinking about work."

Emily scrunched up her nose. "Why would you do that? I thought you were on leave."

"Because at some point I need to go back."

She took off her glasses, blinking as a waft of her flowery perfume hit me in the nose. "Are you sure you're ready?"

Rubbing my forehead, I sighed. "That's just it, I don't know."

Snuggling up closer, she gave a small sigh. "Well, if you don't know, then maybe you should take a little more time and think about it. I know—we could go on vacation."

I don't think I had ever taken a vacation in my life. "Vacation? That sounds nice. Where would we go?"

She pursed her lips. "Someplace tropical."

I rattled off, "Hawaii? Bahamas? Tahiti?"

She clapped her hands. "Ooo! How about Cancún?"

I could probably afford to take a little more time off. "I could do Cancún. I'll buy the tickets tonight. When do you want to go?"

She stroked my leg with a finger. "Let's leave tomorrow. I just need to pop into work to make the arrangements. I have vacation time coming anyway."

I grew more excited by the prospect. "It's settled, then."

Her hand crawled up to my crotch and squeezed. "Now, how about we go to bed early?"

Considering the throbbing between my legs, she didn't need to ask me twice.

I T DIDN'T TAKE LONG to pack all my bags for a week at a tropical resort and change into a loud Hawaiian shirt, cargo shorts, and sandals. I even made a playlist on my phone that included a lot of Beach Boys and Jimmy Buffett. Emily had left about an hour ago to pack and check in at work. We planned to meet back here in another hour to leave in plenty of time to make it through security before our flight.

I hummed to myself, Irish coffee in hand, because... why not? I never wanted to be responsible again. The feeling of forgetting something nagged at the back of my brain, but I pushed it away. Responsibility could kiss my rosy-red butt cheeks.

As I sipped at my new traditional morning beverage, the only thing I could think about, the only thing I wanted, was Emily. I saw us side by side on a sandy white beach in lounge chairs. Her in a bikini, a floppy sunhat, and sunglasses and me in an open button-down shirt, sunglasses, and swim trunks. I'd let her have the window seat on the plane, of course. Unless she had a fear of heights. I really didn't know. I'd have to ask her when she got here. Her intoxicating scent still filled the apartment, and I breathed deep.

It smelled like bliss.

A knock at the door pulled me out of my dream state. I saw the clock and scowled; too early. Maybe she had lost her key?

I ran to the door and threw it open. "Emily? Is that you, sweetheart?"

Two guys in ski masks stood before me. "Sorry, Boo-Boo-Kitty-Fuck, we ain't Emily. Now, we can either do this the easy way or the hard way."

He sounded familiar, but it took me too long to process. The speaker threw a sack over my head and something hit me hard from behind. Before the world went completely black, I heard a stretched baritone voice say, "The easy way."

As I came to, I found myself zip-tied to a chair, the sack still over my head. My bleary mind hit the ground running. How could I have been so careless? How long had I been out? Who would want to kidnap me?

A voice spoke. "This is stupid."

Jaiden?

"We couldn't let him pull a Ted Cruz and go to Cancún. This was the only way."

Charlie had been the voice at the door. Everything started to come clear.

Ed piped up, "You leave Senator Cruz alone!"

Jaiden oozed disapproval. "I can't believe you two went through with this."

"What's not ta' believe, missy? Was kinda fun hittin' Doc o'er the head. Did I ever tell y'all 'bout this one time I was on a black op in Afghanistan?"

Charlie sounded exasperated. "Only about a hundred times, Ed."

Jaiden sighed. "I still think you guys should have let me talk to him first."

Ed hiccupped. "That's yer problem there, missy. Y'all think too much. These here results was realized through decisive action."

"What, kidnapping him?"

I had heard enough. "You guys know I can hear you, right?"

The sack flew off my head. There sat my three team members staring back at me, two sitting in chairs from the table, one perched on his wooden barstool.

I recognized Ed's cabin.

Charlie held a pinky to the corner of his mouth and pursed his lips. "Welcome back, Mr. Powers."

Panic crept into my voice as I looked around. "What the hell did you guys do? Emily…?"

Charlie grimaced. "Yeah, sorry about that."

"Sorry? You're… sorry? We're supposed to go to Cancún!"

"Yeah, about that…"

My glare could have cracked glass. "What? What did you do, Charlie?"

He fidgeted with his fingers while biting his lower lip. "I kinda canceled those."

"You did what?" I struggled in the chair, trying to break out of the zip ties.

"I got you a full refund."

"Oh, you got me a full refund, did you? Charlie, when I get out of here, I'm going to kill you!"

Ed looked stern as he put his hands up. "Whoa, whoa, whoa, slow down there, hoss. Now, Charlie jus' did what 'e thought was best, understand?"

As I fought against my bonds, I fixed him with a scowl. "What he thought was best? Who the fuck told him he could choose what's best for me? Or you, for that matter? She's going to hate me, and it's all your fault!"

Ed sniffed. "Aww, don't worry 'bout that. We left ol' what's 'er name, Emily? Yeah! We done left 'er a message. Kinda weird ya gave 'er a key already, but that ain't none'a ma' business."

I stopped my struggling for a moment. "You left her a message? What the hell did you say?"

Jaiden spoke up. "That you were needed at work, because you are."

I started struggling again. "She's going to kill me. Besides, why the hell would you want a guy that screws everything up?"

Jaiden exploded at me like a cannon shot. "It wasn't just you who screwed up, you selfish fucking prick, it was all of us. So shut the fuck up and listen!" Her breathing sounded like that of an angry gorilla. I stopped and stared at her as she continued. "We all have to live with letting that little girl down, and how dare you suggest otherwise. Ed, Charlie, especially me! I-I had to look her in the eye. I had to... to lie to her and tell her everything was going to be okay. I had to see her face when it didn't turn out... okay."

"Jaiden, I'm..."

She wiped a hand over her cheek then the back of it under her nose, speaking over me. "I don't want your damn apology, at least not in words. I want you to get off your ass and do something about it!"

Ed raised his beer to her speech and took a swig. "Preach on, sister."

Charlie nodded in emphasis. "Drop that science, girl."

Jaiden's eyes never left mine. "Now, we'll untie you, but you can't… you can't run away anymore."

"I…"

"And you can't… you can't quit."

"Jaiden…"

She punched me hard in the shoulder. "And no more withholding information from us!"

I looked at my shoulder in disbelief then back at her. "Ow!"

Charlie shook his head, tsking. "You should have told Ed and Jaiden about your history, Doc."

Dropping my eyes to the floor, I frowned. "It's not like I purposely did that."

She charged on, holding a finger level with my nose so my head came back up as I went cross-eyed looking at it. "And… and, you have to train with us. Do you hear me?"

"Then we're gonna bring this motherfucker down!"

Jaiden sniffed and dabbed the corner of her eye with a sleeve. "What Charlie said."

Ed took a penultimate sip of his beer, keeping his gaze fixed on me. "What's it gonna be, hoss?"

I looked away. "I don't know…"

Charlie moved to put the sack back over my head. "No problem. We can just put this right back on here."

I cringed. "No, no, no! Fine, you guys win."

Charlie dropped the sack and began to cut my restraints. "I totally understand why you wanted to go to Cancún, though."

I rubbed my wrists. "How long have you guys been watching me?"

Ed glanced at the ceiling. "Umm, 'bout two weeks."

Weird I hadn't noticed them. "Two weeks? You mean you guys have been stalking me since that night?"

Ed's face scrunched up. "Weren't stalkin' ya. More like… a stakeout."

Charlie and Jaiden nodded in unison as Charlie continued. "It was part of Ed's training for us."

Jaiden added quickly, "Plus, we were worried about you."

Charlie wiggled his eyebrows. "I take back everything I ever said about you not having game. Dude, she's hotter than an active volcano."

Jaiden shot him a look that could have boiled lava. "That's enough, Charlie."

I looked at all of them, still scowling. "So what's this training regimen?"

Ed took off his hat and scratched his head, then put it back. "Welp, I been teachin' 'em some'a the basics, like how ta' shoot. Jaiden's pretty darn good already."

Charlie looked back and forth between Ed and me like a lost puppy. "I'm not too bad either."

Ed gave him the stink eye. "Boy, y'all couldn't hit the broad side of a battleship."

His cheeks went rosy as he looked away. "Whatever."

"Been teachin' 'em some basic hand-ta'-hand'n self-defense techniques. Also been working with 'em on silent hand signals'n bein' stealthy."

Jaiden sounded enthusiastic. "We've been running an obstacle course, like a boot camp. I've even been working on picking locks under pressure."

Ed chugged down the rest of his beer. "What we don't have is the spook information side'a the house."

Charlie nodded. "Yeah, we need questions answered. There's too much myth and rumor around this subject on the internet. We need empirical facts."

"I don't foresee that being a problem, I love lecturing."

Jaiden smirked. "We noticed."

Charlie looked around the cabin like he wanted to make sure no one was watching us. Then he took an old newspaper article out of his pocket and placed it on the table. "Then, there's this."

My eyes bugged wide as I looked over it. "Charlie, where did you get this?"

He smiled as he polished his nails on his shirt, then blew on them. "Down in that hellhole, but I can't take all the credit. Your sister pointed me in the right direction after I puked."

I gave him an appraising look. "You finally told them?"

He nodded. "Jaiden's right, if we're gonna function as a team, we can't have any secrets."

I nodded slowly. "Okay, I'm in."

Jaiden patted me on the shoulder. "Welcome back, Doctor."

Holding the article in my hands, I began pacing. "Have we done any research on it yet?"

Charlie held up a manila folder. "Jaiden and I put together a file for you when you're ready for it. I must admit there isn't much to go on."

I accepted it absentmindedly, my eyes still glued to the newspaper clipping. "Well, it looks like we have some work ahead of us."

Everyone nodded.

After pulling my eyes away, I finally looked down and noticed my clothing. I frowned. "First and foremost, though, I need to get changed out of this ridiculous shirt."

Jaiden covered her mouth, laughing, as Charlie and Ed joined in. "I wasn't going to say anything, but it is rather tacky."

"Birkenstocks? Really, Doc? We need to get you some style when it comes to your casual wear."

"Git some sun on them legs, hoss. Yer fixin' ta' blind people."

I smiled. It felt good to be back on the team and back on the case.

Chapter 14

CHARLIE AND JAIDEN'S RESEARCH led us to something of a demilitarized zone between the poor and the homeless. Car traffic rumbled sluggishly down a two-way street mixed with streetwalkers, gangsters, and the forgotten souls that begged for existence. The occasional sound of car horns punctuated E-40's "Let's Fuck (featuring Gangsta Boo)" blaring from one of the nearby brownstone apartments, attempting to cover up one couple's morning delight. It smelled of five different styles of cooking inside the old, run-down, moth-eaten building. With scuffed beige walls, dirty brown rubber molding, and thin blue carpet worn black in the high-traffic areas, I wasn't sure how much longer this building would continue to stand, let alone be inhabitable. Charlie and Ed were down in the van waiting for Jaiden and me to check out the apartment as neither had an interest in such things.

I studied the older gentleman next to me. "I really do appreciate this, Mr. Malone."

The landlord wore a brown leather jacket, light blue button-down collared shirt, flat cap, blue jeans, and white tennis shoes. He scratched at his gray hair, looking us up and down. "Well, if you folks really want to rent here, but it looks like you could probably afford a lot more."

"It's really close to work, and I must say the neighborhood is quite…"

A shout came through the wall. "Oh, fuck yeah! Fuck that fuckin' pussy, motherfucker."

"…quaint."

"Yeah…" He hesitated for a second, like he wanted to add something, but then thought better of it.

As we followed him to the apartment, I reflected on the newspaper clipping I carried in my pocket. Supposedly, a man and a woman had died here under mysterious circumstances back in the 1970s. The article mentioned a Joseph and Mary Twitch. Charlie and Jaiden hadn't found much on them: birth certificates, death certificates, the fact Joseph had worked as a construction worker for the city, the address of the building they lived in, and some old unpaid bills. They had found next to nothing on Mary.

Mr. Malone's key ring rattled as he unlocked the door to apartment six. "Go ahead and look around. You guys are probably the first to…"

I blinked, hands clasped behind my back. "First to what, Mr. Malone?"

Trying hard not to let his voice shake, he thought better of what he had been about to say again. He eyeballed me instead. "The apartment is fifteen hundred down, fifteen hundred a month. Also, it's as-is. Got it?"

Jaiden looked around as if she were afraid the building would rub off on her clothing. "You expressed that a few times."

My eyebrow raised and my cheek scrunched to the left. "You're not coming in with us?"

Sweat beaded on his forehead despite the cold. He shook his head nervously. "Nope, I have a few other things to, uh… do on the grounds. Just close the door and come find me after you're done looking at it." I nodded, and he practically ran back down the hallway, calling over his shoulder, "I'll… uh, I'll be downstairs."

Jaiden considered him as he hurried off. "Well, he sure was acting strange."

I shrugged. "Let's find out why, shall we?"

We pushed the door the rest of the way open and entered the apartment. It looked much like any other place: a main hall broke off into a kitchen immediately to the right and a main room straight ahead, then banked left and split into two bedrooms divided by a bathroom, and a small hall closet on the opposite wall. All rooms were done with the same ugly brown carpet, the same beige walls, and brown rubber molding.

Everything seemed rather ordinary for the landlord to be so nervous.

Jaiden stuck her head into a kitchen that boasted blue and white linoleum floors and white cabinets supported by a gray Formica countertop that had been accented by a strip of linoleum as a backsplash. Another exit at the far end led into the main room. "Do you think we're going to find anything here, Doctor? It was so long ago."

I knelt in the entryway toward the main room, examining a dark stain on the rug. A stain this large was weird, considering the asking price. "It's the only lead we have. One Joseph and Mary Twitch who lived here back in the seventies."

As I said their names, the air grew ice-cold in a matter of seconds, and I had to rub my eyes to make sure I saw things properly. The apartment began to change before us, as if trying to remember itself from a former time. It winked in and out at first, like a poorly focused telescope, switching between then and now, but it finally settled on then, becoming a full-on residual haunt. Ugly puke-green shag carpeting now lay beneath our feet and wood paneling adorned the walls in a tacky tribute to the times. A TV with rabbit ears sitting on a wooden stool in front of an ugly brown armchair furnished the otherwise stark front room. An end table sat next to the chair with a bottle of cheap whiskey on it.

I had seen all of this before in the lair of the bogeyman.

Jaiden stifled a scream.

A hand went instinctively to my shoulder holster. "What the hell?"

From the kitchen, I heard running water. Abruptly, it shut off, and out of the kitchen walked the ghostly outline of a woman drying her hands on a dish towel. She had mousy brown hair and wore a sun-yellow dress covered by a white apron.

She looked up at us and gasped, shaking her head. "Oh no! What are you doing here? Joseph doesn't like visitors."

Only slightly sure I wasn't hallucinating, my eyes quickly darted around the room for threats. Easing my hand away from my weapon, I asked, "Mary? Mary Twitch?"

She hissed like an angry alley cat, her voice echoing back from her. "Yes, and if you two know what's good for you, you won't wake him up. Though, you're the first two who have been by to see me in a long time."

I couldn't believe my luck. "Mary, I need to know what happened the day you died."

Mary closed her eyes and shook her head. "No, you both need to get out of here, now."

Jaiden put up her hands. "Mrs. Twitch, please, it's important. We think your husband's spirit is the bogeyman. We... we need to stop him."

A rumbling came from the empty chair.

The housewife bobbed her flattened palms up and down, eyes bulging. "Shh! Don't say that name around him. If he hears you, we're all in trouble."

I tried to watch everywhere at once as Jaiden continued. "Around whom, Mrs. Twitch?"

She spoke in a low whisper, radiating agitation. "Joseph is deep in his bottle. You... can't you see him sleeping in his chair?"

Jaiden glanced at the armchair, her lock of hair flipping to the side as she did so. "There's no one there, Mrs. Twitch. Look, we're pretty sure your husband is the bogeyman, as we found a newspaper clipping in his lair that led us here to you, and..."

Mary shook her head while wringing the dish towel in her hands. "Joseph isn't that creature, the one you mentioned. That's my boy, William."

A growling sound came from over by the armchair again. I still didn't see anything, but my hackles remained up. "There was no mention of a boy in the news article, Mrs. Twitch."

She glanced nervously at the empty armchair again. "Lord, help me. Of course there's no mention of him. He wasn't born in a hospital. We… we just… didn't have the money."

Jaiden took out a notepad and a pen. "How old was he?"

"Six."

"He wasn't enrolled in school at all?"

Mary looked at the ground. "William was… a unique boy, and Joseph didn't want people to know about him because he was… special."

I still hadn't taken my eyes off the growling armchair. "Special how?"

The ghost looked between us and the chair with horror. "All this noise."

I turned to her. "We're sorry, but…"

Suddenly, she reached out and touched both of our foreheads. "Here, see for yourselves."

My brain froze as the world went black.

MARY'S VOICE WAS HOLLOW and echoed in my mind. "I knew William was special right from the start."

The world as she had known it came into focus. I couldn't see Jaiden, but I could feel her presence. As a disembodied spirit, I looked upon Mary in her yellow dress as she zipped up the hooded jacket of a little boy who was no more than six. He had wavy black hair, green eyes, and a forlorn expression rested on his face. His voice sounded like an echo in a long hall. "Why do I have to go outside again, Mama? It's cold."

Mary's voice rang in my head again. "I just never realized how special he really was."

As they stood in the entryway of the apartment building they lived in, Mary from the vision scowled at the boy, eyes bleary from the sherry she had been drinking all day. She finally answered, her voice echoing as well. "Because your daddy's home from work and I don't want you waking him up. Now scoot."

William clutched at her skirt and begged, "I'll be a good boy, Mama. I won't make noise, I promise."

Mary's internal voice sounded thick with regret. "I should have listened. I knew how the other kids treated him. I only knew that out there, he had more of a chance. They had never beaten him as bad as his father had."

Mary in the vision shook her head. "It will only be a few hours until dinner. Go find some of the neighborhood kids to play with."

The little boy turned his scowl on the floor. "They hate me."

His mother snorted. "Then find something to do by yourself, just stay outside. Go on now, before he wakes up with no supper and we're both in trouble."

Pushing William out the door, she called after him, "Make sure you're home by sundown, or your daddy will be upset!"

He muttered, "Yes, Mama."

Mary's voice continued in my mind. "I didn't know what happened at the time, but the universe found fit to punish me with the knowledge of what went on that day. I think it was to make sure that I regret this one decision in my life forever."

William looked around the windy streets of ticky-tacky buildings for something entertaining while he served his sentence in the cold. Counting silently to himself, he hopped up onto a low planter lip in front of a home and walked it like a balance beam.

Mary sounded wistful. "He liked counting. It helped relax him when he got upset."

An unfamiliar voice called out, "Hey, retard! What'cha lookin' at?"

Three older boys converged on him like a pack of wild hyenas, although hyenas might have had kinder intentions. William flinched at the sound of the voice, his body language making it clear that he had been picked on by these boys before.

One of them sneered. "Yeah, dummy, why do you count all the time? That's stupid."

William continued, trying to ignore them. His lips thinned and his body tensed. "Forty-four, forty-five, forty-six…"

The third boy stepped up and shoved William off the planter. "Hey, stupid, he asked you a question. Hey, maybe he's too retarded to answer."

The boys all sniggered. "Yeah, he's never at school. Probably 'cause he's so dumb."

Now cornered, William set his jaw and balled his fists. He looked defiantly at the boys for a moment but quickly dropped his gaze. "I'm… I'm not dumb."

The biggest bully took the lead. "Hey, look. He can speak."

William's voice shook. "L-leave me a-alone."

The lead boy shook his head, laughing. "What are you gonna do about it? Huh, butt-wipe?"

William took a weak swipe with his fist.

The bully continued to laugh, rubbing his cheek, balling up his own. "Oh, man! We are gonna fuck you up."

His two buddies were content to leer at the coming attraction.

William ducked past them and ran.

The lead hoodlum called after him, laughing as they chased him into a dead-end alleyway. "You're only making this worse, twerp!"

The two betas grabbed William by the arms. One of them sneered. "Where do ya think you're going, dumbass?"

The alpha swaggered up, taking his time watching William struggle to free himself. "You made me run, motherfucker."

"S-so?"

He laughed, then a stony look came over the boy's face as he socked William in the gut. "I hate running."

William sputtered, but his leg shot out and kicked the kid square in the balls.

The older boy doubled over. "*Oh!* Oh, man."

William continued to struggle, but the two other boys held him fast.

The bully came up winded, glaring death. He punched William in the face. "You little fuck!"

Blood squirted from his nose, and a second strike caused it to trickle from his lip. William sputtered, "Leave… leave me alone, p-please."

The two other kids laughed as the lead kid began to unzip his pants. "Naw, I got a better idea. You're gonna kiss it."

William was shoved to his knees.

The lead boy shoved his naked genitals in William's face, his sadistic laugh echoing in the alleyway. "Come on. Kiss it and make it feel better, queer."

That's when all hell broke loose.

The lead boy flew back, shoved by an invisible force into some garbage cans.

"No!" William shouted as the wind whipped into a frenzy around him. The two boys holding his arms looked bewildered until they got shoved away in the same manner. One knocked his head against the side of the alley wall, falling unconscious. The other got thrown to the ground as he slid a good five feet away.

"No!" William shouted again. He stood, eyes glowing white as he looked at the lead bully.

The terrified boy shot into the air, hovered for a second, then slammed down to the ground, pants still around his ankles.

"No!" The boy who had been lying on the ground, stood and tried to grab William again.

"No!" William shouted, stretching out a hand. The boy flew into a fire escape five stories up as if tossed by a tornado. He dangled from the railing by one twisted leg with the tibia poking through the shin.

The lead bully groaned as William advanced on him. "Never again!"

The boy rose six feet in the air, levitating as William looked up, considering him for a minute.

Tears flooded the boy's eyes as he gasped for breath. "P-please stop. Don't…"

I heard the sickening crunch of his neck snapping before he got dropped to the ground, lifeless.

The wind died along with the glow in Williams eyes.

He looked around wide-eyed at the carnage he had wrought. I couldn't tell if he realized how the scene had come about or not. Finally, he turned and ran home.

He burst in the door crying. "Mama! Mama!"

Mary came from the kitchen, drying her hands on a dish towel. Her nostrils flared as her glassy eyes bulged and her lips went thin until she saw him clearly. Motherly instinct won over good sense as she rushed to him. "Oh my God, William!"

A voice boomed from the recliner in the family room where a TV showed the San Francisco Giants losing to the New York Yankees. "Who's making all that racket? I'm trying to sleep!"

Immediately, Mary and William stiffened.

The chair creaked as Joseph got up and made his way over. Fit from his job laying Sheetrock for the city, he had the same black hair as William, only greasier, and the same green eyes, only blurry and dead where William's still carried a spark of youthful vibrance. He scratched his chest through his dirty white T-shirt as he considered William's bloody face. Thick eyebrows knitted in a scowl as he observed his wife trying to shield their son with her body

"What the hell happened?"

"I-I... was just about to..."

His sinewy muscles tensed before he backhanded Mary across the face, knocking her to the floor.

Looking down, he pointed a finger. "Shut the fuck up, bitch! I was talkin' to the boy."

Mary began weeping softly.

His face bore no emotion. "Now go finish making my dinner."

Mary scrambled off to the kitchen, holding her cheek.

Joseph turned back to William, pulling a pack of cigarettes from his dingy blue jeans, lit one with a Zippo, then returned them. "You get your ass handed to you again, boy?"

William kept his eyes glued to the floor. "N-n-no, s-s-sir."

His father blew out a plume of smoke and looked at William as if he were an earthworm. His tone became mocking. "Oh, really? Now you're gonna sit there and lie to me?"

William finally lifted his chin. "I-I'm not l-lying, s-sir."

Joseph stuck the cigarette between his lips and put up his dukes. "Okay then, tough guy. Let's see what you got."

William started crying harder. "D-D-Daddy… p-please…"

Pow!

The right jab landed William on the floor.

His father roared, "Get up, weakling. You're nothing but a useless retard!"

"Daddy…" A kick connected with his ribs, and the rest of his reply came out as a grunt.

The upper whites of Joseph's bloodshot eyes bulged, his nostrils flared, his face red with a vein throbbing at the side of his temple as he spoke around his cigarette. "I don't know why I let you live. You're nothing but a whiny, spineless, momma's boy!"

William had a glazed look on his beaten and bloody face as he wheezed. "One… two… three…"

His father seized him by the neck and began to squeeze. "Shut up! You ruined my life! I hate you! I hate you! I hate…"

The snap of William's neck echoed around the suddenly silent apartment. All motion stopped. It was as if someone had pressed pause on the world's most fucked up home video.

Joseph looked at the lifeless body of his son. Emotions flashed across his face in rapid succession as if he couldn't honestly decide what or how to feel about the situation. His voice came, barely above a whisper. "W-William?"

He shook the body as it hung there, limp, William's eyes looking off into space with his mouth hanging open.

Joseph's voice grew angry again. "William? Wake up, boy!"

Mary came out of the kitchen and screamed.

Joseph gave her a clueless look. "Mary, I..."

Before he could finish, a black cloud began to pour from William's open mouth. Hideous laughter reverberated through the room. Lights and electronic devices flickered and fuzzed. The cherry of the cigarette hanging from Joseph's mouth extinguished. He dropped his son's body like a hot coal and stepped back. It landed in a heap on the floor, right in the same spot as the dark stain I had seen earlier.

The cloud took form. Standing before Joseph was a nine-foot hulking shadow of William, deformed and distorted. The light bulbs burst in the lamps and the TV exploded, shrouding the room in darkness. Joseph's and Mary's breaths streamed in clouds from their open mouths as an inky blackness swirled around William.

Mary screamed again.

A huge hand reached out and grabbed his father by the neck. Leering into a horrified face, the bogeyman spoke, "You wanna see what Daddy's got, you mean old bastard?"

"Holy shit! W–William?"

The bogeyman pitched his father across the room and into a wall. Laughing, he leaned over and picked him back up; wrapping both his hands around his neck, William began to squeeze. "Now who's a weakling? Now who's helpless? Now who's worthless?"

Despite Mary's continued screaming, one could hear the strangled gargling of Joseph Twitch. When Joseph's neck broke, it was not the typical single loud pop, but a crackle, like crushing brick.

Looking into his father's dull eyes, he laughed once more as he whispered into Joseph's ear, "Now who's on the Darkside?"

Mary never stopped screaming, tears running from her eyes. "William? What did you do?"

The bogeyman's head ticked to the side as he frowned. "Mama?"

She backed up against a wall, staring wide-eyed and slack-jawed at her son. Her whole body shook as she cried. "Oh, William, no. No, no, no, noooo!"

The specter clenched his fist as his eyes flared. "Why you screamin', selfish-ass bitch?"

He threw his father's lifeless body to the ground and stepped toward her.

Her eyes bulged and rolled as his face came nose to nose with hers, glowing red eyes burning into her soul. A huge, sallow hand covered her mouth as the other reached around and grabbed her by the neck. "Shh-shh-shh. Don't worry, Mama. Daddy will save you too." He snapped her neck quickly rather than crushing it, and watched the light of life leave her eyes. "Now you can be free. Free on the Darkside. Just like you always wanted."

Mary slumped to the floor.

Just as the bogeyman gingerly picked up the lifeless body of his former self and disappeared into the night, everything went black.

MY EYES flew open, and I found myself back in the Twitch's apartment with a strong feeling of remorse flooding every sense I had. I gasped to try and keep my eyes from watering. Jaiden and I both lay on the floor. Checking my iWatch, I found that only a few seconds had passed. As we both climbed to our feet, she sobbed beside me. Mary looked at us with a forlorn expression, glowing blue tears silently tracking down her face, leaving sparkly trails in their wake. "My drinking didn't help either, but what else could I do? It was the only escape I had from the pain. I couldn't leave him, I just... couldn't."

I shook my head, trying to clear the brain freeze I still felt.

"I'm somewhat glad that I got to share all of that with the two of you. It's been so long."

A rare moment, I found myself lost for words. "I-I..."

She sniffled. "I know what you must think of me, and you're right. I was a coward. I just wanted a normal son and a normal life. Before William, Joseph and I used to be so happy. It really is too bad…"

Jaiden cut her off. "Oh, your whole story is just tragic."

Mary dabbed at her eyes with the dish towel. "It really is too bad neither of you will survive to tell it, but it was nice to finally get it off my chest after all these years."

I cleared my throat, trying to regain my composure. "What makes you think something is going to happen to us, Mrs. Twitch?"

Inky-black smoke began to pour from the bottle of booze on the end table as a voice thundered in our brains so loud it almost brought me to my knees again. *Who's making all that racket? I'm trying to sleep!*

Mary gave Jaiden and me a grave look as her ghostly form began to fade. "Because Joseph's awake."

I put myself between Jaiden and the smoke coming from the bottle. "Well… shit."

The door slammed behind us of its own accord.

A voice boomed out loud as the smoke began to take the form of a man with two glowing red eyes. "Whoever it is, they're going to be really, really sorry for disturbing me!"

Chapter 15

Tenderloin District, Hyde Street, Apartment 6, San Francisco, CA—1030 hours

JAIDEN'S VOICE TREMBLED FROM behind me as the temperature dropped to below freezing. "Doctor, what the hell are we looking at this time?"

We stood in the entryway next to the stain on the carpet with the kitchen entrance to our right and the front door behind us. The specter floated in midair in the main room, advancing on us at a leisurely pace. I took a step back. "A shadow. Shadows are echoes of what they were in life: mean, cruel, and foul tempered, they feed off pain, fear, anguish, and despair. They're extremely hard to track as they can shift in and out of darkness in the blink of an eye. Another curious fact about shadows: For some reason, silver and other metals don't work on them. According to the records I have, no one has ever survived one long enough to figure out a weakness, but there are theories."

"So, can we hurt it?"

"Maybe there's no need to." I drew my gun from its holster to blast the door for a quick exit, but an invisible force yanked it from my hand and pitched it across the room.

The shadow taunted me, "Ah-ah-ah, no need for that."

Glancing at my empty hand, my mind raced. "Well... shit."

The shadow's fire-red eyes burned in the smoky form of Joseph Twitch as they considered Jaiden and me like a spider would consider a fly in its web. Its voice sounded high-pitched and raspy, warbling as if in a vortex. "Mortals? How did Mary know I was hungry? The stupid bitch usually fucks up the simplest things."

My eyes never left the shadow. "How fast did you say you could pick a lock?"

"I'm afraid you will find the door quite stuck. You're not going anywhere."

Her voice came from in the kitchen now. "Can we destroy its anchor, like a spirit?"

I shook my head. "Remember, the bottle, the chair, even the TV, they aren't here. How do you destroy an illusion?"

"Good point."

Time for a little therapy session. Maybe if I could keep it talking, I could figure a way out of this mess. "Joseph Twitch, I presume?"

The shadow paused in the darkness, smoky tendrils of negative energy curling off its form like smoke. "That name is nothing to me. The only thing I care about is your agony!"

As I looked into eyes of vehement hatred, it reached into my thoughts and pulled up all my worst memories. My sister, Daisy, being carried off; my parents shutting me out because they thought I had been lying; a téras ghoul ripping off the head of a former partner; two officers ripped apart by a taxi ghoul; checking another partner into a mental hospital and having to explain to her family why.

The shadow groaned in ecstasy. "Yes! Yes! So much torment. So much." I grasped my temples and tried to break eye contact, but I couldn't seem to break its line of vision. The shadow continued pulling up random personal traumas to its delight. "Delicious! Oh, give me more!"

Jaiden popped out of the kitchen with her UV flashlight, shining the beam into its eyes. "Take that, asshole!"

It seemed to do the trick. The shadow roared and dissipated into the inky darkness. Best of all, Jaiden's action broke its connection with my mind.

Doubled over, gasping, I knew what we needed to do. "We... we need some light on this subject."

An invisible force knocked the flashlight from Jaiden's hand as it ricocheted off the front door and onto the ground. The creature's voice sounded deep from within the darkness of the room. "I will kill you slowly."

Jaiden scrambled into the hallway to reclaim her flashlight when the thing materialized in front of her, locking its malicious eyes onto hers. "What delicious tidbits do you have for me?"

This staring contest didn't exactly go in the shadow's favor. It quickly broke eye contact and disappeared with a wail. "*Argh!* What is this?"

I looked at Jaiden, dumbfounded. "How did you do that?"

She dropped to a knee and retrieved her light. "I just thought of happy things, like rainbows, puppies, and unicorns. I figure if it feeds off bad, I should try to feed it good."

Shaking my head, I continued to try and clear the cobwebs. "Positive thoughts will cancel out the negative. It's so simple, so brilliant, so elementary, I wish I had thought of it."

The shadow moaned. "If I cannot feed from you, I will destroy you."

Jaiden tried to click her flashlight on, but it only flickered and faded.

An invisible force shoved her against the wall. Unfortunately, her head hit just right on the kitchen doorjamb, rendering her unconscious.

"Jaiden!" I yelled, but before I could do anything else, the shadow appeared, again locking me in the gaze of its blazing-red eyes.

It sighed. "Yes, this is what I crave!"

It must have been an all-you-can-eat buffet in my brain with all the shit I had been through. My fear of not being good enough, my guilt for not being able to protect the lives of my partners or innocent bystanders, my sorrow at not being able to save the victims like a hero should. The hero I had never been but always dreamed of being.

"Feed me more!"

I hit my hands and knees trying to bring up something positive in my life, but my head felt like it would split in two. A thought of Nicodemus as a kitten and my best friend Stravinsky were like punches to its gut, but it didn't stay the thing for long.

The shadow continued to drain me. I felt so weak, like I just wanted to lie down and sleep forever. "Now, you are mine."

It seemed far away, but a shotgun blast sounded from the front doorway. It slammed open as bright light came pouring into the place. Charlie stood there with a huge handheld spotlight. "Light 'em up, Ed!"

The light, though it didn't seem to hurt the creature, did push it back into the darkness of the main room and broke our eye contact yet again. With a constant stream, it had fewer places to run.

Ed looked down at me. "What'r we dealin' with, hoss?"

I gasped. "Light! We need light."

Charlie gave me a thumbs-up. "Got that shit covered, Doc."

I corrected myself. "No, natural sunlight!"

The shadow accumulated mass in the darkness as it started pulling negative energy into itself. Extending a hand, Charlie's light exploded as he got shoved back through the door, shrouding the place in darkness again. "I will make you all suffer!"

I couldn't see any windows because the residual haunt made it seem like the room didn't have any, but Ed didn't seem to need any direction. He pumped his shotgun and fired twice, shooting the windows out and lighting up the room with midmorning sunlight.

The shadow shrieked, caught in the crossbeams. Not having anywhere left to run, it finally burst into flames and turned into a pile of ash.

I sat, still panting on the floor as Ed began to sweep the room. "Any more of 'em?"

"How... how did you know where they were?"

He lowered his shotgun. "Weren't no luck if that's what'cha thinkin'."

"Then how?"

He helped me up. "I spent long enough outside ta' 'member where them windows were."

"How did you know we were in trouble?"

Squinting, he shoved a toothpick in his mouth. "What? With all the bangin' around'n yellin'n screamin'? Call it a hunch."

"Good one." I limped to Jaiden, who finally began to stir. She rubbed the back of her head and winced as I knelt beside her. "Are you okay?"

"Just a small bump, I'll be fine. Surprised to still be alive, but fine."

Ed called out to Charlie, "Hey, meathead. Ya a'ight?"

Flat on his back, he put his thumb in the air. "Thanks for noticin' me."

We all chuckled until a familiar voice spoke. "I haven't seen the sun in so long."

Mary reappeared in the hallway, her intense, watery eyes glued to the pile of ash that had been her husband. Her chin set firmly, she finally whispered, "Rot in hell, you son of a bitch."

I stood and faced her. "Mrs. Twitch?"

The wood-paneled walls, shag carpeting, and furniture of the residual haunt around us melted back into the present-day setting. Mary turned and considered the four of us as she began to cry harder. She continued to wring the dish towel in her hands as she gave a sniff. "You beautiful, beautiful people, you've finally set me free."

I tipped my hat and nodded. "Glad we could be of service, and I'd like to thank you for sharing that bit of personal history with us. I believe it will help in our investigation."

She floated toward me at a slow pace and clasped her hands together. "I know I have no right to ask, but please, please help my boy the same way you helped me and my husband."

I nodded. "I promise."

Then she turned to Jaiden, glowing blue tears streaming down her face. "And… please, please tell the world about him. Don't let him be forgotten."

Jaiden nodded vigorously as she wiped at her eyes with a sleeve. "I will. I-I promise."

The apparition nodded, then looked back toward the sun one last time. "Thank you all so much. It's been so long."

She turned into light blue particles and vanished in the sunlight.

"Well, I'll be a son of a bitch." A new voice spoke up, one I didn't immediately recognize. In the doorway stood Mr. Malone with his mouth hanging open.

I turned to him. "Yes, I'm afraid we've decided against renting."

Mr. Malone turned to Ed. "Is he always such a wiseass?"

Ed nodded. "Yup."

The landlord considered me with his arms folded and an eyebrow raised. "On one hand, you shot out my door and windows. On the other, you folks did something that even a priest couldn't accomplish."

I wasn't surprised he had gone the religion route, as most people do. I retrieved my weapon from the other side of the room. "So how do we play this?"

He sighed as he considered the carnage. "Well, that stain in the carpet seems to have disappeared, and I just might be able to rent this place out now once the door and windows are fixed. I'll call that a wash."

Coming to stand in front of him, I stuck my hand out as I passed my card with the other. He grasped both. "If you ever have another infestation like this, don't hesitate to call."

He looked down at the card then tucked it in his shirt pocket. "I'll keep that in mind."

I turned to my comrades. "Anyone for pizza? I'm famished."

Pizzeria, North Beach District, San Francisco, CA—1229 hours

The four of us sat around a table, enjoying some of the best pizza San Francisco had to offer. Since we were in the North Beach District, that said something. The fresh smell of baking pizza hung in the air as we all sat around a bench-style table outside under a red and white striped umbrella. Engines revved and horns complained from the jam-packed street of midafternoon traffic. Charlie spoke around a mouthful of pizza. "So let me get this straight. A dude named Joseph and a chick named Mary had a son?" I took a bite and nodded. "And his name wasn't Jesus, it was the bogeyman?"

Ed scowled. "Don't be a blasphemous turd, yah meathead."

"Actually, his name is William, William Twitch. Don't be afraid to use it, as true names hold power over creatures like this."

Charlie took another bite and swallowed. "And… he was some sort of psychic?"

I nodded. "A latent telekinetic."

Ed removed his hat and scratched his head. "What makes 'im a uh… a lament psychotic?"

I drank down some of my strawberry lemonade. "Latent psychic, Ed. It simply means he wasn't gifted from birth. He only had the potential for it. His powers manifested later in life due to stress and trauma."

Charlie spoke slowly and loudly. "That means he developed them over time because people were mean to him. Might wanna think about that."

Ed gave Charlie a sour look from over his beer. "I ain't deff'n I know what manifesto means, yah meathead."

Our intelligence specialist chuckled.

"Judging from his speech pattern, he's also suffering from multiple personality disorder and disorganized schizophrenia."

Charlie whistled. "Damn."

"He wasn't always like that. When alive, he was a Level One on the spectrum."

Ed blinked. "What the heck does that mean?"

"While alive, he was autistic."

"Still ain't followin', hoss."

"He was smart but quirky."

"Got'cha, like you, then."

Scowling, I held my silence.

After a moment of reflection while sipping his soda, Charlie spoke up. "Wow, almost makes you feel kinda sorry for the evil bastard."

I nodded. "Almost."

Jaiden scribbled in her notebook. "To think, his parents were practically the only ones who knew of his existence. This story is going to land me a Pulitzer." I chuckled thinking about the fit Stravinsky would throw over a story like that. She looked up at me from behind her glasses. "Your agency?"

"PIE?" I asked.

She nodded. "Yes, them. They're going to let me write this story, aren't they?"

I shook my head. "It may need a few redactions to be suitable for the public."

Jaiden scowled. "I knew it! Trying to suppress the truth."

Ed eyeballed me. "Back up there, hoss. I don't wanna be perpetuatin' no fake news."

Charlie stifled a laugh. "Perpetuating? What, did the dictionary fall open, Ed?"

Ed kept his eyes on me. "Simmer down, yah ugly-ass Kewpie doll."

Taking another slice of Sicilian style pizza, I shrugged. "It's not like I have the final say, and I really have no idea who does as I've never met the director personally."

Jaiden went back to notes as she grumbled, "Then I'll be talking to Stravinsky. I made a promise."

Ed took a swig of beer. "Now that we know who this thing is'n how 'e ticks, so what?"

I took another bite but swallowed before speaking. "Never underestimate the usefulness of psychological warfare."

Ed shook his head. "That ain't what I meant, hoss. Y'all done a good job on gatherin' intel, but no matter if 'e's a sad case'r not, we still gotta take 'im down, 'n' we don't even know where 'e is 'r when 'e's gonna strike next."

I finished off my last slice of pizza and wiped my mouth on a paper napkin. "One step at a time, Ed. One step at a time."

San Francisco Medical Examiner's Office
Parking Lot, San Francisco, CA—2045 hours

CHARLIE CACKLED AS AN impish grin played at the corners of his mouth. "Dude, this is so not gonna work."

I desperately tried to hold back a sneeze. "I–it b-better, f-for your sake."

After dropping off Jaiden at her office to catch up on a few things, I had Charlie and Ed drive me to see if I could make amends with Emily. After all, they had gotten me into this mess.

Charlie pointed farther down the parking lot from the rose-pink Corvette where they dropped me off. "We'll wait over there, just in case."

The flowers I brought for Emily were making me sneeze. "Sh-sh-sh-aaaaachoooo! She'll be reasonable."

Ed had a toothpick hanging from his mouth. "Y'all obviously don't know women, hoss. We'll wait o'er there, jus' ta' make sure, like meathead done said."

I nodded, preparing myself to eat a shit sandwich while trying desperately to stifle another sneeze. "F-f-fidne."

"Good luck with that shit, Sir Sneeze-a-Lot."

I could still hear Charlie laughing as they pulled away into a distant parking spot, killing the lights and engine.

It didn't take long before I saw Emily walking toward her car, nose in her phone. Upon spotting me, she slipped it into a pocket, folded her arms, and gave me a stern look with those hypnotic green eyes. "Well, look what the cat dragged in."

I responded with a sneeze and a sniffle as I held the flowers up. "H-h-h-*hachoooo!* Hi, Embly. Look, I…"

She hushed me, taking the flowers with a smile. "*Shh!* No, you look. I understand work pulled you away. I read the note your friends left me. We can go to Cancún some other time."

I blinked. That seemed to go too well. "I'm… glad dhat you… udderstand?"

She closed her eyes and brought the bouquet of roses to her nose, inhaled deeply, then brought them away and opened her eyes. "Of course I understand. You're not the only doctor that gets called away at a moment's notice, you know."

"I…"

She held a finger to my lips and gave me a coquettish look. "Really, it's okay. Thank you for the flowers."

I shrugged and sniffed, still a little confused she wasn't mad. "It was da least I could do. So, uh, are you busy todight? Maybe we could get dinner? I could continue to try add make it ub to you."

Her bottom lip pushed out in a pout as she batted her eyes. "Aww, as much fun as that sounds, sorry, Tiger. I promised one of my girlfriends some time. She's going through a real bad breakup. Her husband left her with two kids, can you believe it?"

I supposed I could understand that. I clasped my hands behind my back and smiled. "A rain check, then."

She leaned in and kissed me on the lips, looking deep into my eyes. Immediately, all my reservations melted away as a bit of her perfume broke through my congested sinuses. "One I plan to cash very soon."

I opened her car door. "Well, have fud tonight."

She glanced at Ed and Charlie in the van over my shoulder and gave me a smile. "You too."

As I watched her drive off, I wasn't sure that situation could have gone any better, and with the flowers gone, my nose finally started to clear.

Charlie's voice broke me out of my stupor. "You just gonna stand there all night or what, Doc? I'm fuckin' hungry."

I turned toward the van and made my way to the front passenger side. As I climbed in, I popped my collar. "See? I told you guys she'd understand."

Ed's wide-eyed look of disbelief was visible in the side-view mirror. "Golly. She didn't even raise 'er voice, not once. She even smiled."

"Because she's a reasonable, rational human being, Ed."

Charlie started the van and put it in drive. "Nah, that's what you call the bait and switch 'cause she knew you had friends close by. She's acting normal now, but when she gets you alone… *wham*, she's gonna hit you with the crazy. Just watch."

"No way. You guys are just jealous I got one of the good ones."

"Welp, I hope yer four-leaf clover holds out, hoss, 'cause she sure is a looker."

"Thanks, Ed." I settled in the seat for the drive back to San Jose with Emily on my mind even though my stomach growled for food.

Chapter 16

Santana Row, San Jose, CA—2330 hours

AFTER SOME DINNER, ED decided to crash at Charlie's place instead of going back to his cabin in the woods. He nodded at me as he stepped off the elevator on the first floor. "See ya in the mornin', hoss."

Charlie jumped out after Ed. "Later, Doc."

I rode the elevator up to my floor. As I approached the apartment, I noticed something wrong.

My door stood ajar.

Immediately, I drew my weapon. Nudging it further open with the nose of my pistol, I slipped inside.

Looking around the main room, I saw the place a wreck. Not in the manner of a professional casing, this seemed more like… a temper tantrum. Table and chairs lay in heaps of kindling, the couch had been shredded and broken in two. Pictures and papers had been strewn about my redwood desk that laid across the room from where it should have been, demolished. Peeking into the bedroom, it looked as if it had been hit by a hurricane. The bed frame had been wrecked and the mattress shredded. Drawers laid upended, mirrors and TVs were shattered and smashed. Even the refrigerator had been tipped over and emptied, its contents all over the floor and walls among broken dishes and scattered cutlery.

My thoughts first went to… Emily? Maybe she had been so calm and forgiving because she had already extracted revenge? Reason won over. Emily wouldn't have the strength to do half these things.

Coming out of the bathroom and finding no one around, I put my gun in its holster. The eerie silence nagged at me—there should have been some meowing by now. I began to sift further through the wreckage. "Nicodemus? Here, kitty, kitty, kitty."

All his normal hiding spots like under the bed, under the table, or under the couch had been eradicated, so that narrowed down the search, but he still seemed reluctant to come out. "Nicodemus, buddy, come on out now. Daddy's home."

Deciding to use a different perspective, I took out my UV flashlight and clicked it on. A bright trail of paw prints and the ghostly prints of a work boot led to a smashed back door. "Oh, no. Oh, no, no, no, Nicodemus!"

Looking out on the balcony, my heart stopped as tears flowed beyond my control. Nicodemus hung from a pole by his tail, his belly slit open, and underneath him scrawled clumsily in the cat's own blood, a simple message: *Tag! You're it!*

I took down the fallen warrior and gingerly placed him in a shoebox I found on the bedroom floor. I could tell Nicodemus had gotten in a few swipes as the black ectoplasm on his paws had led me to him. At least he had gone down fighting, poor little guy. I gazed upon my best friend in the whole world for the past ten years for the last time, my tears drenching his fur before I covered him with the lid.

I bowed my head, squinted, and gritted my teeth. "William, you son of a bitch. I'll…"

Interrupted by "Comin' in Hot," I fished my phone out of my pocket and put it to my ear. My voice came out in a wracking sob. "Ch–Charlie?"

He sounded unsurprised. "Oh damn, you got hit too, huh?"

"N–Nicodemus… he…"

"Aww, man. Your cat?"

"It was him. It… it was William."

"Yeah, Ed's buggin' out about checkin' his cabin."

"Has a–anyone c–called Jaiden?"

"Yeah, that was the first thing Ed did."

"And?"

"Yeah, she got hit too. I guess her parakeet got snuffed. She's pretty shaken up."

"We'll… pick her up on the way to Ed's. I'll meet you both downstairs in five."

"Roger, roger." He hung up.

Ed's Cabin, Somewhere in the Hoover
Wilderness between CA and NV—0345 hours

W E ALL STUMBLED INTO Ed's cabin, exhausted from driving all night. As we entered, it didn't look like anything had been touched.

Ed nodded, satisfied after a quick look around. "Another reason I live off-grid."

Charlie moaned as he flopped onto the couch. "I'm just interested in sleep."

Ed gave Charlie a shove, so he fell on the floor. "Git yer filthy carcass off ma' couch."

"Hey! What gives?"

Ed retrieved two sleeping bags from his closet and threw them to Charlie and me. "Best I got."

I set the sleeping bag on the floor. "Thank you, Ed."

Charlie was already spreading his out. "Yeah, thanks."

He looked at Jaiden, then he nodded toward the bedroom. "Missy, y'all go ahead'n take the room."

"T-thanks, Ed." Jaiden looked grateful with tearstained eyes as she yawned, stretched, and closed the door after herself.

Ed stretched out on the couch with his Remington close by.

I cradled the shoebox with Nicodemus. "Say, um, Ed. Do… you have a spot I can…"

He lifted his chin toward the door. "Shovel's outside on the porch. There's a good spot by that lone redwood out yonder. Make sure ta burry 'em deep, 'cause we don't want no critters draggin' 'im up."

I nodded but didn't say anything.

He raised an eyebrow. "Y'all wanna congregation?"

I shook my head. "I-I think I'd… rather do this alone, but thanks."

Ed settled back on his couch. "Suit yerself."

I could already hear Charlie lightly snoring.

As I went out into the cold October night, I couldn't stop the tears from rolling down my cheeks. Grabbing the spade shovel, I headed out to the lone redwood to bury my nearest and dearest friend under a clouded full moon.

I AWOKE TO THE smell of fresh, strong coffee and squinted against the sunlight that poured in from the windows as I yawned and stretched from a miserable night's sleep on the floor. Charlie's sleeping bag lay crumpled near mine. The door to Ed's room stood open, and the only thing left on Ed's couch was a blanket. I heard the unmistakable pop of gunfire coming from outside. Curious, I got up and poured myself a cup of joe then wandered out onto the porch to see what I could see.

I heard Ed in the distance. "Quit lookin' at the target, meathead. Look at the sights! It's all 'bout sight alignment, sight picture."

I rounded the corner of the cabin in time to see Charlie flip Ed the bird. "Hey, take a picture of this."

Eight shots rang out in rapid succession. "Woo-nelly, now that's how ya shoot! Nice group there, missy."

Jaiden, with goggles on, cleared the nine-millimeter Beretta like a professional.

I wandered over to a stretch of land with paper targets hanging on wooden posts that had been hammered into the ground depicting lanes. Both shooters stood behind a makeshift counter constructed from wooden boxes as Ed loomed behind both with big yellow headphones covering his ears. He turned and raised his cup of coffee. "Afternoon, hoss. Care ta' show us how it's done?"

I shrugged as I set my coffee down on a box, took a set of squishy foam earplugs from him, and shoved them in my ears. Drawing my "side cannon"—as Ed liked to call it—from its holster, I cleared and racked a round into the chamber, aimed downrange, then emptied all seven shots into one of his paper targets.

Jaiden gave a scream and jumped at the sheer force of the muzzle blast.

Charlie watched on in wide-eyed wonder.

Ed exclaimed as he looked at the target my Desert Eagle shredded into pieces. "Woo-hoo! Now that's a sidearm, hoss. I done felt that in ma' da'gone bones."

I nodded at him as I removed my earplugs, holstered my gun, and picked my coffee back up. "Nice range you have here."

He spat in the dirt as he hung his headphones around his neck. "She does a'ight. Say, I got a dumb question."

"There are no stupid questions, Ed. Ask away."

Taking out a shotgun shell, he held it up and smiled wickedly. "Sterling silver buckshot. Think they'll do the trick? Made 'em ma'self."

I had never thought about it. "Will it fire?"

Ed's face fell. He loaded a round into his shotgun and sent it downrange no problem.

Jaiden scrunched up her nose. "Isn't that expensive, though?"

Ed sniffed. "Only forty bucks fer nine hundred 'n' twenty-five balls at the hardware store. I can make quite a few with that."

A slow smile crept across Charlie's face. "That's about how much they are on Amazon as well, but I pity the Amazon driver who has to make the trip out here."

"I done got a PO box."

"Do you even know how to order off Amazon? Let alone use a computer?"

Ed looked more serious than a starving polar bear. "Boy, y'all could make a cup'a coffee nervous. 'Sides, why in tarnation would I order 'em from the Amazon anyway? It's a frickin' jungle, yah meathead."

Charlie just laughed.

I nodded, attempting to keep the conversation focused. "Good initiative, Ed. The more things we can bring to the table to help our cause, the better."

Charlie stifled a grin as he glanced at my weapon. "That begs the question: Why does silver work? I thought that was only good against werewolves."

"It's one of the seven pure metals of alchemy. That's why iron works too."

Jaiden raised a finger. "And for those of us who don't know what the seven pure metals of alchemy are, Doctor?"

I set my coffee cup on the makeshift range counter and ticked off on my fingers. "Gold, silver, iron, tin, lead, copper, and mercury."

Ed screwed up his face. "Y'all tellin' me that fire poker I done threw at that flab-nabbin' thing…"

"The djinn?"

"Yeah, that. Y'all mean ta' tell me it's 'cause that poker was iron, that's why it worked where bullets wouldn't?"

I picked my coffee cup back up. "Bullets tend to be brass and an aluminum alloy or steel, which means they're not one of the metals that I cited."

Ed rubbed his chin. "Well, I'll be."

Charlie gave me an impish smile. "But aluminum is on the periodic table."

"Aluminum bonds so well to other elements, even in nature it's never found pure and it's not one of the seven metals of alchemy as I mentioned before. The periodic table has nothing to do with it. Now a metal like gold is even specific to certain entities like banshees, but overexposure to lead and mercury are toxic, and pure tin or gold are rare and expensive. That's why silver, iron, and copper are more commonly used."

"What about depleted uranium?"

"Don't be stupid, Charlie. Where exactly would one get depleted uranium legally?"

He scowled. "Hey, I thought you told Ed there are no stupid questions."

I took a noisy sip of my coffee. "There's always an exception to the rule."

Jaiden interjected, "Why not melt down tin cans for the tin?"

Ed spat in the dirt again. "Naw, tin cans nowadays'r actually made'a aluminum'n other metals."

Charlie sighed. "Is nothing sacred?"

I nodded. "Keep in mind all salt works in a pinch, but kosher salt works best."

Jaiden crossed her arms. "How does that work?"

"Pagans, witches, hell, even the Catholic church when performing an exorcism uses salt. Spirits and the like can't cross over salt lines, it's a pure, natural substance that reacts negatively to ectoplasm. Using it to line doors, windows, making a circle around yourself with it, can prevent spirits from getting to you. When used in a blast, it should make some weaker entities disperse temporarily and may even irritate monsters and specters."

Ed shrugged. "I can always pack some'a them shells with rock salt, hoss."

I sipped at my coffee. "Good idea, but make sure to color code shells. We don't want to be firing off rock salt when we're looking to shoot sterling silver. Make sense?"

Ed nodded at me then gave me the stink eye. "I also 'member ya sayin' the Good Book don't work neither. What's that 'bout?"

"Depends on what you mean. Will holy water and crosses make a vampire burst into flames? No, the most they will do is make it wet and piss it off."

Charlie chuckled. "Sounds like you know from experience."

Jaiden went white, her voice timid. "You mean vampires are real?"

"Yes."

She snorted, shaking her head. "Well, if crosses and holy water don't work on them, then what does? Garlic?"

"The scent of garlic can repel them, and an oaken stake through the heart will paralyze them, but it must be oak. You need to decapitate them to kill them."

"Ugh."

Charlie sputtered his lips. "Next you'll say Jaiden's boyfriend isn't a dweebus-maximus and that Bigfoot is real."

"Hey!"

I gave a chuckle. "Actually we believe that sasquatches live in small tribes throughout many different wildernesses all around the globe. We just haven't been able to catch them on film due to their aboriginal belief that a camera will steal their soul. That, and they're extremely quick and strong for a species, though to the best of our knowledge they are pacifists."

Ed squinted. "Are UFOs real too?"

"I have not officially been to Area 51 and cannot confirm or deny an answer."

He punched his fist in the air triumphantly. "Knew it!"

Charlie rolled his eyes. "The government already admitted to UFOs, Ed. Get with the times."

Ignoring Charlie, I plowed on. "Circling back as to what religion might be good for, it's good to keep the mind busy to avoid possession."

Jaiden nodded. "Like a mantra?"

Ed scratched his head. "A man-tra? Sounds like one'a them hippy yoga poses."

Charlie shook his head. "No, a mantra is something you say over and over again."

I added to Charlie's explanation, "It must hold some meaning for the individual as well, and again, it could be anything someone strongly believes in, religious text, string theory, the Rifleman's Creed. It grounds and centers you in such a way you can't be possessed."

"Huh, a'ight then."

Charlie studied the silver weapon I held in my shoulder holster. "So how does your gun work? The mechanisms can't be silver, too, can they? Or do I want to know where my tax dollars have been going to all this time?"

I shrugged. "Surprisingly the inner workings are also silver, but I couldn't tell you why it works. By all rights, this thing should fall apart. I've done enough study on it to know my bullets are solid bronze."

Jaiden wrinkled her nose. "Bronze isn't one of the alchemistic metals you mentioned, Doctor. I thought you said anything but those tend to be useless."

"When I had them tested, they were an exact mixture of tin and copper, so maybe that's okay? All I know really is this is the sidearm they issued me, and it hasn't failed me yet."

"Your bullets do seem to work on just about everything."

"Not on everything, nor do the alchemistic metals. Remember the shadow?"

She shuddered. "How could I forget?"

"Only pure sunlight could have destroyed that creature, though artificial light seemed to irritate it at least. Your defensive tactic of thinking happy thoughts is something for the books. Very clever."

The corners of her mouth curled. "Elementary, my dear doctor."

Charlie laughed, poking her in the ribs with an elbow. "Good one."

Ed continued to reason things out. "So, the purer'n more natural a substance, the more effective? Sounds like God's work ta' me."

"Debatable, but the bit about natural being best? That seems to be the case in most instances."

Charlie nodded. "Is that why holistic medicine helped my leg? Or eating helped you and Jaiden?"

I took another sip of coffee. "Naturally, negative spiritual energy can drain us of essential vitamins and minerals by kicking our emotions and hormones into overdrive. This is why negative spiritual entities are so dangerous and how they can hurt or even kill. So, when drained after an encounter, one needs to replenish vital nourishment: Jaiden needed Vitamin C after the skoupída specter, I needed calcium after the shadow. The perfume, as you called it, that helped heal your leg was a mixture of alcohol infused with strong antibacterial oils."

Jaiden looked perplexed. "Why dark chocolate after the haunt? That must be something straight out of *Harry Potter*."

"Dark chocolate releases endorphins that help battle depression, so Rowling got it right. Though what she calls dementors are most likely wraiths."

She nodded thoughtfully. "The more you know."

Ed's mustache twitched. "Sounds like a bunch'a satanic, tree-huggin' hippie crap ta' me."

Out of nowhere, Charlie's stomach growled. "Speaking of food, I need to be nourished by a tall stack of Ed's pancakes."

Ed chuckled. "It's all in the buttermilk."

"Food doesn't sound half bad," Jaiden agreed.

I was famished as well and my stomach growled in kind. "I could use more coffee, but buttermilk pancakes would be most welcome. Throw in some bacon, hash browns, and eggs over easy and I'd be a happy camper."

"What'cha think this is, hoss? Memaw's house?"

Charlie bit his lip. "Actually, bacon, eggs, and hash browns don't sound half bad."

Jaiden rolled her eyes. "Oh my God, Charlie. It's like you have a hollow leg or something."

As we moved toward the cabin, I couldn't help but feel a bit of pride in the team I had now. We had come such a long way in such a short time.

San Jose Sewer System, San Jose, CA—1939 hours

WATER DRIPPED IN THE darkness. Cockroaches wiggled their antennae and clung to the walls. Hunks of sludge floated along the water trench like some repulsive lazy river. An army of rats skittered, chittered, and squeaked along the slimy concrete pathway.

The bogeyman bounced up and down on the balls of his feet, clapping his hands. "That… that was fun. Messing up their homes. Smashing things, throwing things, we should do it again."

His hood fell back to the nape of his neck as his eyes flared and his fist clenched. "Daddy… Daddy couldn't find them in their homes, and Daddy wants more. Daddy wants more revenge on the Darkside! Big Brother's cat and the stupid bird weren't enough blood-bloody blood. Daddy wants *their* blood! Daddy wants to smash their bones and gouge their eyes out!"

His head jerked and his face fell. "We… we missed one. We didn't get to play at his house."

Roaring, he stomped his feet. "And that makes Daddy mad! But no matter, what Daddy did will draw them to the Darkside. And this time? This time, on the Darkside, Daddy will be ready for them and then they'll be sorry for hurting the poor little guy."

He twiddled his fingers. "Shouldn't… shouldn't we find another playmate soon?"

"Yes, yes soon. Very soon. Right now, Daddy needs to find a new home, new things… new everything. They even took the poor little guy's story that hung on the wall!" He stomped on a rat, squishing it flat in his ire.

"But… but we found a new chair, and a new TV. Ooo, and the new cages from the animal shelter to put friends in."

"But they're not the same on the Darkside! Daddy wants it to be the same and it's not! Big Brother and his friends are mean, and nasty, and they're gonna pay."

"The poor little guy shouldn't be afraid anymore. Daddy promised we wouldn't be afraid ever again."

"Daddy's not afraid! Don't ever say Daddy's afraid or Daddy will kill you, understand?"

"Sorry."

He scooped up a rat and glared at it. "Daddy wants friends, like Big Brother. Daddy can feel friends close by. Daddy will reach out to them. Call them… calling them to the Darkside. They'll help protect the poor little guy and keep him safe."

He retrieved a huge sack and dumped bones onto the sewer floor. A black, smoky aura of negative energy radiated from him as he stuffed the rat into his mouth and chewed, letting the negative energy do its work.

I AWOKE IN ED'S cabin with a start. I wasn't sweating like I normally did after a bogeyman dream. Ed and Charlie snored as I tried to fall back asleep, but I found it difficult without Nicodemus curled up on my feet purring. A tear escaped my eye at the thought of him.

William had every right to be afraid, because I was coming for him.

My Apartment, Santana Row, San Jose, CA—0910 hours

After spending another night at Ed's, the next morning we each had to go deal with the aftermath of William's attacks. Ed went to go help and keep an eye on Jaiden. Charlie drove both of us to Santana Row. When I let myself into my apartment, I found a surprise waiting for me. The whole place had been put back together just as it had been.

Couch? Fixed.

Bed? Fixed.

Walls? Freshly painted.

Even the refrigerator had been fixed and restocked with its exact contents. I almost called out for Nicodemus.

Something moved in my peripheral vision. My Desert Eagle came out. "Hello?"

The voice of my best friend graced my ears as Stravinsky stepped into view with his hands raised. "Ah, there you are, Doctor."

Immediately, I holstered my weapon. "Stravinsky! What…"

He put his hands down and gestured to everything. "Consider this agency's way of saying, 'welcome back.'"

"What about Charlie and Jaiden?" "Oh! Darling" by The Beatles sounded from my pocket. Stravinsky motioned for me to answer.

Jaiden's voice came from the other end. "My apartment. It's… it's fixed! There's even a new parakeet."

"Courtesy of PIE. I'll call you back."

I hung up, only to have "Comin' In Hot" start playing immediately after. Again, Stravinsky waited patiently for me to answer.

Charlie sounded awestruck. "Doc, this is fucking amazing. It's like it never happened."

"Courtesy of PIE, Charlie. I'll call you back."

I hung up and looked at Stravinsky. "I suppose a thank you is in order?"

He shook his head. "No need for thank you. You know we take care of own. I am very sorry about Nicodemus. *Pozhaluysta primite moy soboleznovaniya.*"

Bowing my head, I sucked in a breath and released it. "Thank you for the condolences, he's already missed."

"Which is why I brought you this."

"What?"

Stravinsky held his hand out as he moved to one side, revealing the cutest German shepherd puppy. He smiled warmly. "*Dlya tebya.* For you."

I locked eyes with her and felt my heart melt. The puppy, only about six months old, bounced up to me and sat at my feet. The color of her fur looked rich and dark for a shepherd, a solid black with tan and cream markings around her face, legs, belly, and paws. Cocking her head, she looked up with one ear in the air and one ear still drooping. I looked down with a similar expression. There was weakness in my protesting. "Stravinsky… I… I can't care for a dog."

He patted me on the shoulder. "I am sure you will both, how you say, 'work it out.' She is half breed. Half German shepherd, half rottweiler. She was runt of litter but is very smart, like new owner."

She began to sniff my foot, thumping her tail on the carpet.

Stravinsky looked between us. "So, what is name?"

I considered the dog's big brown eyes and floppy ears, making her look more rottweiler than shepherd. Judging from her size, she was already about seventy pounds of pure, unadulterated puppy. She gave me a sideways dog look as I rubbed my chin in thought. "Well, I always loved *Garfield*, so I think I'll call her… Pooky."

Stravinsky raised an eyebrow. "Dog in *Garfield* comic? Is Odie. *Tupitsa.*"

I could feel the bond between us, like some magnetic pull that had snapped into place. I smiled and chuckled as she licked my cheek. "A dumbass, am I? You're right, Stravinsky, the dog's name is Odie. This dog isn't a boy, which is why I named her after Garfield's teddy bear. Pooky is gender neutral."

Stravinsky nodded. "Is good name. Now, try giving command."

I stood up straight. "Okay. How about: lie down."

Both ears shot up in the air and her belly hit the ground as her eyes remained focused on me looking like a statue of the Anubis jackal.

"Roll over."

She rolled to the right without additional prompt and returned to her sphynx-like position.

"Good girl. Heel."

She trotted over and sat by my foot.

I raised an eyebrow and patted her head. "Good girl. Now I'm gonna need to carry treats with me."

Stravinsky folded his arms. "Now, try thinking command."

Squinting, my cheek scrunched in disbelief. "You're shitting me."

He gestured with a hand. "Go on, try."

I thought of her retrieving my slippers.

Immediately, she trotted into the bedroom and came back with both dangling from her mouth. She dropped them at my feet, sat, and sent me back an image of her eating a dog biscuit.

My jaw dropped. "What, is she super pooch or something?"

"Is familiar."

"A familiar? You mean like a wizard's familiar?"

His eyes went toward the ceiling as his nose scrunched and his bottom lip jutted out, then he nodded. *"Da."*

My face bunched up. "But I'm an average Joe, why does she respond to me?"

"Perhaps you are more *osobennyy* than you would like to believe, Doctor."

I snorted. "Yeah, sure. Special."

Stravinsky clasped his hands behind his back. "Now, to business."

"You sure do know how to ruin a moment, don't you?"

"This is what ex-wife tells me."

I finally looked up as I laughed out loud. "Stravinsky, you finally made a decent joke."

A hint of a smile played at the corners of his mouth. "Perhaps you are rubbing off on me more than I would like, Doctor. As I say, agency has job for you and team."

Glowering, I took out my notepad and pen. "No word on the bogeyman?"

"*Nyet*, but we are still searching. You will be first call if we find something."

I nodded. "So what'cha got?"

"You are knowing Apple computers?"

"Based in Cupertino? A leader in world technology? I own most of their products? Never heard of them."

He lifted an eyebrow. "Always joking. What is no joke, it appears they have gremlin terrorists in one of their buildings. They make no demands but are threatening to dump server information to telemarketers, putting millions of people's personal data at risk. They are also having hostages, so time is of essence."

"That is a problem. How are we keeping a lid on this?"

Stravinsky moved to the door. "You will go in under guise of negotiator and use team for support, *da?* Oh, and Doctor?"

"Yeah?"

Stravinsky stuck his hand out. "Welcome back, *moy drug.*"

I shook his hand as the puppy looked back and forth between us. "Thanks. It's good to be back, Stravinsky."

Chapter 17

Apple Headquarters, Infinite Loop,
Cupertino, CA—1030 hours

I CLEARED MY THROAT to summon my team's attention. "Okay, people. When you mention a gremlin, most people's minds go to a movie made in the 1980s, and they're not far from the truth. Short, scaly, sadistic little buggers, gremlins are tricky, devious creatures put on this Earth simply to cause as much chaos, havoc, and mayhem as possible. Back in 2012, I had to deal with a gremlin who decided to sabotage a jumbo jet full of people."

Jaiden covered her mouth with a hand. "Wait, Hawaiian Airlines, flight 420 out of SJC back in November of 2012? I remember that story. Oh my God, that disaster was you?"

"Not one of my finer moments, but back to the task at hand. Now, if a gremlin can blow something up, set something on fire, make something crash, or wreak some other sort of devastation with mass casualties, there's no better fun for them. And they're smart, extremely smart."

Charlie smirked. "Smarter than you?"

"I wouldn't go that far, but their intelligence is also one of their weaknesses, it makes them arrogant. They can speak any language and have an amazing aptitude for electronics and mechanical things, which is why technology companies have the most problems with them. Unfortunately, I've never encountered more than one at a time before, so I'm not sure about their social dynamics or why they're working together. Any questions?"

Everyone shook their heads.

"For code names, I figured we'd stick to the basics: I'm Doc, Charlie-Spook, Jaiden-Ace, and Ed-Eagle Eye. Make sense?"

Everyone nodded.

As we sat in the van outside the target building, I designated roles and handed out earpieces so we could keep in contact. "Charlie, I need you in the van on this one. Do everything you can to try to stall them from dumping those servers."

Charlie sat in the back with his laptop. "On it, Doc."

Pooky, complete with a pink silver-spiked collar and a gray bulletproof harness I had gotten from Stravinsky, attacked his shoe as it shifted.

He paused and gave me an exasperated look. "I don't know why you insisted on bringing Marmaduke."

"Her name is Pooky and she's part of the team now. Besides, she needs the socialization and the experience."

Charlie rolled his eyes as he attempted to shake the seventy-pound puppy off his foot. "Whatever."

I turned my attention to Jaiden. "I need you to figure out what the media knows so we can control the story."

Her lips went as thin as graphene as she folded her arms. "Eavesdropping and trying to control the press better not be my only responsibility in this group or we're going to have words, Doctor."

My brow collapsed on itself as my left cheek scrunched up. "Oh, come on, I've put you in plenty of dangerous situations already so it's not fair to say this is your 'only responsibility,' but it is an important one when the press is involved. So, please, be a dear and keep an eye on them for me?" She rolled her eyes and huffed. I turned to my sniper. "Ed." He nodded. "Find a rooftop away from police and post up. That office building over there should do nicely. You have your rifle?"

"Yup."

"You have the special bullets our agency supplied?"

"Yup."

Charlie continued to fend Pooky off from messing with his shoe, almost knocking himself over in the process. "Le'go, ya crazy-ass mutt."

"Pooky, heel."

She put her ears back and came over to sulk by me, her sad puppy dog eyes still on Charlie.

I took in a cleansing breath and exhaled slowly. "Everyone have their earpieces?"

Each of them gave me a thumbs-up.

"Alright, folks. Let's move. Pooky, come." I jumped out of Charlie's van and started toward the building, my dog trotting along beside me.

An officer tried to stop us. "Sorry, sir, I need you to step back from the premises."

My badge came out. "I'm the negotiator, bring me to whoever's in charge, please."

The officer opened his mouth, thought better of it, and held the tape up for me. He led me to a SWAT van where a few suits and a captain stared intently at a video screen that played feed from a body cam. Her head came up at our approach and she reared back at the sight of me. Her eyes finally gravitated onto the officer. "Who's Dick Tracy?"

"Captain, this is the… negotiator." He chuckled and left.

Both eyebrows went up. "That's odd, because we just sent in a negotiator."

No sooner had she said something when audible feed came from the officer's body cam. "Don't shoot. I'm here to negotiate for the Cupertino Police Department?"

"Ratta wonga?"

"What? What the fuck is that? Holy shit, what the…? No, no, no!"

"Ahhhhhhh!" A man in a bulletproof vest crashed through a sixth-story window and landed on a police cruiser. Screams came from below as unintelligible yelling ensued from the window.

The captain reared her head, her eyes going wide. "Jesus!"

I grimaced. "Obviously he didn't speak their language."

The captain turned back to me with her eyebrows raised and her eyes popping out. "You think you can do better, Mr. Gumshoe Magoo?"

Nonchalantly studding my nails, I shined them against my jacket. "It's doctor, and I'm sure I couldn't do any worse."

Folding her arms, she squinted. "Who did you say you were again?"

I flashed my badge. "Dr. Darrell Diamondback, special federal task force."

She looked me up and down. "Federal, huh, and… uh, who's mini-Cujo?"

My eyebrow hitched up. "Don't you know a K-9 unit when you see one?"

This time the captain let out a full belly laugh. "Isn't she a little young to be in the field?"

My new partner began to growl.

"Pooky, back off." She stopped and began panting again. "Sit." She sat, going ridged at my heel. I arched an eyebrow. "Good enough for you?"

The captain looked incredulous. "I'm phoning this in. Wait right there."

I clasped my hands behind my back. "This is a hostage situation and time is ticking, Captain. Do hurry."

She finally spoke into the receiver. "Hello, Mayor Kline, please." She paused. "Hello, Mayor? I have a fed here claiming..." Someone spoke sternly on the other end. "But Mayor..." More rapid-fire talking. The captain didn't seem to like what she heard. "And who's gonna be responsible when he gets tossed out a window?"

This time the mayor yelled so loud I couldn't help but overhear. "Send him up now or you'll be walking a fucking beat for the rest of your goddamn career! Do you understand me, Captain?"

Immediately, she lost her bluster and scowled. "Yes... yes, Mr. Mayor. Sorry, sir. If... that's... what... you... shit."

The captain stared at the phone for a moment looking like someone had just told her to haul a truck full of rotten fish guts to the county dump.

One of the suited detectives folded his arms. "Well, Cap, what do we do with him?"

She glared at me with her bottom lip sticking out. "Fuck it, let him go up."

Another suit objected loudly, "He hasn't even been briefed on the situation."

"Supposedly, he's a federal expert. He can figure out the situation for his damn self."

They began grumbling between themselves.

I tipped my hat. "Thank you, Captain."

"Yeah, whatever."

Spinning around on my heel, I walked out, Pooky following. Time to test the earpieces. "Testing, testing. Can everyone read me?"

Jaiden's voice came in an irritated whisper. "Yes."

A horrible mock-southern accent came from Charlie. "10-4, good buddy. Hot damn, I always wanted to say that."

Ed's voice chimed in. "Got'cha loud'n clear, Doc. An' quit screwin' 'round on the radio, meathead."

"That's Spook to you, Eagle Ass."

I rolled my eyes. "Ace, what's the press saying?"

Jaiden growled. "That this is the work of some new Syrian terrorist group called, uh… *Al Makhalib Alzili*."

"The Shadow Claws? Good, stick to that."

"But…"

Short on time, I cut her off. "How serious are people going to take you when you tell them it's nothing but a gang of gremlins?"

Her scathing reply hissed in my ear. "What happens when we don't pull out any Arabs?"

"Leave that bit to me. Speaking of which, you in position, Eagle Eye?"

"I got you'n Purty Girl approachin' the northeast entrance, Doc. I also got a good view inta' the hole they done made'n I ain't seen nothin' weird yet."

I liked Ed's code name for Pooky. "You won't. They don't like sunlight. It's rather odd they're operating during the day." Filing that information away for later, I switched gears. "Spook, can you see me?"

"I've got you from five different angles, Doc."

"Perfect, open my door, please?"

The electronic door clicked open, allowing me entrance into a huge lobby with marbled tile floors, an empty receptionist's desk with the Apple logo on the wall behind it, and some potted plants to add decoration. My shoes echoed loudly as I headed toward the elevators. "Where are my hostages?"

"Sixth floor. The gremlins have them tied up and gagged. There're three: two men and a woman. They look pretty banged up. Might wanna hurry, they're gonna be breaking through Apple's firewall any second."

I quickened my pace. "I thought I told you your whole mission in life was to keep them from doing that."

"Ruh-row, they noticed me in the systems."

"Keep them busy."

His voice came back strained. "Damn. They're good, Doc."

"Be best." A horrid slogan, but there it was.

"You can count on me."

"That was the idea."

A moment of silence. "Shit, they put the elevators out of commission."

I changed direction to the stairwell door, pushed it open, and started taking two at a time. "Looks like Pretty Girl and I are taking the stairs. Spook, you still hanging in there?"

"By the skin of my teeth, but yeah."

I passed a sign telling me I had made it to level four, Pooky still pacing me. "Open the sixth-floor stairwell door, please. I'm almost there."

The sound of his keystrokes clicked in my ear. "On it… and… done. *Ha!* Fuck these little bastards."

Pushing open the door before it locked on me, Pooky navigated through as I let it swing close. We came out next to the elevators. A potted plant between them, the doors opened and closed of their own accord, the up and down arrows blinked in rapid succession, and I heard "Lights Out" from Hollywood Undead blaring over the interior speaker. The lights overhead flickered on and off, messing with my vision. Looking out into the office area among a plethora of cubicles, phones rang off and on, a copy machine machine-gunned blank pieces of paper all over the floor, and every computer I ran across had the buggy-eyed face of a gremlin staring back at me, menacingly blowing raspberries.

I continued down to a split in the corridor, then turned right, away from the bathrooms at the end of the hall. Making my way forward, I came to an electronically locked door and another stretch of hallway that continued to my right. "Which way, Spook?"

"Quickest way would have been through the locked door."

"You can't get it open? Why did I hire you again?"

"Hey, there's four of them and only one of me. It's amazing I haven't been booted yet."

"You mean no one from Apple's cybersecurity is helping you?"

"Nah, all those lamers were ousted a while ago. So, since it's just me by my lonesome, maybe you should try being a bit nicer."

I sighed. "Just find me a way in, please."

Pooky's nose went to the ground as she darted down the hall, sending a mental picture of me following her.

Charlie's voice piped up again as I moved after my dog. "Keep going and make a left. I have a door open that will lead you to them, but I don't know for how long." Pooky sat by the door Charlie had indicated and once again slipped past as I pushed it open. "Now past the conference room on your left is a short hallway and that should lead you into where the gremlins are, along with the hostages."

Pressing my back against the wall, I tried to move as stealthily as possible, the cubicles obstructing my vision of things. I could see the hole in the window where the gremlins had thrown out the first negotiator, but I couldn't see the little buggers.

"Spook, give me positions."

"Hostages are in an office along the far wall. There're two gremlins in there with them. Then you have four on computers, but I only know where three of them are: one by where the conference room is, one in the farthest corner away from you, and one to your left. Those are the only ones I've seen so far… and there goes visual."

"What?"

"Fucking shit! I'm no longer in control of the cameras, Doc. I'm blind."

Silently cursing, I looked around. A maze of cubicles, the office where the hostages were being held, and a break room were the main features of the area. Reason told me all gremlins had to be posted up away from that hole in the window, added to Charlie's placement of five of them, if I had to guess the last one should be to my right.

I looked down at Pooky holding a picture of a gremlin in my head. "Time to earn your stripes, little girl. Seek."

Pooky put her nose to the ground and darted down to the right, slinking out of sight around a cubicle. After a moment, I heard an exclamation. *"Ratta wonga?"*

A gremlin in a leather biker jacket jumped up on top of a cubicle wall. Only three feet tall, it had large, bat-wing ears, dark green scales covering its body, and clawed hands and feet. It looked down at Pooky with its bulbous eyes and hissed.

I drew my weapon. "I'll tell you what the fuck."

The scaly creature turned its head and looked at me with genuine surprise. Then a slow, wicked smile came across its face. "So, the wizards are finally here."

"I'm not exactly sure what you mean, but I'm pretty sure I never got a letter to Hogwarts."

It chuckled as its forked tongue washed over a bulbous eye. "You carry a magic weapon, you have a familiar, and you speak our language. You even have that nifty jacket of holding and protection. You're a liar, or you're stupid. Maybe both."

"I admit my weapon is state of the art, my dog knows a few tricks, and I've studied your language. And where my jacket seems to have an endless amount of pocket space and is rather durable, now that you mention it, I'm still not convinced of this wizard accusation."

The gremlin gave a guttural laugh. "A stupid liar, then."

I cocked the hammer back on my gun while Pooky growled from the other side of the cubicle. "Manners, or the young lady over there will teach them to you."

It shook its head, literally keeping one eye on me and one on Pooky. "You're not in the position you think you are, wizard. Call off your familiar and lower your weapon or the hostages get it."

Ed spoke in my ear. "I had ta' shift a little, but I done got one'a them things on a computer in ma' sights."

I lowered my gun, releasing the hammer. "Pooky, leave it. I'm here to negotiate anyway."

An image of Pooky following the command flashed in my mind as the creature's eyes shifted to me. It cackled. "Negotiate? I hold all the cards. Why the fuck would I negotiate?"

I sent her back an image of stalking the two Ed didn't have sighted. "Because you're sorely outnumbered and outmatched."

It scoffed. "You mean the humans? There's nothing they can do."

I muttered into the earpiece, "Eagle Eye, go to work."

Crack!

The gremlin jumped as I heard a squeal, and a plume of smoke started pouring from one of the corner cubicles.

I raised an eyebrow. "I could just pick you off one by one."

The gremlin threw its hands over its head, trying to make itself as small as possible, and crouched on the partition. "You're not alone? *Wonga!* This doesn't make sense. Wizards always work alone."

I shook my head. "How many times do I have to tell you? I don't know any wizards."

It glared at me. Then a slow smile crossed its face as it straightened back up. "Oh, that's even more delicious. They're using you as a pawn. I bet you don't even know what you're involved in."

A high-pitched scream came from another gremlin. Glancing over, Pooky's reflection in a window showed one of the things in her jaws, whipping it back and forth like a chew toy before tossing it into the sunlight. It burst into a cloud of ashes and blew out the hole in the window like sand.

I chuckled. "You're easily distracted. Maybe I'm not the one in over his head."

The leader shouted over its shoulder. "Galdu! Hagnok! Kill the humans!"

I waggled a finger at it as I pointed my weapon at the cubicle to the left. "Ah-ah-ah. Do that, and your last hacker goes down along with the point of your little stunt here."

"Call off your familiar!"

"Pooky, stay."

The gremlin lifted a hand. *"Boldag!"*

The word for *hold.*

Charlie's voice came through. "Visual's back up, Doc. Hey, tell *señor* psychopath to back off the hostages, one is gettin' a little rough with 'em."

I raised my voice as I cocked the hammer back. "Better call off gruesome, I'm getting itchy."

The leader raised its voice, still not taking its eyes off me. "Galdu, *boldag!*"

"Okay, we're good now, Doc."

I gave a curt nod. "Good, now we can resume talking like civilized creatures."

It laughed. "There's nothing civilized about us, human. We were summoned here for one reason and one reason only: maximum chaos."

My ears perked up. "Summoned? Who summoned you?"

The gremlin showed me its needlelike teeth in a huge grin. "All that matters is we feel his power. That and the amount carnage he wants us to inflict."

"His who?"

The gremlin laughed maniacally. "The bogeyman!"

My weapon swiveled onto it. "Where the hell is he?"

The gremlin produced a remote detonator from its jacket pocket. "Oh, you don't need to worry about that, foolish pawn. You need to worry about getting out of here alive."

"Eagle Eye, I need you to take out the window to the office on my mark."

"Copy."

"Spook, I need you to knock that gremlin out of the system, like, yesterday."

"Still workin' on it, Doc. Lizard lips is pretty damn good."

The lead gremlin had a crazed look in its eyes. "Speak up, pawn! We're all going to die anyway. I'd love to know your last words."

A smile crossed my face. *"Wonga."*

The gremlin cocked its head. *"Wonga?"*

The gremlin behind the computer swore. *"Wonga!"*

At the same time, the crack of a rifle rang out and the tinted window in the office burst, dousing the room in sunlight.

Shrieks of anguish came from the office. *"Wongaaa!"*

Firing my weapon, I hit the leader right between the eyes. Its head exploded before it could press the detonator button.

I reiterated to the dead gremlin, *"Wonga."* A death squeal sounded from the last gremlin as I picked up my casing and put it under my hat. "Spook, make sure to wipe all video of this incident."

"On it, Doc."

"Eagle Eye, I'm sure you already know this, but police your brass and get out of there before the blues swarm you."

"Already movin', Doc."

Jaiden's voice spoke up. "What do you want me to do?"

"Ace, start spreading the word this was a false alarm."

"What?"

"Please, trust me on this. Pooky, come." Back under control, I made my way down the elevators and out of the building.

T HE CAPTAIN'S EYES BURROWED into me as I climbed the stairs into her command post. "What the hell happened up there?"

I shrugged as Pooky sat by my right foot, panting, and looking between us. "False alarm."

She reared her head. "It was what now?"

I repeated myself, slower this time. "False… alarm."

The captain chuckled like she had lost her mind. "That's what I thought you said."

I laughed along with her.

Her face abruptly went cold and her right eye began to twitch. She ticked off on her fingers, her eyes never leaving mine. "I had a man tossed out a window, gunfire in a building, three obviously abused hostages rambling on about monsters, ash everywhere like someone set something or some*things* on fire, and over ten pounds of plastique removed by my bomb squad from various support girders, and you're telling me 'false alarm'?"

I shrugged as I ticked off on my fingers. "There're obviously no terrorists to apprehend, no fire or fire alarms, no video footage from the cameras due to a misfortunate malfunction, and you had your officers sweep for shell casings. Did they find any?"

Her eyes bulged. "That's not the point! I'm also pretty sure you had a sniper set up somewhere."

"I even let them check my pockets."

The captain's face turned beet red and a vein near her temple throbbed. "I'm about to have you arrested for obstructing my investigation!"

"I'm federal so good luck with that, but I'll let you look under my hat if you like."

A Russian accent interjected, "I do not think that will be necessary."

"Ah, the cavalry."

The captain turned her wrath on Stravinsky. "Who the fuck are you?"

A voice I didn't recognize chimed in, "At ease, Captain."

"Mayor? What..."

A well-dressed middle-aged gentleman in a tailored dark gray suit held his hands up. "This is deeper than you wanna dive, Mendez. Let it go."

"The hostages?"

"The city will pay their medical bills."

"The property damages?"

"The city has been in contact with Mr. Cook."

Captain Mendez spread her arms wide as her jaw went south. "The press?"

The mayor growled. "Have been taken care of. Thank you, Captain. That will be all."

Without another word, she spun on her heel and barked, "Get everyone out of here, now!"

Stravinsky nodded at the mayor. "*Spasibo*, Mayor Kline."

Mayor Kline scowled at Stravinsky. "I expect that campaign contribution, Agent Stravinsky. It's going to cost the city a lot of money to sweep this under the rug."

Stravinsky continued to stare at him, hands clasped behind his back.

The politician looked around as if someone had overheard. Finally, his eyes found Pooky and me. "I hope you and your… agents have a pleasant afternoon."

"You as well, Mayor."

He turned and walked away.

I took the .50 AE shell casing from under my hat and dropped it in my pocket. "It's a good thing she didn't want to look. And remind me to give Charlie a pay bump for wiping that footage so quickly. Now, not to change the subject, but we need to have a chat."

Stravinsky raised an eyebrow. "Oh, *moy drug*? About what?"

"What do you know about wizards?"

He shrugged. "Not much. I am knowing they are secretive, paranoid of exposure, and very mistrusting. Why ask?"

"Oh, just a little gremlin chirping in my ear."

He snorted. "And you are trusting gremlin?"

I tapped my chin with a finger. "I take down all sorts of paranormal things for a living, Stravinsky. You know, I've never run into a wizard."

"That you know of."

"That I know of…"

He laughed aloud. "If you are thinking I am wizard, *moy drug*, you are mistaken."

"No, not you, but you work for them."

He shrugged. "Maybe."

I shook my head. "I thought this was a federal branch."

He nodded while struggling for the right words to say. "It is, it is… of sorts. More like… worldwide."

"I obviously haven't been asking for enough pay."

"*Nyet!* We pay you quite enough."

"One wonders. You know, it would have been nice for you to be up-front with the information."

He lifted an eyebrow and bunched his cheek up. "What would you have done with information, hmm?"

"That's not the point, Stravinsky, and you know it."

"That is exactly point, Doctor. This is why no one, not even me, knows more than they are supposed to."

"This isn't how you build trust."

He gave me a wide-eyed look of disbelief. "You want trust? Badge, jacket, and weapon you carry. Is that not trust?"

"I…"

He gestured at Pooky. "How about new dog? Hmm? Is that not trust?"

Pooky cocked her head at Stravinsky with one ear standing up.

"Well, I'm sure there's a level of trust that I'll take care of her, but…"

"How about tomes of knowledge I give to you when you graduated from police academy, hmmm?"

I crinkled my nose. "Oh, come now. Everyone needs an instruction manual first day on the job and I had questions that needed answering, you know that."

"Every time your *zadnitsa* is in trouble, I pull it out of fire. Is this not trust?"

"Look, I'm not mad…"

He shook his head. "*Nyet*, you just want answers to questions better left alone. *Moy drug*, now is not time for such lines of thinking, but I promise I will try to let you in more."

"Okay, for now."

Jaiden came striding toward us with Charlie and Ed close behind her. "Stravinsky? Stravinsky! We need to talk."

My friend lifted an eyebrow.

Suddenly, I became very interested in my sleeve as I muttered out of the side of my mouth, "Something about a story you won't let her write."

"Der'mo."

"I don't envy you."

"Ah! Ms. Fox, what can I do for…"

Jaiden shot him one of her award-winning glares with her hands planted firmly on her hips. "Cut the bullshit, Stravinsky. Are you going to let me run these stories or not?"

"What stories? I have denied you nothing…"

She rolled over him like a boulder trap. "Because if I'm not here to print the truth, then I'm not sure I want to be here."

Ed took his hat off and ran his fingers through his hair, a look of pure panic on his face. "Y'all didn't tell me we was workin' fer Commies!"

I tried to reassure him. "We don't work for the Commies, Ed."

Charlie eyeballed Stravinsky. "Yeah, I'm with Ed on this one. Who's Igor? Why is he trying to silence the press? What's with the secret ops? This all reeks of a KGB plot."

I shot him a glare. "You're not helping, Charlie."

"Stravinsky, you still haven't answered my question, are you going to let me print this or not? I made a promise and I'm not about to break it."

"Ms. Fox, think of what a story like this would do to career at XYZ…"

"I'm a 'Merican!"

"Not anymore, Ed. Looks like we're changing your name to Edvard and going out for piroshkis and borscht."

Stravinsky looked at me in disbelief as they all began talking at once. "You work… with this?"

With Pooky leaning into my leg, I couldn't help but smile as I patted her head. "It's not so bad once you get used to it."

Chapter 18

Applebee's, Saratoga Avenue, San Jose, CA—1831 hours

OUTSIDE IN THE DOG-FRIENDLY patio area sitting around a bistro table, a big red umbrella loomed overhead. The angry rush-hour traffic on Saratoga Avenue and the 280 still raged on and the smell of exhaust mixed with the food in the air. Charlie studied Ed with half a smile on his face. "Don't worry, he'll come around. I think."

Ed slowly worked on his Bourbon Street steak with loaded baked potato and steamed broccoli, beer close at hand as he sat muttering to himself. "Y'all can't buy me off with yer fancy dinin'n yer craft beer. Damn Democrat done got me twisted up in a Communist plot."

Pooky sat obediently under the table on the cement floor, accepting bits of my twelve-ounce rib eye.

Jaiden rested her cheek on a fist and scowled at her dinner. "There has to be a way…"

Charlie gave a snort of a laugh as he jerked a thumb at Ed. "A way to what? Shut him up?"

Her eyes lit up. "That's it!"

I raised an eyebrow. "Did you have an epiphany?"

"A pen name. That's the answer."

Charlie chewed on a full rack of barbequed pork ribs. "So you change your name, big deal. It still doesn't take you off camera."

She looked at me over her Tex-Mex shrimp bowl. "If I do a blog like the doctor suggests it will."

A smirk formed as I lifted a forkful of mashed potatoes. "Don't forget your tinfoil hat."

Ed looked at me with one eye squinting. "As long as the truth gets out there. I suppose I can go along with it fer now, but if I git wind I'm workin' fer some foreign gov'ment, we gonna have words. Hear me, hoss? I'm a 'Merican!"

I nodded, speaking around a bite of rare steak. "I appreciate your trust, Ed."

Charlie turned his attention to Jaiden. "What name are you gonna write under?"

She shook her head as she finally started eating. "I don't know, but I'll think of something."

"It should be something catchy, like... Ms. Information or something."

Jaiden wrinkled her nose. "Misinformation? I don't want people to think I'm misleading them."

Charlie shook his head as he felt his pockets. "No, no, no, does anyone have a pen?"

Ed produced one and handed it to him.

Writing it out on a paper napkin, he slid it to her. "Ms. Information."

Her eyes sparkled. "Oh, Charlie, that's genius!"

He went red. "Yeah, I am a genius, aren't I?"

"Don't push it, but… thanks."

Charlie handed Ed back his pen, looking down at his plate. "Yeah, sure, whatever."

I raised my beer in toast. "Well, folks. Here's to a big, fat feather in our caps."

I beamed at them as they raised their glasses in kind. "To success."

A scream came from inside.

From my vantage point, things unfolded through the glass of the door. A waitress ran from the kitchen, screaming, "Oh my God, he's gone crazy!"

Everyone else looked over.

A Hispanic male came out of the kitchen close behind the waitress, wearing a chef's jacket and checkered pants, wielding a large knife. He yelled, "*Qatālu!*"

Scrunching up my face, I cocked my head to the side. "*Qatālu?* Isn't that the Akkadian word for 'kill'?"

"Why'n the holy heck would anyone but you know 'bout somethin' like that, hoss?"

I took a closer look at the young man in his early twenties: waxy, greenish-yellow skin, milky pupils the same color as his irises, oily hair, green drool, knowledge of a dead language. Yup, the guy was possessed. He let out a howl and sprang at the waitress, knife flashing.

I set my drink down and stood. "Shit!"

Charlie raised his eyebrows. "I didn't think her service was *that* bad."

Jaiden snorted. "That's because you were too busy staring at her ass."

"He's possessed! We need to stop him."

Ed vaulted to his feet. "What'cha mean by 'stop,' hoss? Do we put 'im down like a rabid dog 'r somethin'?"

I shouted over the cook's howls and the waitress's screams as tables and chairs were overturned in their struggle. "No, I just need you guys to help me catch him and hold him down."

Ed stood. "A'ight."

So did Charlie. "Aww man, now my dinner is gonna get cold."

"Stay," I commanded Pooky as I handed Jaiden her leash and charged through the door and into the main restaurant. I tackled the cook from behind before he could turn the waitress into ceviche. Knocking over a table and some chairs as we fell to the floor, people screamed as their food went flying. I went into a backward roll, planting my foot in his stomach, and tossed him into a booth.

My mind raced to figure out what could be possessing him. It wasn't a poltergeist. There were no signs that one had infested the building: The walls weren't melting, maggots weren't bursting out of baked potatoes, it wasn't cold with the lights flickering. Which meant this had been a wandering entity of some sort, or else the guy had picked up a cursed object. Unfortunately, each scenario had to be handled differently.

Covered in clam chowder, he clambered to his feet. At least I had his attention on me rather than the waitress. My extendable baton slid out of its sheathe, and with a snap of my wrist, it extended to full length. "I just wanted to let you know, primo job on my steak. Thank you."

"Erēqu!" His milky-white eyes considered me as he hissed the Akkadian word for "flee."

"Hold on, buddy. We're gonna get you some help."

He lashed out with the knife. *"Qatālu!"*

I easily batted his hand away with my baton, stepping to the side like a bullfighter as he charged by, tripping as he stumbled past. He wound up crashing into another table. Enhanced reflexes caused by the spirit possessing him allowed him to regain his footing quickly. The cook's fumbling gave me an opportunity to study him further. Stepping out of the way of yet another clumsy charge, I noticed he wasn't wearing any jewelry nor carrying anything else odd on his person. Now satisfied that no cursed objects were in play, I had to assume this to be a hexis spirit, also known as a parasite. Only lethal when it found a suitable host, a hexis spirit entered through any orifice of an emotionally vulnerable person. The angrier, the more depressed and downtrodden a prospective host, the better. The spirit had the poor cook's mind trapped in his own personal hell of sorrow and anguish while the thing controlled his body. A hexis made people do horrible, unspeakable things while possessed, then left them with no memory of what transpired. Nine times out of ten, the life of the person was ruined beyond repair after the spirit moved on to find a new host.

The waitress screamed, "Oh my God, it's like he's possessed 'r something!"

"Very perceptive, now please stay behind me." Funny enough, this was one of the few times Christianity worked as an accidental antidote. See, the trick to ridding a person of one of these spirits happened to be inhaling frankincense. A lot of the times, when people were possessed by a hexis spirit, the Catholic Church got called upon to rid said person of "Satan" by performing an exorcist. If they didn't bleed the poor soul to death, one of the things they did correctly was to burn frankincense during the whole ordeal. It took longer for it to work that way, and a dab of some pure essential oil underneath the nose could snap the spirit right out, but the Catholic Church liked to put on a barbaric show.

Speaking of shows, the restaurant patrons stared, wide-eyed. Some had their phones out recording. Some even had the good sense to move out of the way to give me more space. I had the distinct feeling that the police would be showing up sooner rather than later, so we needed to end this fiasco quickly.

Ed and Charlie stepped up next to me. "What'r we doin' here, hoss?"

"Again, you need to hold him down, but be careful, we don't want to hurt anyone. Watch it because the thing that's possessing him has enhanced strength and speed due to kicking his adrenal glands into overdrive, but one thing it can't give him is the ability to fight, that comes from muscle memory."

Charlie backpedaled from a knife swing, knocking aside a chair. "Someone forgot to send him the memo."

Ed grabbed up two steak knives from a still-upright table and held one in each hand. Nodding, he gave Charlie the game plan. "I'll keep 'im busy, y'all take out his legs."

The cook yelled and lunged at Ed, stabbing down with his weapon. Ed crossed his knives, catching the flimsy stab between them, and twisted the knife out of his hands. A bewildered look landed on his face as his blade went spinning away. Charlie ducked in low, clipping the chef's legs out from underneath him. Ed dropped his knives and followed them down to the ground.

With Ed and Charlie on top of him, I had enough time to take a bottle from my jacket pocket, unscrew the cap, and dab some of its contents on my finger. "Try to hold his head!"

Ed had grabbed the cook in a headlock as the young man struggled and snapped his teeth. "Easier said than done, hoss!"

Charlie flew back about three feet as the cook thrashed his legs around, attempting to invoke a Mesopotamian god of death. *"Namtar! Namtar! Namtar!"*

Despite Ed's weight, the chef had nearly regained his feet. I jumped into the mix, knocking both to the ground again.

Ed grunted as I scrambled over him. The guy gnashed his teeth while sweating bullets and screaming.

I wiped some of the oil under his nose. "Here we go."

Immediately, he went limp.

Grabbing Ed, I rolled us out of the way. "Look out!"

The cook shot into the air like a champagne cork. Suspended about three feet above the floor, he let out a mighty belch and began to spray vomit all over the place. I shielded Ed and myself the best I could with my overcoat.

Finally, after about thirty seconds, the young man fell back to the floor. His natural color was already returning. As I stood, I surveyed the destruction. Tables overturned, food everywhere, a terrified waitress, Charlie and Ed still on the floor, and a bunch of people covered in pea-soup vomit. I did the only thing I could: I took a bow. "We are your impromptu dinner theater for the evening, ladies and gentlemen, and we thank you for your time and attention."

A few people began to clap, then more. Then the whole room broke into applause.

The chef started to stir. He flinched as I hauled him up. "Let's get a big round of applause for this guy right here!" A few people whistled. "Such a fantastic actor! He really should be in Hollywood, folks."

The waitress looked around confused. "This… this was all… staged?"

The bemused cook wiped some puke from his mouth with the back of his sleeve and gave a timid wave to the audience.

Grinning wide for the cameras on us, I asked, "What's your name, buddy?"

He shook his head and shrugged his shoulders.

I tried again. *"¿Cómo te llamas, señor?"*

"He-Hector?" Good. He didn't seem to be speaking in tongues anymore—an excellent sign.

"¿Cuantos dedos, Hector?" I held up three fingers.

"Morado." An odd response, but Spanish at least.

I patted him on the back, continuing to wave at the crowd. *"Eso es bueno. Un poco de perplejidad de palabras está común, pero lo pasará en algunos dias. Asegúrate de beber agua y tomar un poco de sol. ¿Entiendes?"*

The cook nodded meekly at my direction to drink water and get some sunshine.

"Pluma," he replied, still waving at his newfound fans.

Affidavit From Marcy Hulettson: Evidence ID#: SJ-0023 San Felipe Road, San Jose, CA—1922 hours

Marcy Hulettson put the food she had just purchased on the front seat of her Prius. Her six-year-old daughter whined at her from the back seat as she climbed into her booster chair. "Mom, we want McDonald's!"

Marcy's four-year-old son chimed in as she scooped him up to put him in his car seat. "Yeah, McDonald's!"

She sighed and rolled her eyes. "Both of you are gonna drive me crazy. You both like teriyaki chicken and fried rice, so you can have teriyaki chicken and rice when we get home."

Her daughter wailed, "I don't like teri-yucky chicken!"

Her son kicked his feet into her shins and yelled as she buckled him in, "McDonald's!"

"Summer, that's enough! Dillon, stow it! We'll be home in a few minutes, then we can eat."

Both children continued to screech their displeasure. "Mom!"

"McDonald's!"

The crows flooding the parking lot began to squawk and cackle.

The parking lamps flickered as a cold chill crept into the air.

Marcy accidently dropped her keys on the ground. "Shit!"

As she bent down to pick them up, the parking lamps flickered again, the crows went bonkers, and the noise from her children abruptly stopped.

She straightened up and looked at her daughter's empty booster seat. "Summer?" Her son's seat sat empty as well. The straps she had just fastened not two seconds ago hung limp, still fastened. "Dillon?" Marcy's heart jumped into her throat. She raised her shaky voice. "Summer? Summer, come out, honey, and I'll get you some chicken nuggets and french fries. How… how does that sound?" She began to physically shake, looking frantically around the car for her children. Her voice came out in a squeak. "Dillon?"

They were gone.

Applebee's, Saratoga Avenue, San Jose, CA—1922 hours

"SEE? EVERYTHING IS OKAY, *politseyskiy*."

The restaurant's owner looked at the check Stravinsky had just handed him and nodded. "Yup, we're all okay here."

The police officer cuffing me wasn't about to humor him. "That's not the point, sir."

Stravinsky scowled. "Is excellent point. There were no *zhertvy*, no casualties, *da?*"

"Having the dog there without proper paperwork constitutes…"

He held up a folded piece of paper. "Dog was in patio area, which is allowed by restaurant, so is no health code violation. Besides, violation is fine at most, and does not warrant being arrested. So, *pozhaluysta*… please take handcuffs off clients now, before I am filing harassment suit against you. This is federal operation you are interfering with."

The cop hesitated. "Federal, huh?"

Stravinsky's face remained frozen as he gazed at the officer, folding his arms.

Ed nodded, hands cuffed behind him. "Don't let the fact he's a Russki fool ya. We're 'Merican."

Jaiden glanced at Ed with a scowl on her face. "I can vouch as well, Officer."

They had Charlie up against the police cruiser while the officer's partner searched him. "This job is fucking awesome. I love having federal immunity."

The cop finally gave in. "Alright, but can I have a selfie with you, Ms. Fox? The wife is never gonna believe I ran into you."

Jaiden smiled awkwardly as she handed Pooky's leash over to Stravinsky. "Umm… sure."

The handcuffs clicked off my wrists. "Thanks for calling Stravinsky, Jaiden."

She gave me a thumbs-up as she brushed the lock of hair out of her face, shoulder-hugged the cop, and smiled wide for the selfie.

Stravinsky's sour expression turned on me. "This is second time in one day. Are you trying to set record? Having team was supposed to keep you out of trouble, not get you in more."

I took the service-dog permit for Pooky and filed it in my jacket. "Hey, the first one you knew about. I can't help it if shit seems to be hitting the proverbial fan. Besides, I think there's a larger force at work here."

He opened his mouth to say something as his phone rang. He held up a finger and answered. "*Da?* You are sure? Okay, I will have team there as soon as possible."

"Who was that?"

He hung up the phone and put it back in his pocket. "We have break in case. Two children missing under mysterious circumstances."

A tingle shot down my spine. "Where?"

"East Side San Jose. Near Panda Express off San Felipe Road."

I looked at my team. "Once more into the fray?"

Charlie shook his head. "See, it would have been funnier if you had said, 'Time to boogie.'"

Ed shook his head at Charlie as he gave him the stink eye. "Naw, that ain't funny at all."

"Only because you have zero sense of humor, Ed."

We all piled in Charlie's van and headed down 280 toward East Side.

Parking Lot of Panda Express, San Felipe Road, San Jose, CA—2007 hours

A LIGHT RAIN SPRINKLED down on red and blue lights flashing everywhere in the parking lot. Streetlamps radiated ghostly halos as officers bustled around on the other side of the yellow police tape that already marked off the crime scene. I lifted the tape and ushered everyone under as a blue approached us. "Just what the hell…"

I flashed my badge. "Dr. Darrell Diamondback. I'm part of a special government task force. These are my associates."

A flash of recognition crossed the officer's face as he snapped and pointed at me. "Say, I heard of you. Yeah, you're that uh… what was it… that federal spook hunter guy."

I folded my arms. "'Spook hunter guy'?"

"Yeah. Man, you've been busy today, haven't'cha? Did you really tear up the Applebee's in Santa Clara? And an Apple building out in Cupertino before that, right?"

"Look, I really don't have time…"

He laughed as four other officers stepped up behind him. "Hey, look! It's Scooby-Doo and the gang. Where's the Mystery Machine, guys?"

"Now look here, Officer…"

The officer changed his tone, poking me in the chest with an index finger. "No, you look here. This is our case, this is our beat, and you're not welcome here. We heard about the crap you guys pulled in San Francisco costing two detectives their lives. Well, it's not happening on our watch."

My scowl could have parted the Red Sea. "Where's your chief?"

The officer sneered back as he folded his arms. "Chief Watanabe doesn't wanna talk to you, and said, and I quote, 'You can go fuck yourself.' I suggest you sit this one out, ghost boy."

"Ghost... boy?"

"You heard me."

My fists clenched. "You're making a grave mistake, Officer."

"No, you are. If you and your spook team don't beat it, we have orders to arrest the lot'a ya."

I sighed. "Leave it to Watanabe to still be a bitch after all these years. Look, you understand you're impeding a federal investigation. I could have you..."

"Tell it to someone who cares."

Pooky started to growl.

I raised a hand. "Back off."

At my command, she went silent.

I turned my attention back to the officer. "Every second you waste of mine puts those children further at risk."

He flipped me off. "Yeah? Sit on it and spin."

The other officers continued to chuckle behind him.

I looked at my team and lifted my chin toward the way we had just come. "Come on, guys. Let's go."

We moved back to the other side of the police tape. As we walked out of earshot of the officers, Charlie spoke up. "Who the fuck is Watanabe?"

"Someone from my days at SJPD that for sure won't do us any favors. We're not going to find any help from them."

"You ain't goin' out like that, are you, Doc?"

"Of course not. Does everyone still have their earpieces?" They all nodded. "Time to divide and conquer then. Jaiden." She lifted an eyebrow as she folded her arms. "I need you to get to that witness and find out what happened. Try to get names and full descriptions of the children. See? No eavesdropping or attempting to control the press, just pure investigative journalism."

"Can do." She gave me a smirk then went off to find the mother.

"Charlie."

He saluted me. "Oh captain, my captain."

"I need you in the van. Get me schematics of the surrounding sewer system."

"You got it, Doc." He did a one eighty.

"Also look for places he could be hiding. Try to narrow down the search for me." He waved back as he continued to run toward his van. I took out my UV light. "Ed, Pooky, we're going hunting."

Ed nodded. "Now yer speakin' ma' language, hoss."

"You have your rifle with those special bullets you got from the gremlin fiasco?"

"Only got a few of 'em left. It's all back at the van. Let me go'n grab 'em right quick." He double-timed away.

I looked down at my animal companion, who cocked her head and raised a single ear, waiting for instructions. I patted her on the head. "You need to find me a trail."

Ed reappeared at my side with his rifle slung over his shoulder, breathing heavy.

"Ready?"

He nodded.

I took the newspaper clipping from William's hideout out of my pocket and held it to Pooky's nose. "Seek."

Her eyes bugged as she inhaled, catching the scent, then took off at a trot for a nearby McDonald's. Ed and I followed as I silently hoped she wasn't tracking a Big Mac.

Chapter 19

Affidavit From Jaiden Fox: Evidence ID#: SJ-0025 Panda Express Parking Lot, San Felipe Road, San Jose, CA—2016 hours

"Ma'am?" Even though Jaiden tried to keep her voice nonthreatening, the woman jumped at the sound of it. Wet auburn hair hung in her face as her brown eyes locked onto the reporter. The hood from her light blue rain jacket had been pulled up against the drizzle and her blue jeans and sneakers were damp as she stood there shaking.

She shied away. "I-I d-don't w-want to talk to the p-press."

Jaiden put a hand up. "Wait. You know who I am, right?"

The lady nodded slowly. "You're that reporter for XYZ News San Francisco, Jaiden Fox."

"Then you know I'm working on a string of kidnappings in the area, right?"

Her eyes grew wide. "You know something about my children?"

"That's why I need your help, Ms.…."

"Marcy… Marcy Hulettson. Where are my children?"

Jaiden gently put a hand on her shoulder. "We have people looking for them right now, Ms. Hulettson, but I need you to stay calm and answer a few questions for me. Can you do that?" Marcy nodded vigorously. "Good. First, what are the names of the children?"

"Uh… Summer… Summer and Dillon Hulettson. Please, I told all of this to the officers already."

Jaiden removed her hand from Marcy's shoulder and nodded. "I know, I know, and now you're helping me and my team."

She looked confused. "Your… team?"

"Exactly. Now I need a description of each."

Tears started to well up in her eyes again. "I-I gave their pictures to the cops. Please, I just want to see my children again."

"You will, you will. I just need you to give me a description of them."

The poor woman's eyes shifted around as she rubbed her clasped hands together. "Uh, Summer has blonde hair and b-brown eyes. She was w-wearing a pink jacket, blue jeans, white sneakers, and a uh, a white-and-pink shirt with Pinkalicious on the front."

Jaiden nodded. "What about Dillon?"

She wiped her nose on the back of her sleeve. "Dillon has c-curly brown hair and b-brown eyes. He was wearing a b-blue hoodie with a dump truck on it, black pants, and b-blue sneakers."

"And how long ago did you notice the children missing?"

"A-about an hour and a half, maybe."

"What exactly happened?"

She choked back another sob. "I was s-strapping them into their c-car seats. I-I dropped my keys. When I looked up, they were both… gone, just like that."

"You didn't see anything else?"

"N-no." Marcy began bawling uncontrollably.

Jaiden touched her earpiece. "You get all that, Doc? I don't think I'm going to get much more out of her."

McDonald's Parking Lot, San Felipe Road, San Jose, CA—2021 hours

I NODDED DESPITE THE fact she couldn't see me. "Thanks, Ace. Try to get her to stay at the scene. When we pull the children out, we're gonna need her nearby."

"Copy that. Don't worry, I don't think she's going anywhere."

"Spook, what do you have for me?"

"I've got an entrance point. Over by McDonald's there should be a manhole for the sewer."

My UV light had also picked up a bright trail that the rain couldn't wash away. "10-4, Pretty Girl is leading us in that direction."

"Well, what do you need me here for, then? Have I already been replaced by a dog?"

"Negative, Spook. Pretty Girl can't give me schematics to the sewer system. Besides, you were able to confirm my suspicions. I don't like wasting time in the dark."

"That dog can smell crack in a hooker's ass from a thousand feet away, she'll be able to find him quicker than I will. I should be down there with you guys."

"Negative. Hold your position."

"Whatever, Doc."

Ed's voice sounded behind me. "He means well."

I nodded. "I just don't need him or Jaiden getting hurt this time."

"Y'all need ta' focus less on that'n more 'bout what's going on, hoss. Don't make the same mistake twice."

"Trust me, Ed. I don't intend to."

San Jose Sewer System, San Jose, CA—2021
hours

SUMMER HULETTSON SCREAMED AT the top of her
lungs, "I-I w-want m-my mommy!"

Her brother Dillon screamed as well. "Teri-yucky!"

Rats scrambled to and fro on the floor of his new
hovel. They paused to sniff at the crying children in
cages, sat on a smelly old armchair in the center of the
room, their whiskers twitching. An end table next to
the chair held a small, broken '80s-style record player
and a bottle of Jack. A hanging overhead lamp had
been strung up and tried to drive away the darkness
by its lonesome as it flickered, threatening to die at
any given moment. A cracked flat-screen with the
cord missing sat on a stand in front of the armchair.
The bogeyman looked around with a twisted sneer as
he snatched the bottle off the table and took a drink.
He set it back down, sighed, and smiled a wicked
grin. "Life for Daddy is good-goody-good again. The
sounds of the tormented ringing in Daddy's ears, the
fresh smell of innocence waiting to be broken by the
Darkside. Yes, this is what Daddy needed. To relax
and have some fun… fun on the Darkside."

"And we have friends. Powerful friends that can help
Daddy…"

He pounded the armrest with a fist, then pointed at nothing. "Shut your goddamn filthy mouth! Daddy needs no help. How dare you suggest Daddy needs help. Daddy will teach you a lesson if you ever talk like that again."

"Sorry. Maybe… maybe we should play some music to make Daddy happy?"

"Yes… yes. Daddy found the record on the Darkside. Play it for Daddy." He reached over and started the record player. "Folsom Prison Blues" warbled through the dank corridors.

"Does… does Daddy remember what life was like without the poor little guy?"

He grabbed his bottle and took another drink. "Of course Daddy remembers. Daddy remembers everything. Did you know that mean old bastard and the selfish bitch were happier without the poor little guy? Daddy would hear them fight at night, blaming the poor little guy for their problems, their mistakes, their insecurities on the Darkside. It wasn't fair! They could have been a family. The poor little guy wasn't so bad, maybe different, but not so bad. They just needed to spend time with the poor little guy, care for the poor little guy, to… to love the poor little guy, but they didn't! They didn't, and it made Daddy rage inside. It made Daddy furious to know they hated the poor little guy. That's why Daddy swore to protect the poor little guy in the Darkside, no matter what."

"Why… why did the mean old bastard and the selfish bitch hate him?"

"Because the poor little guy was special, that's why. That's what they always said."

"Does… does it make Daddy sad?"

"No, Daddy doesn't get sad. Daddy gets mad! Mad, mad, mad!"

The bogeyman got up from his chair, threw open a cage door, and reached inside. "Come to Daddy, yah little shit."

The young boy had stopped crying and now stared at him wide-eyed, tears and snot running down his face. "W-where's m-my m-mommy?"

His sister rattled her cage. "You leave him alone!"

The twisted specter chuckled and pointed a finger at her. "Shut it, 'cause you're next!"

He carried the screaming, struggling toddler over to his chair where a switch lay. Picking it up, he put his face level with the child as it continued to whimper. "This is gonna hurt you a lot more than its gonna hurt Daddy, but it's for your own good. Now shut it and take your medicine like a man."

McDonald's Parking Lot, San Felipe Road, San Jose, CA—2030 hours

I SNAPPED OUT OF my dizzy spell as I heard Ed's voice. "A'ight there, hoss? That's the second time I done see ya go lame. Y'all got a wire disconnected 'r somethin'?"

"Sorry, Ed. I'm okay. Really. Let me help you with that."

Ed and I moved the manhole cover. "I don't really relish the idea'a goin' down there."

I handed him my Vicks after dabbing some under my nose. "You can still walk away from this 'Communist' plot if you like, I won't stop you."

He considered me for a second, then accepted the jar, following suit. "Quit bein' a fuckin' moron'n git in the damn hole, yah damn Democrat."

I descended the ladder and had Ed hoist Pooky down by her harness. He followed. When he hit bottom, I held the article to Pooky's nose again. "Seek!"

Pooky sniffed the air, then immediately put her head down and covered her nose with her paws. She began to whine. I shined my UV all over, but no good. I found an ectoplasmic trail leading in each direction. I frowned. "Shit."

Ed looked at me. "What now, hoss?"

Sighing, I touched my earpiece. "Time for plan C. Spook?"

His voice sounded in my ear. "What's up, Doc?"

"I think Pretty Girl is too overwhelmed down here, and I've got a false ectoplasmic trail, so I'm going to need your lead."

He took on a note of bravado. "While I was sitting here with nothing to do, I created an algorithm to help narrow down possible hideouts."

I had the distinct feeling that a catch hung in the balance. "Just like I told you to do? Impressive, but what's the bad news?"

"There are two possible locations, each in different directions."

"Your thoughts?"

His keyboard clicked in the background. "One second, I'll send what I got to your phone."

My phone vibrated, and I brought it out, pulling up the screenshot of the map Charlie had created. Two red lines in two different directions had been crudely drawn out.

"What parameters did you use for your algorithm?"

Charlie began the list. "Dimensions he'd need to fit everything he had, for one."

I nodded. "Good, he's a creature of habit and will want to replicate his den as close as he can to the last one."

"It also needs to be deep enough in that he feels comfortable."

"Very good. Which one has a second manhole nearby? He'll want an easy escape route if things go south."

"Doc, you're brilliant."

My lip twitched up into a grin. "I know. You're not so bad yourself. You may have missed your calling as a profiler."

"Go left. There's an alcove down and to the right that fits."

Ed, Pooky, and I moved down the dark, stinky tunnel at a quick pace. As we progressed, Pooky began to dance and growl with her ears flat back and her tail down.

Ed stopped, whispering, "Is it… hot? Hotter than it should be?"

It wasn't like Ed to break the silence, but I noticed it as well. The sewer had been growing unbearably hot as the smell of rotting flesh and brimstone began to mix with the stink of hydrogen sulfide. No wonder Pooky hadn't been able to track William's scent from the newspaper clipping; her sensitive nose must have run for cover against the reek. My flashlight caught the sight of the sewer water boiling before it fizzled out, Ed's light following suit, leaving us in pitch dark.

A soft blue glow began to emanate from under my jacket, lighting up our surroundings. As I drew my weapon from its holster, I saw a series of Nordic runes down the barrel and handle shining against the dark. On the bottom of the pommel, a glowing *valknut*, the sign of Odin in Norse mythology. I sighed. "Well… shit."

The ghostly light allowed me to see Ed's sweaty face. "Yer peashooter ain't never done that b'fore, has it?"

"Only in the presence of strong magic."

"In the presence'a say-what-now?"

Pooky took a stance and barked fiercely at the shadows.

A voice that sounded like a thousand children echoing each other came from the darkness. "Friends, come and play with us… play with us… play with us."

Before my eyes, a creature completely constructed from bone clambered out of the abyss. It's long, sharp, demonic face had two wicked-looking eye sockets glowing with brilliant red orbs. Below a thin nasal cavity, a gaping mouth full of jagged, sharp teeth clicked opened and closed as it considered us. Its bulky white frame filled most of the tunnel as its long-clawed fingers grasped the archway, preventing any forward progress. A tail crafted from vertebrae with spikes sticking out of the tip swished back and forth, supported by two legs oddly bent at the knees, making it look as if it would spring at us at any given moment. Negative energy swirled and flowed between the bones, as if they were smoldering.

Ed's lips began to tremble out the Lord's Prayer. "Our F-Father, who a-art in H-Heaven, hallowed be thy n-name…"

The eerie, childlike voice echoed through the sewer again. "Olly olly oxen free… olly olly oxen free… olly olly oxen free."

Before me loomed something I had only ever read about in the tomes Stravinsky had given me after graduating from the police academy. "An ostéon."

"A-a say what now?"

"A bone demon."

Ed's hands gripped his rifle as he shouted at me, "Don't'cha tell me nothin', yah damn Democrat!"

I backed up, scowling. "Ed, get a hold of yourself! Don't succumb to the aura of anger its projecting."

He shook his head, blinking rapidly. "Sorry, hoss. Damn thing's messin' with ma' noggin."

"It was most likely summoned by William, forged from the bones of his victims. It's straight from the fifth plane of hell, which explains the excessive heat and overwhelming stench. It feeds on fear, jealousy, and resentment, so it will try to draw those feelings out of you. Make sure to keep yourself in check, as we don't want to start fighting each other."

Ed squinted. "I've had practice controllin' ma' emotions b'fore, hoss. Some intense trainin' called the Marine Corps, it jus' caught me off guard is all. How do we kill this damn thing?"

The tip of the bone demon's tail appeared over its shoulder and fired a barrage of spikes at us. "Do you like games… games… games?"

Pooky jumped in front of us.

I screamed in horror. "Pooky, no!"

Instead of getting impaled, Pooky encased us in a blue sparkling hemisphere, the bone shards that meant to skewer us bouncing harmlessly away.

The demon wailed. "No fair! No fair! No fair!"

Ed looked himself over, his eyes wide. "I don't know what the hell's goin' on here, but we gonna have ourselves a long talk if we git out'a this alive, hoss."

"Over a beer, but for now, you kill it like this." Pooky dropped her magic shield as I leveled my weapon and fired, blowing two holes in its sternum.

The demon emitted a high-pitched, earsplitting screech.

Ed brought his rifle to his shoulder, letting loose a round that cracked its skull, but didn't puncture it. "Why didn't it punch through like yers did?"

"Not sure, but at least it will help keep it busy." I lost my footing on the slick, narrow walkway, teetering on the edge of the ravine of sewer water.

Its voice began a childish chant as its hand reared back. "One potato, two potato, three potato, four…"

Ed jumped in front of me. "Look out!"

Its backhand sent him tumbling against the wall, the rifle flying from his hands.

I screamed as the demon gave a childlike laugh. "Ed!"

The negative energy around it began to tendril out farther from its body as it raised a hand to smite me where I stood. "Five potato, six potato, seven potato, more…"

As its hand came down, I fired two more shots, blowing off one of its phalanges to prevent it from squashing me. As its hand slammed down, it shook the ground and cracked the pavement. Unfortunately, the quake dropped me to the ground as well.

Pooky ran up the hand like a ramp and clamped her jaws on its ulna, growling while whipping her head back and forth.

The ostéon primed its middle finger behind its thumb, ready to flick her off like a flea. "Our mother told us to pick the very best one…"

"And you're not it, motherfucker!" Charlie's voice sounded from the shadows as he stepped out from the darkness with a shotgun leveled. He fired twice, blowing off chips of bone from its hand with the silver buckshot. The demon screeched as I laid on my back and aimed, then emptied the last three shots from my clip into its left eye socket. I wound up blowing a hole through the back of the skull.

"No! Help us, help us, help us…" The bone demon wailed as the red in its eyes faded and individual bones began to rain down. Pooky leaped to me and used her magic shield to cover us.

Charlie called out, "Doc? You okay?"

Grunting, I pushed one of the demon's ribs out of my way. "Yeah, you?

"Yeah, I'm good."

I stood panting as the smell of rotting flesh faded to be replaced with the overwhelming scent of sewer gas again. "Thank you for the assist, Charlie, even though it was against orders.'"

"Orders? Are you fuckin' for real right now?"

Pooky whimpered and nudged Ed with her nose.

"Ed!"

He still wasn't moving.

Charlie ran over and dropped to his knees, putting the tips of his index and middle fingers at Ed's radial artery. "He's still alive."

He moved away as I came to kneel beside the wounded. After feeling the back of his head, I checked the responsiveness of his pupils by pulling his eyelids open and shining a light into them. "He's got a concussion, and his arm is broken. We need to get him an ambulance, now." Pooky whined again and began to lick Ed's face, still trying to get him to move. I touched my earpiece. "Ace, you copy?"

"Yeah, what's going on down there?"

"I need you to get an ambulance here, stat."

"What happened."

"It's Ed. He's alive but needs a neck brace and a stretcher."

"10-4, calling one now."

I removed the empty clip and loaded another into the well.

Charlie raised an eyebrow. "Has it always done that?"

Racking a bullet into the chamber, I put it away. "No, it does it when I'm close to magical things. I need you to stay here with Ed until help comes."

"Just me alone?"

"No, you'll have Pooky too."

"You're leaving me with Clifford the big-ass puppy? Jeez thanks, Doc. I feel so much safer now. What the fuck are you gonna do?"

A sigh escaped me as I looked farther down the tunnel. "Me? I've got to take down William."

He crossed his arms and scrunched his eyebrows. "You sure?"

I shook my head. "He's not getting away this time."

Charlie shrugged. "If you're sure."

I turned to Pooky. "Okay, girl, I need you to guard Ed and Charlie until help comes. You hear me?" She whined and bumped my leg, sending me a mental picture of her going with me. I knelt, put my hands under her jowls, and looked her in the eye. "No, I need you to do this for me." She licked my nose in affirmation. I gave her a hug and kissed her on the top of the head. "I'll be topside before you know it."

She barked and settled down with her big brown eyes focused on Ed.

As I began to make my way down the damp corridor, Charlie called after, "Remember, you're not alone. Your sister's with you."

I paused and gave a long look over my shoulder. "Thanks."

"No, for real, Doc. She's right fuckin' there."

I looked down at my side and for the briefest moment, I swore I could see Daisy in her pink jacket, blue jeans, and LA Gears standing beside me.

Chapter 20

BOTH LOCKED IN THEIR cages, the unconscious children made no noise.

"Good, Daddy can rest in the Darkside."

"That… that was fun. How much longer until we can play again?"

"Daddy wants to rest. Yes, rest." His eyes began to close

A crack like thunder and the tunnels shaking violently startled him out of his stupor.

He sat up, gripping the armrests, head on a swivel like an oscillating fan. "What? What was that Daddy heard… heard in the Darkside?"

"We don't know."

A rat jumped onto his hand as he brought it eye level. His eyes flared. "Of course you don't know, only Daddy knows. You! Check the Darkside for Daddy and make sure no one is there. Go, go now!"

The rat ran down his leg and out into the darkness beyond.

"Maybe… maybe it was our demon pet, the one Daddy made from the old bones of our friends."

The bogeyman shook his head and sniffed at the air. "No! No, no, no, he smells like farts, and Daddy thinks farts are funny. Daddy can't smell farts. Daddy smells… something spicy, something leathery, something… from the Darkside." A high-pitched squeal cut through the gloom. "What? What's going on? Daddy can't see in the Darkside anymore. What was that? It looked like…"

The Lair of the Bogeyman, San Jose Sewer System, San Jose, CA—2043 hours

M Y VOICE SPOKE FROM the shadows as I let go of the vision. "Hello again, William."

He growled. "Big Brother."

I stepped into the light. "That's right, William. It's time to end this."

He laughed. "That's true, Big Brother. Are you and your mean friends here to try to get rid of Daddy again? To try and send him back… back to the Darkside? You'll fail! Fail, fail, fail, just like you did last time."

I shook my head as I stepped deeper into the maintenance alcove. "No, William. It's just you and me."

"Stop using that name! That's not Daddy's name anymore. Not Daddy's name in the Darkside."

"It's what your mother named you, isn't it?"

He roared. "That selfish bitch is dead. So is the mean old bastard. So is William! Daddy killed them, Daddy killed them all! There is only Daddy and the Darkside!"

"Poor William. Poor little guy."

A laugh escaped his lips as he mimicked my sister's voice. "You're going to die, Dare. You're going to come to the Darkside with me. Come play with me, Dare. Come play with me on the Darkside!"

Ignoring his attempt to shake me, I redoubled my efforts to stay in his head. "What about your father, William? Is he dead too?"

The malicious specter finally stood from his chair. "Of course. Daddy sent that mean old bastard to the Darkside."

"You see, William, I'm not so sure you did."

William scoffed. "Daddy crushed that mean old bastard's neck and felt him go… go to the Darkside. That mean old bastard even shit his pants! Of course he's dead, stupid, stupid Big Brother."

"That's funny, because I see him standing right in front of me."

The bogeyman's face screwed up. "What?"

"See, I met the guy, your father. Well, I met his deformed energy in the form of a shadow. I'm sure he wasn't any more pleasant in death than he was in life. The thing is, you look and sound exactly like he did."

William's face contorted into an ugly mask of rage as he stamped his foot like an angry child, making the ground quake. "You don't know anything! You don't know anything about Daddy, about the Darkside. You found their souls and set them free, didn't you? You weren't supposed to find them. They were supposed to suffer forever. How did you find them? How? How? How?"

I held out a crumpled newspaper clipping. "Lose something?"

William's eyes flared as a sneer crossed his face. "The poor little guy's story from the Darkside. Daddy wondered where that went."

"It helped me to better understand you."

He gave me a supercilious look. "It doesn't matter. Soon you'll be on the Darkside and so will your friends, 'cause Daddy will find them… find them and send them to the Darkside forever. Then Daddy will continue to eat the sweet, tender flesh of the innocent. Like countless playmates before that. Daddy is the bogeyman! Daddy is the eternal Darkside!"

"Is that really what you want, William? To be just like your father? Or those boys who taunted and abused you?"

William covered his ears and stamped his foot again, cracking the grimy concrete. "Shut up!"

"Yeah, William, I know about them too. I know a lot more about the scared, broken little boy you really are."

His face went rigid, then a smile spread across his lips as he began to laugh. "Only because, with Daddy's help, you had a taste of the Darkside. A taste of what the poor little guy went through. Daddy made you scared and broken too, Big Brother!"

I nodded. "Maybe I was, I admit it. You killed my sister, Daisy. My parents didn't believe me when I told them what happened."

He laughed maniacally. "And they shunned you! They shunned you just like everyone shunned the poor little guy. You have no one here to save you from the Darkside. No one."

"I overcame it, William. I became something more, and I have friends now. Real, genuine friendship, and I'm not willing to put them in harm's way again. I don't need them to bring you down. This is between you and me."

He looked at the cages, then back at me. "Take Daddy down? Ha ha ha ha! You can't hurt Daddy, Big Brother! You've already failed so many times. You couldn't save your sister, you couldn't save any of Daddy's playmates, you couldn't save your nasty cat, and you won't save them."

"Her name was Maddison Bell, William."

"Daddy doesn't care what its name was!"

I nodded at the cages. "Their names are Summer and Dillon Hulettson."

He chuckled. "Their names are Dinner and Breakfast."

My eyes narrowed. "And I did fail at first, I admit."

"That makes you weak and worthless! Only the strong don't fail, like Daddy."

I drew my weapon, still glowing, and brought it to my side. "But I always kept trying, William. I didn't give up like you did."

He clenched his fists, his eyes casting an eerie red glow in the low light. "I-I was murdered by my own father! What was I supposed to do?"

"And that gives you the right to be a bigger dick then he was? That makes you want to hurt people when all you supposedly wanted was love, a family, companionship?"

"Shut up!"

Sighing, I shook my head. "I'm going to offer you something you never had in life: my friendship. Please, stop this madness, William. Only you can choose to break the cycle. Only you can choose not to be like your father. Take my hand and take my advice, let it go."

The bogeyman let out an earsplitting roar and charged.

Affidavit From Charlie Mopps, Evidence ID#: SJ-0030 Manhole by the McDonald's Parking Lot, San Felipe Road, San Jose, CA—2055 hours

CHARLIE SHOOK HIS HEAD, hands on his knees and breathing hard after putting Ed's rifle and shotgun back in the van. "I should have gone with him."

Jaiden sat watching Ed with a neck brace, strapped to a stretcher, being loaded into the back of an ambulance. "I needed your help with all this, especially getting Princess Fat Butt up the ladder and getting rid of the weapons so we don't get in trouble for them."

Pooky leaned in and licked her nose.

She closed her eyes, scrunched her face, and waved her hands. "*Ack!* Crazy dog."

A not so pleasant voice interrupted. "What the hell do you people think you're doing?"

Pooky set herself in a protective stance and began to growl. The officers stopped, hands moving toward their weapons.

Charlie shot a dirty look at the cop as he pulled out his phone and began to record. "Hey, look, Jaiden. It's Officer McButtmunch."

The cop pointed at Charlie. "Watch your fat-ass mouth, and put that stupid thing away."

Charlie continued to film. "It's not interfering with you doing your duty so, no, I don't think I'll comply with that request. I'm also notifying you that I'm recording so it will stand up in court. As for calling you Officer McButtmunch, Officer McButtmunch, I'm stating my opinion. That's a form of free speech and protected by the First Amendment, so suck it."

The officer sneered at Charlie as his hand moved away from his pistol. "You know what isn't protected by the First Amendment, wiseass? Trespassing on city property. Want me to arrest you?"

Jaiden scowled. "That will never stand up in court, and you know it. There's no law that says we can't go down there, even though it may not be safe to go spelunking in a sewer system, but that's not the point: It's not illegal."

Charlie nodded. "Now how about being a good pig and go do something useful? Like maybe your job."

"Which is what, according to you?"

One hand on his phone, the other made air quotes. "Oh, you know, 'serve and protect' or some shit like that?"

Just then, the unmistakable crack of gunfire echoed from the manhole.

Pistols began to jump into the hands of the officers. "What the hell was that?"

Charlie's eyes went wide. "Umm, I wouldn't go down there if I were you."

The last thing Charlie ever saw of the guy was his scowl. "Shut the fuck up, you little pissant. If I wanted your opinion, I'd give it to ya."

All five officers clambered down the ladder.

Jaiden looked at Charlie, adjusting her glasses and brushing her hair back. "What now?"

He didn't hesitate as he quit recording and dialed 9-1-1. "Fuck them, I'm calling another ambulance 'cause I got a feeling they're gonna need one. You call Stravinsky."

Jaiden fished her phone out of her pocket. "I sure hope the doctor's okay."

San Jose Sewer System, Lair of the Bogeyman,
San Jose, CA—2101 hours

"I'LL KILL YOU, BIG Brother!" The light flickered as William disappeared amid his charge.

I saw his intent in my mind's eye and ducked.

He appeared beside me, his fist sailing over my head. I danced away and leveled my weapon. "William, don't!"

He charged me like an angry rhino. "Die!"

Again, I anticipated the move, spinning away from his crushing grip just in time to shuffle backward and out of reach. "William, please don't make me do this. Think of your mother."

He pointed a huge, gnarled finger. "You! You leave the selfish bitch out of this. That selfish bitch didn't love Daddy! She didn't love anyone but herself."

"Didn't she? How many beatings did she take for you, William?"

He covered his ears again. "Shut up!"

"How many times did you watch her throw herself in front of your father's wrath, just to protect you?"

His hands still covering his ears, William started counting. "One, two, three…"

"You watched him beat her bloody so many times while you stood by, screaming, crying, powerless to do anything about it, fighting the impulse to help because you knew if you did, his viciousness would fall back on you tenfold. Yet you snapped her neck without a second thought. Don't you have any remorse for what you did to the only person who ever loved you? Don't you feel any regret for the only person that ever cared about you? The only person that could truly empathize with your situation?"

He looked around wildly. "She…"

"Her final wish was for you to be set free, William."

He howled like a wounded animal. "I am free! Daddy set me free in the Darkside!"

I shook my head, cocking the hammer of my gun. "No, no you're not. But I'm here to free you."

He reached out to grab me. "You? You're here for a one-way trip to the Darkside, Big Brother!"

I fired, hitting him in the chest as he roared. I almost dropped my weapon to cover my ears. My heart had made that sound when I watched him carry off Daisy.

Five cops burst into the area with their guns drawn. "Freeze!"

I looked around, but William had disappeared into the shadows. "What are you idiots doing?"

"Arresting you for negligent discharge of a firearm, asshole!"

I recognized the douchebag cop who had denied me access to the crime scene earlier. My face fell. "You've got to be kidding me."

"Drop your weapon and put your hands up, now!"

I whispered as I shook my head, "You damn fools."

The lead officer noticed the children in cages. He lowered his weapon as he squinted. "What the fuck?"

Heavy breathing echoed in the darkness as the light overhead continued to buzz and flicker. The temperature dropped to thirty degrees in nothing flat as a pungent breeze stirred up from nowhere.

One of the officers got pulled into the shadows by the scruff of his neck, screaming.

It cracked like a macadamia nut.

I put my back to the wall as the remaining four officers fired wildly into the darkness.

A bloody hand reached out and grabbed another officer by his ankle, pulling him off his feet and dragging him screaming into the void.

He yelled, "No! No, no, please, no…"

A scream followed by a squelching sound, a heap of bloody entrails splattered all over the floor as the bogeyman threw the officer back into the light in front of the others, bleeding out with a hole in his stomach.

Then there were three.

The lead officer stammered as he looked upon the mutilated body. "Holy fuck! Holy fuck! Holy fuck!"

The muzzle flash of another officer's weapon illuminated William briefly, grinning, standing behind him. He promptly ripped the officer's head from his body, the spine still dangling from it and threw it aside as the body fell.

"*Aaarrrrggghhh!*" The second-to-the-last officer decided to go out like Rambo, emptying his magazine into William until his gun clicked in protest.

William grabbed him by the face with a single hand, gritted his teeth in a sneer, and squeezed until the guy's head squished like an overripe berry.

"Holy fuck!" The lead officer let his weapon clatter to the ground, his hands shaking uncontrollably.

The murderous specter finally stepped in front of the last one, his fists, overalls, and jacket covered in fresh blood and viscera. His greasy hair hung in his face as he snarled with scorching red eyes at the quaking man.

Bottom lip trembling, he looked up. "Wh-what in the h-holy fuck are you?"

William shoved his face into the cop's and bellowed, spittle flying everywhere, "I'm the motherfuckin' bogeyman, bitch!"

The officer screamed as the specter lifted him off the floor by his neck then squeezed until he crushed the officer's windpipe along with the upper vertebrae. Staring into the cop's panic-stricken face, William drooled with pleasure as he watched the life fade from his victim's eyes. He tossed the body away like a broken toy, his breathing raspy and shallow from the wound in his chest. Black ectoplasm mixed with the blood on his overalls as he turned to face me.

I stood, hanging my head. "Just like your father."

His glared could have scared a Siberian prisoner straight. "Daddy has had enough of your games, Big Brother. Time for you to join… join the Darkside!"

I raised my weapon, but this time, William disappeared in a cloud of negative energy. He phased through the wall behind me and shoved me to the concrete, knocking the Desert Eagle from my hand. It skidded away across the muck-covered ground.

Wheezing, he advanced. "This looks familiar, doesn't it? You've been here before with Daddy, haven't you, Big Brother? On the ground, defenseless with no one around to help you!" His foot lashed out and caught me in the face. "Getting the shit kicked out of you!" I skidded across the floor on my back, dizzy, blood welling from my nose. "Laying broken!" He picked me up and threw me into a wall. My ribs cracked as I slumped against it, gasping in pain. "Alone!" Picking me up by the shirt, he punched me in the face, causing it to swell. I dropped in a heap at his feet. "Bleeding!" I coughed up blood as he grabbed me by the scruff of the neck and hoisted me to my knees. His face looked down on mine, so close I could smell his rancid breath. "Any last words before you go to the Darkside forever, Big Brother?"

A heavy clatter sounded and I caught movement out of the corner of my eye. My gun skidded across the pavement toward me.

I snatched the weapon up, pressed it against his forehead, and looked him in his hateful red orbs. "I release you, William Twitch."

His head exploded in a gore of black ectoplasm and the body slumped to the ground. Smoke billowed from it, as it did when he had died as a child. It swirled quickly in a vortex until it dissipated with an audible *pop*, replaced by the sound of soft weeping and the ghostly blue outline of William as a boy lying on the ground with a gaping wound through his heart and another through his forehead. What looked like blood surrounded both, but nothing issued from the wounds themselves. He sobbed even harder as I gazed at his young face, glowing blue tears streaming down his cheeks. "I-I never meant to hurt anyone."

I could feel his life force fading. "I know, William."

"I j-just wanted people to l-like me."

I nodded, keeping my voice gentle. "I understand."

"I j-just w-wanted someone to l-love… me." His head fell to the side, his eyes still open, distant and staring.

My eyes welled up with tears. "I'm sorry, poor little guy. This is just where I fit into the story. Rest in peace now."

"You did it."

I looked up. "D-Daisy?"

A blue outline of my sister stood over William and me as hundreds of other kids milled about. Some watching us, some staring at William, most of them crying. Ian Johnson, Kayla Sanchez, Montel Evens, and Maddison Bell were among them. My sister continued to beam at me like the sun among the echoes of, "He freed us. We're free."

"I knew you could do it, Dare."

Tears began to leak down my face as my esophagus constricted. "Day! I-I'm sorry. I'm s-so, so sorry."

She shook her head. "You have nothing to be sorry for."

I looked into her eyes, stammering as sobs wracked my body. "N-no! I f-failed y-you."

Her nose, lips, cheeks, and eyes all scrunched together at once. "Darrell James Diamondback. You stop it right now."

"But…"

"No nuts, no butts, no coconuts, you never failed me. Except you couldn't make sense of those dreams I sent you. God, you're so dumb."

I gave a chuckle as I dabbed at my eyes with my sleeves. "I thought it might be you after Charlie and I talked, but I couldn't be sure. I'm sorry you've been anchored to him all this time."

She hugged me. "You never gave up on me, big brother. I couldn't be prouder of you."

I hugged her back. "I miss you so much."

"I know, and I know Mom and Dad do too."

"They had every right to stop talking to me."

"Stop beating yourself up and go talk to them."

I shook my head. "They don't want to see me. Dad doesn't believe and Mom just goes catatonic every time I bring you up."

She squinted as she frowned. "Didn't I tell you not to be stupid? Besides, they need to know you solved my case and caught the bad guy."

I shook my head. "I…"

She looked at me with those deep-blue eyes. "Promise me you'll try?"

Finally, I gave her a curt nod. "I-I'll try, I promise."

William began to disappear, evaporating into thousands of small dazzling blue lights.

Daisy looked at his dissipating body as she began to dissipate herself in the same manner. "I've gotta go now, Dare. Please tell Charlie goodbye for me. I really liked him."

I reached out my hand. "No, wait! Don't leave yet!"

She waved solemnly. "Sorry, Dare, but it's calling me. I gotta go. I love you, big brother. I love you. I…"

"I love you too, Daisy," I whispered into the empty dark as the record of "Folsom Prison Blues" skipped, making The Man in Black repeatedly sing the word "cry."

Manhole by the McDonald's Parking Lot, San Felipe Road, San Jose, CA—2147 hours

I EMERGED FROM THE sewer with Summer Hulettson's arms clasped around my neck and Dillon cradled in one arm on the opposite side of my bad ribs. Our agents controlled the crime scene as people swarmed everywhere. I noted an ambulance nearby and stumbled toward it, laboring for breath. Someone tried to take one of the children from me—it might have been an EMT, I wasn't sure. They got an elbow to the face for their efforts.

Jaiden came running up. "It's okay, Doctor. I have them."

I blinked at her for a moment then finally let go. She took Summer from my back then took Dillon and handed them off to an EMT. Next, she dropped a blanket around me and helped me sit on the bumper of the ambulance. She didn't say anything, just sat there quietly with me, her perfume washing the stink of the sewers from my nose, her face radiating the warmth of the sun in the cold October rain, her eyes silently telling me it would all be okay, and I believed them.

Pooky leaned into my leg as she rested her chin on my knee, her eyes looking back and forth between Jaiden and me.

Charlie walked over and the episode with the bone demon flashed in my mind. My voice came out in a croak. "How's Ed?"

Charlie nodded. "On his way to Kaiser Santa Clara. He'll live."

"Why not Kaiser San Jose?"

"Dude, have you seen Kaiser San Jose? It's hella ghetto."

Jaiden glanced sideways at me, the flashing lights reflecting off the lenses of her glasses. "What happened to William?"

"Gone."

Charlie looked around. "I don't see your sister anymore."

"She said to tell you goodbye. She liked you."

"Aww, dude. You saw her?"

Nodding, I pulled the blanket around me a little tighter. "She saved my life."

Stravinsky came striding toward me. "Congratulations on rescuing *deti*, Doctor. Did you happen to see five officers?"

"Dead."

His face stitched into a scowl as he swore. "*Der'mo.* Now I am having to speak with Watanabe."

I looked at Jaiden. "Are the children alright?"

She nodded as she took my hand. "They're scared out of their wits, and they'll both have physical and emotional scars, but they're back with their mother now. You were brave."

I shrugged. "I just did what I promised William's mother I'd do."

As we sat there watching the responders buzz around the scene, it began to rain harder. I looked up as the drops pelted my face and thought of my little sister. She had been far braver than I in the end.

Pooky bumped against my leg again and looked up at me, sending me a picture of us getting out of the downpour. "Yes, my pretty, good girl. We'll be leaving soon. Give me a minute, I need to get my ribs taped." I scratched her behind the ears as she closed her eyes and lolled her tongue out in pleasure.

An EMT approached me warily, his nose bandaged. "Mind if I help you out now?"

"Yeah, sorry about earlier."

As he patched me up, I thought about my new team. They had really come together when it counted, and we had gotten the job done. Charlie with his heartfelt intentions expressed by a foul mouth. Jaiden with her fiery attitude tempered by a tender heart. Ed with his steadfast support enhanced by his gruff exterior. Even Pooky with loyalty and love that only a dog could show. Perhaps it didn't start out that way, but now I had friends, I had love, I had peace, and for the first time in a long time, I was happy.

Chapter 21

Ravenswood Way, San Jose, CA—1005 hours

EVERYTHING LOOKED JUST AS I remembered it. The bougainvillea trying to take over the side of the house, the neatly manicured front lawn, the Italian oak Mom had gotten Dad for his birthday one year as a sapling.

It had grown to be much larger now.

Standing, staring at the ornate, custom-made door with stained-glass windows, my mouth was dry and my stomach in knots. The hum of the pool filter and the splash of the waterfall came from the backyard of the two-story home.

I hadn't seen my parents in twenty-six years.

Promising Daisy I'd speak to them had seemed like the right thing to do at the time, but now felt tougher than facing down a bone demon or taking down the bogeyman.

For the fourth time in a row, I tried to raise my hand to knock when it swung open. "Can I help… you? D-Darrell?"

The woman standing at the door froze, staring at my face. The wooden spoon in her hand clattered to the ground.

I saw my mom in the older lady that stood before me. Her mousy brown hair looked the same from being dyed, but she had crow's feet under her eyes and wrinkles spiderwebbed across her face and hands. The years of drinking hadn't done her much good.

"Hi… Mom."

She blinked at me through cheap wire-framed glasses as her jaw went slack. "Wha-what? W-will… do you… how…?"

"Sorry to drop by unexpected, but I uh… I have some-something for you."

She looked nervously over her shoulder, I assumed for my father. "I…"

I held up my hand. "It's okay, Mom. I won't take up much of your time."

"Darrell?"

I held out the gold heart locket that I had been carrying for thirty years. It gleamed in the morning sun. "I found him."

My mother looked at it, horrified. "Y-you… found… him?"

Nodding, I put the locket in her hand and pushed it closed with my own. "Yeah, I uh… I found Daisy's killer. Here, she… she wanted you to have this."

Her knees buckled and she fell against the doorjamb. She opened her hand and stared at the locket as if it were a ghost, bringing the other to her mouth as tears streamed from her eyes.

I stepped back off the porch, still facing her. "Uh, tell… tell Dad for me, would ya? I'm not sure it would go this well if… if we spoke."

Turning away quickly to hide the tears in my eyes, I brushed them away with my arm. I had promised myself I wouldn't cry.

After a moment, my mom cried out, "Darrell!"

I stopped without looking back. "I love you, Mom."

Her voice sounded meek. "Darrell? I-I don't understand what's going on."

"Tell Dad I love him too."

Pooky's head hung out the window as I walked the rest of the way to my Spyder. I got in, started the car, and drove off, leaving my mother kneeling in her doorway, sobbing uncontrollably.

Affidavit from Ed Anderson: Evidence ID#:
SJ-0031 Ed Anderson's Cabin, Somewhere
in the Hoover Wilderness between CA and
NV—1005 hours

E D SAT IN HIS armchair, enjoying his coffee and newspaper with his left arm still in a support sling. Fresh air, chirping birds, and a stupid trash panda rooting through his garbage—that's what a man needed. Peace and quiet.

A knock sounded at the door. He set down his paper and got up. "Who is it?"

He opened the door and found Charlie standing there with his hands shoved in his pockets. "Hey, Ed. How ya doin'?"

Ed scowled. "I'm tryin' ta' relax, like the Doc done told me to."

He looked around. "Need anything? It's been quiet at the apartment since you came back up here."

"Naw, I'm good and uh, thanks fer lettin' me stay at yer place fer a bit till I was back on ma' feet again."

"Yeah, sure, no problem. Well, hey. Since I'm here, you mind if I use the range?"

Ed waved his good hand. "Suit yerself, jus' make sure ya follow range rules 'n' ya better make sure ya clean any firearm ya shoot, hear me? Don't go leavin' it fer me ta' scrub."

"Yeah, yeah, thanks." Charlie backed off the porch and ran off toward the range.

Ed shook his head as he called after him, "And police yer damn brass, meathead!"

He closed the door and made his way back to his chair. He had just settled in and unfolded his paper again when a knock sounded at the door. Ed slowly brought the paper down, his eyebrows in a straight line, mustache twitching. He finally called out, "It's open!"

Jaiden knocked on the door again as she opened it, dancing in place. "Ed?"

"Well, hey there, missy. What brings ya all the way out here?"

"Sorry to bother you…" The pop of gunfire made her jump.

Ed waved his good hand. "Don't pay that no never mind, it's jus' Charlie out at the range practicin'."

She brushed her hair out of her face while continuing to cross her legs. "Oh, he's here too? Well, like I was saying: Sorry to bother you, but I wanted to pick your brain on firearms for a story I'm doing. But first, can I please use your bathroom as it is an awful long hike out here and…"

He jerked a thumb. "Think nothin' of it. Y'all know where it's at."

"Thank you." She closed the door behind her and expediently made her way toward the bedroom.

"And ya better not be doin' a piece infringin' on the Second Amendment neither."

"Wouldn't dream of it, Ed." He heard the bathroom door close.

He looked around before bringing his paper back up. "Anyone else?" He flicked the paper straight and began to read. Not two words in and another knock came at the door. He dropped the paper into his lap as he gave a sigh. "This place is busier than a da'gone sweatshop in Communist China… Door's open!"

As it swung open, Pooky came scrambling through and began rubbing her head against his leg, tail wagging. Doc's voice came from the doorway. "Ed? You in here?"

Ed tossed his paper over his shoulder as he acknowledged Pooky with a pat on the head. "Course I'm in here, yah damn Democrat. Where else would I be? Ya told me ta' git some rest didn't'cha?"

"I just came by to see if you needed anything from town. I see Jaiden and Charlie are here."

"Yup, they're crawlin' up ma' keister too."

"Say, since I'm here, do you have any coffee made?"

"In the kitchen, help yerself." The toilet flushed in the background and more gunfire echoed from outside.

Doc made his way to the kitchen. "I was thinking I'd give Pooky some exercise and maybe give Charlie some pointers on his shooting."

Ed snorted. "Suit yerself."

Jaiden came out of the bedroom. "Ah! Doctor, you're here. I wanted to talk to you about…"

Ed tuned out as he shook his head, chuckling to himself, continuing to scratch the dog behind her ears. He'd never known why he listened to Doc and Jaiden in the first place. Sure, he liked his new… coworkers? No, that didn't sound right. Friends. Doc and his weird, dramatic ways. Jaiden and her quirky, fiery personality. Even the techno meathead Charlie. Truth be told, Ed was rather proud of them. They had all come a long way in a little time.

He paid some attention to his coffee, just looking out the window at God's country all around him. Honor, courage, commitment… they meant something, and as far as his friends were concerned, even the Good Book said, "Behold, how good and pleasant it is when brothers dwell in unity."

Ed wasn't sure what the future held, but he would try to meet it from now on with his mind open and his rifle ready, just like always.

Affidavit From Charlie Mopps: Evidence ID#: SJ-0032 Charlie's Apartment, Santana Row, San Jose, CA—1120 hours

THANK GOODNESS A LOT of what he had to do for work could be done from home, or Charlie would have found himself jobless in the last month. His boss could be a bigger dick than Tom Cruz, but he begrudgingly had to admit that this time the guy might have had a point when chewing his ass for missing so many days. He also had his side clients piling up and that never boded well for business. He had bills to pay. Doc had said he would be receiving a paycheck from PIE, but Charlie hadn't seen it yet.

He sighed as he removed his headphones and stared at the textured walls, finding himself not really caring about the money, which wasn't like him at all. Truth be told, he wouldn't trade chasing ghosts with his new friends for all the money in the world. Now he had found three other people who accepted him for him. People who didn't judge or ridicule him, except for maybe Ed, but he was more like an angry uncle he could ignore at the worst of times. It for sure beat tracking down n00b script kiddies and spanking them or spending all day on chat games with losers he had never met. Doc, Jaiden, and Ed even seemed to appreciate his wit and company, unlike his peers in the computer security subculture who recognized his skillz but always were self-centered or competitive.

A knock at the door pulled him out of his reverie. Grabbing the maple baseball bat with iron nails hammered through it that Ed had help him make, he made his way slowly toward the door. One thing his time with Doc had taught him: vigilance.

He checked out the peephole and saw a DHL delivery driver standing outside in the hall. Scrunching his eyebrows, he set the bat down, leaning it against the wall.

The delivery guy knocked again then turned to leave as Charlie cracked the door open. "Yeah?"

Chawing on a wad of gum like a yak, the delivery dude spoke around it. "Yeah, I got a letter here for a uh… Charlie Mopps?"

"I'm Charlie."

The guy shoved a tablet at him. "Sign here, please."

Charlie took the e-pen, scribbled his name on the screen, attached it back to the pad, and received a tan envelope in return.

The delivery driver tipped his hat as he walked away. "Have a good day, buddy."

"Yeah, you too." Charlie closed the door, staring at the envelope.

The return address had to be fake: The People's Democratic Bank in the Cayman Islands? Who the fuck?

Taking a letter opener from the MIT stein that held stuff on his desk, he ripped open the top of the envelope and took out a check. His eyes popped. "Holy fuck, would you look at that? Alexa, call work."

After a few rings, his boss answered, "Pro Tech Inc. This is Darren speaking."

"Hey, Darren? It's Charlie."

"Charlie? Yeah, what's up? Don't tell me you're not showing up to work again tomorrow because I wasn't lying. I don't care how good you are, you miss another day and you're fired."

Charlie chuckled. "Dude, I fucking quit, yo."

"What the hell? Are you serious? Charlie? Char—"

"Alexa, end call." He had always wanted to do that. He grinned as he continued to stare at all those beautiful zeros.

Affidavit From Vladimir Stravinsky: Evidence ID#: SJ-0033 PIE Headquarters, San Francisco, CA—1120 hours

S TRAVINSKY'S SHINY LEATHER BOX-TOED shoes clicked on the checkered tile of the building. He had become accustomed to navigating this place, but sometimes it was still like a labyrinth to him with all its twists and turns. Finally, he found the office he had been searching for.

He waited until the huge golden double doors with the likenesses of Brokkr and Sindri, blacksmiths to the Norse gods, etched on them swung open. Rich red carpet lined the floors beyond. Gold trim gleamed, dividing the carpet from the stark white textured walls. Two granite pillars jutted to the ceiling, one white, one black, framing a huge oaken desk at the center of them. Behind it, a bay window so sheer it looked like he could just walk out onto the clouds drifting by on the wind. Pictures of stuffy old men in business suits and prim ladies in dresses with petticoats decorated the walls of the room. A computer sat on the desk, along with a partial glass of what Stravinsky figured, if he knew his friend, to be rum and Coke sitting on a golden coaster. Mechanical gadgets hummed, warbled, clicked, whistled, or whirred around, each set on a different task. "Coffin Dance" by Bemax played from hidden speakers.

Stravinsky approached the center of the room, ducking a motorized hand attached to a helicopter blade and narrowly dodging an overzealous carpet buddy. He found his longtime friend and the director of PIE staring out the window, hands clasped behind his back. He wore a dark purple corduroy suit with tails, a crisp white button-down shirt, and a gold tie. His pristine bowling shoes sinking into the carpet as he patiently lifted one foot and then the other for the carpet buddy to scuttle by. Stravinsky wasn't sure he had ever seen the man in anything else. Despite his wavy white hair and long white beard, his keen brown eyes gleamed with sharp intelligence.

He never took his eyes off the greater Bay Area skyline. "Good news, I hope?"

Stravinsky nodded. "Everything is in order, just as requested."

The wizened man nodded his head. "Good. Why is it I feel like that is not the only reason you're here?"

Stravinsky stepped next to the man in the corduroy suit, taking in the view himself. It was amazing and terrifying at the same time. "Is true."

The director now turned his head and raised an eyebrow. "You still think it's a good idea I meet with the doctor?"

Stravinsky clasped his hands behind his back. "This is also true."

He snorted. "To what end?"

The Russian gentleman shrugged. "Maybe he will help you be less of introvert?"

"Why, Stravinsky. If I didn't know any better, I'd say you were developing a sense of humor."

"Is another thing you can learn from the good doctor."

The man sighed and looked back out the window. "I don't particularly like senses of humor, but… alright. I'll… consider it."

"Have you given any thought to suggestion?"

"Change the agency's name? Whatever for?"

Stravinsky shrugged. "New team, new name?"

"Tell me again, what does he want to change it to?"

"Paranormal Investigation and Termination Crew, or PIT Crew. Is more… serious, so I have been told. Is also less offensive to women, is cooler, and is play off NASCAR which is favorable among team members. Besides, when is last time we educated anyone on anything?"

The man reached out a hand toward his desk. A steampunk robotic butler rattled up, picked up the drink, and handed it to him. "I don't ever remember this being a democracy and we really should reinstitute that side of the program now that you mention it. You think this is a good idea, do you?"

Stravinsky shrugged again. "Is hard to get law enforcement to take one seriously when you are calling yourself PIE. Agency is not a dessert."

The man arched a bushy eyebrow. "There are other agents who might have complained about similar problems… and you think PIT will fare better?"

"As young Charlie says, at least is cooler."

He nodded. "Very well, then. It just means more work for you, after all."

"I would expect nothing less. This is still far cry better than Soviet Russia and Putin's bandit Communism."

He turned back toward the city. "Fine. File the paperwork and have new credentials made and issued to everyone."

"As you wish."

He shook his head and chuckled. "The PIT Crew, it does roll off the tongue."

"Spasibo, moy drug."

"Stravinsky."

Stravinsky looked over his shoulder. *"Da?"*

"Good work all around." The director fell into silent contemplation once again.

Stravinsky nodded and saw himself out, the doors banging closed behind him.

Affidavit From Jaiden Fox: Evidence ID#: SJ-0034 Jaiden's Apartment, San Francisco, CA—0105

J AIDEN HAD BEEN UP all night working on her blog. Ever since college, whenever she had a story burning in her brain she couldn't sleep. With a fresh pot of coffee steaming in the kitchen and Jakob snoring in the bed, Jaiden drummed her fingers as she considered what she had just written on her laptop:

I never believed in monsters. I was always the skeptic. Surely there were no goblins, no ghosts, nothing supernatural waiting in the dark to grab me. Nothing hid under my bed or in the closet waiting to jump out. It was all just metaphorical to help teach me right from wrong. I even believed that people innately had a guiding light of good inside them.

A boy named William Twitch taught me I was wrong on all accounts.

William Twitch was born to Joseph and Mary Twitch in the Tenderloin District in San Francisco back in 1964. Joseph worked in construction for the city, and Mary, of course, had become a housewife. You won't find any birth certificate for William because he was born in his parents' apartment on Hyde Street with only a few of Mary's friends to help her through delivery, and even they were told the baby died shortly after birth.

William proved himself special from the beginning as a Level One on the spectrum, marking him as autistic. Unfortunately, they had no diagnosis for such a thing in those days. His parents, incorrectly thinking him "slow," never enrolled him in school. Therefore, you won't find any school records for him either.

Both Joseph and Mary had drinking problems. One drank to escape the pressures of a family they had created but no longer cherished. To escape the hardships of a labor-intensive job that demanded so much yet gave so little. To escape the average demands of life that can wear the soul down until nothing is left but bitterness, envy, and a longing for days gone past.

The other drank to escape as well. To escape the pain and anguish of feeling trapped in a helpless situation. To escape the physical and emotional abuse they had to endure day in and day out. To escape the responsibility of trying to hold together a toxic family without any help from anyone. What do you do when your life is an escape room and you can't seem to break out? If given long enough, depression and desperation can kill even the most resilient of souls.

Joseph had a foul temper, which added more trauma to the already dysfunctional family dynamics of the typical, all-American '70s household. Taking his frustrations out on his wife and child unjustly easily paints him as the monster he was. Never taking the time to appreciate what he had been blessed with in life, he mistakenly blamed a wife and child for his shortcomings, never pointing a finger at himself. He made poor choices that destroyed any chance he could have had at a happy, well-adjusted life. But how many times as adults do we fail to imagine how our choices in life will impact our children, let alone our own future?

Sadly enough, our choices do impact them, and probably more than we'd like to admit.

Both Joseph and Mary were victims as well, there's no denying that, and on the fateful day of November 23, 1970, both were murdered. But in that moment, they were more victims of their own brutality and apathy toward their own son than of murder.

Let me explain.

I would like you to consider two separate cold cases. The first, the deaths of Joseph and Mary Twitch themselves. You can find an article mentioning the murders on page E4 of the November 24, 1970, edition of the *San Francisco Chronicle*. The police opened an investigation into the strange, brutal crime, but gave up after two weeks with no leads.

The second cold case involved three boys: Phillip Whitmore, Kenneth Hynes, and Stephen Smith. An apparently unrelated article at the top of the same page of the *Chronicle* mentions how two of the boys, Phillip and Stephen, were found dead in an alleyway off Hyde Street. One from a broken neck and the other from bleeding out due to a compound fracture, both exhibiting signs of extreme blunt-force trauma. The third one, Kenneth Hynes, was treated at the Public Health Service Hospital in San Francisco for cranial injuries then was moved to

Agnews Developmental Center for severe brain damage. In 2009, Agnews shut down and he got transferred to a mental hospital facility in San Jose where he remains to this day.

You'd never know there was a link between them until you add William.

They never found William's body. To be fair, they never knew they should be looking for him. Only his parents and his bullies even knew he was alive—that's the reason you won't find a death certificate for him. However, on November 23, 1970, he became one of the largest serial killers to ever rock the California Bay Area.

Earlier that day, after killing two of his tormentors and injuring one to the point of mental impairment, William doubled back and killed his parents as well. Then from 1970 to the present, if one accounts for his method of taking a victim every month, it is believed he is responsible for more than 612 kidnappings and over 700 deaths ranging everywhere from San Francisco to San Jose.

Children were his victims of choice: easy to lure, naive, trusting. Children like Daisy Diamondback, Ian Johnson, Kayla Sanchez, Montel Evens, and Maddison Bell, to name only the few that we know of. Adults he brutalized and tortured only when they got in the way of his true passion: hunting the innocent.

This monster was finally brought down by federal authorities last night after abducting two final children: a brother and a sister whose names I'm withholding for their protection. They were lucky to escape with their lives.

When I first discovered the story of "Bloody-Bones William," it was easy to hate him, easy to fear him, easy to blame him. Considering all the horrible things he did, it's easy to forget that William was created by the neglect and failings of his parents and a lack of basic human decency. Joseph and Mary surely didn't intend to create a monster, but their intentions don't change the fact of what they did or what results their choices yielded. Nor were their actions solely and entirely responsible for William, yet without their part the other parts would not have bore fruit, and vice versa.

This tragedy overlaps with a ghost story as well. You see, on that day of November 23, William Twitch also died, not just metaphorically but physically. William's father snapped his neck. By all rights, William Twitch should have died that day, but his pain, fear, and trauma took a stable form, and he lived on.

He lived on as the urban legend of why children fear the dark and want to sleep with the lights on. He lived on as the creature that comes in the night, snatching up little kids from their homes to torture, then eat them.

He lived on as the bogeyman.

His warped, twisted soul continued to haunt this earth for decades. He spread fear, panic, and death, and what one must wonder is: Could this all have been avoided?

Maybe if Joseph and Mary Twitch had sought help for their troubles from a councilor or clergyman? Maybe if the neighborhood boys that had bullied, tormented, and sexually abused poor William had instead been more tolerant and friendly? Maybe if there had been someone to show poor William a different way to live? Would he have followed it?

It's still hard to believe he was only six years old.

Too many times through apathy, poor choices, and tormenting those who are perceived as weaker or different than we are, we have created the monsters that plague our very lives. Too many times we feed into the cycle of perpetual violence laid out before us by others. Most times it's unintentional, and by the time we realize what we're doing, a habit has taken root. We don't want to believe we are monsters. How could the people we know, love, and trust have steered us onto a path of hate and self-destruction? How could we possibly fall from grace? Aren't we the hero of this story? But the self-serving biases, the white lies, and half-truths that plague our justifications for the damage we inflict pile up, so much so, we wind up believing them and cling to them with all hope, less our lives come crashing down around us in a never-ending waterfall of misguidance and despair.

I'll tell you. After observing Joseph Twitch and his actions, I no longer believe in tough love.

Why don't we want better lives for our children? For ourselves? For our community? How long will it take for us to wake up as a society and start making the right choices in life, even if they're tough? How long before we quit creating the Williams in the world for others to deal with?

Some people will call me crazy. Some people will mock me for putting this story out. I don't care because I feel it's important enough to consider, even if you take out the supernatural aspect of it all.

So, for all of you skeptics, you nonbelievers, you naysayers who don't believe in ghosts, who don't believe in monsters. Take it from someone who has seen them firsthand, and check in the mirror, because there may be a monster staring right back at you.

-Ms. Information

Footage from Emily McCormick's Video Journal:
Evidence ID#: SJ–0035 My Place, Santana Row,
San Jose, CA—0105 hours

E MILY SAT ON MY black leather couch recording
herself. I had fallen asleep with my head resting in
her lap. She made kissy lips at the camera. "Hey, party
people. I made him put the stupid mutt outside. I already
know it's going to be trouble. For some reason, he's
resisting my suggestions to get rid of the stupid thing. I
think their bond is already too strong."

She gave an exasperated sigh, then a wicked smile
crossed her face. "That just means I'll have to find another
way to get rid of it. The cat was bad enough, but the
allergy ploy worked just fine until the bogeyman did me
a favor by killing the damn thing. I'm sure the allergies
excuse will work again."

She shrugged, closed her eyes, and visibly shuddered.
"I've never gotten my claws into someone like this before,
but party people, let me tell you: so far, worth it! This will
be something new, something exhilarating. The doubts
I'm able to play on. The fears I'm able to feast on. The
insecurity I'm able to revel in."

She ran a finger up my hip with a coy smile. "It's all so
intoxicating, and I mean to… ride out this high as long
as possible."

One could see her legs rubbing together, the prospect
of my torment making her sexually aroused. Her eyes

flashed red as she gazed down. "This will be my most delicious kill yet, party people. Just wait and see."

She blew a kiss at the screen. "TTFN, ta-tas for now."

I gave a snore.

She giggled as she jiggled her titties in the camera, then clicked it off.

Epilogue

STRAVINSKY BROUGHT POOKY AND me to an old, abandoned building. The chain-link fence with the padlock and the "Keep Out" sign was all too familiar. He unlocked the gate and pushed it open. Pooky sat obediently at my feet, panting and staring at our handler. "Umm, Stravinsky?"

He spared me a backward glance. *"Da?"*

I looked around for cameras, thinking it strange there weren't any. "Normally when I ignore the 'Keep Out' sign, next thing I know you're hauling me out of a holding cell."

He held the door open. "That is you. This is me."

It was, for lack of better words, a dilapidated dump of a building. Cobwebs, dust, broken beams... It appeared ready to fall down any second. Clusters of old cubicles littered with outdated electronics stood beneath a skeleton ceiling. Wires and cables hung through the gaps like jungle vines. Chunks of plaster and Sheetrock provided rough terrain in the gloom, and the dust from them ground under our feet as if we walked on sandpaper. Pooky chased a few rats into a hole before I could give her a negative marker.

"Umm, Stravinsky…"

He turned to me, arching an eyebrow and letting his jaw go slack for a moment before saying, "Look, would you like to meet *blagotvoritel*…uh, benefactor, or *nyet?*"

I frowned, folded my arms, and nodded.

"Good. Then follow." Stravinsky turned and led us to the back of the building. He began rotating a small cog made of copper embedded in the wall like the dial to a safe; soon, I heard a click from deep inside.

"Oh shit!" I felt my stomach lurch as the floor fell away.

About the author
J.M. Tilbury

Jarrod M. Tilbury writes paranormal horror, dark fantasy, and is an editorial assistant for Grendel Press. Born in Huntsville, AL he was raised in San Jose, CA and continues to haunt the Bay Area to this day.